TH
KHANDAVAPRASTHA
CONSPIRACY

Book 3 of The Mahabharata Quest Series

Christopher C. Doyle is an author who transports the reader into a fascinating world where ancient secrets buried in legends blend with science and history to create a gripping story.

His debut novel, *The Mahabharata Secret*, featured among the top ten books of 2013 and was nominated for the Raymond Crossword Book Award, 2014. He followed it up with the bestselling The Mahabharata Quest series, featuring *The Alexander Secret* and *The Secret of the Druids* and the bestselling The Pataala Prophecy series featuring *Son of Bhrigu* and *The Mists of Brahma*, all of which have won rave reviews from readers.

Christopher can be contacted at:

Website: www.authorchristophercdoyle.com

Email: contact@christophercdoyle.com

Facebook: www.facebook.com/authorchristophercdoyle

The Quest Club: www.authorchristophercdoyle.com/the-quest-club

Other books by Christopher C. Doyle

The Mahabharata Quest Series

The Alexander Secret

The Secret of the Druids

The Pataala Prophecy

Son of Bhrigu

The Mists of Brahma

BOOK 3

THE
MAHABHARATA
QUEST

THE KHANDAVAPRASTHA
CONSPIRACY

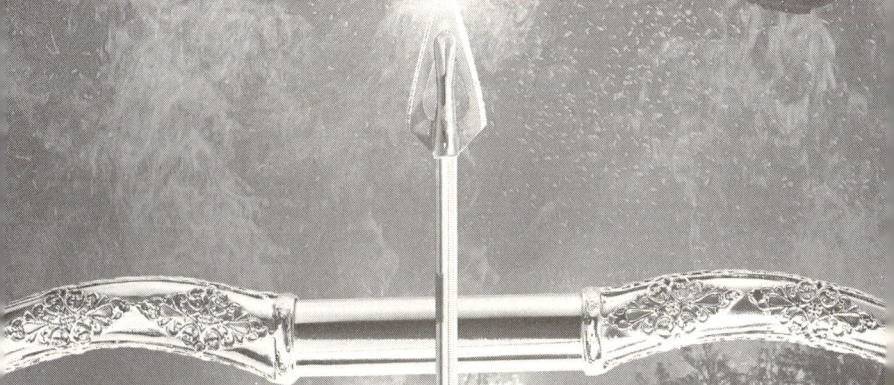

CHRISTOPHER C. DOYLE

First published by Westland Books, a division of Nasadiya
Technologies Private Limited, in 2022

No. 269/2B, First Floor, 'Irai Arul', Vimalraj Street, Nethaji Nagar,
Allappakkam Main Road, Maduravoyal, Chennai 600095

Westland and the Westland logo are the trademarks of Nasadiya
Technologies Private Limited, or its affiliates.

Christopher C. Doyle asserts the moral right to be identified as the
author of this work.

ISBN: 978-93-95767-15-6

10 9 8 7 6 5 4 3 2 1

This is a work of fiction. Names, characters, organisations, places,
events and incidents are either products of the author's imagination
or used fictitiously. Any resemblance to actual events, locales,
organisations or persons, living or dead is entirely coincidental.

Typeset by Jojy Philip, New Delhi 110 015
Printed at Thomson Press (India) Ltd.

In ancient times, the dreaded Khandavaprastha forest was burned down and all living beings who inhabited the forest were killed without mercy.

And there was a reason for this slaughter.

For, in that terrible forest called Khandavaprastha, lay buried, for thousands of years, a deadly secret, which we now call The Khandavaprastha Curse.

And the Naga King Takshaka, who lived in the forest, discovered the secret and hid it away from the eyes of the world. It is the secret of The Khandavaprastha Curse that I will reveal now.

Susruta, in The Owen Manuscript, Chapter 1

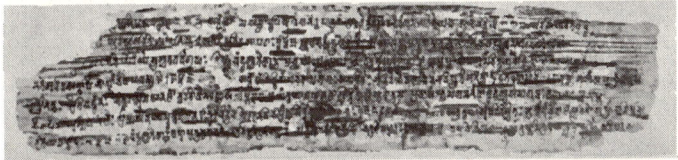

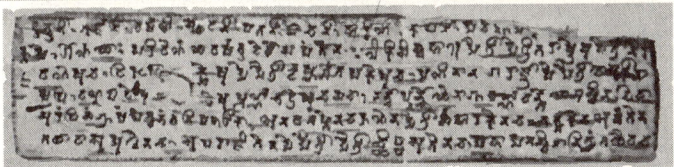

To Anand Prakash,
One of the most brilliant creative minds I have known,
Thank you, Andy, for your friendship and advice,
For your unstinting and selfless support,
And for everything you've done for me

ACRONYMS & DEFINITIONS

CCP	Chinese Communist Party
CMO	Chief Medical Officer
PLA	People's Liberation Army (of China)
Estim	Electrical Stimulation
Wet Science	Scientific experiments and analysis in a laboratory where drugs, chemicals and biological matter can be tested and analysed using liquids and fluids
PMO	(Indian) Prime Minister's Office

PROLOGUE

3340 BCE
Present-day Miaozigou
Inner Mongolia, China

Yun looked back, tears streaming down his face, as he trudged along with the ragged group of survivors. It was the last time they would see the village they were abandoning forever.

It wasn't just the huts they were leaving behind.

Less than three months had passed since the discovery of the accursed rocks. A find that had, at first, been welcomed as an auspicious omen. Almost a godsend.

He could still recall, vividly, the events of the day his friends Chang and Xang had intrepidly ventured out to the semi-arid desolation that lay a few miles east of their village; a tract of land where no one had ever lived or farmed, and which was shunned by the villagers.

And for good reason.

Legend had it that this barren belt was *Jingshén zhī dì*—the dwelling place of spirits. According to the myth, an ancient conflagration had rendered the land unfit for tilling, and inimical to human survival, leaving it fit only for spirits to infest. No one in the village had been brave or foolhardy enough to test the myth, but stories were told of daring men in antiquity who had audaciously attempted to cultivate that land, despite the legend, and had died horribly.

Young and not entirely convinced of these old superstitions, Chang and Xang had decided to brave their way to *Jīngshén zhī dì*. They believed there was water to be found beneath the infertile surface soil. Water had been a scarce commodity that year. If new water sources were not found, the entire village would have to move.

Yun, uneasy about the legend and the stories, had tried to dissuade his friends. But they had refused to pay heed.

'We will dig for water at the edge of *Jīngshén zhī dì*,' Xang had laughed away Yun's reservations. 'It is such a large expanse of land! Surely the spirits will not mind us searching for water at the very fringe?'

'And we will honour and propitiate the spirits before we commence our exploration.' Chang took Yun's apprehensions a bit more seriously. 'Don't worry, Yun, we will not offend them.'

And so the two had started for the barren strip of land, inhabited only by spirits.

Their efforts had soon borne fruit. A few feet of digging had unearthed water.

A jubilant Chang and Xang had scrambled back to the village and shared the good news. The spirits appeared to have smiled upon them and aided their efforts.

But water was not all they had discovered.

Yun had an inkling that his friends had stirred up trouble. He didn't know what it was about the small black rocks that they had found while digging for water, but he couldn't help feeling that something was amiss.

But he had kept his misgivings to himself as the ecstatic villagers rejoiced in their deliverance from the drought. He didn't want to cast a pall over the celebrations.

Some of them thought the black rocks were old, hardened wolf droppings. Others thought they were old pieces of charcoal. Either way, it was intriguing because the area was not frequented by wolves nor were rocks of this kind found there. But the village elder was the most perspicacious.

'Why have you brought these cursed objects here? Have you no fear?' he had exclaimed, holding out his hands dramatically as though to ward off the small black fragments. 'They are accursed! Possessed by spirits!'

Despite his own suspicions, Yun, with all the irreverence of youth, had sniggered quietly on witnessing the old man's histrionics. Today, however, as he tore his gaze from the huts, he knew the village elder had been correct.

Within two months of the discovery of the rocks and the water, the village had become a living hell.

It had started with the madness. People losing their minds. It was different for different people. For some, it was limited to memory loss, disorientation, confusion and incoherence. For others it was more serious. An inexplicable aggression would take hold of them without any perceptible provocation.

Fortunately, only a few were afflicted.

Then came the bodily deterioration. A baffling series of physical disabilities began to spread through the village. Some lost their vision, others lost the use of their limbs. And there were those with puzzling tremors, some so badly affected that they could not walk or even stand on their own.

Before the villagers could even begin to understand what was happening, people had started dying.

A fever would come on without warning, even in men and women who seemed hale and hearty. It would burn high for a day.

At the end of it, the tormented individual would be dead.

Within a few weeks of the beginning of the mysterious affliction, most of the villagers were either ill or dead.

The handful of survivors had huddled together, desperate for a way to escape their inevitable fate.

It was then that Yun had voiced his fears about the rocks.

A murmur of agreement had spread through the rest of the group.

'It must be as Yun says,' one of them had said. 'The sickness came upon us only after the rocks came to the village. They are cursed. *We* are cursed!'

A decision was made quickly that day. There was no time to lose.

The village had to be abandoned.

And another, more difficult, decision was also arrived at.

They quickly scoured the village, collected the dead who had not yet been buried and dumped the bodies into pits that were hastily dug around the huts. There was no time to transport the dead to the ancestral graveyard, which lay a short distance away.

The survivors then packed the bare essentials they needed for their journey: a few utensils and clothing.

Nothing else was touched.

Everything else was to be left behind. Including those unfortunate people who were sick in mind and body, but not yet dead.

The most difficult decision had been to abandon not just the village, but all the afflicted.

They were left to die where they lay.

And the mysterious disease—the curse—would die with them.

June 1800 CE

Angostura

Chinese Turkestan

Present-day Ciudad Bolívar, Venezuela

Baron Alexander von Humboldt groaned as José, his faithful servant, hammered at the door.

'What is it, José?' he grumbled hoarsely. It had been barely two weeks since Humboldt and Aimé Bonpland—the French scientist who was his travelling companion in the Americas, and who would become one of his best friends—had suddenly been taken by a strange fever.

For seventy-five days and 1,400 miles, they had travelled, first on the Rio Apure, and then along the Orinoco, collecting specimens from the dense Amazon forests along the rivers. They had braved jaguars and mosquitoes, survived hunger and other dangers in their journey through the rainforest; but the fever had struck them down when they reached Angostura, confining them to their beds for almost two weeks now.

Humboldt chafed at the bit. His restless nature, accustomed to constant action and little rest, threatened to get the better of his fever. Had it not been for the weakness in his body, he would have been up and about.

He failed to keep the frustration and irritation out of his voice now. 'Go away, José! You know I can't get out of bed!'

'The monkey!' José's voice, quivering with an undistinguishable emotion, came through the closed door. 'You must come quick!'

Humboldt sat up on hearing this. A sudden burst of energy propelled him out of bed, and he fumbled with his gown as he tried to open the door at the same time.

José's face was flushed, a worried look creasing his forehead. He had only just about recovered from near death due to the same fever that had subsequently felled Humboldt and Bonpland.

'What's the matter, man?' Humboldt demanded, grabbing his servant by the arms.

José could only shake his head. But the horror in his eyes spoke louder than words.

Humboldt took the lead and rushed to the room where the titi monkey was kept in a large cage of its own.

The German had grown quite fond of the little fellow—the titi monkeys were his favourites, with their long tails, soft greyish fur and white faces that looked like heart shaped masks, according to Humboldt. He loved their graceful movements which had earned them their German name of *Springaffe* or jumping monkey.

And this particular monkey had endeared itself to Humboldt for a number of reasons.

The first was the circumstances in which he had discovered it. Titi monkeys were difficult to catch alive. In April, though, a few weeks after leaving the Rio Apure, as they had paddled along the Orinoco, Humboldt and Bonpland had come upon a troop of *Springaffe* in a remote part of the rainforest.

The monkeys were all dead—or so Humboldt had thought—a mass of blood and gore, almost as if they had been massacred. So grim was the sight that Humboldt and Bonpland had concluded, sadly, that not one could have survived what appeared to be an aggressive attack by a predator.

Just as they were about to leave, José had spotted movement among the bloodied bodies.

A small titi monkey was discovered, little more than a baby, still clinging to its dead mother. A part of one of its hind legs had been ripped off, presumably by the same predator that had decimated the rest of the monkeys, leaving a bleeding stump.

José had immediately been given the task of nursing the monkey back to health.

Over the next few weeks, under José's tender care, the baby recovered not just its health but also its lively spirit.

It was then that they discovered the most amazing thing—a miracle, as Bonpland had described it—something that was impossible, and which they would never have believed had they not seen it for themselves.

Over the next few weeks, they watched, astounded and baffled as the miracle unfolded before their eyes.

Around this time, Humboldt and the monkey became fast friends. Once it recovered, José would bring it, still inside its cage, to the stern of the small canoe in which they were travelling, where Humboldt would show it his scientific books.

The little monkey would grab at the engravings of the insects—grasshoppers and wasps—as if wanting to feed on them, for the titi monkeys ate insects.

Now, wondering what it was that had so agitated José, Humboldt rushed into the room where the caged monkey was kept.

And stopped short.

A chill ran down his spine.

Dread gripped his heart at the scene that greeted him. He understood the horror he had seen in the depths of his servant's eyes.

The monkey was sitting in its cage and tearing out chunks of flesh from its arms and legs with its teeth. There was flesh strewn around the cage and the bars were splattered with blood.

As Humboldt entered, the monkey bared its fangs and rushed towards him, furiously banging against the bars of the cage. It bit the iron bars and let out a howl of fury.

It was like the animal had gone mad. The mischievous monkey who had grabbed at pictures of insects on the boat was gone. It had been replaced by what appeared to be a blood-thirsty monster, one that was intent on tearing itself to pieces.

For a few moments, Humboldt stood, transfixed, unable to comprehend what he saw. Then it dawned on him.

The troop of monkeys in the rain forest.

They had not been attacked by a predator.

The monkeys had turned on themselves and torn each other apart. Somehow, this one had survived.

But what had driven those monkeys, and now this one, to this terrible fate?

In his mind, Humboldt knew what he was gazing upon now was linked in some way to the miracle he and Bonpland had witnessed during the journey here. How, he didn't know and couldn't explain, but there was a certainty about the feeling that racked him.

In that moment, he knew he had to discover what was behind the frenzied butchery he was witnessing.

Even as he turned away and with a heavy heart gave José instructions to put the monkey out of its misery, he couldn't help but notice once again the miracle they had witnessed on the boat.

He knew that, somehow, it held the key.

When he had rescued the monkey, it had part of one hind leg missing.

Now, as it tore itself apart, the little monkey stood on two completely formed hind legs.

The missing part of the leg had grown back during their journey to Angostura.

April 1804 CE
South of the T'ien Shan, Chinese Turkestan
Present-day Xinjiang Province, China

The five men gazed uncertainly at the dome-like tower that loomed sixty feet above them in the darkness of the night. A pale half-moon lit up the sky and the landscape around them with a ghostly glow. Now that they were here, their plan didn't look as attractive as it had when they were drinking and planning this expedition.

The ancient tower that stood before them had a legend around it.

A story from antiquity.

Of treasure.

No one really knew what the tower was. A Buddhist stupa? A tomb?

And the mysterious nature of the edifice lent the legend a greater sense of authenticity than it perhaps deserved.

It was believed that the tower was associated with the mythical king of yore, Afrásiáb, and the ruins that lay half buried around them were the remains of his capital.

Today, these five friends had decided they would have a go at finding that treasure.

One of them nervously licked his lips and looked at the others.

'Well? Shall we start?' He didn't sound very enthusiastic about the proposition. But none of them wanted to backtrack either. It was more a matter of pride than anything else.

Another hefted his pickaxe. 'Let's do it. We haven't come all this way just to gape at the tower. We need to tunnel in and get our hands on whatever we can before the night is over.'

The matter settled, they got to work, tunnelling a hole in the ancient sun-dried brickwork of the tower. After about an hour, they had a decent-sized opening through which to enter.

Torches were lit and the group of men filed through the entrance they had created.

A musty, stale smell greeted them as they entered a large room. As they held their torches aloft, they noticed a heap of old texts lying in the centre of the floor.

The light of the torches also revealed a bizarre sight: the mummified remains of several animals positioned in such a way that they seemed to be standing guard.

One of the men walked up to a mummified cow and poked it to determine whether it was real or not.

To his horror, the animal crumbled to dust under his touch. He looked at his colleagues fearfully, but they could offer no solace; each of them had the same terrified look on their face.

What was this room and why had it been built?

'Look at this!' One of the men stood before a wall, examining something on it.

The others crowded around him, half eager, half apprehensive. They gazed at the strange inscriptions that were revealed in the light of the torch. The characters on the wall were unfamiliar.

'There's no treasure here,' one of them said finally, his voice betraying his disappointment.

'The books,' another suggested. 'They are old. Let us take them to the qazi. Maybe they are worth something?'

The others agreed and they gathered up as many texts as they could and trooped out of the tower.

None of these men could guess that, more than two hundred years later, these ancient texts would mean for a world besieged.

June 2013
Canyonlands National Park, Utah, USA

Howard Barnsfield, PhD, slowly drove his car to the very edge of the dirt road where the cliff fell away, a sheer precipice with a few boulders jutting out of it at random intervals, as though stone inhabitants of the cliff's interior were peeping out at the steep drop below them.

He stopped the car, its tyres millimetres away from the edge and let the engine idle as he took a swig from his hip flask, steeling himself for what lay ahead.

For he had made up his mind. It had been a big decision to make, an irreversible one. But he had had enough.

He was a brilliant scientist and had made a name for himself at Craggett University where he taught genetics. He was known for his path-breaking work in genomic science and biomedicine, especially in the field of synthetic biology.

He should have been one of the most feted scientists in the world—perhaps even a Nobel Prize winner for his innovations and discoveries.

Yet, fame and fortune had passed him by.

Not that he was unduly concerned about the latter. Money didn't interest him unless it was in the form of a grant for one of his radical research projects.

And it wasn't as if he had not received any recognition at all; he was respected in the scientific community for his experimental work and unconventional approach to his research.

But that was all in the past. Deep in the past. And he wasn't getting any younger.

Besides, Barnsfield's work in the last few years had won him derision and even rebuke from some of his more outspoken peers. His work had veered from the mainstream to more radical niches, prodding, poking and exploring corners of the biological world that others in the scientific community felt were out of bounds. Or futile to pursue since it was impossible to achieve anything concrete in those areas of research.

And for his efforts to create a truly synthetic organism from scratch—not one word of appreciation from the scientific community.

If not for the funding he had received from his benefactors, his work would have stopped long ago.

Now it was time. He had to take the final plunge. This was it. After this, there would be no more censure, no more ridicule. It would all end.

Barnsfield took another swig from his hip flask and patted the suicide note kept on the passenger seat next to him, just to make sure it was there. He had also emailed a scanned copy to a score of his peers, just in case. It was quite possible that this handwritten note would burn up in the likely conflagration that would result when the car went over the edge of the cliff.

He smirked. It would come as a shock to his colleagues. They would regret the taunts and the snide remarks. He went over the contents of the note in his mind.

It is time for me to bid goodbye to an unappreciative world. I have, for the last six years, been trying to build a fully synthetic organism—not like Craig Venter's M. Mycoides synthetic genome transplanted into an M. Capricolum recipient cell to transform it into an M. Mycoides cell. My quest was for a truly synthetic organism that lived. Authentic artificial life. Unfortunately, my detractors, of whom there are many, turned out to be right. I was on the wrong path in my research. I ignored what lay before me and pursued what was impossible. I was blind to Nature. Now I have learnt my lesson. This life I have lived is no longer worth living. And so I bid goodbye to all of you. God bless you all!

Barnsfield took another swig, then put his flask down as he disengaged the handbrake and laughed.

Now there was no turning back.

His manic laughter echoed through the night as the car plunged down the cliff, bouncing off the protruding boulders, finally crashing into the valley floor and bursting into flames.

PART I

GENESIS

September 3

Hotan

Xinjiang Province, China

Beth gazed happily at the sprawling expanse of stalls, artisans and hawkers that spread out before her.

She was in China as part of the Silk Wheels team—a group of young people who were cycling across Tibet and Xinjiang along China's Silk Road. Beth had flown in from Connecticut and joined the rest of the team in Kashgar. After a week of planning and preparation, the team had set off for Western Tibet on the first leg of what was to be a two-week tour.

Somewhere down the line, the team had chosen to explore different paths. And, as much as she hated to admit it, Beth had decided to take the advice that her parents had given her before she left home, and temper her ambition. Not for her the cycling routes to Tibet, which comprised the most difficult leg of their itinerary. She had realised, on the second day of the cycling tour, that, for her, it was possibly the most challenging route in the world.

Instead, Beth's path now lay in Western China, through the places she had originally come to see: Xinjiang, the old silk routes and Kham. While she was eager to meet the rest of the group later, she had retraced her steps through Xinjiang, riding along the southern rim of the Taklamakan desert—where she had encountered the customary sandstorm—and arrived in Hotan just in time for the legendary Sunday market.

By now, she had become quite comfortable on her bike. Her body was beginning to get accustomed to the constant cycling and the long hours on the bicycle seat. In fact, she was quite enjoying the trip now, after getting over the inevitable loneliness that had accompanied her parting of ways from the others.

As she took in the famous Hotan Sunday market, she felt she had fallen into a sea of chaos. There was a staggering array of wares for sale: carpets, silk, clothing, the Uzbek hats called *doppi*, knives, vegetables, furniture, medicines, yarn, wool, bikes, stoves, motorcycles, cows, horses, donkeys, sheep, goats, and a wide variety of food. The market existed primarily to serve the needs of the Uyghurs, Tajiks, Uzbeks, Kyrgyz and Chinese who made up the population of the town.

Beth walked through the maze of scattered and disorganised stalls, the spaces between them filled by throngs of people and animals.

People came up to her all the time; some to hawk jade or doppis, and others to look at her long golden hair, which she had tied in a loose ponytail. She felt quite self-conscious, especially since her hair was dishevelled and gritty with sand after the hard ride along the desert trail.

The tantalising aroma of food wafted over to her and she followed it to a stall where a hawker grinned amiably at her.

She pointed out what she wanted to eat and paid for it. The hawker nodded and set to work loading a plate with roasted goat meat, flat bread and berries.

But Beth was not destined to enjoy the delicacy.

Even as she stretched out her hand for the plate, loud shouts cut through the din of the market.

Someone screamed.

A ripple ran through the crowd as people jostled to see what was happening.

There was a series of loud bangs, as if someone had set off firecrackers within the throng.

More screams.

Someone was shouting again. Beth didn't recognise the language. Was it Chinese? Uzbek? She didn't know.

Whether it was a reaction to the shouting or something else, the crowd suddenly shifted and swirled.

There were more loud bangs.

The crowd scattered. People jumped into the stalls near them or ran helter-skelter in all directions, jostling and shoving in their haste to get away.

But from what?

Beth turned to the hawker, but he too had disappeared. For the first time since she had come to China, Beth was afraid. She had no idea what was going on.

But as the crowd thinned, she saw it.

A man, running as though his life depended on it, with a posse of Chinese police in hot pursuit, guns drawn.

Horrified, Beth realised that the police had been shooting at the man.

She looked around desperately and tried to find somewhere to hide as the pursuit drew closer to her.

The only suitable place in sight was the stall that the hawker had just vacated.

Beth vaulted over the counter into the stall and crouched there. She wasn't quite hidden. The counter was not very high and she was tall, so she could see what was happening.

More shots rang out. But these sounded different. They formed a continuous staccato.

To Beth's surprise, two of the Chinese policemen went down, the fronts of their uniforms staining red as they fell.

Someone was shooting at them!

Her head spun. It was surreal. She seemed to be caught right in the middle of a shoot out!

The other police personnel immediately took cover, shooting back at their unseen attackers.

The man they were chasing paused and glanced around, as terrified as a rabbit, clearly unsure of what he should do next.

It was then that Beth saw that the man being chased had been clutching something tightly to his chest. She couldn't make out what it was, but he was hanging on to it for dear life.

The man's uncertainty lasted just a split second and then he was haring off again; but his hesitation proved costly.

There was a flurry of shots from the direction of the policemen and the man lurched as he was hit.

Beth couldn't bear to watch anymore. She quickly dropped to the ground and lay there, waiting, her heart pounding.

She could still hear everything.

There was an immediate response of staccato shots from the other party; shooting that went on for a while without a break.

Then it abruptly stopped. A silence followed.

Beth heard shuffling sounds as the man who had been shot staggered past the stall where she had sought refuge. There was a loud thud as he hit the ground.

Beth could hear the sound of boots on the ground. It sounded like a small group of people had run up to the fallen man.

She heard him groan. Then there was silence again.

Beth waited for several minutes before she gathered the courage to peek over the counter once again.

Where she expected to find the bullet-ridden body there was only a pool of blood soaking into the mud, marking the spot where the man had fallen.

She glanced in the direction where the policemen had taken shelter during the shootout. There was no sign of them either. Even the bodies of the policemen she had seen shot had disappeared.

Who were the mysterious gunmen who had fired at the Chinese police? Had they carried off the man who was being pursued by the police? Or had the police carried him off along with the bodies of the Chinese policemen? Her head spun.

Slowly, the crowd began to seep out of the stalls and passages and fill up the open spaces once more. But just as quickly, it melted away, even hawkers abandoning their stalls. They knew Beijing would come down heavily on Hotan as retribution for the killing of the policemen. No one wanted to be called upon as a witness to what had just happened. Not that anyone really knew what had happened anyway.

There was no way that Beth, or anyone else there could have fathomed the extent of the disaster that had just sucked them into its wake. A disaster that would leave the human race tottering on the brink of extinction.

October 7
Hartford Institute
Hartford, Connecticut, USA

David Burke, president and CEO of Hartford Institute, stared at his chief clinical officer, the creases on his forehead betraying his disquietude. 'There must be some mistake,' he insisted, glancing back at the document open on his laptop. 'How is this even possible?'

Sanjay Mathur, MD, looked equally worried. 'I've never seen anything like this before. We've run every kind of test possible, including tissue biopsies. We've collected hundreds of samples. Every effort has been made to isolate the pathogen.' He shrugged. 'Nothing.'

'No pathogens detected,' Burke summarised the report on his laptop that had been sent to him by Mathur a short while earlier while requesting this meeting. 'No virus, bacteria, archaea or protozoa revealed in any of the cases. No antigens. No antibodies. Only elevated levels of neurotransmitters and bacterial toxins, with no indication of what is producing them.' He looked at Mathur. 'How long since we've been getting these patients?'

'Well, most of them came in over the past week or ten days. Except the one who I suspect is patient zero. She came in around three weeks ago. I've had them all moved to an isolation ward in the ICU. All staff dealing with them have been put on a mandatory PPE protocol. I didn't want to waste any more time waiting for tests to throw up something positive. We've lost enough time as it is.'

Burke nodded. 'Good thinking.' He took a deep breath. 'I'll contact the CDC immediately.'

Mathur grimaced. 'I just hope it isn't too late.' He sighed. 'Until we find the damn thing, how do we even try to figure out how it is transmitted?'

Burke leaned back in his chair, with a thoughtful gaze fixed on Mathur. 'You say you believe that the same pathogen is causing all the symptoms reported in different patients?'

Mathur hesitated before replying. 'That's what I think. But I can't be sure.'

Burke waved a hand at his laptop screen. 'It is hard to believe. There doesn't seem to be a consistent set of symptoms across patients.' He ticked off the symptoms mentioned in the report on his fingers. 'Cognitive decline. Nerve deterioration. Muscle atrophy. Failure of major organs—and even here, different people seem to be affected in different ways.'

'I know,' Mathur admitted. 'It is unthinkable that a single pathogen could result in so many different symptoms. But these are the only patients in the Institute for whom we cannot isolate the cause of their condition. And there's one key fact that points to a common pathogen for all these patients, despite their different symptoms. In every single case, the initial symptoms were identical. They all experienced the same neurological disorders in the beginning. The onset of the other symptoms that you see in the reports was much later. And the patients are all either known to each other, or live in the same apartment block, using the same elevators and common services. They've all met or come in contact with each other in the last few weeks. That's what gave me the idea that it could be a single bug.'

'And we don't have any clue about how it is transmitted?'

Mathur's face showed his uncertainty. 'All we can do for now is guess. If it weren't for the cytokine storms, we wouldn't even know there is a pathogen at work.' He paused and met Burke's gaze. 'But if I'm right, then we're dealing with something new, strange and deadly. A previously undiscovered microbe that is somehow completely invisible to our immune systems. Which means that no vaccine will work against it.'

Burke raised his eyebrows. 'A pathogen that can bypass our immune systems. Sounds crazy, even impossible.' He gestured to the report. 'Yet something has caused these patients to end up here in the state they are in.'

He looked at Mathur. 'How do we even begin to look for a cure?'

October 15
Putney, London Borough of Wandsworth
UK

Alex Wilson had a spring in his step as he left The Spotted Horse, an eighteenth century pub, after an evening with his friends. It was fine weather, a rare event for that time of year, and he had decided to enjoy it by walking home.

He felt good. Accomplished. An excerpt from his forthcoming book, an explosive biography of Alexander von Humboldt, the famous German naturalist, geographer and explorer, had been very well received by the media. The pre-orders were stacking up well. His book was already a bestseller weeks before its official release.

Humboldt himself had been a prolific writer and much had been written about him during his lifetime and after his death in 1859. Which was not surprising, given how influential he had been as a scientist and thinker in his era, with people like Thomas Jefferson, Charles Darwin and Simon Bolivar, among hundreds of other luminaries, counting themselves as his friends or fans.

Yet, despite being the most famous scientist in the world while alive, Humboldt, today, had been forgotten. His name lived on in the countless things that had been named after him. But it was no longer as easily recognisable as it had once been.

Wilson's book would change all that. Despite the volumes written about Humboldt, there were mysteries that still lingered. In the course of his research, Wilson had found clues to some of these enigmas—the case of the missing parts of Humboldt's voluminous journals, for one. And he had also made some discoveries through sheer dogged enquiry and innate inquisitiveness that revealed things about Humboldt and his travels which no one had known. These would also raise new questions, but that was good for it would increase book sales.

Wilson had hinted at some of these mysteries in the excerpt his publishers had released. The excerpt had featured in the morning newspapers, creating a buzz about his book that no amount of advertising could have done.

He whistled a tuneless song as he walked. The streets were deserted. People were either at home or in the pubs at this hour.

Wilson welcomed the peace and solitude after a busy day of fielding questions from the media.

So busy was he with his thoughts that he didn't notice a black van with darkened windows pull up alongside him.

By the time he became aware of its presence it was too late.

Five men, wearing balaclavas that left only their eyes visible, sprang out of the moving vehicle, giving him no time to react.

It was all over in a matter of seconds. Wilson was overpowered, gagged, bound and shoved into the van which then sped away. There were no witnesses to his abduction.

Wilson was going to make the headlines, but not in the way he had intended.

The Dorchester Hotel
London, UK

Christian van Klueck studied the glass of whisky in his hand. The complex design etched in the crystal lent a glow to the rich amber liquid within. He took a sip, savouring the smoky flavour of the single malt, and ruminated on the conclusion he had reached.

His cellphone rang. He looked at the number and accepted the call.

The caller got straight to the point. 'I saw the report you sent me.'

'You agree?'

'It certainly seems right. The pattern is difficult to miss.'

'That's what I thought.' Van Klueck took another sip of his whisky. 'Too many correlations to be a coincidence.'

'Yet we have no idea who is coordinating all this. If these are not coincidences, then there has to be a single agency at work.'

Van Klueck grimaced. He too had come to the same conclusion after studying the operations of the Order which had been thwarted in recent years. It had perplexed him. Though these operations had been disrupted by the government agencies of different countries, the level of cooperation required among these agencies for them to succeed just didn't exist in the real world.

'So, what is your plan?'

'Well,' van Klueck chose his words carefully. 'Now that you have seen the evidence and agree with me, we do what we've always done. Eliminate the traitor.'

There was a moment's silence. Van Klueck knew exactly what his caller was thinking.

It wasn't the first time that the Order had had a traitor in its ranks. In the centuries of its existence, even the Order had not proved impregnable. But this time it was different.

'We've never had someone from within the bloodline betray the Order before.' The caller voiced what van Klueck was thinking.

It was van Klueck's turn to be silent. He was not of the bloodline. And he didn't want to be seen as turning on one who was.

'What do you suggest, then?' he asked finally.

'A final test. A validation of your conclusion. If your suspicions are correct, then even the bloodline cannot be a reason to make an exception.'

'Agreed.' Van Klueck saw another advantage to this strategy. 'And it may also lead us to the agency that has been a thorn in our side.'

'You have the perfect test case, have you not?'

'Yes,' van Klueck agreed.

'Let it be done then.' The caller signed off.

After disconnecting the call, Van Klueck spent a few moments lost in thought.

Then he picked up his phone again and dialled a number.

A female voice answered. 'Hello, Christian.'

'Dee,' van Klueck addressed her. 'I have a job for you.'

PART II

A RACE AGAINST TIME

DAY ONE

October 21
The White House
Washington DC, USA

'We now know that this disease is a global one and not just limited to the USA,' Amy Bryant, the director of the Centers for Disease Control & Prevention (CDC) told her audience, which included the president, the vice president, the secretary for the Department of Health and Human Services (HHS) which oversees the CDC, the director of the CIA and other members of the president's innermost circle.

Bill Patterson, director of the Global Task Force —or the GTF as it was now referred to—listened in horror as Bryant updated the group, that had hastily been mobilised for an emergency briefing on the mysterious contagion that was slowly, but surely, spreading through the world. Patterson was not a regular member of this group, but had been specially summoned by the vice president to attend the meeting.

'Thousands of people have been infected all over the world,' Bryant told the group. 'Transmission is likely both airborne and via contact with contaminated surfaces, though we have no way to be sure. The initial symptoms are neurological—memory loss, disorientation, confusion, incoherence for those with mild symptoms—but almost all patients then go on to develop further complications ranging from gastrointestinal disorders, physiological problems, deterioration of the nervous system and cognitive disorders to organ failures and muscular dysfunction. There seems to be a general consensus amongst the experts who have studied the cases known so far that it is very likely, that despite the wide range of symptoms, a single pathogen is responsible. The exact symptoms experienced seem to depend on the health and constitution of the individual, comorbidities and genetic make-up. From what we've seen so far, it takes around seven days for the symptoms to develop. We have no idea yet whether asymptomatic transmission is possible or not, though there is a fair chance that it is.'

James Ryan, the president of the United States of America, wore a calm expression that did little to reveal the sense of foreboding in his mind. 'And it is possible that there are people out there who are infected but have not yet been found?' He voiced the fear that lurked in the minds of all the people in the room.

Bryant looked away for a moment, uncomfortable. Then she took a deep breath and held Ryan's gaze. 'Yes, Mr President.'

'What's the prognosis, Amy?' President Ryan urged in his slow Texan drawl, his voice steady. 'Let's hear it.'

'The prognosis is not good, Mr President,' Amy Bryant informed him, her face grim. 'There have been no deaths so far, but some of the patients are critical and in the ICU. It is only a matter of time for them. Unless a cure is found—within days, not weeks—we expect a hundred per cent mortality rate for this disease.'

A deathly silence descended on the group. Her words had chilled everyone to the bone.

Bryant took a deep breath and continued. 'We've spent the last two weeks on our toes ever since the first reports of this infection came to our attention from Connecticut. We've been working with the WHO and health ministries of other countries where similar cases have been detected.'

She paused, clearly disturbed by the update she was giving. 'We've roped in the best epidemiologists and infectious disease experts, not just in the States, but across the world. Despite our best efforts, we've drawn a blank. We cannot identify what is causing the infection.'

She pursed her lips and sat back.

'What about the WHO?' Ryan demanded. 'Put pressure on them to declare a pandemic. Get member countries to begin locking down and sealing the borders. We're their largest source of funds. Surely we can do this much?'

'The WHO has refused to declare a pandemic. There aren't enough cases, they say, so it will be difficult to convince all member countries about the seriousness of the disease, especially with no clearly identified pathogen. Enough countries will believe conspiracy theories about the USA wanting to destroy their economies and political systems using this as an excuse to lockdown their economies and borders.' Bryant looked at Ryan helplessly. 'And there are some WHO experts who are questioning if this is even a pathogenic infection at all. They say it just isn't possible for a single bug to cause such varied symptoms and have refused to rule out the possibility that it is a genetic disease rather than an infectious disease.'

'Yet you are sure it is the latter?'

Bryant nodded. 'Yes, Mr President. We have good reason to believe it is.'

'Let's hear it then.' Ryan folded his arms and sat back in his chair.

Bryant glanced at Michael Austin, the secretary of HHS and her direct boss.

Austin nodded and took up the briefing. 'We've been coordinating at an unprecedented level with the governments of the countries in which the patients live. Through an elaborate system of tracking and contact tracing, it has been established in more than 90 per cent of the cases that patient zero in each country had been in China in the first week of September, about a week prior to the manifestation of their symptoms. Specifically, in Hotan.'

Austin looked meaningfully at the president.

'And the remaining 10 per cent?' Justin Bedford, the vice president wanted to know. 'What about them?'

'We haven't been able to trace patient zero in those cases,' Austin replied.

'So, it is a 100 per cent match in the cases where you have been able to identify patient zero,' Bedford concluded.

Austin nodded.

'What is the probability that the patient zero in the remaining 10 per cent is Chinese?' Bedford asked thoughtfully. 'Someone in Hotan?'

'It is possible, though we cannot be certain, of course,' Austin assented.

Ryan considered this for a moment, then addressed David Walsh, the CIA director. 'Does this mean that the China Telegrams aren't fake after all? I thought experts had certified them as a hoax?'

Walsh looked uncomfortable and exchanged a glance with Steve Martinéz, the secretary of Defence. 'That's what we need to find out, Mr President. It is complicated. Since the China Telegrams were published last month, some classified information has come to light that seems to substantiate the hypothesis that the agent causing the infection is a bioweapon developed by China and somehow let loose in Hotan either deliberately or accidentally—it is difficult to say which. What we have learnt now is that a complete lockdown has been enforced in Xinjiang. It hasn't reached the news channels or social media since the CCP was quick to impose censorship. Internet access has been shut down in Xinjiang, just like it was in 2009. We've been talking to the Chinese government agencies for several days now, but they've been tight-lipped, denying anything of the sort. Only now, when we presented them with evidence, have they finally admitted there is a problem. Even so, they claim that there was a terrorist attack by Islamic radicals in Hotan in the first week of September which started the epidemic in Xinjiang. They're blaming it on bio-terrorism.'

President Ryan looked thoughtful. 'And that validates your theory about this being an infectious disease.'

He looked at Martinéz. The glance between the CIA director and the secretary of Defence had not escaped his attention. 'What is this classified information that has come to light? Did we know about this all along? Why haven't I been briefed already?'

It was Martinéz's turn to look uncomfortable. 'Well, Mr President,' he began. 'As you know, we have a classified programme to develop countermeasures against bio-threats. As part of that programme, we outsourced some sensitive lab work to non USA-governmental organisations.'

Ryan nodded. 'Titan Pharmaceuticals is one of them. As I remember, they are still working on stuff for us.' He leaned forward and rested his arms on the conference table. 'But good heavens, Steve, that's a defensive programme! Not a bioweapons programme!'

'I know, Mr President.' Martinéz shrugged. 'There's a fine line, I guess. To many countries it would look like an offensive bioweapons programme.'

President Ryan leaned back and gestured for Martinéz to continue his explanation. 'So where does China come in?'

The White House
Washington DC, USA

'Around fifteen years ago, we began outsourcing some lab work to China. Nothing high-tech; just basic research. It was cheap, the risk was low and the quality of their output was high. They were keen to deliver. It worked for us. It worked for them. Win-win.' Martinéz shrugged again. 'Then a few years after they started, they came to us for funding for a new line of research in synthetic biology. It was a nascent area of research at that time and even today the progress made in that area is insignificant compared to the potential. It was interesting and it could get bigger, so we agreed to fund them.' He paused.

'And?' Ryan pressed him.

'It was slightly anticlimactic. After five or six years of funding, they told us they weren't making progress and shut down the project. It was the same year that Howard Barnsfield drove his car off a cliff because he wasn't making headway with his efforts to build a synthetic organism.'

There were nods around the table. Everyone recalled the headlines Barnsfield's suicide had made. He had been a brilliant scientist, working at Craggett University, and one of the leading lights in the field of genetics and synthetic biology. His death, especially the manner of it, had come as a shock to the scientific community.

'So, you're saying the Chinese labs lied to us,' Ryan got to the nub of the matter. 'They actually did make a breakthrough and develop some kind of a synthetic bug, which they hid from us. And they've been evolving it over the years until it somehow escaped or was let loose last month in Hotan and is now causing the pandemic we are witnessing. And the China Telegrams are not a hoax as we originally thought. Did I get that right?'

'It is a possibility, Mr President. But we can't be certain. We know nothing. No facts. We have no evidence.' Martinéz looked at Walsh.

'We're shooting in the dark,' Austin observed, soberly. 'Even if we did fund the Chinese synthetic agent programme, I find it very hard to believe that with just a few years of research the Chinese labs were not only able to develop a synthetic microbe that has devastating effects, but also one that can slip past the human immune system and disappear without a trace. There was a reason why Barnsfield failed and took his life. He wrote it in his suicide note. And Barnsfield was one of the leading scientists, perhaps the best, in the field of synthetic biology. And he failed after years of trying. What chance would any other scientist have of succeeding in just a few years?

'Yet we have an infection on our hands that we cannot diagnose and cannot treat,' President Ryan mused. 'That seems to be the only thing we know about this damn bug!'

There was silence again.

Patterson's brain was awhirl. The GTF director now understood why he had been asked to attend this meeting.

'C'mon, folks,' President Ryan spread his hands, as if imploring his team to give him some good news. 'Give us a break, will ya? Surely you're not saying there is nothing we can do to avert the extinction of the human race?'

The faces in the room were grim. Ryan was not exaggerating. It was clear to every person there that if the unknown microbe was not identified and a means to destroy it found, the contagion would spread from person to person, country to country, killing everyone it touched, until there was no one left to infect. Or kill.

'We're on pretty thin ice with China as it is, Mr President,' Walsh said. 'It is a difficult country to operate in from an intelligence point of view. We have no way of validating the China Telegrams. Unless …' He looked at Patterson meaningfully.

'Patterson?' President Ryan turned to him. 'This looks like a task for your team. Not the CIA. What's your plan?'

Patterson nodded. This was what the GTF had been set up for. He had an answer ready. 'If we can get China to agree to a WHO team visiting Hotan for first-hand information, meeting Chinese researchers who have worked on the epidemic so far along with medical staff on the frontline—no "wet science"—I can slip in a couple of my people to see if we can find the source of the contagion.'

'Fine.' Ryan pursed his lips. 'I'll make the call. We need to do this. We have a responsibility to make this right. Make sure your team is ready to fly out.'

DAY TWO

October 22
Intelligence Bureau Headquarters
New Delhi, India

Bill Patterson's face was serious as he stared out of the large television screen at Vijay and Imran Kidwai. From an adjacent screen mounted on the wall, Alastair Duncan, the UK commander of the GTF, looked on. A third monitor showed the face of Colin Baker, who had also been summoned for this meeting.

The GTF had been originally set up as a bilateral organisation—the USA–India Task Force—to tackle technology-based terrorism around the world. The team had quickly morphed into an international set-up with several other countries joining and giving the GTF considerable heft and a global reach.

Since its inception, the GTF had done a commendable job of battling techno-terrorism. The last two years particularly had been very productive for the task force, especially when it came to its efforts against the Order—a shadowy, amorphous organisation about which very little intelligence existed with any government on earth. The GTF had managed to successfully uncover and thwart several small projects sponsored by the Order, ensnaring, in the process, several agents of that enigmatic organisation. Imran, who was on deputation from the Indian Intelligence Bureau as deputy director of the GTF, had played a major role in rooting out these projects, directing and monitoring intelligence operations across the globe.

But the Order itself remained beyond reach and as impenetrable as ever. None of the agents who had been apprehended were senior enough to have information about the organisation beyond their immediate mission.

Initially, both Vijay and Colin had taken a dislike to Patterson. Both of them were civilian members of the GTF, along with Dr Shukla, a linguistics expert with considerable knowledge of ancient Indian texts. Together, they had played a big part in thwarting two major projects of the Order in the past few years. Colin, a natural rebel, had instantly abhorred Patterson's overbearing attitude, brusque manner and insistence on military-style discipline. Vijay had taken just a bit longer, sharing Colin's opinion about Patterson after being reprimanded in no uncertain terms by the director upon violating the GTF code almost off the starting block.

But over time they had come to like the man. Beneath that gruff, tough exterior, honed by years as a USA Navy SEAL, lay a warm human being who was committed to doing his job well and had a high level of integrity. Both these qualities meant no compromise under any circumstances, which manifested in his tone, language and seeming rigidity.

The past few months had seen a lull in the GTF's caseload, enabling the civilian members of the force, Vijay, Colin and Dr Shukla, to return to their normal lives. The rest of the members of the GTF were either former military or intelligence men whose normal lives involved keeping tabs on what was happening around the world, obtaining and analysing a constant feed of news to ensure that they were able to pre-empt any major issues on the world stage.

As had happened now.

Vijay and Imran had received a summons for this meeting of the GTF an hour earlier. Now, with everyone logged into the videoconference, they waited for Patterson to speak.

'It never rains,' the director began. 'It pours. All these months, there was nothing. Now, suddenly, we have two completely unrelated concerns that have been flagged. The one that concerns you guys is from the United Kingdom.'

Vijay looked at Imran. Was the Order at work again?

'Duncan will brief you.' Patterson muted himself as the GTF's UK commander nodded.

'Aye, thanks, Director Patterson.' Duncan spoke with a marked Scottish brogue. 'Well, we have a strange one on our hands, don't we? And it has taken its own sweet time in coming to our notice, but there you are.'

He glanced at his notes. 'Here are the bare facts: last week, an author named Alex Wilson disappeared.' He took a pause, looked up and continued. 'Wrote biographies, I am told. He was last seen at the Spotted Horse in Putney, not too far from his house, where he'd had a couple of pints with his mates.' He looked up from his notes. 'This should have been a case for the local police—and so it was—until the day after his disappearance, when his publisher received a terrorist threat. Wilson had a book that was about to be released. The terrorists threatened to blow up the publisher's offices if they released the book. The publishers dithered for a few days and finally went to the police. It took a couple of days for the matter to reach the home secretary, who decided to call us in.'

'Because nothing about this made any sense,' Patterson interjected as Duncan paused. 'The police had no idea what to do with the case since there were no leads.'

'Aye, director,' Duncan agreed. 'Why would a terrorist organisation—which has remained anonymous, by the way— be interested in holding back the release of a book?'

Vijay raised his hand.

'Yes, Vijay?'

'Director Patterson, what was the book about? It could give us a clue as to why Wilson disappeared. Maybe he was abducted? There must be something in it that the terrorists are worried about going public.'

Patterson nodded. 'You're thinking along the same lines as we did, Vijay. The trouble is that the subject of the book is quite innocuous. It is a biography of Baron Alexander von Humboldt, a nineteenth-century naturalist, geographer and explorer. Hardly cause for trouble, I should think. Especially since tomes have been written about him already.'

He paused. 'You think it is the Order.' It was a statement, not a question. Patterson had noticed the glance that Vijay and Imran had exchanged.

'There has been no intelligence chatter about anything like this,' Imran said slowly, a frown creasing his forehead. 'But it is strange that the terrorists issuing the threat have not revealed their identity. Nor have they indulged in any terrorist activity. No one has been attacked, nothing has been blown up. It is almost as though they don't want any attention directed to themselves. But they do want leverage. It does seem that suppressing the publication of the book is really what they want. This sounds more like the modus operandi of the Order than a regular terrorist organisation. And we haven't dredged up any activity by their agents for several months now. It isn't like the Order to stay quiet for so long. Unless we're missing something.'

Vijay nodded grimly. The Order had been responsible for the murder of Radha, his fiancée, whose body had never been recovered. He had relished every opportunity he had been given to sabotage their operations ever since, despite the danger it entailed and getting shot twice on different missions against the Order. 'Sounds right,' he agreed. He ticked off the points on his fingers. 'An innocuous nineteenth-century naturalist. An anonymous threat. No obvious motive. A perfect fit.'

'That's what you and Colin have to find out,' Patterson told him. 'If it is the Order, Wilson's disappearance could lead us to something bigger that they're planning.'

'Roger,' Colin acknowledged the assignment.

Vijay nodded his acceptance as well.

'The complete dossier on the case is available in the task force shared folder. You fly to London today. Duncan will coordinate with you both,' Patterson concluded.

'What's the second case, Director?' Imran was curious.

Patterson's face took on a grim expression. 'I'm going to China. We've been given the task of validating the information in the China Telegrams.'

Craggett University
Boston, USA

'Dr Tsai will join you in a minute.' The young woman who had ushered Patterson into the office smiled at him.

'Thank you,' Patterson smiled back at her.

As he waited, his mind ran through the dossier on Iris Tsai who was to be his partner on this mission to China. While she was not a formal member of the GTF, she had been co-opted for this mission for two reasons.

First, she had been born in China, having moved to the USA only fifteen years earlier, and was fluent in Mandarin, which made her perfect for the role Patterson had in mind for her.

Second, Patterson and Iris Tsai were scientists whose fields of study overlapped. Patterson had earned PhDs in molecular biology and chemical biology, in addition to his former career as a USA Navy SEAL. It was one of the reasons he had decided to go to China himself instead of deputing someone else for the job. It was just more credible. And no one would have to forge papers or bone up on science they had no idea about.

Iris Tsai was a brilliant scientist. Just short of turning thirty, she had made a name for herself in the world of neurobiology, genetic engineering and synthetic biology. With degrees from Harvard and MIT, including a PhD from Harvard, she was now head of the Tsai Lab and an assistant professor in the departments of Brain and Cognitive Sciences and Biological Engineering at Craggett University. The Tsai Lab held quite a few patents even for the short time it had existed and, according to its website, was engaged in cutting-edge research on using synthetic biology and precision gene editing to develop molecular and cellular tools and delivery systems for these tools to develop a new generation of therapeutics.

Both Tsai and Patterson were to pose as members of the WHO team; which would not require much subterfuge. The WHO itself lacked the staffing to undertake a full-scale investigation of this nature on its own and was accustomed to rely on external experts for fieldwork. The real deception was the objective of Patterson's own mission. While Iris Tsai was going as a bona fide scientist, Patterson had a second, secret objective.

The China Telegrams.

The door opened, and a voice intruded on his thoughts.

'Dr Patterson? I'm Iris Tsai.' The speaker was an attractive Chinese woman with a dazzling smile.

Patterson rose to his feet and shook her extended hand. 'Call me Bill, please.'

Iris smiled at him and sat down. 'I got a call from the White House, saying they wanted me to be part of a top-secret mission. I'm guessing you are a secret service agent, but of course you aren't going to tell me that, are you?' She laughed.

Patterson smiled. 'I can honestly say I'm no secret service agent. Like you, I've been requested to be part of this mission. I'm a biologist.'

'I see. So, what is this mission about? I was told you would give me the details. All I know is that we're supposed to travel to China on short notice.'

'And here I am,' Patterson smiled at her again. 'Are you packed? Our plane's waiting. I'll brief you on board. We'll have plenty of time to discuss the mission en route to Beijing.'

In the air over Europe

Vijay shut his laptop with a sigh. He had been reading the manuscript of Alex Wilson's book on Alexander von Humboldt, which had been obtained from the publisher. It was a well-written biography, there was no doubt about that. Wilson was clearly an accomplished writer.

But he really couldn't see what the book contained for any terrorist organisation to worry about or want to suppress.

Vijay had been stunned by the magnitude of Humboldt's achievements as detailed by Wilson. To begin with, he had had no idea that so many glaciers, mountain ranges, rivers, waterfalls, parks and towns were named after the German scientist, not to mention nearly three hundred plants and more than one hundred animals and several minerals. Even an area on the moon—the *Mare Humboldtianum*—was named after him.

Humboldt had been a prolific writer, but that was the least of his accomplishments. Apart from his pioneering travels across the world, he was possibly the first real environmentalist, conceiving the impact of deforestation and industrial activity on climate change. His work was an important precursor to Darwin's theory of evolution. Indeed, Charles Darwin had been in awe of the German naturalist and had eagerly read all his books. Humboldt was often called a 'pre-Darwinian Darwinist'.

It was Humboldt who had discovered the idea of a keystone species. It was he who had written that nature is a living whole, thus providing a new perspective on the natural world. Humboldt had invented isotherms, discovered the magnetic equator and the cold current off Chile and Peru now called the Humboldt current. He had talked about an ancient connection between the continents of Africa and South America, and explored how islands—now separated by vast distances—had once been connected or had been part of a larger landmass long before theories of continental drift had been formulated. He had written about subterranean forces causing continental shifts two hundred years before the theory of tectonic plates was developed.

Humboldt's explorations in South America had convinced him that the continent had had an ancient and sophisticated culture in the distant past, contrary to the image of wild savages portrayed for centuries in Europe.

To Vijay's surprise, Humboldt had also had strong sympathies towards Indians, along with South Americans, due to their exploitation by colonial masters. It was his critical attitude to colonialism that had traditionally been thought to have cost Humboldt the opportunity to visit India, which he had long desired to do. Although Wilson provided strong hints in the book that there was a deeper, more sinister reason for the East India Company's refusal to allow Humboldt to visit India in the early nineteenth century.

Poets like Wordsworth and Coleridge had used Humboldt's works as inspiration for their poetry. In fact, Humboldt had been good friends with Johann Wolfgang Goethe, the famous literary figure. Wilson had written much about their close friendship but what had surprised Vijay was the revelations about Goethe in the book. Goethe's literary works were famous—*Faust* being possibly the most prominent—but Vijay had had no idea that Goethe had also been a passionate botanist, with his own theories about plants. In fact, one of the revelations that Wilson had made in his book was about a previously unknown letter that Humboldt had written to Goethe in 1830, two years before the latter's death.

Yet, Vijay could find nothing incendiary in the book, that would incite terrorists to issue threats to stop its publication.

He knew he was missing something. But what?

A thought struck him. Maybe if he took a different tack, it might help. He had been reading the book as any reader would and had been overwhelmed by the sheer volume of information about Humboldt that Wilson had painstakingly put together.

But what if there really was no terrorist threat and therefore, no terrorists?

Vijay began to warm to this idea. What if he assumed that it was indeed the Order behind the so-called terrorist threat? That it was they who didn't want the book to be published and not a bunch of terrorists who couldn't care less who Humboldt was or what he did.

How would that assumption affect the analysis of what he had just read?

Vijay turned over the information he had just perused in his mind. His excellent memory came in handy at times like this since he didn't need to refer to his notes. He sat for a while, thinking hard.

What would the Order be interested in hiding? If they didn't want the book published, it meant there was some revelation that they didn't want the world to know about.

Mysteries. Secrets. That's what the Order was all about.

Wilson had in fact written about a few mysteries. But Vijay had not paid them much attention because, unlike the rest of the book, the sections that dealt with these mysteries appeared to have been cursorily written. There were few details provided by Wilson and the overall tone of the narrative seemed to suggest more speculation than fact.

What if there was more to those passages than met the eye?

He studied them again.

There was, to start with, the missing parts of Humboldt's travel journals. According to Wilson, Humboldt had reorganised his journals a few years before his death, which was when many portions of the journals, describing a large part of his travels, had gone missing.

While Vijay had come across secret journals and missing texts in the past, in this case, if something was missing, why would it perturb the Order? It didn't make sense.

Then there was the mystery of why the East India Company had refused to allow Humboldt to travel to India, despite his dogged attempts to get permission. He had travelled four times to London to meet the directors of the East India Company. He had solicited the support of powerful men in London, including the Prince Regent. But nothing had worked. And Wilson was quite clear that the accepted view that Humboldt's anti-colonial writings were responsible for his failure to visit India was incorrect. According to Wilson, it was the discovery of an ancient manuscript by a British soldier that lay at the root of the East India Company's refusal to allow Humboldt into India.

Could this be it?

It did sound like something the Order would be interested in. The Order was an ancient organisation, apparently going back thousands of years, and many of their projects, including the ones that the GTF had aborted over the past few years, revolved around a search for, or discovery of, ancient manuscripts and accidental discoveries from antiquity. But Wilson had not shared any more details regarding the manuscript, except for its name—the Owen manuscript—after Captain Owen, the soldier who had unearthed it.

Why would the Order be interested in suppressing this? There was barely enough information as it were.

What about the letter Humboldt had written to Goethe? It was unpublished. Again, Wilson had provided scant information about the contents of the letter. All he had mentioned was that Humboldt had written the letter after his tour of Russia in 1829 and that he had very excitedly described to Goethe a strong link he had stumbled upon between the Owen manuscript and a mystery he had encountered in South America more than 25 years earlier. The nature of that link or details of the mystery in South America were, however, not elucidated by Wilson.

Then it hit Vijay like a bolt of lightning. Of course!

He opened his laptop and connected to the aircraft's Wi-Fi, browsing for almost an hour before he found it.

He couldn't be a hundred per cent certain, but he had a hunch.

Vijay picked up his satellite phone and made a call.

'Alastair!' he greeted Duncan breathlessly. 'We need to visit Oxford tonight!'

He quickly told Duncan what he needed, then put the phone down and sat lost in thought.

A familiar thrill coursed through his veins. Was he on the cusp of uncovering another big operation of the Order?

He couldn't wait to find out.

Weston Library
University of Oxford
Oxford, UK

Vijay, Colin and Duncan sat at one of the tables in the deserted café in the foyer of the Weston Library, outside the Admissions Office, waiting. After Vijay had called Duncan from the plane, the Scotsman had immediately followed up on his request.

Colin had arrived at London Luton airport from the USA at almost the same time as Vijay. Both had flown in on aircrafts chartered by the GTF and met at the airport. It was only then that Colin had learned of Vijay's plan to drive directly to Oxford from the airport.

After meeting Duncan at the airport, the three had started on their expedition. On the way, Vijay had updated his colleagues on his theory.

Now they were waiting for their guide to meet them as appointed.

Presently, a woman in a floral skirt and white blouse, with a florid complexion and hair liberally streaked with grey, hurried to where they were seated and beamed at them apologetically.

'Oh dear,' she said. 'I am so, so sorry to have kept you waiting. It's all the permissions, you see. We don't allow non-members into the Radcliffe Camera, unless they buy the tour, or apply for a Reader Card, so …' She stopped abruptly and stood there, hands clasped. Clearly, this was an unusual and uncomfortable situation for her. Duncan had used his military connections and credentials to swing this special request their way. The University would not be able to refuse, but the paperwork could not be waived either.

Duncan smiled at her. 'No worries, my dear. I'm Alastair Duncan and these are my colleagues, Vijay Singh and Colin Baker. We do appreciate your accommodating our request at such short notice.'

'Oh my! So remiss of me!' Her hand went to her mouth, embarrassed at her lapse. 'I didn't even introduce myself, I was so flustered. I'm Julie Hunt, and I will show you to the Radcliffe Camera and assist you with your request.'

Vijay and Colin shook hands with her and smiled.

'Come on, then!' Julie gestured and set off with the three men in tow. 'It's just a couple of minutes from here!'

As they walked, she gave them a brief introduction to the building they were about to enter. 'This is the most beautiful building in Oxford, with the third largest dome in Britain. It was built between 1737 and 1749 as the Radcliffe Science Library. In 1860, it was taken over by the Bodleian Library and renamed the Radcliffe Camera. Today it serves as a reading room for the Bodleian Library.'

'Is that where the letters are kept?' Duncan asked.

'Not usually.' Julie shook her head. 'All our old manuscripts are normally kept in the Weston Library, in special temperature and humidity controlled rooms. Though the oldest part of the Bodleian is the Old Library, which is almost 600 years old.' She gestured to the building on their right, as they walked down Catte Street. 'But we acquired this set of unpublished letters just last year, so they've been temporarily housed in the Radcliffe Camera.'

She looked at Duncan and then at Vijay and Colin. 'You had specifically asked for the unpublished Humboldt letters that Alex Wilson had requested to see when he applied for his Reader Card.'

Access to the collection of manuscripts and old papers at the Bodleian Library was limited to people who held a formal affiliation to colleges, departments or institutions at the University of Oxford. Anyone who was not affiliated needed to apply for a Reader Card if they wanted access to these collections.

When Vijay had discovered, while trawling the internet on the plane, that a set of unpublished letters written by Humboldt was among the collections at the library, he had asked Duncan to contact the University and check if Alex Wilson had researched this collection.

It had been a long shot, but they struck gold. Wilson had indeed applied for a Reader Card—and in his application he had requested access to the collection of Humboldt's letters that Vijay learnt was in the Bodleian Library. It was this collection they had come to peruse now, to see what it was that Wilson had discovered that could be important enough for the Order to cover up.

As they rounded the corner of the Bodleian Library complex and the Old Schools Quadrangle and turned right into Radcliffe Square, they caught their first glimpse of the circular building named after Dr John Radcliffe. Dr Radcliffe had decreed in his will that a portion of his funds be used to build a library.

Julie Hunt had not exaggerated when she had described it as a beautiful building. But Vijay was not interested in its architectural splendour or historical significance. All he could think about was what the circular building contained.

Humboldt's letters.

What would they find there?

Radcliffe Camera

Radcliffe Camera

University of Oxford

Oxford, UK

Four heads bent over the sheaf of letters written by Humboldt to his various acquaintances.

'Is there something specific you are looking for?' Julie asked, as she carefully sifted through the letters. 'Or would you like to go through each one?' By the look on her face, it was obvious she hoped they didn't. Humboldt's handwriting was illegible and they could be here all night trying to read this collection of letters.

'Actually, we were looking for a letter from Humboldt to Goethe.' Vijay was glad she had asked and kicked himself for not having thought of being more specific. But then he had had no idea if Julie would be able to help them find the letter they wanted to read. 'Would you be able to help us find it?'

A look of relief spread across Julie's face. 'Oh, that's quite simple! There's just one letter from Humboldt to Goethe here. I was asked to show you around because I'm familiar with this particular collection, having handled it from the time of its purchase.'

She slowly flipped over each letter until she came to one that was written on a single page. 'Here you go.'

They stared at the squiggles on the page masquerading as letters and words.

Not only was Humboldt's writing hard to read, but the thought that Humboldt may not have written this letter in English had not crossed their minds.

'Do any of you read French?' Julie looked up at them as they peered over her shoulder at the letter.

'Weren't both Humboldt and Goethe German?' Duncan wondered. 'Why would Humboldt write to Goethe in French?'

Julie shrugged. 'Both were Germans, as you rightly pointed out. But Humboldt wrote in many languages—French, German, Spanish, Latin, English. And Goethe was fluent in French right from his childhood. In fact, it is said that the last book Goethe read the day before he died was a volume by Balzac, the French novelist and playwright. Would you like me to translate this letter for you?'

'Yes, please!' Vijay responded eagerly. 'Are you able to read it though?'

'It won't be easy,' Julie laughed. 'Humboldt was notorious for being the only one who could really read his own handwriting. But I do have the advantage of familiarity.'

'That's perfect, thank you so much.' Vijay was dying to hear what the letter contained.

There was silence for a while, as Julie scanned the letter, trying to decipher Humboldt's miniscule handwriting. Vijay, Colin and Duncan waited patiently.

After around half an hour, Julie finally looked up, her brow furrowed. 'I'm sorry,' she said. 'There are many words I just cannot make out. So I'll give you a general translation rather than a word-for-word translation.'

She glanced back at the letter, trying to pull her thoughts together.

'The letter was written in 1830,' Julie began. 'I can't make out the exact date, but the year is readable. Humboldt sounds quite excited. He rambles a bit, but essentially is updating Goethe about another letter he had written to Goethe several years ago—Humboldt reminds him of that letter, referring to a story about a monkey who grew back his leg in South America in 1800.' She raised her eyebrows, but continued without stopping. 'Apparently this monkey had lost a part of his leg and, over a period of two months, it regenerated. Then Humboldt talks about the discovery in 1807 of the Owen manuscript, and his attempts to visit India to investigate a link that he thought existed between the manuscript and the regeneration of the monkey's leg.' She looked up uncertainly. 'You know, this is rather weird—he actually uses the word "regeneration", as if it was a real occurrence, rather than a story.'

She turned her attention back to the letter. 'The East India Company denied his requests repeatedly, so he was unable to personally investigate this link. But he says, "Last year, my theory was validated, if not by fact, then by anecdotal evidence, by an Indian fakir who I met in Astrakan." Which means that he met the fakir in 1829. He ends the letter by saying that he is both excited and worried, for his discovery—he doesn't say what this discovery is—could lead to a new, greater future for the human race, but could equally become its doom.'

Julie looked up. 'That's all I could make out. There could be more detail about some of the things I've mentioned but if there is, I can't read it, I'm sorry.'

Vijay's eyes were shining. 'Please don't apologise. I think we've learnt what we needed to know. You have been immensely helpful. I don't know how to thank you.'

'Really?' Julie beamed, delighted with his praise and appreciation. 'I helped, did I? Well, you're welcome any time! Is there anything else I can do for you?'

'Actually, there is,' Vijay told her. 'Can we get a peek at the Owen manuscript?'

On the M40

En route from Oxford to London

UK

'So what do you think?' Vijay asked as they sped towards London in Duncan's BMW. Vijay sat in the passenger seat next to him, as he drove, while Colin sat in the backseat.

Julie had proved to be very helpful. At Vijay's request, she had looked up SOLO (Search Oxford Libraries Online), the online catalogue provided by the Bodleian Library, that listed all printed materials in the Oxford libraries, and located the Owen manuscript.

The three men had gazed upon the ancient, ragged, strips of birch bark, bound together and held in place by two wooden boards.

'Wow!' Colin had breathed, awestruck by the fact that they were looking at a document that was almost two thousand years old. It had been dated back to the second or third century CE. 'Is this Sanskrit?'

'Yes, Sanskrit written in the Brahmi script.' Vijay had read up on the Owen manuscript on the flight to London. 'Apparently, a form of Sanskrit that not everyone could translate. Several Indian scholars tried and failed; it fell to a German scholar—Friedrich Fischer, who was born in Agra and died, coincidentally, in Oxford—to painstakingly translate the manuscript.'

After gazing upon the ancient document, there had been nothing more to see or learn at Oxford, so they had thanked Julie for her help, and were about to leave when she had dropped a bombshell.

'*You know,*' she said with a nervous laugh, wringing her hands, '*I'm not usually inquisitive, but …*' She hesitated, then seemed to overcome her indecision. '*I'm wondering what is suddenly so interesting about Humboldt's letter and the Owen manuscript. I mean, I don't know about the manuscript, but the letter has been with us for several months now and no one had ever asked to see it. And now, in the space of just a few months, you are the third party to show an interest in using both sets of documents for their research.*'

Duncan was instantly alert. '*Wilson, us and who else? Who is the third?*'

'*Oh, well, I don't recall the name of the person who had applied for a Reader Card to access these documents for his research. But I do know it was a very pleasant Chinese gentleman. He came in just last week to file his application.*'

The three men looked at each other, but didn't allow their bewilderment to show.

'*Would you be able to share the name of this gentleman with us?*' Duncan asked her, the genial smile on his face masking the intention behind his request.

'*Well …*' Julie paused to think for a moment. '*Usually, it would be against the rules, but since you are here on government work, I suppose it's all right.*'

Having obtained her promise to email the name first thing the next morning, the GTF group said their goodbyes and set off for London.

'Well,' Duncan spoke up now. 'I can't figure out if this Chinese angle is something we should be suspicious of or not—I mean it could be entirely innocuous. And we'll find out more once we get the name from Julie. But it certainly looks like you were on to something, Vijay. I don't know the Order as well as you two, given the number of times you've both crossed swords with them, but now your theory does make sense.'

'Yes,' Colin agreed. 'When you told us what you were thinking, it seemed to be a stretch. But after hearing the contents of Humboldt's letter, it does seem that the Order could be involved. If the East India Company had discovered something in the Owen manuscript—which is about as ancient as it gets—and they wanted to keep it hidden away, it would explain their stubborn refusal to allow Humboldt to visit India. And it is quite clear from the letter that Humboldt did have an interest in visiting India.' He leaned forward and put a hand on the backrest of Vijay's seat. 'But what I don't understand is the story of the monkey. Humboldt was a scientist. A respected scientist. How could he believe in the regeneration of limbs? That just doesn't happen! Could he have meant something else?'

'Yes,' Vijay agreed. 'I'm a bit baffled by that piece of the puzzle. It doesn't fit in. And, at least from whatever I could find about it on the internet, the Owen manuscript doesn't talk about regeneration either. So, what is the link that Humboldt refers to in his letter to Goethe? Is that link important to the Order? And do they want to suppress Humboldt's knowledge of that link? But why? What would happen even if the world did get to know what Humboldt told Goethe?' He shook his head. 'Too many questions. I think we've hit a dead end.'

'Hang on, mate,' Duncan protested. 'Not so fast. You caught on to the importance of the Owen manuscript. Colin and I didn't. Why did you want to see the manuscript?'

Vijay smiled sheepishly. 'Oh, that. That was only because I wanted the thrill of gazing upon a two-thousand-year-old document. In the flesh, in a manner of speaking. Gave me a kick.'

Colin rolled his eyes. 'Seriously! Vijay, sometimes you can be really ...' his voice trailed off as he searched for the appropriate word.

'Okay, how about I tell you what I found out about the Owen manuscript?' Vijay proposed.

On the M40
En route from Oxford to London

'Aye, that's pure barry,' Duncan responded.

'Huh?' Colin was flummoxed. 'Who's Barry?'

Duncan chuckled. 'Sorry, mate. That's Scottish slang for "utterly wonderful and fantastic".'

'Don't people in Scotland speak English?' Colin countered.

'About as much as you Americans do,' Duncan retorted.

'Touché.' Colin sat back and folded his arms. 'We're all ears, Vijay. Pure barry, as Duncan put it.'

Duncan chuckled again. 'Learning fast, laddie.'

'Okay, so the story of the Owen manuscript is quite intriguing,' Vijay began. 'It starts with a murder, as all good stories do. Back in 1806, a Scottish trader was murdered in the Karakoram mountains by a Pathan from Quetta. The murderer was most likely a thug, if one goes by the description in *The Geographical Journal* published by the Royal Geographical Society; more than six feet tall and powerfully built. The Scotsman didn't have a chance. So Captain Owen, who was travelling through a place he calls Yarkand—I have no idea where that is—was commissioned to capture this Pathan. This was in 1807, a year after the murder.'

'Ah,' Duncan piped up. 'A Scotsman to avenge a Scotsman.'

Vijay smiled and continued the story. 'While on this mission to track down the Pathan, Owen reached a village south of the T'ien Shan mountains in what is today Xinjiang and at that time Chinese Turkestan. There, he was befriended by a local who told him about a book that he and his friends— all of them locals—had discovered in the remains of an ancient city not far away. Apparently, this book was unearthed from within an ancient tower of some kind—Owen doesn't know whether it was a tomb or a stupa, a fortification or a victory tower; he even visited it in the dead of night—and he bought the ancient book from this local guy. This book was what we saw today at the library—the Owen manuscript.'

'What a story,' Duncan said. 'Amazing!'

'There's more,' Vijay continued. 'Owen finally tracked down the murderer, but that isn't the important part. He brought the manuscript back to India in 1807 and handed it to a Colonel Wilson, who in turn sent it to Henry Thomas Colebrooke, who was the president of the Asiatic Society at that time. Colebrooke was a Sanskrit scholar who immediately saw the value of the manuscript and he set about having it deciphered. As I said earlier, some Indian scholars attempted to translate it, but failed. One of them wrote to the Asiatic Society, speculating that this manuscript might be the sole surviving remnant of Indo-Tartar Sanskrit, which was prevalent in Khotan—now known as Hotan—and Kashgar in the first couple of centuries CE.'

Duncan and Colin listened with rapt attention to this fascinating tale. Vijay had explained to them during the drive from Luton airport to Oxford that he had drawn a blank on his first reading of Wilson's book. He had told them about how he had eliminated possibilities until he had zeroed in on Humboldt's letter to Goethe and the Owen manuscript, and how he had then researched until he had learnt that both the letter and the manuscript were in the possession of the Bodleian Library at Oxford.

'Finally,' Vijay continued, 'Fischer, who was also a Sanskrit scholar and the secretary of the Asiatic Society, got his hands on the manuscript after returning from Europe, where he had been on furlough, and deciphered it after several months of study.'

'So what does the manuscript say?' Colin couldn't hold back his curiosity any more. 'Did you manage to find a translation or a synopsis online?'

'That's the problem.' Vijay frowned. 'I couldn't find a copy of Fischer's translation online that I could download. There are a few references to the contents of the manuscript, but they are cryptic and don't really shed much light on anything that could have interested Humboldt so much. Yet, his letter makes it clear that he was really excited about something in the Owen manuscript.'

'Tell us what you found,' Colin pressed, wanting to know more.

Vijay shrugged. 'Like I said, not much. Apparently the fifty-six pages of the manuscript are not one text. It is actually seven different texts or, as Fischer put it according to one source, a collective manuscript of seven parts. Some of the parts seem to make up a treatise on medicine, others on the art of divination and the rest contain mantras against diseases. From what I could find on the internet, the parts dealing with medicine are fragments—there are leaves missing or incomplete. And apparently, by the time the manuscript reached Fischer, the leaves were disordered, possibly due to the fact that it had passed through several hands, each of whom may have cut or loosened the strings that bound the entire book together. And the *British Medical Journal* of 1808 was dismissive of the medical tracts, essentially calling them useless from a medical perspective. What was the word they used?' His brow furrowed as he tried to recall what he had read. 'Oh yes! Farragos. They called the texts a collection of farragos.'

'That doesn't tell us much.' Duncan couldn't hide his disappointment.

'No, it doesn't,' Vijay agreed. 'That's what baffles me. There must have been something in the text that caught Humboldt's attention. But what was it? He wouldn't have had any knowledge at all about ancient Indian medicine.'

'Maybe Wilson found something?' Colin suggested. 'It would be great if we could take a look at Wilson's research notes.'

Vijay stared at Colin. 'You are a genius, Colin. Have I ever told you that?'

'Not often enough,' Colin sighed. 'Alastair, is it possible for us to access Wilson's research notes?'

'Aye, that we can,' Duncan affirmed. 'We can do that now if you want. All his stuff is still at his house. We'd have done it earlier, but the paperwork took time. One of the challenges of being an unofficial and secret organisation. We were planning to pick it up tomorrow. We can head there right away. I'll get someone to organise the keys; we can pick them up on the way.'

He made a quick call and organised their access to Wilson's house.

Vijay had a hard time controlling his excitement. He was convinced that there was a missing link between the Owen manuscript and Humboldt's letter. What was it?

Putney, London Borough of Wandsworth
UK

The BMW drew up outside the two-storey townhouse. Someone on Duncan's team had met them en route and handed over the keys to the house. Colin figured that Wilson must have been quite well off. The house was fairly large—it looked like it had four or five bedrooms, with two large bay windows that overlooked the street and a short driveway with small green patches on either side leading to a porch.

It was almost midnight and the street was quiet.

Duncan unfastened his seatbelt and frowned. 'That's funny.' He opened the glove compartment of the BMW and pulled out three Glocks, handing one each to Vijay and Colin.

'Trouble?' Vijay wondered.

'I thought I saw a light inside the house,' Duncan replied as he glanced around anxiously. 'There shouldn't be anyone here. The house is locked.'

Colin stared at the house. 'Are you certain? Doesn't look like any of the lights are on.'

'Exactly.' Duncan frowned, a bit less sure now. 'I could have sworn the lights winked out just as we arrived.'

'Do you think it could be the Order?' Vijay felt his hair stand on end as he spoke. Had the Order beaten them to it?

But that was the mystery. Beaten them to *what*?

'I'll take the back of the house, you two take the front,' Duncan instructed them. He handed them the keys to the front door and looked at each of them in turn. 'You know the drill, right?'

Vijay and Colin nodded. While they weren't hardened field agents, they were no longer the novices they had been when the GTF was created. Over the last two years, they had received enough training both in the classroom and in the field, as well as first-hand experience on missions, to know what they were supposed to do in a situation like this.

And they had both been in situations like this before.

'Let's go.' Duncan clambered out of the car, leaving the door open to avoid making a noise.

Vijay and Colin followed his example and left their doors open as well.

Duncan disappeared, heading for the rear of the house as Vijay and Colin noiselessly made for the front door.

Everything was still and silent.

Even the night.

Not a leaf stirred in the trees around them.

It was almost as if the world was holding its breath to see what would happen next.

The two friends vaulted over the boundary wall which was around two and a half feet in height, landing softly on the grass.

Keeping to the shadows, they advanced to the porch and arrived at the front door.

The porch was dark.

'Damn!' Colin hissed.

They had no option. To unlock the door, they needed light.

'Be quick,' Vijay whispered.

Colin nodded. He took out his mobile phone and switched on the torchlight. Quickly inserting the key into the front door lock, he switched the torchlight off and silently turned the key, hoping the light had not been noticed by anyone.

He pushed the door. It swung open silently.

Vijay hoped that the locked front door meant Duncan had been mistaken about the light he had seen in the house. The house was so silent he could almost believe it.

But something told him they weren't going to be so lucky.

The two men crept inside. In the dim light from the streetlamp that filtered through the entrance, they could make out that they were standing in a short passageway that opened into a kind of lobby. On one side, directly in front of them, a staircase wound up to the first floor. Two doors, leading out of the lobby, were visible. One was set in the wall next to the staircase, the other was in the wall that stretched from the passageway into the lobby, perpendicular to the staircase.

They looked at each other. There was nothing to do but to keep going.

Colin wondered how Duncan was faring. There was probably a backyard to this house. How would the Scotsman enter?

He waved the distraction aside and tried to focus on their situation.

The wooden floor underfoot creaked as they left the entrance passage and stood in the lobby, abreast with the glass door in the left wall, the room beyond it a well of darkness.

Vijay grimaced at the noise their movements made. If there was indeed someone in the house, there was no way they had not been alerted to the intrusion. And if the entire ground floor had wooden flooring, then stealth was no longer an option.

Colin jerked his thumb to the right, pointing out two more doors. One was fully wooden and the second had a wooden lower half with a glass fitted on top. Beyond it there was darkness.

Both men instantly flattened themselves against the wall nearest them, trying to stay within the shadows. The lobby

Backyard with small lawn

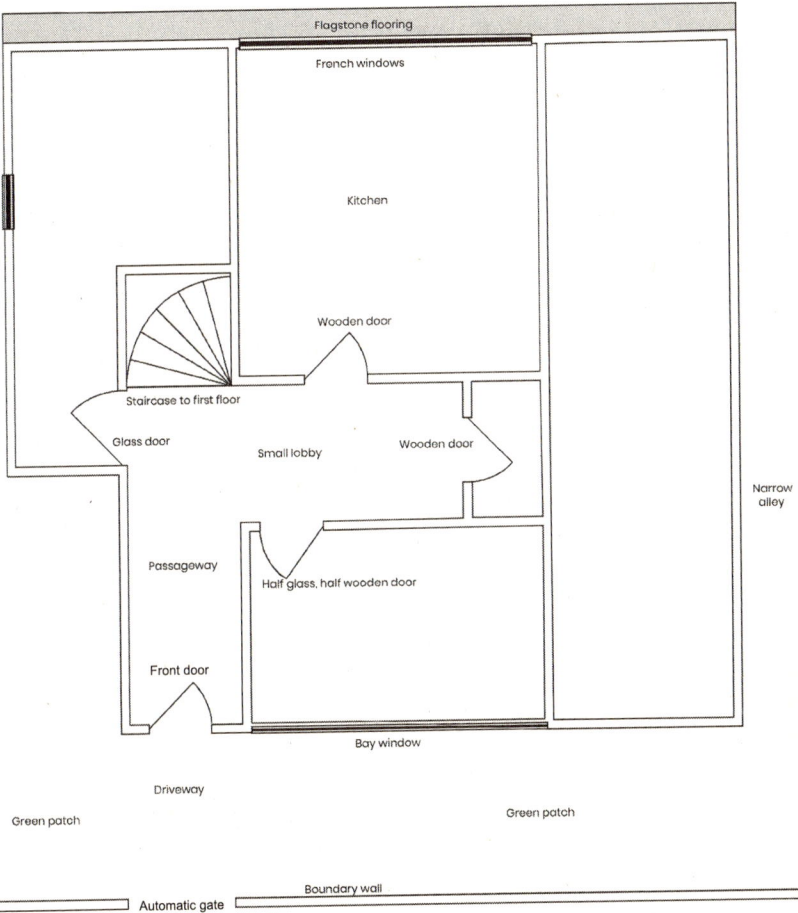

Flagstone flooring

French windows

Kitchen

Wooden door

Staircase to first floor

Glass door

Wooden door

Small lobby

Narrow
alley

Passageway

Half glass, half wooden door

Front door

Bay window

Driveway

Green patch

Green patch

Boundary wall

Automatic gate

Wilson's house plan – Ground floor

was an insidious trap—exposed from all sides—if there were intruders hiding in any of the rooms that led off it.

And then there was the matter of the staircase and the first floor.

Vijay gestured to Colin. *You take the first floor.*

Colin nodded.

He stealthily crept to the staircase and began making his way up, trying not to step too fast or too heavily on the wooden stairs lest they creak with his weight.

As Colin disappeared up the stairs, Vijay decided to begin by checking out the room with the glass-topped door.

Still keeping to the shadows, he lowered himself to the ground and edged his way to the door, ensuring that his head stayed within the wooden lower half and below the glass upper half. Reaching the door, he stretched out a hand and slowly turned the handle.

It squealed as he turned it.

Vijay cursed silently. But he remembered his training. It was always better to wait for the opponent to make the first move when you were going in blind. That way you knew what you were dealing with.

The door opened and he swivelled back against the wall, out of the line of the doorway, and waited.

When nothing happened for a while, he rolled into the room, heading for the wall adjoining the entrance passage, his eyes watchful for any sign of movement. As he touched the wall, he sat up, his gun held in front of him.

Nothing moved.

The room was empty.

Vijay sighed with relief.

Time to check the other rooms.

Where was Duncan?

Vijay slithered out of the room and crawled towards the wooden door set in the opposite wall, next to the staircase.

He slowly turned the handle, hoping this one wouldn't squeak.

It didn't. The door opened slightly on well-oiled hinges.

Thank God!

Light from outside the house filtered through large French windows on the far side of the room, casting shadows across what was clearly a large kitchen.

Vijay slid inside, sticking to the wall.

One of the shadows in the kitchen abruptly moved as a sudden burst of light revealed a man outside the house, running past the French windows, and there were three soft coughs in quick succession. The glass of the French windows shattered.

The light winked out and darkness descended once more upon the backyard beyond the kitchen windows.

Then all hell broke loose.

Putney, London Borough of Wandsworth
UK

Duncan was familiar with the layout of the house, having been there before. Leaving Vijay and Colin behind, he swiftly vaulted the boundary wall and slipped through the darkness to a rough wooden door that led to a narrow alley within the premises, which ran along the side of the house to the backyard.

He passed a small wooden toolshed and emerged into a spacious backyard with a lawn separated from the house by flagstone flooring. Bracing himself against the wall, he looked around, thinking through his next move.

In front of him was the garden, bordered by a wooden fence. To his left, a set of French windows led into the kitchen. The problem was that there was no way to open them from the outside.

He decided to secure the kitchen even if he couldn't enter it. Slowly, carefully, he edged his way to the French windows and peered inside.

The kitchen was dark.

Nothing moved.

He had to risk it. Now or never.

Duncan sprinted past the French windows, keeping low and looking into the shadows in the kitchen as he ran, trying to gauge if it was unoccupied.

As it turned out, he needn't have looked.

As he ran, a diffused light came on above, on the first floor, casting a glow on the garden. And him.

He cursed. It illuminated him for just a moment, then was gone. But it was enough.

The glass of each of the French windows shattered in turn as he sped past them. The only other indication that someone was shooting at him was the soft cough of a suppressor on the assailant's gun, not unlike a car door slamming shut.

Duncan dived and rolled on the flagstones as he reached the last French window, scrambling to get out of the line of fire and to the shelter of a wall. He pulled himself up to a seated position with his back to the wall and waited, breathing heavily.

He grinned despite himself.

At least the problem of opening the French windows was solved.

Was his attacker going to come outside to finish the job?

Putney, London Borough of Wandsworth
UK

Inside the kitchen, Vijay pounced on the gunman who had shot at Duncan. There was no question of mistaken identities—the Glocks the GTF team carried were not fitted with suppressors.

The gunman turned out to be a tough adversary. As Vijay attacked him, knocking his gun out of his hand, the man twisted around and punched Vijay on the chin, making him see stars. He followed up the punch with clean chops that sent Vijay's gun clattering to the ground, then pivoted for a vicious roundhouse kick that, had it been better aimed, would have instantly knocked out Vijay.

As it happened, the shooter had been distracted by Duncan and not anticipated Vijay's sudden assault, and his roundhouse kick landed on Vijay's arm.

With the impact of the kick, Vijay lost his balance and fell heavily to the floor.

His training kicked in and, as he went down, he twisted to land on his back and lashed out with his legs, tripping up his opponent who joined him on the ground.

Vijay leapt on top of the man, grappling with him as the two of them rolled around the kitchen, each trying to get the better of the other.

Putney, London Borough of Wandsworth
UK

Duncan stood up and listened. The sound of a slugfest came to his ears from the kitchen.

What was happening?

He swung around so he could look inside the kitchen, his gun aimed, and saw two figures grappling on the floor. One of them had to be Vijay or Colin, but there was no way of telling who was who.

Duncan decided to enter the fray and leapt through the shard-lined frame of the French window nearest him.

As he entered the kitchen and drew closer to the two men wrestling on the floor, the door to the kitchen opened and another figure burst in.

Was it one of his team? Or another intruder?

Realising that the situation was now precarious, Duncan thought swiftly and remembered that there was a light switch on the wall next to him. He flicked it on and the garden lights came on, illuminating the kitchen enough for him to see that it was Vijay on the floor, grappling with a masked opponent, and the man who had entered was also masked and had a haversack on his back.

The new intruder had aimed his gun at the two men on the ground, probably trying to figure out which one was his teammate, but when the lights came on and he saw Duncan's gun aimed at him, he swung his weapon towards Duncan instead.

But he was a split second too late.

Duncan fired but he was shooting while moving and caught the second intruder in the shoulder with his bullet. Luckily, it was the man's gun arm and he dropped the weapon, stumbling back with the impact of the bullet.

Pressing his advantage, Duncan charged like a bull and used a classic rugby crash tackle, sending the injured gunman flying backwards and causing him to crash onto the floor.

Panting, Duncan looked back to see that Vijay too had got the better of his adversary and had pinned him to the ground.

The Scotsman grinned with satisfaction, then turned to his stunned opponent and pulled off his mask.

A Chinese face glowered back at him.

Duncan turned to the man who was pinned down by Vijay and pulled off his mask as well.

A second Chinese man.

Vijay and Duncan looked at each other, bewildered.

Were these men working for the Order?

Vijay opened his mouth to speak, but before he could say anything, footsteps rang out as someone clattered down the wooden staircase.

Duncan and Vijay were instantly on alert.

Was there a third intruder?

Putney, London Borough of Wandsworth
UK

Colin reached the landing at the top of the staircase. It was a tiny one, leading into a room—presumably a bedroom—through a door to his left, and into a narrow corridor that angled to the right a few feet in front of him.

Everything was silent. It was unnerving.

Grasping his gun tightly, he slowly crept into the bedroom on his left.

It was dark. To secure the bedroom, he would have to switch the light on.

He felt along the wall, trying to find a switch. But there was nothing.

Colin moved forward and tried another wall. This time, he was in luck. His fingers found a switch and he flicked it on.

Bright light streamed from a ceiling lamp with five bulbs. He quickly switched it off, but not before noticing a window with the blinds down. The room was empty, as was the ensuite bathroom.

As the light went out, he heard a commotion downstairs.

Colin had no idea that he had just shone a light on Duncan as he had sprinted past the French windows leading from the kitchen to the lawn.

Were those gunshots? So there was someone else in the house apart from them.

What was happening down there?

For a moment he was torn between going down to investigate and continuing to secure this floor. Then he

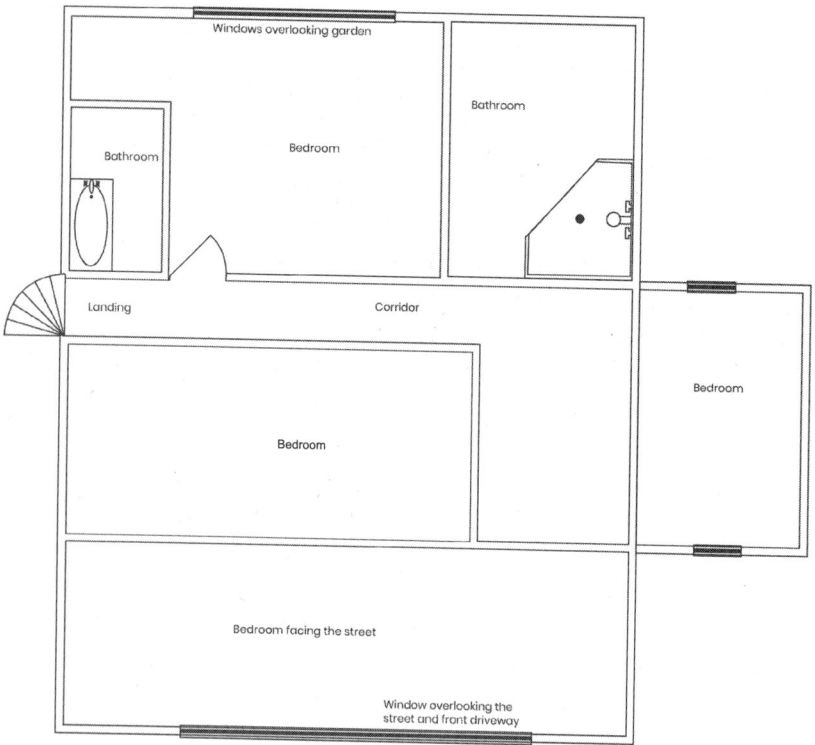

Windows overlooking garden

Bathroom

Bedroom

Bathroom

Landing

Corridor

Bedroom

Bedroom

Bedroom

Bedroom facing the street

Window overlooking the
street and front driveway

Wilson's house plan – First floor

decided to finish the job at hand first. Operations like this were all about teamwork. If someone was hiding upstairs and he neglected to secure the first floor, it wouldn't help that he had rushed to aid his teammates.

Anyway, both Duncan and Vijay were downstairs, so they could backup each other.

Colin slowly made his way out of the room and down the corridor. There were three doors leading off the corridor.

He stepped forward carefully, trying to make as little noise as possible. If someone had decided to hide in one of these rooms, they would have definitely heard the noise from below and would want to investigate. He didn't want to be taken by surprise.

To his relief, as he went through the three bedrooms one by one, he found nothing.

As he stood in the last bedroom, which faced the street, he heard a loud bang from the floor below.

That was definitely a gunshot.

He turned to go, then froze.

Through the window of the bedroom, which overlooked the street, he saw their BMW, its three doors still open. Someone had switched on a light downstairs, and some of it spilled into the driveway and front gardens.

The tumult from downstairs had ended. But that was not what had arrested his attention.

A large black van had silently drawn up. It was probably an electric vehicle, which was why he hadn't heard it drive up.

The van disgorged four masked men, all carrying automatic weapons. They immediately took up defensive positions outside the house. They seemed to have not expected anyone to be in the house.

Were these reinforcements for whoever Duncan and Vijay had encountered on the ground floor?

Whoever they were, they spelled trouble.

Colin knew they had minutes, if not seconds, before the armed men who had just arrived launched an assault on the house. Whatever they had come here for, the GTF team was going to be in the way. And it was painfully obvious that the GTF team was outnumbered and outgunned.

He sprinted down the corridor, and dashed down the staircase, bursting into the kitchen and skidding to a halt.

Vijay was kneeling on one man, having pinioned his arms behind him, while Duncan was restraining another, who was bleeding from a gunshot wound and propped up against a wall.

But there was no time for this.

'We have to leave. Now.' There was an urgency in Colin's voice that could not be ignored. He nodded towards the Chinese men. 'I think they've got reinforcements.'

A puzzled look flitted across the face of the injured shooter. He said something in Mandarin to the other gunman and got a short reply in return.

A glance passed between Vijay and Duncan and they both nodded.

'Now!' Duncan and Vijay rose with one accord and the three men sprinted through the French windows, cutting across the garden and pulling themselves over the wooden fence at the back.

To their great surprise, the two Chinese men, instead of running towards the entrance to meet the reinforcements, were also bolting from the house.

It was as if all five men had temporarily set their differences aside and were fleeing together. They all hit the ground beyond the fence and ran through the garden of a neighbouring house, past another wooden fence, until they reached a parallel street.

As if on cue, probably summoned by one of the Chinese gunmen, a black van sped up, the rear door opened as it slowed slightly and both gunmen leapt into it, haversack, gunshot wound and all. Then the van sped up again and was gone.

The GTF team jogged down the street as Duncan called for another car to pick them up, noting on his phone their exact GPS position.

'Are we safe here?' Colin wondered as they stood in the shadows, facing the direction of Wilson's house in case anyone had pursued them.

Before he could get an answer, the sky above the house lit up with a bright orange glow.

'It's on fire,' Duncan said grimly. 'They're burning it down. Someone doesn't want us to find out what Wilson discovered.'

In the air over the Pacific Ocean

'So, in Beijing, we will be debriefed by the Chinese researchers who have been working on this disease and learn what they have discovered so far. Then we will be taken to Hotan where we will do our own fieldwork—no access to any labs, mind you, and accompanied all the while by a Chinese escort—after which we return home.' Patterson shut his laptop, put it on the seat next to him, stowed away his meal tray, and leaned back.

'In brief, our mission is to go in for a few days, do the rounds of hospitals and doctors and find out as much as we can about what's happening there. It will be a quick trip. In and out.' Patterson concluded his detailed brief on the epidemic in China, the cases that had been detected around the world, the symptoms, the progress of the disease, the mysterious absence of any possible pathogen that could lead to symptoms—along with the equally baffling absence of antigens and antibodies or any kind of immune response apart from the cytokine storms—and finally their assigned responsibility as part of the WHO team that was assembling in Beijing.

There was silence for a few moments as Iris seemed to mull over the reports and data that Patterson had shown her during the flight over mainland USA. She had been full of questions and Patterson had dutifully provided answers. Where he had had them, of course.

Patterson wondered what she was thinking. He hadn't disclosed everything to her, keeping his own role in the mission to himself. Quite apart from the classified nature of his own assignment, the less Iris knew, the better. It would keep her safe. She was of Chinese origin, but that meant nothing to a totalitarian state that took umbrage at the slightest challenge to its authority.

Finally, Iris spoke. 'So, I was chosen as part of the team because our intelligence experts believe that China has developed a synthetic pathogen which has somehow got loose and might cause a pandemic. And the Chinese government is not admitting to anything, so we're going to see what we can dig up about this pathogen.'

Patterson smiled to himself. He had expected nothing less. It was her perspicacity that had led him to suggest her name for this mission.

'You didn't take much time to figure that out,' he laughed. 'And you're right. As I told you, this is a clandestine mission, but it made more sense to include you for your expertise, than a CIA agent. And who could make it all look any more authentic?'

Iris smiled. 'It's obvious, isn't it? Neither of us is an epidemiologist. True, my research is targeted at therapeutic outcomes, but I'm hardly an expert on infectious diseases. And neither are you, Bill. Now, I can't say why they asked you to be part of this team, but something tells me that my research in synthetic biology is one of the reasons why *I* was considered for the job. For a top-secret mission like this one.'

'That's right,' Patterson admitted. 'We don't believe that the claim of an Islamist terrorist attack is genuine. For a while now, the CIA has been hearing rumours about a secret scientific experiment being run by the Xia Yu Pharmaceutical Group—the largest state-run pharmaceutical company in China. Not only have they been sponsoring a lot of research in academic institutions across China, but intelligence leaks indicate that they have their own secret labs across the country working hard to develop a synthetic bioweapon, one that can be used not only in war against other countries, but also in the occupied territories of Tibet and Xinjiang. Maybe even Hong Kong and Taiwan.'

Iris eyed him doubtfully. 'But there are no high-tech labs in Xinjiang that I've heard of. Or are you saying there is a secret lab somewhere in Xinjiang—perhaps in Hotan—that is engaged in cutting-edge research on synthetic biology?'

'There could be. But we don't have any evidence.'

'So, one of our mission objectives is to try and find evidence, right?'

'Correct.'

'How do we know that we aren't barking up the wrong tree? I can't believe that the USA government would pull me out of my lab and assign me to a job like this unless they had a very good reason. I think I contribute much more through my research than by running around in China on a wild goose chase.' She fixed Patterson with a steady gaze. 'Which tells me that it can't be a wild goose chase, then. What makes the White House believe that China has developed a synthetic pathogen? I mean, the fact that no pathogen has been detected so far despite hard evidence that something is causing this mysterious disease is definitely an indication that *someone* has created a synthetic microbe that can somehow slip past the human immune system—hard to believe practically, but there could be any number of theoretical ways this could be achieved. But why China? Why not North Korea or Iran?'

Patterson held her gaze. He had hoped he would not need to divulge more than he already had. But, if his mission was to be successful, he needed her full cooperation and it was clear to him that she would be satisfied only if all her questions were answered.

'You are right,' he nodded. 'This is no hunch, no random call to investigate what might turn out to be a dead end.' He hesitated before continuing. 'The evidence lies in the China Telegrams.'

In the air over the Pacific Ocean

'The China Telegrams?' Iris frowned. 'What are they? Telegrams from whom? And to who?'

Patterson chuckled. 'They're not actually telegrams. They're a bunch of more than four hundred documents— highly classified and marked "top secret", which is the highest level of official secrecy in China—that were leaked last month, and obtained by the ICIJ—the International Consortium of Investigative Journalists. The papers were shared with the ICIJ by a member of the Chinese political establishment who preferred to stay anonymous but wanted to warn the world of a looming danger that no one suspected.'

He opened up his laptop again and clicked on the trackpad a few times until he found what he was looking for. He turned the screen to face Iris so she could see the document he had opened.

'Autonomous Region State Organ Telegram,' Iris read the title. She looked at Patterson, still confused.

'The leaked documents included a classified list of guidelines which were personally approved by Wu Xingxu, deputy secretary of the CCP, Xinjiang Uyghur Autonomous Region.' He pointed to the screen. 'You can see his name inscribed at the top. This Telegram is effectively a manual for a new bioweapon programme being spearheaded by Xia Yu. This manual is called a "Telegram" in the Chinese communication system. It covers the operation of top-secret labs as well as procedures for procuring human subjects for live experiments as part of the development process, and running the camps in which these human guinea pigs are housed. The telegram instructs the personnel in charge of running the bioweapons programme on lab operations, including ensuring total secrecy about the labs and the camps, methods for preventing escapes from these camps and even when to allow detainees to use the toilet. Apart from the Telegram—which consisted of nine pages in Mandarin dating back five years— the leaked papers include six intelligence briefings, called "bulletins", also in Mandarin, providing guidance on the daily use of the Integrated Joint Operation Platform or IJOP—a mass surveillance and predictive policing programme used to analyse data from Xinjiang; around one hundred pages of speeches by leading figures in the CCP and another two hundred pages of directives and reports on the surveillance and control of the Uyghur population in Xinjiang. Together, these documents were nicknamed the China Telegrams.'

Iris was overwhelmed. And shocked. 'You mean we've had this information for the last three months and we've done nothing about it?'

Patterson saw the anger in her eyes. He shrugged. 'This was widely reported by the media partners of the ICIJ,' he told her. 'And the China Telegrams created quite a stir; it was a big deal in intelligence circles—the first set of internal Chinese documents that explicitly talked about a Chinese bioweapons programme. But the Chinese government launched a massive campaign to prove that the China Telegrams were fabricated. The CCP is good at manipulating the media. Bloody good at it. The documents were examined by experts, but it seems even their opinions were swayed by the powerful media campaign launched by the CCP. Eventually, the Telegrams were declared as forged and the matter died a natural death. No one took them seriously until now.'

'So, we're supposed to try and find out if this bioweapon mentioned in the telegrams is a pathogen that is invisible to the human immune system. A microbe that cannot be detected by any known means that we possess today. A synthetic pathogen that somehow escaped and made its way out of a top-secret lab, and is now spreading around the world.' There was still a ring of disbelief in her voice.

'Look, we know something happened in Hotan last month,' Patterson told her. 'The Chinese government has admitted that there was an incident. Okay, they call it a terrorist attack. But there's no denying that this pathogen, whatever it is, was released during that incident. And there's no denying that a pathogen is causing this disease. Not with the scale of infection that we're dealing with. So why is it so hard to believe that the CCP was responsible?'

Iris looked at him, uncertainty in her eyes. 'What do *you* believe, Bill?'

Patterson could see the struggle she was going through. 'I find it hard to believe that an Islamic terrorist organisation would have the capability of developing a microbe that is as sophisticated as the one we're dealing with here.' He paused. 'I believe there is a top-secret facility hidden somewhere near Hotan, if not *in* Hotan.'

'And we have to find it?'

Patterson shook his head. 'We'd never be able to snoop around enough in Hotan. All across Xinjiang are innumerable checkpoints and CCTVs with facial recognition. The police and other authorities run apps that communicate with IJOP in real time. And there is a lockdown there now. It would be impossible to try and locate a top-secret lab—if one exists—anywhere in Xinjiang.'

Iris contemplated this.

'Better get some sleep,' Patterson told her. 'We arrive in the afternoon and get to work immediately.'

'So, all we need to do is to collect evidence for the existence of this synthetic pathogen? Or anything that indicates that it was created in China?'

'That's right.'

Iris settled back into her seat. 'That doesn't sound so dangerous.' She smiled at Patterson. 'As you said, we'll be in and out. A quick trip.' She closed her eyes and was asleep in a minute.

Little did she know what lay ahead.

DAY THREE

October 23
London
UK

'What were the Chinese men doing there?' Vijay wondered aloud, rubbing his chin. His skin was beginning to bruise where he had taken a punch. 'I don't think they were working for the Order.'

The three men were sitting in Duncan's office, having been picked up by a GTF vehicle and transported to safety. The fire service had been alerted and was still battling the flames at Wilson's house, trying not only to salvage what was left of it but also stop the conflagration from spreading to adjacent houses on the street.

'No, they weren't,' Colin agreed. 'I thought the new arrivals were their reinforcements, but I suspect they were sent by the Order.'

'Aye,' Duncan concurred. 'The Chinese intruders wouldn't have shot off like jackrabbits in the opposite direction if their reinforcements had arrived. They knew they were also in danger. I wonder if they knew who burned down Wilson's house.'

He looked at Vijay and Colin. 'You could be right, you know. If the Order issued the threat to the publishers, then it is logical that they would want to destroy anything else Wilson may have discovered, including his notes.' He sighed.

'If only the GTF had been allowed to take possession of the papers earlier.'

'Yes, but why would the Order want to destroy Wilson's papers and possessions?' Vijay was thoughtful. 'Why would they want to suppress information about Wilson's research or his book? And what is the link between the Chinese researcher Julie told us about, and the Chinese intruders? I don't think it is a coincidence that a Chinese researcher turned up at Oxford, expressing interest in Humboldt's letter and the Owen manuscript, just around the time Wilson disappeared, and then we find two Chinese men going through Wilson's house. There are too many mysteries here.'

There was silence as Duncan and Colin contemplated these questions. Clearly, they were overlooking something.

But what?

'There's only one way to find out,' Vijay said at last. 'There is something in the Owen manuscript that interested Humboldt. We need to know what that was. Remember, both Fischer and Humboldt were German, and contemporaries. Given the number of people Humboldt knew, including luminaries like Thomas Jefferson, when he was President of the USA, it is quite possible that Humboldt may have known and met Fischer. We have to read Fischer's translation of the Owen manuscript.'

'Aye, that's braw.' Duncan approved of the idea.

'Not pure barry?' Colin quipped.

'Skedaddle aff,' Duncan responded cheerily. 'Stay with me a while longer and you'll ken enough Scottish slang to find your way around Edinburgh.' His face grew serious as he turned to Vijay. 'I presume you know where we can get hold of an authentic copy of the translation.'

'Of course,' Vijay grinned at him. 'The Fischer Collection at the British Library.'

The Jingxi Hotel
Beijing
China

Zhu Jingting fixed Wu Xingxu with a stony gaze. 'We now know who was behind the attempted theft in Hotan.' He shook his head. 'Took us long enough to find out.'

'It was difficult, Zhu zǒng.' Wu bowed respectfully, using the term of respect for high-ranking government officials.

Zhu Jingting was his boss, the CCP committee secretary, Xinjiang Uyghur Autonomous Region. Zhu had been transferred from Tibet four years ago to govern Xinjiang. He was a hardliner and a tough taskmaster who made no secret of his ambition to rule China someday.

'Difficult!' Zhu snorted. 'Excuses!'

'They covered their tracks very well, Zhu zǒng,' Wu persisted. 'But no one can hide from our brilliant spies. Our strategy of planting people all over the Western world in the course of the last thirty years has ensured that.'

'You are sure about this?' Chen Gangxin spoke up. The managing director and CEO of Xia Yu Pharmaceutical Group, like Zhu Jingting, a member of the politburo of the CCP, was the third member of this little group in the suite. 'It was Titan Pharmaceuticals?'

Wu nodded. 'It was.'

'Kurt Wallace.' Chen spat and scowled.

'Actually, we're not sure if Wallace was involved in this operation,' Wu clarified. 'We do know that the CMO of Titan Pharma, Varun Saxena, gave the order.'

Chen nodded. 'Saxena had approached us two years ago, asking if we would like to collaborate on this technology. How he learnt of what we were doing, I don't know. But he wouldn't have approached us if he didn't know.'

Wu frowned. 'There's more to this than meets the eye.'

'Indians.' Chen spat again. 'So proud of their sham democracy. Yet fifty years behind China in everything.'

'True,' Wu agreed. 'The ancient Indians were worthy of admiration. They equalled us Chinese in every respect—science, philosophy, culture, technology, even economic status. But the Indians of today? They aren't worthy of a second glance.'

'Which is why they are so unimportant to us,' Zhu interjected softly. 'Don't waste time and words on the Indians. They are like flies—irritating, but not deadly. We'll continue to feed their egos; keep them thinking they are the most important thing for China, let them be happy with their petty preoccupations on the border and think that they are thwarting our ambitions, while the glorious CCP focuses on what is really important for China: global domination and global respect. Neither the Indians nor the rest of the world can stop us.' He turned to Wu. 'Any news from our team in London?'

'Yes,' Chen chimed in. 'Have they got anything yet?'

Wu nodded. 'They reported in an hour ago. They were able to break into Wilson's house and find some papers. Our experts in London are studying them now. I expect a full report in a few hours.'

'Good.' Zhu sounded satisfied. At least something was moving. He had been tense ever since the Hotan incident. The cut-off point for complete deterioration was drawing near and if they didn't find what they were looking for, he would have a bigger problem on his hands than the attempted theft in Hotan. They had successfully seen off the China Telegrams, but if another week passed and there was no success, the world's attention would be focused on China, and more importantly, on the failure of the CCP. This could not be allowed to happen. The CCP had to demonstrate that it was the most effective political organisation in the world. Infallible and invulnerable. This was important for international respect as well as domestic tranquillity. The Chinese people would accept the harsh terms of CCP rule only as long as it was efficient and competent. Any chinks in the armour of the CCP would be the equivalent of the Titanic hitting the iceberg.

And Zhu did not want to be the man responsible for that.

Wu hesitated. 'There were others at Wilson's house ...'

Zhu straightened up. He had allowed himself to relax in his chair. 'Others?'

'Yes, Zhu zŏng. Two other parties. Both armed. Our team managed to get away even though they were outnumbered. But they couldn't find out who the others were.'

'Someone else had the same idea.' Chen was thoughtful. 'Perhaps Titan?'

'Perhaps. But who was the third party then?'

'It doesn't matter.' Zhu dismissed the question. 'Apart from Titan, no one else can possibly know what we seek.' He looked at Wu. 'The team must move fast,' he urged. 'Time is not on our side any longer.'

Wu bowed.

Zhu changed the subject. 'Is everything in place for the WHO team?'

'Yes,' Chen confirmed. 'We've planned the presentations. Our top researchers will be interacting with them.'

'And Hotan?'

'We've arranged for hospital visits,' Chen assured him. 'And a visit to the Hotan market as well. They will leave convinced that we are the victims, not the perpetrators.'

Zhu's face was hard as stone. 'They had better. If there is any other outcome …'

He left the threat dangling.

But both Wu and Chen knew exactly what he meant.

The GTF Base
Hounslow
London, UK

Duncan exhaled in satisfaction as he read the name. Julie had been as good as her word and emailed him the name of the Chinese researcher who had applied for a Reader Card.

Li Ping.

He quickly typed out a note of thanks to her and then sat back, thinking.

For the first time in this perplexing case, he had a concrete lead. A name, no less.

A name could be used to locate its owner. And that owner could be watched.

Which was exactly what Duncan now planned to do.

Like it or not, Li Ping was going to get a shadow.

Duncan picked up his phone and gave instructions to find Li Ping and place him under 24/7 surveillance. 'I want to know what he does, where he goes, who he meets. I want to know when he goes to the loo. I want every minute of his day recorded.'

He put the phone down. He had no idea if this too was a blind end, but it was the only thing to go on at this time.

Duncan rose. Time to head to the British Library.

The Fischer Collection awaited.

What were they going to find there?

Beijing
China

Patterson walked briskly down the street, his mind awhirl with sorting, sifting and analysing everything he and Iris had experienced since their arrival in Beijing a few hours earlier. They had caught up with the rest of the WHO team, a motley bunch of scientists from different countries cobbled together by the WHO to investigate the mysterious outbreak that was spreading around the world.

Getting China to agree to a WHO team to visit had itself been a great accomplishment—and a clear indication that the Chinese government was up against something it did not understand or know how to control.

But Patterson was not convinced that the CCP would do all it could to ensure that the WHO team got the necessary information to determine the cause and source of the epidemic. It was simple—he did not trust the CCP. Patterson knew it was an old bias from his time in the Navy. He had tried to get rid of it. But action in part of the Chinese government agencies could dispel his belief that they were not being completely above board about this whole affair. There was definitely more to it than met the eye.

It was because of his suspicions that he was walking down the street now, en route to his rendezvous. To a meeting that could be critical to deciphering this mystery.

He knew he had to be careful. This was not America. This was not a free country.

This was China.

The WHO team was without a doubt under close observation by the Secret Police. If they were shadowing him now, they were doing a damn fine job of it. He couldn't see anyone he could suspect of being from the police. Everyone around him looked like nice, normal, friendly people.

It was uncanny. As a Navy SEAL, Patterson's nickname had been Spiderman. He had had an extraordinary ability to sense things, especially the presence of other people in places where they didn't belong. It was his sixth sense that had saved his life and those of his teammates on too many occasions to remember. Today, however, either his spider sense wasn't working, or he actually didn't have a tail.

Patterson realised how long it had been since he had been in the field and made a mental note to get away from his office in the GTF headquarters more often. He was not a 'desk job' kind of guy, but had somehow managed to get himself into that position. Things had to change.

He stood for a moment and looked left and right, getting his bearings. He had memorised the directions he had been given during his briefing, an ability developed through years of working in conflict zones, where knowing where you were could make the difference between life and death.

Next turn right.

At least he didn't have to worry about the GTF. Imran was in charge, coordinating and monitoring operations around the globe. Knowing that his phone might be tapped, Patterson had been clear that he didn't want any briefings while he was in China, who had not been approached to become a member of the GTF. Several countries, including India, had raised objections when the idea was mooted. And, so it was dropped.

China didn't know that the GTF even existed. And it was necessary that it should remain that way, especially in these circumstances. So Patterson had instructed Imran to take full control of operations while he was in China.

He turned right into a side street and looked at his watch. Almost time. There were few people on this street. Which of them was the contact?

Abruptly, there was a squeal of tyres and a car came speeding down the street, screeching to a stop beside him. A head poked out of a window and shouted to him. 'Get in. Now!'

'Who ...' Patterson began, but the Chinese man repeated. 'Get in. We go. Now.'

Patterson was accustomed to making split-second decisions. He had made so many of them during his SEAL days. Some of them had turned out well. Others hadn't. It was part of the job description.

Today, like so many of those other days, something helped him make his choice.

His sixth sense was buzzing.

He did have a shadow.

Patterson didn't wait a second longer. He opened the car door and slid inside. The driver accelerated even before he had shut the door.

Patterson knew he had bought a precious few seconds before the authorities traced his movements, but perhaps a few seconds were all he needed.

The man sitting next to him was dangling a black hood.

Patterson sighed. At least he was on the right track. If he had been taken hostage, they wouldn't be asking.

Hopefully, it also meant he was going to meet the person he was supposed to meet.

He nodded and the world went black as the hood was slid over his head.

Beijing
China

The car pulled up with a jolt, having sped through the streets of Beijing for the last hour or more; at least it had seemed that long to Patterson.

One thing was clear to him: he didn't know where he was, but it was someplace outside of the city.

'Come on!' His escort in the back seat urged him. 'We reach.'

Patterson felt the man's hand grasp his. It was soft and limp, like a dead fish, and Patterson instinctively recoiled. Then, checking himself, he gripped the hand and stepped out of the car.

At least they hadn't tied him up!

He was guided along a smooth path—concrete, Patterson surmised—then up a flight of stairs. It was not a short walk. And there were times when he felt like he was walking on metal—a suspended walkway?

Finally, the hand on his arm applied pressure, indicating he was to stop.

Patterson heard the sound of a chair scraping the floor.

'Sit.'

He obeyed. Abruptly, the hood was jerked off his head.

Patterson blinked as he emerged from complete darkness into light. Fortunately, the light was not extremely bright. Not, he realised, from any consideration for him, but more because these people did not wish to be conspicuous.

He seemed to be in an old, abandoned warehouse somewhere outside Beijing. But he didn't waste time wondering where he was. That was not of consequence. What *was* important was the reason he had been brought here.

Was it going to be worth it?

'Mr Patterson.' A voice came from beyond the lights.

'Bill. Call me Bill. Please.' Patterson blinked and strained his eyes as he tried to focus on the darkness to see who was speaking.

Was it who he thought it was?

But Patterson knew better than to reveal his hand. This was a mistake a lot of rookies made in situations like this. Faced with someone whose identity they were only partially certain of, they would blurt out the name of who they thought they were speaking to. That was the easiest way to be deceived. It was like stealing milk from a baby. If you mentioned a name, the other person would immediately assume that identity—and there was no way you could verify it.

But Patterson was no rookie.

If it was *him*, then he would identify himself.

And if it was not, well, then, Patterson was in trouble.

Deep trouble.

Just outside Beijing

China

'At last we meet … Bill.' The voice seemed to hesitate before taking his name, as if not used to addressing someone by their first name. The speaker came into the light, revealing his features. He wore horn-rimmed glasses and had a crew-cut—a picture perfect CCP technocrat.

Patterson recognised the face from the photographs he had been given as part of the intelligence briefing at the White House.

But he still had to be sure.

'How come you are free?' he demanded. 'You should be incarcerated, if not dead. Prove to me that you are who you claim to be.'

The stranger laughed. 'It is good to see that you are alert. It is what I expected.' He nodded. 'This is China. It is good to ask questions. Never trust anyone. Even if they claim to be your mother.' He cocked his head and looked at Patterson. 'But surely the fact that you are not bound hand and foot should indicate that you are not a victim of some elaborate deception?'

'Yeah,' Patterson retorted. 'Sure. With twenty guns pointed at my head, why would you need to tie me up?'

'Fair point,' the other man conceded. 'Let's not waste any more time with pleasantries. I am Lin Feng. As to why and how I am free, it is a long story and we do not have time to talk about it. Let us spend our time productively … Bill.'

Patterson considered this. The man was right. He knew that it was only a matter of time before the secret police caught up with him. For all he knew, they had tailed him with drones instead of human shadows.

'Fine. Lin zǒng.' Patterson made his decision. 'I'm going to trust you. Somehow, you are free, despite having disappeared four years ago after what you did in Xinjiang.'

Lin bowed. 'Thank you. And you do not need to address me as zǒng.' A shadow fell across his face. 'I am no longer a senior official in the government or the CCP. I am disgraced. For showing a conscience.'

Patterson's dossier had contained the key details about this man. Lin had been the CCP secretary in Xinjiang before the incumbent, Zhu.

Lin had been tasked with rounding up Uyghurs for detention and had, at first, appeared to embrace the task with characteristic zeal, building new detention facilities and increasing funding for security, along with giving rousing speeches about the extermination of terrorists.

'We must wipe them out completely,' he had said, according to the dossier that drew upon information in the China Telegrams. 'Destroy them root and branch.'

But he had also promoted economic development. And he had made the mistake of declaring publicly that there was nothing wrong with having a Quran at home. He had even encouraged party officials to read the Quran to better understand Uyghur traditions.

But it was not these transgressions that had led to his downfall.

It was something else.

Lin had secretly ordered the release of thousands of inmates from the detention camps. This was his fatal mistake, which had led to him being stripped of power and prosecuted.

He had then quietly disappeared from public view. The CCP had denounced him and initiated an investigation against him for disobeying the party's central leadership strategy on Xinjiang. He was painted as irredeemably corrupt and rebellious.

But he had been a party official with a conscience. Or so the China Telegrams had indicated.

And, until the Telegrams were denounced as forgeries, Lin, in Western secret service circles, had been regarded as China's Schindler. The man who had saved thousands of lives.

Patterson reckoned that if the Telegrams were right about the bioweapon, then Lin's act had been no less than that of Schindler—saving the Uyghurs he had released from a certain, agonising death.

It was this man that Patterson gazed upon now. And it was this man who, according to the ICIJ, had been the source of the China Telegrams leak.

'I want to thank you,' Lin told Patterson, 'for taking the risk of meeting me here. It is fraught with danger for both of us. I am a hunted man. But it was important to meet. I have so much to tell you and so little time in which to do so.'

'Tell me about the bioweapon,' Patterson's face was grim. 'I want to know everything.'

'Even I do not know everything,' Lin sighed. 'The one who knows all is Zhu, my successor. But I will tell you all I know. Even that may be enough.'

Patterson listened as the disgraced Chinese party leader revealed what he knew.

It was then that the director of the GTF realised what the world was really up against.

London
UK

Vijay was disconsolate. 'It's a dead end.' He couldn't keep the disappointment from creeping into his voice. 'There's nothing there. The *British Medical Journal* was right.'

Vijay, Duncan and Colin had spent the day at the British Library. Duncan had used his heft to organise special access to Fischer's translation of the Owen manuscript, along with a copy of the translation for each of them. They had then divided the manuscript among the three of them and settled down to review it to try and find out what, in this collection of texts, had so excited Humboldt.

Now, several hours later, they had convened to discuss their respective findings.

Vijay had spoken up first. He had been so disheartened by his lack of progress that he had not waited for anyone else to speak.

'What do you mean?' Colin asked.

Vijay shrugged. 'The journal said it was a collection of meaningless farragos. And they were right. It is a bunch of recipes for concoctions which probably mean nothing. I couldn't see anything which would interest a scientist as renowned as Humboldt. I mean, there isn't anything even remotely scientific in the text that I read!'

Duncan nodded. 'Aye, I couldn't find anything either. Just a bunch of spells that claim to provide protection against things like snakebite and stuff like that.' He had got the texts that dealt with divination and mantras.

'I didn't have much luck either,' Colin echoed them. 'I think I got the last bit of the manuscript. Or rather, the texts. It ended pretty abruptly. Fischer did make a note of this, saying he believed that the manuscript was incomplete; that there was more to it, but it was missing. He conjectured that it was probably damaged when it was retrieved, or that the missing portions had been left behind in the chamber where the manuscript had been discovered. He felt it wasn't possible that they would have disintegrated over time since the rest of the manuscript was intact and the dry weather of the Taklamakan desert would have preserved the entire manuscript.'

'So, your portion also had useless medical recipes?' Vijay asked glumly.

'Most of it. But the final section was a bit different. It is supposed to be a copy of a text written by some guy called Shush ... Suss ... ' Colin looked at Vijay. 'Help me here.'

Vijay looked at Colin's notebook. 'Susruta.'

'Yeah, right. Heard of him?'

Vijay made a face. 'Heard the name. But I've no clue who he is.'

'Dr Shukla would know.' Colin's eyes lit up. 'Let's call him!'

'Sure.' Vijay still sounded downbeat about their failure to learn anything of importance. 'At least we'll hear something interesting about ancient India, if nothing else.'

Colin opened his laptop and called Shukla using the encrypted video conferencing app developed by the GTF for use by their team members. It was secure, private, and used minimal bandwidth, so it could be used from almost anywhere in the world without a problem.

After several rings, the video conference connected and Shukla's face appeared on the screen.

'I hope it is important,' he grumbled good-naturedly. 'I was about to retire for the night and was looking forward to my sleep. Unfortunately, I hadn't switched my phone off. Or fortunately; depends on whose point of view. Do you know what time it is in India?'

'Sorry, Dr Shukla,' Colin said. 'We know it is late, but we came across something that requires your expertise. Who is Sush ... Suss ... ' He threw Vijay a glance. 'Heck, just say the damn name!'

Vijay chuckled. He couldn't help being amused at Colin's irritation. 'Susruta,' he informed Shukla.

'Ah, Susruta.' Shukla seemed to perk up. 'Well, he was an Indian physician who lived sometime in the first millennium BCE. Probably around 600 to 800 BCE—almost three thousand years ago. He is supposed to be India's first surgeon. His book, the *Susruta Samhita*, is a collection of surgical procedures, diagnostics, pre- and post-operative care therapies and even contains descriptions of surgical instruments used by him and his contemporaries. Some of the surgical tools and procedures described in the *Samhita* are still in use today.'

'You don't say,' Duncan said. 'I never knew that.'

'Lots of people don't,' Shukla told him.

'I didn't either,' Vijay admitted.

'So, we're supposed to take this surgeon guy seriously, huh?' Colin sounded unsure. 'I wasn't sure if he existed in the first place, leave alone believe what he said.'

Shukla shrugged. 'Well, the *Samhita* is real. The surgical procedures are real. But why are you asking about Susruta?' His curiosity was piqued.

Colin quickly brought Shukla up to speed on the Owen manuscript. Shukla's eyes flashed. An ancient document, the mention of Susruta—these were all things guaranteed to make his sleep disappear.

'What does this text by Susruta say?' Shukla enquired.

London
UK

'That's just what I'd begun telling them,' Colin said. 'This incomplete text—it was written by this surgeon dude who lived three thousand years ago.'

'Susruta,' Vijay interjected, unable to help himself.

Colin glared at him and resumed. 'Apparently the person who transcribed the text that is included in the Owen manuscript had copied it from an older text which probably hasn't survived.'

'If Susruta lived three thousand years ago, that's hardly surprising,' Vijay commented. 'Sorry, go on.'

'If you let me.' Colin scowled. 'Okay, so the surgeon dude says in this text that he is going to reveal a secret that was known only to the Nagas. I don't know who these guys were, but they seem to be important.'

'The Nagas were serpents,' Shukla explained. 'They were the offspring of the Maharishi Kashyapa and his wife Kadru. They were powerful and, according to the ancient texts, they now reside in two levels of Pataala Lok—the underworld.'

'Maharishi … So he was one of those ascetic dudes, right?' Colin guessed.

Vijay chuckled, despite himself. 'That's a pretty interesting description of Kashyapa, but yes, you are correct.'

'Cool,' Colin resumed, ignoring him. 'So, these serpent dudes apparently had a secret. And the surgeon dude says that he is going to reveal all.'

'Why were people in ancient India so fond of secrets?' Vijay complained.

'Well, the Nagas weren't exactly the good guys,' Shukla countered. 'If they had some kind of secret, you can be sure it was something nefarious. They would naturally want to keep it hidden away.'

'True,' Vijay agreed. He turned to Colin. 'But this is pretty vague. Doesn't Susruta say what the secret is?'

Colin shrugged. 'Hey, I don't know. Like I said, the text is incomplete. Fischer says so.' He looked at his notes. 'Hang on, there was one more thing. He said something about the Nagas and the curse of … Khan … Kahnd … Kandavp … damn it, Vijay, I've had it with these tongue twisters.'

He shoved his notebook at Vijay, who picked it up and read from it. 'Khandavaprastha.' He looked up from the notebook, his mouth open. 'That's the name of the forest that was burned down by Arjuna and Krishna.'

'Yes, yes, that's right!' Colin nodded. 'That's what the surgeon dude says. He mentions an entire forest being burned down and all the living beings inside the forest being killed.'

'Why would Susruta talk about the Khandavaprastha forest?' Shukla wondered.

'Hang on,' Duncan interrupted. 'Wur tearin' the tartan, and that's braw, but I dinnae ken what you're going on about.'

'Er, um, in English, please. I didn't understand a word of what you just said,' Colin told him.

Duncan shook his head. 'Exactly. Neither did I. What I said was that it's fantastic that we are having such a riveting conversation but I have no clue what you are talking about. What's this forest and what does it have to do with serpents and an Indian surgeon who lived three thousand years ago? I don't see an obvious connection between any of these things.'

'Sorry,' Vijay sounded contrite. 'Just got carried away. Of course, you and Colin wouldn't be familiar with Indian texts like the Mahabharata.' He looked at Shukla. 'Dr Shukla, maybe you can help them understand better than I can?'

'Certainly, Vijay.' Shukla's eyes were shining now. Explaining the intricacies of ancient texts was something he particularly enjoyed doing.

'The burning of the Khandavaprastha forest is one of the most famous stories from the Mahabharata,' Shukla said. 'But this is the first time I've heard it being mentioned in any ancient text that purports to be scientific in nature. To hear Susruta talking about it makes my hair stand on end. I want to know more, Colin. But first, let me tell Duncan and you the story of the burning of Khandavaprastha.'

London

UK

'So the Pandavas were given half the kingdom and asked to go to Khandavaprastha by their uncle, the king, Dhritarashtra, where they built a splendid city which was compared to Amravati—the city of the celestials,' Shukla concluded, after giving a quick background of the story of the Pandavas and Kauravas more for Duncan's benefit than Colin's.

Colin nodded as Shukla spoke; it was a refresher for him, since he had become more familiar with the story of the Kurukshetra war after having tangled in the past with the Order over secrets from the time of the Mahabharata.

'Wait a minute,' Vijay objected. 'I thought that the Pandavas—specifically Arjuna, with Krishna's help—burned down Khandavaprastha in order to build Indraprastha?'

Shukla smiled. 'A common misconception. But the Mahabharata is very clear about the chronology. Indraprastha was built well before the forest of Khandavaprastha was burned down.' He saw Vijay's puzzled face and held up a finger. 'Wait a minute. I'll prove it to you.'

He disappeared from the screen and returned a few moments later, bearing a thick volume. 'The Adi Parva,' Shukla explained, 'is the first of the eighteen books of the Mahabharata. This is where the story of Khandavaprastha is narrated.'

Shukla flipped through the pages until he found what he was looking for. 'Here. Listen to this.' He read out the Sanskrit shlokas:

अस्माभि: खाण्डवप्रस्थे युष्मद्वासोऽनुचिन्तित: ।
तस्माज्जनपदोपेतं सुविभक्तमहापदम् ॥
वासाय खाण्डवप्रस्थं व्रजध्वं गतमत्सरा: ।
तयोस्ते वचनाज्जग्मु: सह सर्वै: सुहृज्जनै: ॥
नगरं खाण्डवप्रस्थं रत्नान्यादाय सर्वश: ।
तत्र ते न्यवसन्पार्था: संवत्सरगणान्बहून् ॥

'Here Dhritarashtra is telling the Pandavas that it has been decided they will live in Khandavaprastha. The Pandavas then go to Khandavaprastha, taking with them jewels and the best of things, and they live there for many years. Khandavaprastha is described in these shlokas as being a place which contains people—*janpadopetama*—and which is a well-divided space —*suvibhaktamahapadam*—possibly alluding to a table land upon a height—*prastha*,' Shukla explained.

He looked up from the book. 'Quite clearly a well-planned and inhabited district by the sound of this.' He flipped some more pages.

'And here:

न च वो वसतस्तत्र कश्चिच्छक्त: प्रबाधितुम् ।
संरक्ष्यमाणान् पार्थेन त्रिदशानिव वज्रिणा ॥
अर्धं राज्यस्य सम्प्राप्य खाण्डवप्रस्थमाविश ।

'This is from a later chapter in the Adi Parva, where the story is being narrated in greater detail. Once again, Dhritarashtra is telling them to take half the kingdom and live in Khandavaprastha, protected by Arjuna, just as the Devas are protected by Indra. That's what these shlokas say. And of course there *was* a forest at Khandavaprastha—that is also mentioned in these shlokas:

वैशम्पायन उवाच

प्रतिगृह्य तु तद्वाक्यं नृपं सर्वे प्रणम्य च ॥
प्रतस्थिरे ततो घोरं वनं तन्मनुजर्षभाः ।
अर्धं राज्यस्य सम्प्राप्य खाण्डवप्रस्थमाविशन् ॥
ततस्ते पाण्डवास्तत्र गत्वा कृष्णपुरोगमाः ।
मण्डयाञ्चक्रिरे तद् वै परं स्वर्गवदच्युताः ॥

'In these verses, Vaishampayana, one of the narrators
of the Mahabharata, is saying that the Pandavas agreed to
Dhritarashtra's instructions and started for Khandavaprastha,
having received half the kingdom. And after entering the
dense forest, they made it as glorious as heaven. There's more:

तत: पुण्ये शिवे देशे शान्तिं कृत्वा महारथाः।
नगरं मापयामासुर्द्वैपायनपुरोगमाः॥

'This shloka says: those great warriors selected with the
assistance of Dvaipayana, a sacred and auspicious place,
performed the propitiatory ceremonies and measured out a
piece of land to found a city. And then this chapter goes on to
describe the city, its moat and walls, its whiteness, the gates
and mansions, the streets and even the palace of the Pandavas.
Again, this is before the forest was burned down. So, it is quite
clear that the city was built before burning down the forest
and not after.'

Shukla flipped some more pages. 'Here's one last piece of
evidence, if you will.' He read out the shloka.

वैशम्पायन उवाच

इन्द्रप्रस्थे वसन्तस्ते जघ्नुरन्यान् नराधिपान्।
शासनाद् धृतराष्ट्रस्य राज्ञः शान्तनवस्य च॥

'This verse,' Shukla told them, 'says that after the Pandavas took up their residence at Indraprastha—on the command of King Dhritarashtra—they conquered many other kings and monarchs. This shloka makes it quite clear that they not only established Indraprastha, but also annexed other kingdoms, which means that some amount of time would have passed to enable them to achieve their conquests after they settled in Indraprastha.'

London

UK

Shukla wagged a finger at them. 'All this was before the Khandavaprastha conflagration. There cannot be any doubt in anyone's mind about the chronology. The forest was burned down many years *after* Indraprastha was established.'

He shut the book.

Vijay's eyes widened. 'I had no idea. Somehow, everything I've read seems to indicate that Indraprastha was built after Khandavaprastha was burned down. There are academics who claim that the story reflects a conflict between the agrarians and the forest tribes, and that the forest was burned down to clear the land for agriculture and development.'

'With not a whit of evidence,' Shukla snorted. 'A lot of speculation. As an academic myself, I do find it strange when academics disregard the Mahabharata, calling it mythology, and then go on to create their own mythologies, without any archaeological evidence to back their speculations. Moreover, this theory of conflict between an agrarian society and tribal or forest dwellers cannot explain one of the biggest mysteries of the Khandavaprastha story: why did Krishna and Arjuna kill every single living being in the forest, with the exception of Takshaka's son, Ashvasena, who escaped; the Asura, Maya; and the four Sharangakas and their mother? What was the reason behind such a gory slaughter, especially with Lord Krishna's involvement?'

He shook his head. 'I am jumping the gun. This is no way to tell a story. It will only confuse you more.'

'Aye,' Duncan agreed. 'I'm getting cross-eyed already, trying to keep track of all the names.'

Shukla smiled. 'I'll try and make it simpler then. The Pandavas went to Khandavaprastha, which was more than just a forest, and built their city which they called Indraprastha. They ruled there for several years before Arjuna asked Krishna to accompany him and their friends to the Yamuna for—as the Mahabharata puts it—"sport". It was there, while Arjuna and Krishna were engrossed in conversation and each other's company, that Agni—the Deva who is synonymous with fire—approached them in the guise of a Brahmana, asking for food. When they asked what kind of food he wanted, he revealed his true form as Agni and expressed his desire to consume Khandava—the forest.'

'Ah, I get it now.' Duncan smiled. 'Agni burned down the forest, aided by Krishna and Arjuna.'

'Correct.' Shukla smiled back at him. 'And this is where it gets a bit mysterious. The reason Agni gives for wanting to destroy the forest is that he had been consuming ghee—clarified butter—for twelve years during a sacrifice conducted by King Shvetaki. That's another story for another time, and this sacrifice apparently happened some hundreds or thousands of years before Agni approached Krishna and Arjuna on the banks of the Yamuna. But as a consequence of twelve years of bingeing on ghee, Agni lost his lustre and went to Brahma—the Creator—for help. Brahma advised him to consume Khandavaprastha along with the *fat of all the creatures living in the forest*, in order for him to regain his lustre. For some strange reason, Brahma specifically insisted that Agni had to consume the forest *and* every one of its living creatures in order to recover, and regain his strength. So, Agni went off to Khandavaprastha and made several attempts to destroy the forest but failed, since the forest dwellers extinguished the fire every time. Moreover, the forest was protected by Indra—the king of the Devas. It was then that Brahma advised him to wait until Krishna and Arjuna appeared upon Earth as incarnations of Narayana and Nara, respectively. When Agni heard that they were so incarnated, he went to Brahma again, and Brahma advised him to seek their help in consuming the forest and all its inhabitants.'

'Wow!' Colin, who had been listening with rapt attention, exclaimed. 'That's some story. And Sush ... Suss ... the surgeon says that it all started at this place ... this forest.'

'What exactly does Susruta say?' Shukla enquired.

'In the portion of the manuscript that is still there, he says the Nagas discovered something in this forest—he calls it the curse of Kand ...' Colin stumbled over the pronunciation again, and decided to avoid the name, '... the forest; and then he mentions that they had a secret; and just when he starts warming up, the translation ends and Fischer says that the rest of the text is missing. I'm guessing that in the part that's lost, Susruta went into some detail of what exactly the Nagas discovered and what the secret was about.'

'That really isn't much.' Shukla couldn't keep the disappointment out of his voice.

'What is the curse of Khandavaprastha that Susruta refers to?' Vijay wondered. 'I've never heard of any curse associated with the story.'

'There is none,' Shukla said slowly, thoughtfully, shaking his head. 'I'm quite sure there is nothing in the Mahabharata about a curse of Khandavaprastha, as you say Susruta puts it.'

'He does,' Colin asserted. 'Do you think it could have some connection with the secret he says he is going to reveal?'

'Perhaps,' Shukla agreed. 'But we need to have the rest of the manuscript to know for sure.' He shrugged. 'For all we know, Susruta is simply narrating a myth that was passed down over thousands of years; a story that found no place in the Mahabharata.'

'That's the trouble,' Vijay complained. 'We've hit a dead end. I'm pretty sure that the Order is involved in some way. I'm convinced that the second lot of goons with guns were sent by the Order. But what they are after mystifies me.'

'I thought that there would be something about the regeneration of limbs in the Owen manuscript,' Duncan disclosed, 'which would have interested Humboldt, given his story of the monkey who grew a limb. But there isn't even a set of spells that refers to regeneration.'

'There certainly doesn't seem to be anything in the manuscript that explains Humboldt's excitement in his letter to Goethe,' Colin agreed. 'But surely there must have been something for him to be so effusive about the manuscript?'

'Oh, well, then, I'm going to turn in for the night, boys.' Shukla stifled a yawn. He'd had enough of idle speculation. 'Do you need anything else from me?'

Colin shook his head. 'Not at the moment, Dr Shukla. Thanks a lot for staying up.'

They said their goodnights and Shukla disconnected.

Vijay sighed. 'Better report to Imran.'

They connected to Imran, and Duncan gave him a detailed update, ending with the conversation with Shukla, and their conclusion about the Owen manuscript being a dead end.

Imran nodded. 'Doesn't look like there is anything more to go on,' he agreed. 'But don't worry. We've just got an intelligence tip. Our hunch about the Order's involvement with the Owen manuscript was correct. We've got more information on the location of the monument where the Owen manuscript was found. Apparently, the Order has been hunting for the missing text as well. Our intel says that the Order believes the missing parts of the manuscript are still buried somewhere beneath the structure Owen had visited. The men who discovered the manuscript and even Owen may have missed it somehow.'

'Are you going to ask Director Patterson to check it out?' Vijay asked.

'That's what I had in mind. The place isn't far from Hotan. And Director Patterson will be in Hotan tomorrow. There isn't a better opportunity to see if we can beat the Order to finding the missing parts of the document.'

Just outside Beijing
China

'I will be brief,' Lin told Patterson. 'They will be here soon.'

Patterson didn't need any explanation to understand who 'they' were. He waited.

'Between 1985 and 1987,' Lin began, 'Chinese archaeologists excavated a site called Miaozigou Area I, where they uncovered the remains of a five-thousand-year-old village: the foundations of around fifty houses, ash holes and tombs, along with the usual pottery, stone, bone and horn articles.'

He paused to satisfy himself that he had Patterson's complete attention, then continued. 'Along with all of this, they discovered more than seventy human skeletons. What was strange about these was that most of them were not buried in the graveyard near the site. These skeletons were discovered in the village itself, including within some of the houses. It was apparent that the village in Miaozigou had been destroyed by some sudden disaster. Analysis of the site ruled out earthquake, war, and fire as probable causes. Famine and pestilence were the only other possible reasons. Especially pestilence. If the village had been attacked by an epidemic, there would have been no time to transport the dead to the graveyard. What was very revealing was the fact that a group of skeletons was found hastily buried in large pits around the remains of the dwellings. Then there were other skeletons which had been carelessly dumped into the pits. These, along with the skeletons that were discovered in the dwellings, were strong indications of a contagion of some sort. As the plague spread, orderly burying was no longer possible, so the bodies would have been dumped into the pits. And then when the disease became rampant, it would have been impossible to bury the dead. Clearly, the survivors decided to flee, leaving the sick and the dead behind with no one to care for them or bury them. There were skeletons of people who had died in their homes, alone and untended.'

Patterson was beginning to guess where Lin was going with the story. But he said nothing, waiting for more.

'All of this was documented, of course,' Lin told him. 'But what was left out of the official records was the fact that five of the archaeologists from the Miaozigou team fell ill right after the excavation.' He looked pointedly at Patterson.

'Let me guess,' the GTF director said drily. 'A week after the excavations, they developed neurological problems. Then their condition deteriorated. And no one could figure out what was causing the disease.'

'Doesn't take much to connect the dots, does it?' Lin smiled mirthlessly.

'So, you are absolving the CCP of any responsibility for what's happening now?' Patterson demanded. 'You're saying that this epidemic, which may well develop into a pandemic, was not caused by the government but by some accidental infection more than thirty years ago?'

'Of course not.' Lin sounded aggrieved. 'Haven't you read what the Western media calls the "China Telegrams"?'

Patterson caught on. 'You cultured the pathogen. You finally discovered what it was and grew it in a lab.'

Lin sighed and shook his head. 'You make it sound so easy. Remember that this was a mystery to everyone at that time. I was a junior member of the CCP then. Before the archaeologists died …'

'So they did die.' Patterson's face was as hard as stone.

'Yes. Eventually.' Lin's voice rose slightly as if to emphasise his next words. 'And they died horribly. Two of them started to cannibalise themselves. The others were reduced to vegetables, unable to move, speak or even …' his voice trailed off. 'Death came as salvation for them. They would have welcomed it, had they been in a state to know what was happening to them.'

Patterson was speechless. The horror of what lay in wait for the world if this disease got out of control was just too much to confront.

Lin found his voice. 'Before the archaeologists died, our scientists took biopsies and preserved them for future investigation. Autopsies were also conducted and organs that were affected were preserved for further study.'

'When did you discover what caused their death?' Patterson enquired. 'If you cultured it, you must know what it was.'

Lin nodded. 'Yes. But it took time to work out what the pathogen was. As it happened, we chanced upon the discovery quite by accident. In the 1990s, perhaps a decade after the Miaozigou discovery, some new ideas began emerging in Western scientific circles. About a new kind of life. Different from life as we know it. "Weird Life" was the term used to label it.'

Patterson's blood ran cold. He knew what Lin was referring to.

'No,' he remonstrated. 'That just isn't possible.'

Lin looked him in the eye. 'You have no idea.'

'And you cultured this organism in the lab?'

'Yes. It took us a couple of decades to get there. You know how difficult it is to identify an organism like this. Virtually impossible using our current methods and technology, advanced as they are. But we kept at it and finally identified it. All this work was done in a top-secret lab in Hotan.'

'But that is crazy,' Patterson struggled to come to terms with what he was hearing. Was Lin lying? He had to be. But then again, he had no reason to dissemble. 'But if you have a cure, why is Hotan under lockdown? Why aren't you using the antidote to stop the transmission of the disease?'

A thought struck him. 'The Uyghurs. The CCP wants to exterminate them. Is that it?'

Lin looked sadly at him. 'The truth is more complex than that … Bill. We don't have a cure. There is no antidote.'

Patterson sat back as the implications of Lin's words sank in.

If what the disgraced Chinese leader was saying was true, then there was no way to stop what was inevitably going to blow up into a pandemic that would consume the world.

Just outside Beijing
China

'You have to understand,' Lin continued, 'this is not a synthetic organism manufactured in a lab. I know that's what Western intelligence circles think, but that isn't true. This is a real, natural form of life. We just happened to stumble upon it by accident. And while we've been able to culture it, our scientists still don't understand how it works.'

His eyes flashed in a rare show of emotion. 'Do you know why this organism was cultured?'

Without waiting for Patterson to answer, he continued. 'Not because we want to rule the world! No, that's not what the CCP wants. Its sole preoccupation is with itself—its power, its existence. Nothing should pose a threat to the absolute authority of the CCP. Even the PLA is not a Chinese army—it is the army of the CCP. A lot of people don't know this.' He waved a hand. 'Look around you. There are threats that need to be suppressed. Hong Kong, Xinjiang ... and Taiwan. If a way could be found to bring insurgency under control, the CCP would protect its status and position and continue to command the respect of the Chinese people. The CCP cannot afford to be seen as weak. It is our internal strength that gives us the power to exert influence over others. Who wants to rule the world? Not the CCP. China is enough. With our economic heft, a united China—with no dissidence—would be a force to reckon with.'

Patterson nodded. Even with the territories Lin had mentioned nibbling at the CCP's authority China had focused on building its economic power, becoming the second largest economy in the world in just a few decades. He could see why the CCP wanted to be completely unchallenged—it would be unstoppable.

'This organism was seen as the perfect way to bring people under control.' Patterson's voice was steady but the horror of what he was hearing nauseated him.

'Exactly. Imagine an aerial spray to control crowds in Hong Kong or the masses in Xinjiang. A pathogen that leads to cognitive decline. To docile masses accepting the rule of the CCP. What better way to unite China and its so-called autonomous territories? Or even Taiwan?'

'But you don't have a cure.'

'Exactly. The organism is just too powerful. If it stopped at the mild cognitive decline that all patients exhibit as initial symptoms, it would be perfect. But it goes far beyond that. It causes a complete degeneration of the brain. If only there was some way to arrest the progress of the disease … but we haven't found one yet. Oh, our scientists in Hotan have spent years running all kinds of tests, but to no avail. And of what use is a bioweapon if it cannot be controlled?'

'Why are you telling me this?' Patterson asked. 'What's your motive? Asylum?'

Lin shook his head. 'That would be impossible even if I wanted it. I would never make it to the American embassy alive. I have no illusions… Bill. I've managed to get this far, but there is a limit to human endeavour, especially in the face of a powerful adversary like the CCP. It is just a matter of time.' His voice was calm and his face expressionless as he looked at Patterson. 'But before they finally get me, I wanted the world to know the truth about the CCP.'

'Why?'

'You must understand … Bill, that all Chinese are not what you in the West perceive them to be. We are a peace-loving people. This notion of annexing territories in far-flung places is not part of our ancient culture. China has always been insular. When, in history, have you found a powerful empire in China waging war against other cultures, other civilisations across the world, seeking to bring them under their control, establishing colonies thousands of miles away from the motherland? That dubious distinction goes to Western powers. France, Britain, Spain, Portugal, the Netherlands … *they* were colonisers, not us. Remember history … Bill. China was colonised by Japan. Not to forget the Opium Wars—a different sort of colonisation; not military, but colonisation, nevertheless. China has always looked inwards. We pride ourselves on our ancient culture, our civilisation that is one of the oldest in the world. We want to be respected. Admired. And while the ends are not disputed, not everyone in the CCP agrees with the means to achieve these ends. Despite what the world thinks, there are differences within the CCP. Palpable differences. And there are those of us who would work to promote a China that is benevolent, yet dominates and influences the world, rather than a China that is feared and hated.'

'That is why you leaked the China Telegrams.' Patterson finally understood the dynamics within the CCP.

'Yes.' Lin assessed Patterson. The man was smart. He hadn't expected this level of political awareness from a scientist. It was actually more than he had expected. Which was good. It suited his purpose perfectly. 'I am disgraced anyway. But there are others like me who want change, but are hesitant to come out openly against the party. I understand why.' He waved a hand. 'They are the ones who supplied me with the information—as a convict and a wanted man, I had no access to top-secret files. But I was already exposed. So, I decided it wouldn't make a difference if I channelled the Telegrams to the Western world.'

Patterson was silent. While he was aware of the authoritarian nature of the CCP's rule in China, he had no idea of the dissent within the party.

Lin knew his words had hit home. 'The world must know,' he repeated. 'The world has to stop this madness. There is only one lab in all of China that has samples of this organism—in Hotan. It must be destroyed.'

Patterson knew what Lin had left unsaid.

If the lab was not destroyed, the world would never be safe.

But even if the lab was destroyed, unless an antidote was found, nothing would stand in the way of the extinction of the human race.

DAY FOUR

October 24

Hotan

Xinjiang Province, China

'I'm not going back!' Iris Tsai's eyes flashed angrily as she spoke. 'Why should I abandon the investigation into the epidemic at this point? I was asked to join the mission by the White House. I have received no instructions from them to return. Who are you to tell me I should drop out at this stage?'

Patterson sighed. 'I know, Iris. This is an unofficial, informal *request*. I have no right to order you to do anything. And I know that the White House reached out to you directly. But it was on my request that they did so. You would never have agreed to accompany me on this mission if I had approached you. So, I had the White House step in, because of the importance of this operation.'

'Then what has changed?' Iris demanded. 'Why are you asking me to go back home? We only just arrived in Hotan today—we have ten more days of meeting doctors and making the rounds of hospitals before we are scheduled to return.'

Patterson hesitated. He didn't want to put her in any more danger. After meeting Lin at the warehouse the previous night and receiving Imran's message regarding the Owen manuscript, he knew that the situation had already become precarious. There were too many variables and unknowns to be considered. This was not a place for a scientist to be.

Iris misunderstood his hesitation. 'Do you believe I will betray America?' Her voice could have cut through steel. 'Because I was born in China? Do you really think that my loyalties lie with the CCP?'

'No, not at all,' Patterson protested. This was not the direction in which he had wanted the conversation to go.

'I will have you know that though I am ethnically Chinese, I am an American first. Yes, I have emotions for this country too. I love China. I was born here, after all, and lived almost half my life here. But I can never support the political system in China. I am now a proud citizen of a democracy—the greatest democracy in the world—and I can never have loyalties for a system that oppresses its people and decides what they should know and what they shouldn't.'

'I know, Iris.' Patterson's voice was gentle now. He realised her insecurity. And it wasn't unjustified. It was well known in intelligence circles that China had planted spies in America years ago—students, professors, researchers—all people who could be easily absorbed into regular American life, yet live double lives as conduits for information to China. It was a strategy of patience, stretching over decades—fifty years was a short time in this plan. Yet, there were many people of Chinese origin in America who were not part of this cabal—who were genuinely American patriots.

But how was anyone to tell the difference?

How could you tell who was who?

Maybe that was the problem, Patterson surmised. Did he, somewhere deep down, doubt Iris' allegiance?

Had she somehow sensed it?

'Then why?' Iris demanded, her hands on her hips, her face hard.

Patterson had known since his first meeting with her that she was a strong woman. There was no easy way to wriggle out of this. He had to justify what he had told her.

Now he had to decide how much he trusted her.

'Well?' Iris was waiting for his answer.

There were only two options. Apologise and retract. Or disclose.

Patterson made up his mind.

DAY FIVE

October 25

Hotan

Xinjiang Province, China

Patterson looked around as he pushed open the door leading to the service entrance of the hotel.

It was past midnight and there was no one around. A half moon hung in the sky, casting deep shadows everywhere.

Everything was silent and still. While there was no curfew in Hotan, a complete lockdown had been in place, ever since the first case had surfaced after the so-called terrorist attack at the Hotan Sunday market. Adherence to the lockdown was complete, given the iron hand of the CCP, especially in this part of the country.

Patterson glanced back at Iris. 'Are you sure you want to do this?'

He had eventually decided to come clean and brief her on what was really happening. The WHO mission was eyewash from the Chinese side as well as from the WHO's end. Everyone knew that nothing would happen. The Chinese government would not share any information that implicated them and the WHO would not ask difficult questions. The current head of the WHO had been appointed with strong support from China, and she was not about to go against her benefactor.

That was why the USA president had brought the GTF into the picture. It was the only way to cleanly launch a real investigation into what had happened in Hotan. The GTF was deniable.

So Patterson had decided to let Iris make her own choice. He had to trust her. She had been chosen for a specific reason. He had suspected, for a while, what Lin had finally confirmed last night. And so, he had wanted Iris in this mission for her expertise. It didn't make sense any more to hide anything from her.

When he told her, her eyes had widened.

'You really are a secret agent,' she had laughed, after getting over the shock of his revelations. 'But seriously, if what you say is correct, then I'm with you on this.'

She had insisted on coming along on this expedition as well.

'If I'm in, I have to be all in,' she had told Patterson.

'It is going to be dangerous,' he had warned her. 'You don't have the training for this. I'd rather you focus on what you are really good at than walk into danger without preparation. Remember, there's a lockdown in place. We're not supposed to be up and about without an official escort. If we're caught, they won't go easy on us.'

But Iris had fiercely resisted his suggestion. For her, this was a chance to prove her loyalty to her adopted country.

Now they slipped out of the hotel, keeping to the shadows.

'Do what I say, follow what I do,' Patterson had instructed her.

Iris had nodded, and she walked in his footsteps now.

The service entrance had a large automatic gate, with a smaller swivel gate built into it. Patterson picked the lock on the swivel gate.

It took a few minutes, but finally he was done, and the two of them stole out of the hotel compound.

It was not an easy task to make it to the outskirts of the city. Armed patrols of the PLA kept making their rounds. But Patterson was a veteran of clandestine missions, and through years of experience and training had become a master of stealth. Tonight, he demonstrated that he had not lost any of his skills.

They crept along the road, slowly, painfully; sometimes crawling, at other times moving forward while squatting on their haunches, clinging to the shadows along the road. Fortunately, the night was dark with only a half moon in the sky, which made camouflage that much easier.

There was a close call, when a PLA patrol came upon them suddenly and Patterson had to grab Iris and swiftly take cover behind a low wall to the side of the road that lay deeply submerged in shadows.

They made minimal noise in the process, but the patrol stopped, suspecting that someone was up and about. Patterson and—at his signal—Iris, instantly froze in their tracks, concealed behind the wall, holding their breath as the patrol broke up and the soldiers began combing the road.

Fortunately for them, a stray dog emerged from a side road, snuffling around, foraging for food. The patrol relaxed on seeing the dog, though they stayed put for several minutes after that just to make sure. But they didn't bother to check the wall behind which Patterson and Iris had taken refuge.

Finally, after what seemed like eternity, the patrol moved on, satisfied that there was no one around. One of the soldiers aimed a kick at the dog, which yelped and scurried off as the soldiers marched away in the opposite direction.

The Americans had been lucky.

But it wasn't only luck that had saved them. The CCP ruled Xinjiang with an iron hand, tolerating no dissent and coming down hard on anyone considered to be a violator of the rules set by Beijing. The PLA soldiers would never have dreamt that anyone in Hotan would have the temerity to break the rules of the lockdown, given the price they would pay if discovered.

Patterson and Iris had heaved huge sighs of relief once the patrol had disappeared and continued their laboured progress towards the edge of the city.

After about an hour, they finally left the city behind them and began the trek to the ancient ruins where the Owen manuscript had been found.

Near Hotan
Xinjiang Province, China

Patterson checked his GPS. It had been a two-hour trek, and he had been impressed with Iris' stamina and determination. Not only had she matched his endurance and skills in the slog from the hotel to the edge of the city, evading the patrols along the way, but she had lost none of her spirit on the long walk to their destination.

This was the location that Imran had sent him. In the light of the half-moon that hung above them, he could see indeterminate shapes on the landscape beyond.

'I think this is the place,' he whispered.

'Why are we whispering?' she whispered back. 'There's no one around!'

Patterson bit back a laugh. She was right. He was so used to operating under conditions that required complete secrecy and camouflage that he had spoken in muted tones out of sheer force of habit.

And there was no reason for anyone to be around either. This area beyond Hotan was desolate, almost part of the Taklamakan desert. People rarely ventured there since there was nothing of use to be found.

'Let's look for a tower of some sort,' he told Iris in low tones. His sixth sense was tingling for some reason. It didn't make sense at all but he trusted his finely-tuned intuition, which had kept him alive so far.

'Will it still be around after all these years?' Iris looked around, but couldn't see anything that matched the description of a tower.

Patterson shrugged. 'You may be right. After two hundred years, it is possible that nothing remains. Still, let's look.'

They started hunting amongst the ruins that stretched before them, but no tower or stupa or tomb—the only possible structures that could match Owen's description—could be found.

After about an hour, Patterson was ready to give up. 'Maybe we should just go back. This is impossible.'

'Let's search some more,' Iris urged. 'After coming so far and taking such a huge risk, it would be a shame if we missed it.'

Patterson agreed and they continued searching.

A sharp gasp from Iris drew his attention. She was pointing to something.

A jagged wall, made of sun-dried bricks, stood some two feet above the ground.

The wall was circular; the only wall of that shape among a plethora of ruined walls marking ancient structures that had stood there thousands of years ago.

'Do you think this could be it?' Iris began walking towards the circular wall without waiting for Patterson's answer.

'Perhaps.' Patterson took long strides to catch up with her.

When they reached the wall, Patterson pulled out a torch from his waist pouch and shone it on the surface of the structure.

'There doesn't seem to be any entrance,' Iris stated matter of factly.

Patterson had to agree. Apart from the wall, there was nothing to be seen except for hard-packed mud. If there was a doorway hidden beneath the mud, then it needed to be dug out with tools that they did not have with them that night, and which would take some time to organise.

'We will have to return after a couple of days,' Patterson concluded. 'We will have to dig up the ground within the wall and around it. Who knows what we might find?'

Iris nodded. 'Makes sense.' She looked at him. 'How will we organise the equipment to dig here?'

'It won't be easy, but it isn't impossible. I'll get cracking on it when we get back to the hotel. We're the best chance of finding the missing portions of the manuscript. Getting another team here will be dicey with the lockdown.'

They had ten more days in Hotan, which gave them the opportunity to return with the equipment for the dig. There was of course the problem of procuring the equipment, but that was a lesser challenge in Patterson's mind. The bigger problem was revisiting this place without being detected. They had gone unchallenged tonight, but would they be as lucky on their next visit?

'Let's go.' Patterson turned, followed by Iris, to begin the two-hour trek back to Hotan.

He had only taken a few steps when he stopped.

Dark shadows rose from behind the ruins around them.

Patterson saw the unmistakeable shapes of automatic weapons.

He silently cursed.

This had been a trap.

Intelligence Bureau Headquarters
New Delhi, India

Imran stared at his phone in shock.

He couldn't believe it.

How was this even possible?

Everything had been under wraps. The only people who had known about Patterson's little expedition to the stupa, apart from Patterson and Imran, were Vijay, Colin and Duncan. No one else.

And Imran knew for sure that none of the GTF team members would ever leak information, even if their lives depended on it.

Something had gone wrong. But what?

The SOS was unmistakeable. It was impossible to even imagine the possibility that Patterson may have sent the emergency signal by mistake. Every GTF agent had a special app on their mobile phones that could send a voice-activated SOS if they were ever in trouble. Imran didn't know what had happened, but if Patterson had sent the SOS, he could only come to one conclusion.

The director of the GTF had been ambushed. It had to be the CCP. Who else could it be?

But how would the CCP have known what Patterson was up to?

True, Duncan had reported a Chinese angle to the Owen manuscript that the GTF had not been aware of until now. But it would require enormous leaps of deduction on the part of the CCP to connect Patterson's presence in China with the GTF's search in London. Especially when the very existence of the GTF was not known to most of the world.

And why would the CCP have had Patterson and Iris Tsai followed or waylaid in the godforsaken corner of Xinjiang that they had set out for?

A cold dread slowly took hold of Imran as a grim realisation dawned on him. The intelligence tip he had received.

The GTF had been set up. And he knew who was responsible.

The Order.

His trepidation increased. Had the Order finally discovered the existence of the GTF? Why else would they have laid this trap?

Whatever the reason, he knew what this meant.

Imran swiftly jabbed the intercom on his desk and spoke into it in urgent tones. 'I need a plane.' He looked at his watch. It was 2.30 a.m. 'Departure 7 a.m. Have it fuelled and ready. Two passengers.'

He paused and then answered the question addressed to him. 'London.'

Then he dialled a number on his mobile phone.

His call was answered after one ring.

Imran spoke without waiting for a greeting. 'Patterson was ambushed. You were fed a tip to set him up. They know. Disappear. Now. I'll meet you in London.' He paused, then repeated. 'Disappear. *Now!*'

Hampstead

London

UK

The streets were deserted at this time of night; most of the residents of this upmarket residential area of North London, home to celebrities and other glitterati, had retired for the night, their houses dark from within and lit up only by the streetlamps outside.

There was a light drizzle, not unusual for London at any time of the year.

Inside a neat looking townhouse, Van Klueck sat on a sofa in the living room, a smug expression on his face, as he gave instructions to Dee, who occupied a chair opposite him.

'Our agent in China has confirmed that the PLA has indeed taken two people prisoner. They were poking about in the early hours of the morning, China time, in the exact place that the Owen manuscript was said to have been found. No coincidence then. I was right.'

Dee nodded indifferently. She had not yet got over her last meeting with Vijay and his friends. Her own failure two years ago still gnawed at her. Had she not shown presence of mind and quick thinking, she would not have been alive to tell the tale.

When she had realised what was happening, she had grabbed a parachute from below her helicopter seat and dived out of the chopper in one smooth motion, plunging for a while until she opened her parachute perilously close to the ground, and even then almost losing the parachute when it was ripped in places by the debris that rained down around and upon her when the helicopter exploded.

She had been lucky. Very, very lucky.

She had escaped by a whisker. And she knew who was responsible for her narrow shave.

Vijay Singh.

He had baited her, and she had fallen for it, hook, line and sinker.

Vijay had known what was going to happen and he had sent her to what would have been a sure death had she not acted as she did.

But what had transpired after she returned to the Order was way worse.

She had failed spectacularly in a critical mission for the Order.

Bloodline or not, it was a disgrace. And it rankled.

Especially when Van Klueck was effusive with his sympathies and his platitudes of 'Never mind, there will be more opportunities to prove yourself.'

She was better than the likes of Van Klueck. But in the eyes of the Order, she was a failure.

What was more, the Order seemed to have found a replacement for her.

Another with the bloodline.

As good as Dee apparently, if not better. This other had demonstrated significant successes, many more than Dee had chalked up.

It was humiliating.

Until now, she had been unique. Her skills, combined with her being of the bloodline, were her passport to the higher echelons of the Order—maybe even to the very top someday.

For two years, she had fought and competed. But the competition had been tough.

And now, she thought grimly to herself, her competition would have its comeuppance.

She ignored the fact that she was not getting any credit for the one thing she had successfully worked out. *She* had been the one who had pointed out to Van Klueck that they were dealing with an organisation. That Vijay and his friends were being backed by a mysterious, shadowy force. Dee had reached this conclusion two years ago when she had repeatedly been thwarted in her mission, and had shared her suspicions with Van Klueck. And now he was hogging all the credit for himself.

'So, this precious asset with the bloodline is a traitor.' Dee couldn't help herself. The feelings she harboured, repressed for the last two years, sprang to the fore.

Van Klueck knew what was going through Dee's mind. He had never liked her. A loyal soldier to the Order, he knew he would never have a chance to rise as high as she would; he didn't belong to the bloodline. But he considered Dee an arrogant upstart who had much to learn.

He regretted the fact that the task he was about to assign to her would give her much satisfaction. He wished he could withhold it, but it had to be done.

Van Klueck nodded. 'Yes. And you know what to do, Dee.'

A cruel grin spread over Dee's face. 'Of course. I've waited for this day.'

Hotan
Xinjiang Province, China

Patterson grimaced as he and Iris, their hands cuffed behind their backs, sat in the rear cabin of the Mengshi—the Dongfeng EQ2050, the Chinese equivalent of the American HMMWV, popularly called the Humvee—surrounded by soldiers of the PLA.

He still couldn't believe what had just happened. The last thing either of them had expected was an ambush. There was no way the CCP could have known that Patterson and Iris had chosen that night to venture out to, of all places, this desolate location.

It was impossible that there was a mole in the GTF. The only people who knew about this midnight expedition would never have betrayed the GTF.

That left the source of the intel. But the source had been rock solid, and had led to many successful missions against the Order in the last two years. The source was unimpeachable.

Which led to a bigger question. Had the source been compromised? He shuddered to think what would happen if that were the case.

There were more immediate things on his mind for now. He and Iris were prisoners of the PLA, and that would not be easy to wriggle out of.

While Patterson had managed to surreptitiously send an SOS to Imran seconds before the PLA men took him and Iris into custody, he didn't have much hope. Even if Imran did guess what had happened, there was little he could do to help.

Plausible deniability.

That was what the GTF was about. No government would come to their rescue, especially not when it meant revealing to China that they were being spied on by two members of a purported team from the WHO.

All Imran could do was to try and cobble together a rescue party. But even that was a long shot. Sneaking into China via its western border was not going to be the easiest thing, though trafficking of drugs, weapons and humans did take place along China's porous border with Tajikistan, Kyrgyzstan and Kazakhstan. There was also the route via the Sino-Indian border through Changthang, but that meant crossing Tibet.

But the possibility still held hope.

Patterson was not worried for himself, but for Iris. He cast a quick glance at her face, wan and disconsolate, bravely fighting the fear he knew she must feel. Her Chinese origins didn't count for much in a situation like this, he knew. If anything, they would make things more difficult for her.

Patterson knew that Iris was aware of this.

He wondered where they were being taken. He had not seen any PLA installation in Hotan.

But then again, he had not seen much of Hotan at all.

Lin's words came back to him. He had mentioned a lab in Hotan. A lab which needed to be destroyed.

Was it this lab where he and Iris were now being taken?

Patterson suddenly realised that the convoy of Mengshis was now threading its way through a cluster of buildings that had materialised out of the darkness. He had been so lost in his thoughts that he had not been concentrating on the route they were taking.

He chided himself on his carelessness. He was rusty. As a SEAL, he would never have allowed himself to get distracted. Too long behind a desk, he told himself. That was the problem.

Forcing himself to focus on their surroundings, he finally got his bearings. They were traversing an industrial park that had sprung up on the edge of the desert. It was suspected by Western governments—based on satellite images and the Xinjiang government's propaganda—that one or more political re-education camps for Uyghurs lay hidden among the factories in the park.

Were they being taken to such a camp?

As if on cue, the massive black gates to one of the factories rolled aside, and the convoy turned into the compound of the factory.

So there *was* an Uyghur camp here.

To Patterson's surprise however, instead of making for the main entrance to the factory, the Mengshi in which they were seated turned towards the rear of the building.

As they rounded the corner, he heard a grating sound. It was still dark and the headlights of the Menghsi had been switched off the moment they had entered the factory compound.

Squinting through the darkness, Patterson made out the outline of a structure that was rising from the ground directly ahead of their vehicle. The Mengshi came to a halt in front of it.

They stood there for a few moments until the sound of gears grinding against each other stopped.

Their vehicle moved forward and stopped again.

The sound of a metal door closing came to Patterson's ears and they were immediately enveloped in a darkness that was deeper than that of the night.

The grating sound that he had heard earlier resumed and the vehicle lurched slightly as he felt the ground beneath the Mengshi subside.

Patterson realised that they were in a car lift.

Not just any car lift.

A secret, hidden, perhaps camouflaged, car lift. One that had lain undetected by satellites.

His hopes sank.

Whatever odds he had calculated against Imran mounting a rescue mission suddenly multiplied manifold.

If this was a secret facility, what chance did Imran have to even find them?

Hotan
Xinjiang Province, China

'I'm sorry I got you into this,' Patterson told Iris as they sat on a sofa in an austere office buried deep under the factory.

They were no longer handcuffed, but four PLA soldiers in camouflage uniform, armed with QBZ-191 assault rifles, watched over them. Handcuffs were unnecessary. They had nowhere to run.

Iris shook her head. 'I made a choice. And you can't be responsible for a coincidence like this. Neither of us had expected anyone to be there, least of all Chinese soldiers.'

Before any more words could be exchanged, the door was flung open and a short man dressed in a crisp PLA uniform strode into the room, an air of arrogant authority about him indicating that he was in charge. The four guards saluted him smartly.

'Dismissed.' The PLA officer nodded curtly and the four soldiers obediently trooped out of the room.

The newcomer smiled at his two captives and proffered his hand. 'Major General Jiang Zitao,' he introduced himself. 'People's Liberation Army.'

Patterson rose and took Jiang's hand in a firm handshake, towering over the Major General as he did so. Iris, after hesitating at first, followed his lead.

'I hope my boys were not too hard on you.' Jiang did not sound the least bit concerned despite his words. 'After all, you are scientists.'

Without waiting for a reply, he walked over to his desk and sat down on his leather swivel chair, turning to face the two Americans.

'But I am curious,' he continued in his accented English. 'What were two scientists—from the WHO no less—doing at such a late hour at a place that few people visit even during the day? Please enlighten me.'

Iris looked at Patterson. He would have to take the lead in answering any questions this man had. But Patterson kept mum. In this kind of a situation, he felt that the less he revealed the better it would be.

The smile disappeared from Jiang's face and his voice took on a harder tone. 'I see.' He leaned back in his chair, his gaze fixed on them. 'You have decided not to cooperate. No matter. We have ways of getting the information we need.'

He barked some instructions in Mandarin and the four PLA soldiers who had left the room earlier trooped back in and stood stiffly.

'We'll work on you later,' he told Patterson and Iris. 'Until then, enjoy our hospitality.' He laughed. It was a mirthless laugh that made Patterson wonder what their 'hospitality' was like.

He didn't have to wonder long. The guards marched them into a lift that descended even deeper underground and then along a maze of corridors until they came to a row of metal doors lining a long corridor.

One of the guards kicked a door open and looked at Iris, who looked fearfully at Patterson. He could see the tears in her eyes.

Patterson nodded to her and Iris entered the room. The guard slammed the door shut behind her and shot the bolts. There was no lock and, evidently, none was required.

They marched down, passing several doors, until another door was kicked open. Patterson entered, but it seemed that they had decided to make it more difficult for him.

One of the guards gestured towards the bed and, as Patterson sat down, two of the guards handcuffed his hands and ankles to chains that hung from a steel rail running along the side of the bed. The chains were just long enough for a prisoner to walk around the room without reaching the door, and access the toilet bowl and sink in the cell.

Major General Jiang Zitao was no fool. He had assessed that Patterson was the bigger threat and was taking no chances.

The guards left the room, leaving Patterson to his thoughts.

It was obvious that the CCP had been prepared for them. But what was the link between the Order and the CCP? The tip off about Patterson's early morning expedition to the ruins could only have come from the Order. Were they working with the CCP on something? And Patterson couldn't understand what Jiang wanted from them. He had clearly been waiting for them—there was no other reason why a senior PLA officer would be on hand to meet them when they were brought in. When they were ambushed, he had dreaded to think about what awaited them wherever they were being taken. But Jiang's welcome had been at least ostensibly warm. A smile—however forced—introductions, a handshake. Just what was going on? It was not what Patterson had expected. And this room wasn't a cell in a dungeon, which was what he had assumed awaited them. It was austere; a prison cell no doubt, but there was a bed, a toilet, good ventilation.

So far, they had not been ill-treated. It could have been worse.

Something was going on and Patterson had to find out what it was.

The London Hilton on Park Lane
London, UK

The young man at the reception gazed at the passport that had been handed to him by the guest checking in.

The photograph in the passport showed a beautiful young woman with dark eyes and hair, a haughty expression on her face, staring into the camera as if challenging it to distort her beauty in any way.

In the young man's eyes, the camera had lost. Badly.

He lifted his eyes to glance at the guest and validate the proof of identity.

It was a tough job.

She wore a hijab that covered her hair and neck, exposing only a part of her face, which was overshadowed by the oversized dark glasses she wore. Two things stood out about her: the shocking red lipstick that did little to quell the young man's nervousness, and the fact that her face seemed to glow, almost like it radiated a light of its own.

He dithered a while, wondering how to ask the guest to take off her glasses so he could identify her. The hotel was accustomed to guests from the Middle East, so the staff were all sensitised to Arab customs. And he could see from the remarks on the guest profile in the hotel's property management system that she was a member of the Qatari royal family.

Treat her with kid gloves.

'Er … cash or card, madam?' he ventured finally.

The guest smiled at him and put a wad of sterling on the reception desk. 'Cash, my dear. Of course.'

To his consternation, she lowered her dark glasses slightly and winked at him as he picked up the notes.

Unnerved, he dropped some of the cash and bent to pick them up, apologising profusely to her.

As he disappeared below the counter, the woman in the hijab took the opportunity to quickly scan the lobby, her eyes swiftly glancing off the few guests and hotel staff present at this time of the night before turning back to face the young man who had resurfaced and was now a bright shade of red.

He placed a keycard on the reception desk. 'I've checked you into a Clarence suite on the twenty-seventh floor. It has lounge access and fabulous views.'

'I know.' She picked up the card and smiled at him to soften the dismissal. 'Thank you, you've been very helpful.'

She turned and walked towards the lifts as the young man wistfully watched her go.

Then he shook his head, took a deep breath and looked at the computer monitor. 'Okay, what was I doing before she got here?'

The Dorchester Hotel
London
UK

Van Klueck's mobile phone rang. He picked it up and answered the call. 'Van Klueck.'

'She's checked into the London Hilton.' It was Dee. 'My men have the hotel under surveillance and we also have a contact inside. We'll get her when she comes out.'

There was a note of satisfaction in her voice, like a predator who has finally trapped its prey.

'No.' Van Klueck sighed inwardly. The inexperience and impetuousness of youth. It was not the first time that Dee's impatience for action had exasperated him. 'There's a better way to handle it. Let's wait and watch. If she's taken refuge at the Hilton, it means someone has alerted her.' His voice took on a sharper edge. 'Remember, it isn't her we want. It is the bigger fish we are after. Whoever she fed the information to. They will definitely come to meet her. Once we find out who we are dealing with here, we'll move in.' He decided to throw in a carrot for Dee. 'And then you can do what you wish with her.'

'Fine.' There was distinct unhappiness in Dee's voice at the compromise. 'That makes sense.'

Van Klueck hung up and stared into the distance. It wasn't going to be much longer now before they discovered who had been buzzing like an annoying mosquito around the immense bulk of the Order. And once they found that mosquito, he would swat it out of existence.

DAY SIX

October 26
London Luton Airport
London, UK

Imran Kidwai strode to the exit doors of the airport terminal, wheeling his trolley bag behind him. One of the advantages of a non-scheduled flight was the ability to do away with baggage allowances and size of luggage, which enabled one to skip the mandatory wait at the baggage carousel.

He felt mild trepidation about how the rest of the day would pan out. But it wasn't on account of the discovery by the Order of the GTF's mole. It was the reason he had had to fly to London with such urgency.

Vijay Singh.

Imran had developed a fondness for Vijay and his fiancée, Radha, ever since his first meeting with them five years ago. Over the years, he had grown to know Vijay well. He knew that Vijay was a logical, stable person, not given to bouts of irrationality or emotion—a bit mule-headed at times, but generally genial and easy to get along with.

But today, Imran wondered whether he would see a side of Vijay he had never seen before.

Imran had tried to plan it as best as he could. While on the flight, he had messaged Duncan to pick up Vijay and Colin and meet him at the airport. He had wanted to make the best use of the hour or so it would take to get to their destination in London.

But even so, this was not how he had wanted the situation to play out. Imran had always thought that he would have time to plan, prepare and ensure that things went smoothly. The ambush at Hotan had forced his hand.

With the way things were right now, he had no option.

He took a deep breath and steeled himself.

Whatever happened, he would have to deal with it. It was his responsibility and no one else's.

And he would directly face whatever came his way. It was the way he always worked.

He slowed down slightly to ensure that he didn't walk too far ahead of his fellow passenger on the flight from Delhi to London. Neither of them had slept much on the flight. He wondered what the older man was thinking.

Dr Shukla was lost in thought, an inscrutable expression on his face. Imran had briefed him on the plane. Shukla had taken it surprisingly well, at least on the face of it.

They took the lift to the car park and did not have to wait long for the BMW, with Duncan at the wheel, to pull up. They dumped their luggage in the boot and got in, Imran sitting next to Vijay, with Colin in the passenger seat in front. Imran had given Duncan clear instructions.

Vijay turned to Imran as soon as the car started up again, his expression tense and worried. 'What do we do about Director Patterson? Do you know where he is being held?'

Imran had briefed Duncan about the ambush at the same time as he had messaged him about arriving in London.

Imran shook his head. 'No, Vijay. He's disappeared. We are unable to contact Dr Tsai as well. I'm hoping that nothing has happened to her.'

None of them knew that Iris had decided to accompany Patterson on his little expedition.

He took a deep breath. 'There is a reason why I'm in London, Vijay. I have a confession to make.'

The Dorchester Hotel
London
UK

Van Klueck sipped his coffee as he watched the video Dee had sent him a short while ago.

He was baffled.

The video showed a black BMW drawing up at the entrance of the London Hilton and four men getting out of the car.

The surveillance software had flagged some of the faces as known, using face recognition AI technology.

To Van Klueck's great surprise, one of the men was Vijay Singh, his old adversary. Accompanying him were his usual companions—the American, Colin; the elderly Dr Shukla, and the officer from the Indian Intelligence Bureau, Imran Kidwai.

Van Klueck had tangled with all of them in the past, directly or indirectly, though mostly with Vijay.

He didn't understand it.

What were these four men doing here?

Hotan
Xinjiang Province, China

Iris heard the bolts on her cell door being shot back and involuntarily cringed on her bed, drawing back against the wall as if it offered some sort of invisible protection. She felt ashamed of her fearfulness, which she perceived as a weakness, but this was a situation that her training as a scientist had never prepared her for. She had marvelled at Patterson's fortitude and calm demeanour throughout their ordeal and realised that he was trained for, and experienced in, this sort of thing. Sure, he was a scientist, but he was also a trained soldier. Despite knowing that, she could not bring herself to accept her own pusillanimity when confronted with danger.

The door creaked open and to her surprise, instead of the PLA soldiers, a man wearing a white coat entered, his white hair dishevelled and his spectacles awkwardly balanced on his nose.

Iris recognised him immediately.

'Dr Barnsfield!' she gasped. 'Oh my God! I thought you were dead.'

Barnsfield looked sheepish. 'Please call me Howard. I'm sorry about that ruse, my dear. I am very much alive, as you can see. Unfortunately, that was the only way I could disappear without any questions being asked.' His face crinkled with concern. 'But I hope they have taken care of you, my dear? Are you alright?'

'Y … Yes,' Iris stammered out her response. She was confused. This man standing before her was known to have died by suicide five years ago. His body, charred beyond recognition, had been found in what remained of his car at the Canyonlands National Park in Utah. She had met him a few times when she was still a postgraduate student at Craggett University, with dreams of pursuing a PhD in the same field; dreams she had finally brought to fruition.

Barnsfield had been her idol, her inspiration. And when he had died—or, rather, faked his death, as was now apparent— she had been shattered. Her dreams of doing a PhD under his guidance would never materialise. It was something she had always regretted.

To see him in the flesh, standing before her in this gloomy little cell, was something she had never expected would happen.

Barnsfield extended a hand. 'Come, my dear. There is much to discuss.' His eyes shone with the light of success. 'You will find my work very interesting. There is so much I have been able to achieve here which I never would have done back in America.'

Wondering what he was talking about, Iris took his proffered hand and slid off the bed, slipping on her shoes, and allowed herself to be led out of her cell into the corridor.

Clearly Barnsfield commanded some respect here, for the PLA soldiers guarding her cell never remonstrated with him for bringing her out of captivity.

She followed the American as he led her into a lift and then emerged on a floor which was clearly a laboratory area.

'Here,' Barnsfield told her, 'let's sit in my office and talk. There is much to catch up on and I think you will be excited by what we've been doing here.'

He led her through a frosted glass door into a large office and sat down at his desk, indicating that she take the seat opposite him.

Iris sat down, still wondering.

Barnsfield beamed at her. 'You don't know how happy I am to see you, my dear. Of course, the circumstances are depressing, but there is a way we can turn things around. There is always a way, you know.'

Iris wondered what he was talking about. She couldn't see any means to change the situation she was in. And what was Barnsfield doing in a top-secret Chinese facility anyway? Why had he faked his death?

Barnsfield seemed to read her mind. Or perhaps the questions were obvious. 'You know about my research,' he began, leaning back in his chair, 'and my endeavours to build a completely synthetic organism from scratch. Well, what is not very well known, because I never published the results, was that I had come a long way in putting together a process to put the fundamental biological components together to create such an organism. I had explored many alternatives— replacing the phosphorus in the DNA backbone with arsenic, reverse chirality, using ammonia as a solvent instead of water and silicon as a binding molecule instead of carbon—and finally hit upon the solution that had eluded all of us for so long. The Holy Grail of synthetic biology was finally within my reach. All I needed was the raw material to start with.'

He gestured around. 'Xia Yu Pharmaceutical Group was extremely accommodating of my research. They funded me through my many experiments and failures. Somehow, they had immense faith in my project. And then they provided me with the raw material I needed. That's when I had to leave America and come here. But of course that is easier said than done, isn't it? I didn't want to be arrested in the States for my links with China. So, with the help of my connections in China, I faked my death, planted suicide notes and came here. But why am I telling you all this when I should be showing you? When I *can* show you!'

Barnsfield tapped on his laptop keyboard, then turned the screen towards Iris.

'Here,' he said. 'Take a look at this. This is what the world said was not possible. The so-called leading lights of synthetic biology said that achieving this would take another fifty years, if at all. Yet, here it is, proving them all wrong. See for yourself.'

Iris glanced at the screen, then gasped as she watched the images slide by. The amino acids, the nucleic acids, they were all wrong. And suddenly the realisation dawned on her.

'You did it!' she whispered. 'You created the organism you always wanted to. But how?'

The London Hilton on Park Lane
London, UK

Vijay got out of the car in a daze, still stunned by the revelations that Imran had shared with him during the journey.

His initial reaction to Imran's disclosures had been one of shock and disbelief, which had quickly given way to a strong sense of resentment and anger. A heated conversation had followed, continuing through the journey with only Vijay and Imran participating. Though Colin had also been astounded, he thought it prudent to stay quiet and Duncan stared straight ahead without reacting. Shukla had remained lost in his own world, staring out of the car window but seeing nothing as the city whizzed past.

Eventually Vijay had calmed down, as Imran had hoped he would.

'I'll park and join you,' Duncan told them after dropping them at the porch of the hotel.

The four men made their way through the lobby to the lifts in silence, each lost in thought.

The lift doors opened and Imran led the way to the suite. He rang the doorbell.

The door opened a crack, restrained by the door chain.

Vijay couldn't help but notice the muzzle of a revolver peeking from behind the door jamb.

'It's me.' Imran nodded. He jerked a thumb behind him. 'They're all with me.'

There was a moment's pause. Then the door chain was unlocked.

The four men entered the living room of the suite. It was semi-dark even though it was almost noon; the heavy curtains were drawn and the lights turned off, with only one dim lamp illuminating the room.

In front of the lamp, its features lost in the darkness, a figure stood, arms crossed, facing them.

There were a few moments of uncomfortable silence.

Then Shukla shuffled forward, leaning on his cane, and approached the figure.

'Is it really you?' he quavered.

Vijay shook himself out of his stupor and advanced to the windows, flinging the curtains aside and allowing the daylight to flood the room.

Tears flowed down Shukla's cheeks as he rushed forward and embraced his daughter. He had given up on seeing her ever again—whether living or dead.

Radha too had tears streaming from her eyes, as she hugged him tightly. 'Papa,' she whispered. 'How I've missed you.'

The London Hilton on Park Lane
London, UK

Vijay flung open the curtains, allowing the light from outside to flood the room. He turned around and froze.

Imran had already told him about Radha on their way here. But nothing had prepared him for what he saw now.

Imran took a deep breath. 'There is a reason I'm in London, Vijay. I have a confession to make.'

Vijay looked at Imran questioningly.

'Two years ago,' Imran began, 'I received a call from a private number. Some instinct told me I should take the call, so I did. It was Radha. At first, I didn't believe it. Then, I was overwhelmed. It seemed unreal to me that she was alive. She told me how the Order had gone to great lengths to save, revive and rehabilitate her over the two years since she had been shot. She had no idea where she was when she spoke to me, but had somehow found a way to contact me. For some reason, the Order trusted her implicitly—she had even helped them, while she recuperated, in their search for some ancient artefacts. It was then that an idea struck me. We would never have another chance to infiltrate their organisation—this was our best bet. It was a gift to us on a platter and we would be fools if we didn't make full use of it for the good of the world. I shared my thoughts with Radha and gave her a choice—she could reject my idea and we would bide our time until we found an opportune moment to get her out of the clutches of the Order, or she could implement my plan. She would have to go deeper into the Order and help us get more information about them. Despite the obvious dangers involved, she didn't hesitate to choose *the second option. She was our mole in the Order. Where do you think all the leads came from in the last two years that enabled us to crack so many of their operations? Who do you think was feeding us that information? There was only one source we could trust implicitly—Radha. The successes of the GTF are all because of her undercover role within the Order.'*

'*You lied to me!*' Vijay thundered. '*You told me the trail had gone cold at Abu Dhabi. That she had been declared dead. You knew well even then that she was alive. You put her at risk for your own gains!*'

Imran shrugged. 'I know you're angry, Vijay. And I'm sorry. I really am. But there was no option. For Radha's safety, we had to keep this under wraps. Even Dr Shukla didn't know. I told him only on the flight here. Bill Patterson and I were the only ones who knew. We couldn't risk it leaking out. It was the best way to camouflage what she was doing. If the Order had had even the slightest hint that you knew she was alive, it would have been the end of the road for Radha. You know that as well as I do.'

Vijay had argued long and hard from the sheer frustration of not having known that Radha had been alive all these years and from anger at Imran for having lied to him. But he had gradually realised the truth of Imran's words. Radha had made a choice. She had known what she was signing up for when she had agreed to Imran's idea. And for the ruse to succeed, the Order had had to be convinced that everyone thought she was dead. Who knew how many lives had been saved in the last two years because Radha had volunteered to spy on the Order?

As they had approached the Hilton, Imran had had one final thing to say to Vijay. 'They pumped her with a powerful cocktail of drugs,' he told him. 'You will notice some effects of the treatment that saved her life.'

Vijay hadn't known at that time what Imran had meant. But now he saw it.

And he didn't understand.

Radha's skin had glowed softly as if it had a life of its own.

He had seen this in only one other person.

Dee.

The London Hilton on Park Lane
London, UK

Vijay looked on at the tearful reunion of father and daughter. He had never seen Dr Shukla display such raw emotions. He looked away, uncertain if he was intruding on a private moment.

Finally, Shukla moved away and looked at Vijay, his eyes wet. Realising that Vijay, too, had waited four years for this moment, he stepped back.

Imran gestured to the others, and they melted away into the bedroom, shutting the door after them, to give Radha and Vijay privacy.

The couple watched them go without a word.

After a long moment, Radha slowly turned to face Vijay. 'Well? Now you know why the curtains were drawn.'

Her voice was strangely matter of fact, seemingly devoid of any emotion.

Vijay stood, at a loss for words, his feet rooted to the spot.

A taut silence stretched between them, even as a maelstrom of emotions raged within both.

Finally, Vijay, overcoming his immobility, spoke. Tears welled up in his eyes as he gazed upon Radha's face.

'You don't know how difficult each day has been for me, these last four years,' he told her.

'I do,' Radha said, simply. 'I do know. It has been the same for me. It was only the thought that I was doing something useful with my life, something for the greater good, that kept me going. That, and the thought that, someday, if I managed to escape the Order with my life, I would be able to return to you.'

She shook her head, her tears flowing freely now. 'I can't believe you haven't found someone else—you thought I was dead and yet … You don't know how much that means to me.'

Radha's words hung in the air.

A yawning chasm lay between them. Neither of them seemed to know how to bridge it.

A chasm created by time.

And events.

'Why?' Vijay asked. 'Why didn't you tell me that you were alive? Why Imran?'

After Imran had revealed to Vijay that Radha was alive, he had had an outburst. It was only after a lot of yelling and crying that he had realised that it wasn't only Imran he had been upset with. It was Radha's decision to contact Imran rather than call Vijay. He didn't understand it.

Radha held his gaze. 'Because I love you, Vijay. And I know that you love me. You would never have rested until you found me. You would have done everything you could to rescue me from the clutches of the Order. You would have put yourself in danger in the process. Imran is like a brother to me. Why wouldn't I think of calling him? He has rescued me before when I was in trouble.'

She paused, but Vijay was silent, unmoving, his expression inscrutable.

It was not that he did not understand what she was trying to explain to him. While the hurt inflicted by her decision burnt deep within him, he knew that she was right. He would have gone to the ends of the earth to find Radha and help her escape from the Order, without regard for his own safety. And it was true that Radha and Imran were as close as a brother and sister could ever be. Imran had, indeed, saved Radha earlier when she was in danger of losing her life.

But there was something else that gnawed at the back of his mind.

The Radha who stood before him was not the Radha he had known four years ago.

Sure, she still loved him; that was only too evident. She was still as strong-willed as she had been, and caring too, putting the interests of others before her own.

But there was something different about her, and it wasn't just the glow on her face. Something about her had changed.

Something that he didn't understand.

Vijay couldn't quite articulate what it was. But it was perceptible.

And it made him uncomfortable.

Radha closed her eyes. She, too, hesitated. She longed, with every inch of her being, to rush to Vijay and hold him tight. She had waited for this moment for so long. Yet, now that they were here, back together, her worst fears were coming true. Something was holding her back. And she knew what it was.

The past four years with the Order had been hell. She had done things that she would never have dreamt of doing before. Those years had taken their toll on her. They had changed her. As much as she wanted to hide it, Vijay knew her too well. It was impossible to pretend in front of him.

Radha despaired.

How was she going to reconcile with Vijay?

Would they be able to confront their respective demons?

The London Hilton on Park Lane
London, UK

'I had gone into shock,' Radha told the group as they sat around the dining table in the suite later that day.

After Vijay and Radha's emotional reunion, the rest of the group had joined them. Colin had given Radha a warm hug and told her how glad he was to have her back and Radha was now telling them the extraordinary tale of her survival despite being shot multiple times.

'In normal circumstances, I wouldn't have lived. But I was told later by the doctors who attended me in different places that, apparently, they did several things immediately after I'd been shot that saved my life.' She looked around the table at the members of the group, her glance settling on Vijay who took her hand in his as she spoke.

'The doctors told me that they took an extremely aggressive approach based on a totally untested strategy that they knew might ultimately fail. But they also felt that if it succeeded in saving me, it would be worth it.' She looked around the table. 'They said they *wanted* to save me. They told me the Order did not intend to kill me; that they *did not* want me to die.'

Imran spoke up. 'I've wondered about that for a long time. Why were they so keen to save you?'

She shook her head. 'I have no idea why, but they *did* go all out to save me.'

'I'm glad they did,' Vijay told her and squeezed her hand.

'So,' Radha continued, 'the doctors told me that they induced a coma to put my central nervous system on hold to protect my brain from injury while they treated me. Once I was in a coma, they administered the bacteria and virus mix they had recovered from Alexander's mummy, along with antibiotics to counter the bacteria.'

'But wasn't it that mix that killed all their test subjects?' Vijay was surprised.

Radha nodded. 'Yes, it was. But it was the only option available. They gave me an especially heavy dose, they said. Basically, they hoped the virus would somehow kick in and there would be some beneficial effects as a result, however small, that would help the internal repair that was required. Then they continued to administer the antibiotics along with a cocktail of sedatives to maintain the coma and ensure that my central nervous system remained suppressed.'

She paused and looked at Vijay. 'I was told that you had helped the Order find the original virus in Kazakhstan and that they had managed to spirit it away.'

Vijay nodded grimly. It was not an experience that he wanted to remember, even though it would haunt him all his life.

'Sorry.' Radha realised how Vijay felt.

'It's okay,' he reassured her. 'It is the truth after all. They did get away.'

Radha gave him a wan smile and continued. 'Well, I'm glad you helped them, for a selfish reason. The Order managed to isolate the virus and then administered a fresh dose of it to me, this time in its original form and not as a dormant prophage.'

'Wow!' Colin said. 'So, you got the real thing after all! We were wondering what they would do with the virus after they escaped.'

'Yes. I was a guinea pig for their experiments with the original virus,' Radha agreed. 'But it worked. A week into the treatment, the doctors found an increase in antibodies to the bacteria and a reduction in the toxins. The virus had got a hold in my body and was doing its job.'

'Well,' Colin chuckled, 'I'm not surprised. You had an advantage over Alexander. The poor guy got the second-hand virus, while you got the real thing.'

Radha laughed. 'I guess you're right. The virus had perhaps mutated over the centuries, but it was still effective. After that, they gradually brought me out of the coma. It was a couple of weeks before I opened my eyes. I still remember that moment.' Her eyes misted up as she reminisced. 'I opened my eyes, blinked and looked around the room. But I couldn't do much more than that. It took two more weeks before I could even raise my eyebrows in response to anything they said to me.'

She paused again, the memories of her struggle to regain her life too painful to relive. 'It was agonisingly slow, but physical movement began returning. It started with my being able to wiggle my toes and move my hands slightly. They told me after I had fully recovered that there were some abnormalities as they brought me back to a fully conscious state, but my progress was steady and positive. After several months, I got back more movement and they put me on a regimen of physiotherapy so I could regain my motor skills and build muscle strength once again. And then they put me through intensive training to build muscle—martial arts and physical training routines that were painful and difficult, but which helped a lot. It took two full years, but at the end of it, I had fully recovered. And what you now see is a different Radha. It isn't just my appearance that is different. I don't know what else has changed, but I feel different. I can sense it inside me.'

'Well, I'm glad to have you back with us,' Imran smiled at her. 'You did a damn good job working undercover with the Order. It was dangerous at every step and risky as hell. They could have discovered your deception at any time and who knows what might have happened. I am so proud of you.'

'Thank you, Imran. I think I was just lucky that my cover was blown while I was in London and you had a back-up plan organised for me.' Radha gestured at the suite they were sitting in. 'But what are you going to do about Director Patterson?'

Imran shrugged. 'There's nothing we can do. We don't know what has happened or where he is. Unfortunately, he is on his own now. We can only wait.'

There was silence for a moment as everyone took in the bad news. It was difficult for any of them to even entertain the possibility that Patterson might not return from China. They had all got so used to his leadership that a GTF without Patterson was unthinkable.

Imran changed the subject. 'Tell us what you know about the Owen manuscript and what the Order wants with it.'

Radha perked up a bit on hearing his request. 'Oh, yes. I don't know a lot, but I'll tell you what I do know. The Order's interest in the Owen manuscript is as old as the discovery of the text, but everything the Order has done recently stems from a letter that Thomas Manning wrote to Alexander von Humboldt in 1817.'

Hotan
Xinjiang Province, China

Barnsfield basked in the appreciation from a fellow scientist he respected, even though she was younger than him. He had known that Iris Tsai would make a name for herself ever since he had first met her as a postgraduate student at Craggett University.

'I had a bit of help from nature, of course,' he admitted modestly. 'Around six years ago, Xia Yu Pharmaceutical

Group contacted me. My earlier work and research at that time on synthetic organisms had obviously reached them. They offered to fund my research and threw in a bonus— they would provide me with clues to an organism that would aid my research.' He wagged a finger at her. 'Clues, mind you. They still didn't know what the microbe was. They gave me the money on the condition that I would find out and reconstruct it. Engineer it from scratch.'

Iris glanced at the screen, horrified at what she was hearing.

'It took a lot of work,' Barnsfield said, oblivious to her reaction. 'But I finally managed to isolate the bloody thing.' He leaned forward. 'And here's the thing. I should have won the Nobel Prize for this. Just imagine the prize at stake here. Imagine the drugs that we can create artificially using this organism. Drugs that can be synthesised in their billions and tested in parallel for anti-tumour and antibiotic properties. And once we get a hit, trillions of variations of the molecule can be generated, the good ones identified and then evolved. Then there's biofuel, nano-sized organic circuitry, and even extrusion of organic cement!' He counted off points on his fingers. 'There's more, lots more. We could recognise and repair birth defects, heal injuries with regenerative medicine—imagine being able to regenerate limbs and organs—reprogramme tumours by managing bio-electrics. And there's always synthetic morphology: creating living, functioning artificial biological machines. Imagine growing organs in culture or making little bio-bots that have never existed before to perform tasks in our bodies. The world would be transformed. Lives would be saved. Humanity would live better!'

He paused and sat back to gauge the impact of his words on her.

'What do you mean by clues?' Iris was still trying to digest the enormity of what she had heard. 'Do you mean this organism existed before you created it?'

It was hard enough to accept that Barnsfield had created a synthetic organism of the kind that he had shown her on his laptop screen, but to believe that he had taken a naturally occurring organism and cultured it in the laboratory was even more difficult.

'I would love to take complete credit,' Barnsfield admitted, 'but that wouldn't be the truth. In the 1980s, Chinese archaeologists accidentally stumbled upon a mysterious infection that killed a few of them. Your people are smart, Iris. They didn't know what killed those archaeologists, but they knew they had to preserve enough to be able to find out when the technology did become available.'

Iris ignored the reference to her Chinese roots.

'So,' Barnsfield continued, 'when they realised that there was a new kind of organism involved, they contacted me. And I worked out how to culture the organism in the laboratory.' He shrugged. 'I leveraged all the work I had done in the years before to figure it out. It wasn't easy. You see, all I had to go on was spores. But spores, even normal bacterial ones, store information about the individual growth history of their progenitor cells, as I found out. This enables them to retain a kind of a ...' he paused, searching for the right word. 'A ... memory that links the different stages of the bacterial life cycle. Now, as we know, the spores of many bacterial species can remain in their dormant and resistant states for years, but exposure to nutrients during the process of germination can re-infuse life in them within minutes.'

'So, this thing,' Iris gestured to the images on the laptop screen, 'is a bacterium?'

Barnsfield shrugged. 'I'd be lying if I told you I know for sure exactly what it is. Remember, it is not life as we know it. So, it doesn't fit neatly into any of the known biological kingdoms. Much more study needs to be done to classify this organism. What I do know is this: not only was I given tissue samples from the Chinese archaeologists who died from the mysterious infection in the 1980s, but they also gave me pieces of hard, black stuff to analyse. I would have said they were rock, only they weren't.' He paused, his eyes shining with excitement.

'And that was when I discovered it,' he continued, 'after a lot of frustration and experimentation, of course. It helped that I knew what I was looking for—my research was what had drawn attention to me in China in the first place, remember— so the learning curve was shorter. Anyway, to cut a long story short, I found this little microscopic critter in the black stuff they gave me—they were chunks of a carbonaceous chondrite: a meteorite that had fallen to earth thousands of years ago. Once I figured out they were spores, it didn't take long to work out the exact biochemistry of the organism, which I know you've understood after looking at the video I showed you on my laptop. And here we are.'

Iris realised that this was the source of the mystery pandemic that was slowly spreading through the world; the contagion that she and Patterson had come to China to investigate. She was shocked that it had taken so little for her to stumble upon the source of the infection. She couldn't believe what Barnsfield had just told her.

'But why, Howard, why?' Iris choked on her words, unable to fathom the man's intent. 'Why did you come here to work with the CCP on something as deadly as this? Why abandon your country? Why forsake your fellow Americans and take up this research here? You could have done this in America where it would have been safer for the world!'

Barnsfield was silent for a few moments as he regarded Iris thoughtfully. Then he spoke slowly. 'Clearly, my dear, you don't understand.' His voice was bitter, his face hard as stone now. 'My work is important here. What was there for me in America? My country, you say? My fellow Americans? Bah!' He spat out the words. 'What did they give me but humiliation and reproach?' He half got up from his chair in agitation, before sitting down again. 'But the Chinese—they gave me their trust. Recognition, support, encouragement. Importance. Everything my supposed fellow Americans did not give me, your people gave me.' He jabbed a finger at her for emphasis. '*Your* people!'

'These are *not* my people!' Iris exploded. 'I was born in this country, yes, but *my* people are not murderers. They do not trample the rights of the downtrodden and disadvantaged for the sake of consolidating their own power and privileges. I would never sell my soul to them!'

There was an awkward silence.

A thought struck Iris. The scientist in her needed to know and she knew Barnsfield would answer her question. The scientist in him would prevail.

'One thing doesn't make sense to me, Howard,' she said slowly. 'The organism you have created—re-engineered, actually; I now understand why it is able to slip past the immune system without inviting an immunological response. But the very attributes that render it invisible to the immune system also ensure that it cannot harm life as we know it. It cannot infect humans, forget about killing us. So why are people falling ill? Why are they in the ICU? Why are they suffering neurological disorders and multiple organ failure?'

Howard held her gaze and smiled triumphantly. 'You haven't lost your edge,' he told Iris. 'You're right. This organism is completely harmless to all life on earth. It couldn't hurt a fly, forget humans. Just can't. And that puzzled me for a long time. I couldn't understand why the symptoms we were observing were manifesting themselves in the absence of a proper infection. Especially the cytokine storms. How can something that is completely non-immunogenic provoke a cytokine storm, which is essentially an immune response? It just didn't make any sense. Until I worked out what was happening inside our bodies once the organism was able to enter through the nose, eyes or even mouth.'

Iris waited for the explanation.

Howard pulled the laptop towards himself, then tapped at the keys until he found what he was looking for and pushed the laptop towards Iris so she could see what was on the screen.

'This is why,' he told her.

The London Hilton on Park Lane
London, UK

'Who is Thomas Manning?' Colin looked puzzled. 'Radha, please don't throw names at us, especially of men who lived two hundred years ago. You know history is not my strong point.'

Radha laughed. 'I don't expect you to know who Thomas Manning is. I didn't either, until I looked him up after I learnt about the letter he wrote to Humboldt. But before I tell you about Manning, I need to know your side of the story. What do you know about the Owen manuscript? These last few weeks I haven't really been able to stay in touch with Imran because I was trying to minimise my chances of being discovered—I had a feeling that the Order suspected something. I only connected with Imran when I learnt that the Order was interested in the Owen manuscript. I passed on the lead to Imran as I always do.' Her face fell. 'And that led to Director Patterson's ambush.'

Imran looked at Radha's glum face. 'It wasn't your fault,' he assured her. 'You couldn't have known the lead was a dud. You did what you've always done in the last two years. You heard about something the Order was interested in and told us. And we did what we always do—investigate the lead.'

'Let me tell you what we know.' Vijay quickly changed the subject. He brought Radha up to date on Wilson's kidnapping, the terrorist threat, his visit to Oxford with Colin and Duncan and their run in with the Chinese men at Wilson's house.

Radha's forehead creased with thought as she listened. 'The Order are definitely not working with China as far as the Owen manuscript is concerned,' she told them, when Vijay had finished. 'That much I can tell you for sure. What is the interest of the Chinese in the text, I can't guess, though I can now see the motivation behind some of the things the Order did. But you guessed correctly about the Order burning down Wilson's house. It was Dee who was in charge of destroying all evidence related to Wilson.' She looked at Vijay. 'You remember Dee. You had a run-in with her two years ago, here in the UK when you guys were looking for the secret of the Druids.'

Vijay's face registered shock. He had thought Dee was dead—killed in a helicopter explosion two years ago. He paled as he recalled those events. His memories of her were not pleasant.

'Fill in the gaps for us, please,' Imran said. 'What is the Order's interest in the document? And why did they burn down Wilson's house? What were they trying to cover up?'

'Yeah, and who is—or was—Thomas Manning?' Colin added. 'You've got to clear that up for me.'

'Okay,' Radha glanced at Vijay to see if he had recovered from his shock at hearing about Dee. Vijay seemed to have recovered his composure, though she knew that, inside, he was still wrestling with his emotions.

'I don't know everything—or at least not as much as I knew about the other leads I passed to Imran,' Radha continued. 'They didn't share a lot of information with me on this project—I guess because they suspected me of being an informer. And also perhaps because they were setting a trap for us. But what I do know is that the Order have known about the Owen manuscript ever since it was discovered in 1807. And they have also known about Humboldt's interest in the Owen manuscript since 1817, when Thomas Manning wrote to Humboldt.' She knit her brows as she parsed the facts in her mind. 'Though they didn't know about Humboldt's letter to Goethe—that came as a surprise to them when Wilson mentioned it.'

'Go on,' Colin prodded, as she paused to collect her thoughts. 'Thomas Manning ...'

'I swear I'll throw something at you if you say that again,' Radha feigned irritation. She was glad to be back again among friends. The last four years had been hell with her rehabilitation and constant fear of being found out by the Order. She felt she could finally be herself.

Colin grinned sheepishly at her.

'Okay, so Thomas Manning. Let me give you a quick brief on him.' She made a face at Colin as he raised his eyes to the sky and held up his hands in mock thanksgiving. 'He was the first Englishman to visit Lhasa and meet the Dalai Lama, in 1811. A bit of a mysterious person, actually. He was keenly interested in China and studied the Chinese language—presumably Mandarin—in France and later in London. Interestingly, while in France, he was unable to travel back to England because of the war between the two countries in 1803, but Manning actually wrote to Napoleon and got what was possibly the only passport signed by Napoleon for an Englishman after the war began. He then went to China and lived in the English factory run by the East India Company at Canton. However, he was unsuccessful in his efforts to travel to Peking, as Beijing was known then, and went to Calcutta instead, hoping to travel to China via Tibet. The East India Company never supported him in any major way and instead, he travelled on his own with his Chinese servant and succeeded in reaching Lhasa where he met the Dalai Lama.'

She frowned. 'His journey thereafter is shrouded in a bit of mystery, at least from the sources I could find, which aren't many. He resided in Lhasa for a while, but then abruptly had to return to India the way he came on orders from the Imperial Court in Peking. For some reason, the Chinese suddenly decided that Manning was no longer welcome in Tibet. Apparently, according to a letter—now lost—written to a Dr Marshman, Manning had been travelling in unexplored parts of Tibet and the Emperor of China had sent for his head, as it was quaintly put. So, he returned to Calcutta where he very strangely did not share any details about his journey with anyone, and then returned to Canton by sea. He finally did manage to travel to Peking as part of Lord Amherst's embassy in 1817, but they apparently spent just a few hours in Peking before they were sent packing on account of a perceived slight to the Emperor by Lord Amherst. On his way back to England, Manning had an interview with the exiled Napoleon at St Helena. And on his return to England, Manning never published any accounts of his travels through India, Tibet or China, which was unusual for an explorer of those times. They were usually keen to publish their travel journals or memoirs, unless they died before being able to do so. Anyway, on his return to England he apparently retired to a cottage near Dartford called Orange Grove and lived a very eccentric life.'

'So,' Vijay spoke up, as Radha paused for breath. 'A bunch of mysteries here. An eccentric English traveller who explored Tibet and travelled through China but never revealed to the world the nature of his travels. And you mentioned a letter from him to Humboldt in 1817. I remember from my research on Humboldt that he had visited England in 1817 on what I think was his second attempt to convince the East India Company to grant him permission to visit India. So what did this letter say?'

Hotan
Xinjiang Province, China

Iris sat on the single bed, hugging her knees, her back against the wall, tears streaming down her face. She could not come to terms with the gruesome images that had been burnt into her mind as Howard guided her through the experiments he had conducted, showing her videos and images.

The explanation he had given her until that point was insignificant compared to the real nature of the horror, as she began to understand the mechanics that underlay the contagion.

After his detailed technical explanation, Barnsfield had taken her on a brief tour of parts of the facility. Iris was not sure what had shocked her more—the live patients of clinical trials using the organism that Barnsfield had engineered, or Barnsfield's calm demeanour as he had described the different wards in which the subjects of the trials lay.

'Do you think America would have allowed experiments on live subjects like this?' Barnsfield had casually remarked.

'Never. Here, on the other hand, they have gone out of their way to provide an endless supply of subjects.' He shrugged. 'Convicts, Uyghurs, Islamic radicals from Xinjiang, human rights lawyers and activists, Christians, homosexuals and other undesirables. No one's going to miss them. At least their lives are put to some use this way.'

Iris shook her head, as if trying to empty her mind of the scenes in those wards—men and women alike, some in comas, others in death throes; all in extreme pain. All the wards were isolated from each other by glass partitions and disinfection chambers, and the staff within the wards wore state-of-the-art biohazard suits.

Each time Barnsfield had spoken of the Chinese involvement in this horror show, Iris had felt an anger deep within herself, and a sense of shame. Anger at the fact that the actions of a small group of people from the CCP were being used to demonise the entire Chinese people. And shame because the CCP officials responsible for these atrocities were, after all, Chinese.

'See here,' Barnsfield had shown her another ward where some of the subjects had missing limbs, and others had grotesquely shaped stumps where their limbs should have been.

'Here's another benefit of this organism that can reap rich rewards for the human race. We discovered, quite by accident to be honest, that this organism promotes regeneration in higher eukaryotes without resulting in cancer. Quite remarkable, don't you think? Just imagine a future where people losing limbs or organs can have them grown back right on their bodies! Science fiction today, but here is the means to make it happen.'

Iris had asked him if the subjects had naturally lost their limbs and had been horrified by the answer.

'Of course not,' Barnsfield had assured her. 'These subjects are the dregs of what we get in here—the scum of the earth, so to speak. In certain Islamic countries, they cut off hands and feet as punishment for various crimes. Here, we amputate in the service of medical advancement and the future of the human race. But see,' he had pointed out a man whose hand was a stump until the elbow, beyond which it was bandaged—'their limbs grow back. In a couple of months' time this fellow will have his entire arm back. It won't be absolutely perfect, of course, but that's what we are studying here; how to improve the process to ensure a perfect regrowth of limbs and organs. And we've also been experimenting with electrical stimulation. You'll be surprised at the results we've got for limb regeneration when Estim is applied.'

What had really seared Iris' conscience was the final ward Barnsfield had shown her. In this ward, there were little glass cells with people shackled to their beds, unable to move.

'These subjects are in an advanced stage of the infection,' Barnsfield had explained. 'The infection manifests itself differently in people. Some, like these people, become aggressive to the point of inflicting self-harm. If we don't shackle them, they will tear themselves apart and eat their own flesh. We discovered this extreme form of the infection only when some of them actually began ripping off chunks of their flesh.' He wrinkled his nose. 'Extremely distasteful.'

After the tour, as Barnsfield escorted Iris back to her cell, apologising for not being able to do anything to get her freed, Iris had asked him the question that had been playing on her mind.

'What is the antidote to control this? You'll never get all the benefits you've been talking about if people die horribly. That isn't much of a treatment, is it?'

'That's the one thing missing,' Barnsfield had admitted, shaking his head. 'The one thing that stands between us and all the benefits that we can reap from this discovery. We need an antidote.'

Then he had brightened. 'But we'll find it. My Chinese collaborators have promised me that they are working on it and will have something for me to study and replicate very soon.' His voiced had exuded confidence. 'I have no reason to doubt them. If nature allowed a life form like this to evolve, then it must have created something to keep it in check. Death always finds a way.' He had chuckled at his own joke.

A feeling of helplessness had descended on her as she heard his reply. She did not share his confidence about the antidote.

The CCP officials had chanced upon the organism that Barnsfield had cultured through sheer luck. To similarly stumble upon an antidote, if one did exist, would be hoping for too much.

If this was true, then there was no hope for the human race.

This plague was unlike anything that had been seen before. Unchecked, it would sweep the planet, devouring everything in its way.

Human life would cease to exist. And nothing would stop this from happening.

The London Hilton on Park Lane
London, UK

'In his letter to Humboldt,' Radha told them, 'Manning was very cryptic, very secretive. It was a short letter. All he said was that, in India, he had come across an ancient text which had been christened the Owen manuscript, and that he wanted to meet Humboldt to seek his advice on certain misgivings he had regarding the contents of the manuscript.'

'That was it?' Imran was surprised.

Radha shrugged. 'That was it.'

'Did they meet?' Duncan enquired.

Radha shrugged again. 'I don't know. This letter had disappeared for years. In 2014, a trove of Manning's letters was discovered with an antiquary and was purchased by the Royal Asiatic Society in 2015. Apparently, the Order somehow got wind of this letter and picked it up before the Royal Asiatic Society found out. The Order has tentacles everywhere. They know a lot about what happens anywhere in the world.'

'What did the Order do when they discovered the letter?' Vijay wanted to know. '2014 is quite recent.'

'That's just it,' Radha gestured with her hands, indicating her inability to understand. 'Strangely, they didn't pursue it as a priority project. I mean, they always knew that a part of the Owen manuscript was missing—apparently the most important part. But they never really tried to search for the lost portions of the text as far as I could learn. It was like they didn't really see any point in hunting for it—and we know how tenacious they can be when they do want to find something. It seems the Order wasn't really aware of the Humboldt connection until they got hold of Manning's letter. And even when they did acquire the letter and discovered the link, nothing really happened. But when Wilson's book was announced and the extract was published, the Order suddenly went into overdrive. They wanted to stop the publication of the book and ensure that nothing about the connection between Humboldt and the Owen manuscript was ever made public.'

'But why?' Duncan frowned. 'If the most important portion of the text is missing, how would any of this make a difference? We read through the translation of the manuscript and found nothing.'

Radha nodded. 'The manuscript by itself is useless. But apparently, Humboldt's connection to the manuscript had been a well-kept secret. Until Wilson ferreted out this information, no one had ever dreamt that Humboldt had even known about the Owen manuscript, leave alone being interested in it. And now that you have told me that there were Chinese men at Wilson's house, my guess is that the Order somehow learnt that China, or a group of Chinese, were interested in the Owen manuscript and so they had to stop the knowledge of Humboldt's association with it from leaking. Which is why they sent a terrorist threat to the publisher. You know the rest.'

Imran looked thoughtful. 'The Order kidnapped Wilson to doubly ensure that there was no chance of this piece of information being leaked.'

Radha shook her head. 'No. The Order did not kidnap Wilson. I'm quite sure of that. They were confident that their threat to the publisher would suffice. Any action concerning Wilson would have been a fallback option in case the terrorist threat did not work. And as you have told me, Wilson was kidnapped *before* the terrorist threat reached the publisher, not after.'

Duncan's eyes widened. 'Aye, lassie,' he said, 'you're right. All this time we've been thinking that the kidnapping and the terrorist threat were linked; that they were both attributable to the Order. But we were wrong. Could this group from China have kidnapped Wilson?'

'That's my guess as well,' Radha agreed.

'One mystery leads to another,' Vijay mused. 'Now we know why the Order issued what seemed to be a futile, meaningless, terrorist threat. But we still don't know what is so important about this damn text. And why the Chinese group is interested in the Owen manuscript.'

The London Hilton on Park Lane
London, UK

'Perhaps,' Shukla suggested, 'it has to do with Khandavaprastha, or more specifically the Khandavaprastha curse, as mentioned in the Owen manuscript.'

All eyes turned to Shukla. He had been sitting quietly until now, not really participating in the conversation so far, but just listening to the discussion.

For a father who had believed his daughter dead, nothing gave him more pleasure than being reunited with Radha. For him, she was not the woman who sat before them today, but the little girl who would come running to him to be swung into his arms when he returned from work; who he would carry in his arms when she was tired; and who he would put to sleep every night, humming some song or the other as a lullaby.

For fathers, daughters never grow up.

Now, he felt there was an angle to this discussion that everyone was missing.

'We know,' he said slowly, concentrating his thoughts to articulate them clearly, 'that Susruta mentions a secret that he is going to reveal. Presumably he does that in the missing portion of the text. And he also alludes to the Khandavaprastha curse, or something like that.'

'The curse of Khan ... Kandav ... yup, you're right.' Colin agreed. 'That's what this surgeon dude says.'

'I think,' Shukla continued, 'that if we can figure out what the Khandavaprastha curse is, we'll know what the Order—and perhaps the Chinese group—are after.'

There were nods around the table. Everyone had been so caught up in Radha's revelations and the partial unravelling of the mystery around the Owen manuscript that they hadn't stopped to consider what they did know about what was in the text.

'Fine.' Imran slapped the table. 'We have our work cut out for us. So, here's what we need to do.' He looked at Shukla. 'Dr Shukla, can you investigate the Khandavaprastha angle?'

Shukla's eyes brightened. 'I'm sure I can find enough material here in London.' His voice betrayed his excitement at the prospect of studying ancient documents and texts related to the Mahabharata. 'Between the British Library and the British Museum, I will have enough resources to go through. I have no idea what I'm going to be looking for though, so there are no guarantees about what I'll come up with.'

'Understood.' Imran turned to Duncan. 'Will you accompany Dr Shukla and help him with access to the library and the museum?'

'Aye.' Duncan gave a thumbs up sign.

'Vijay, Radha, Colin,' Imran addressed the other members of the group. 'Check out everything you can about Humboldt and Thomas Manning. Let's see if we can find the Humboldt connection with the Owen manuscript. Maybe Humboldt and Manning met in London. If they did, there could be some record, some document somewhere, that at least hints at what Manning wanted Humboldt's advice on.'

'What about you?' Vijay asked.

'I'm going back to India. I'd love to join you in this fascinating investigation but there's a task force to run.' A dark shadow crossed his face. 'And I'm hoping to be able to get more information on what happened to Director Patterson.'

Hampstead
London, UK

Dee gazed at the live video feed on the banks of television monitors in the large bedroom that had been converted into a monitoring station and barked orders into her phone.

She had begun to understand what was happening. She had seen Vijay, Colin, Imran and Shukla enter the London Hilton more than an hour ago, and had involuntarily clenched her jaw at the memory of what Vijay had almost succeeded in doing two years ago. Her suspicions then, about an organisation backing Vijay Singh and his friends, seemed to be confirmed now. There was no way they would have known about Radha unless they were the ones she had been passing information to.

As if to confirm her conclusion, Radha had just emerged from the hotel with Vijay and Colin in tow.

Immediately following the trio, Imran Kidwai had left the hotel unaccompanied, and hailed a cab. Close on his heels was Shukla. Even as she watched, a BMW drove up with an unidentified man at the wheel—she made a note to check if it was the same car they had all arrived in—and Shukla got in.

Something was happening.

Now, Dee was giving instructions to follow the separate groups and ensure that they did not lose sight of the targets.

She put the phone down and stared into space. Something was going on. Something strange. But what it was, she hadn't the foggiest notion.

Dee sighed and picked up her phone again, dialling Van Klueck's number.

This was the part she always hated. But she had to report this in.

The Dorchester Hotel
London, UK

Van Klueck listened as Dee updated him on the phone.

'Very good,' he told her, a trifle condescendingly. 'Well done. Now bring them all in.'

Dee was puzzled. 'I thought you wanted them followed to find out which organisation is behind them.'

Van Klueck shook his head impatiently. 'No, I didn't want you to bring Radha in. But now we know she was passing on information to this group. After the last video you sent me, I ran a quick check to find out when Kidwai arrived in London. And guess what? He arrived just this morning in a private jet from India, along with the old professor, Radha's father. Do you know what that means?'

'That they are both working for an organisation that can afford to fly them in a private jet from India to the UK?' Dee ventured.

'Exactly. And one more thing. They must have left India early this morning. Which ties in very neatly to Radha's attempt at evading us and the springing of the trap that we had set for them in China. It all fits together so well.'

Dee understood. 'I'll round them up and bring them in. I will personally interrogate each one of them and get the truth out of them. Whatever it takes.'

'Do it.' Van Klueck hung up and reflected on the developments. He was finally going to find out who had been sponsoring Vijay Singh and his friends. They had been a nuisance to the Order for long enough. It was time to end this source of irritation.

The Royal Asiatic Society
Stephenson Way
London, UK

Vijay, Radha and Colin sat in the Reading Room of the Royal Asiatic Society, poring over the documents that had been made accessible to them. Normally, access to the Reading Room is available on an appointment basis and only on certain days of the week at specified times, but Duncan had once again pulled a rabbit out of a hat and got them quick access to the society's collections.

They had been greeted on arrival by the director of the society, a charming lady named Eleanor Davis, who had introduced them to the librarian, Oliver Finch.

Finch had handed them fifteen sets of documents—papers, notes, letters, newspaper cuttings, receipts, address labels and calling cards—that comprised the collection that had been acquired by the society in 2015.

'This is everything we have,' he had told them as they gratefully took the papers and settled down to peruse them.

'Let's take five sets each,' Radha had suggested, to make the process of reading the documents faster.

There were just three other people in the room, so the trio were able to choose a table that was reasonably secluded, away from the entrance, and where they could discuss in whispers, if need be, anything they found.

Colin was first off the mark, though not with a discovery. 'Why did all these nineteenth-century dudes have such terrible handwriting?' he grumbled.

He was justified to some extent. Although Manning's handwriting was not as badly illegible as Humboldt's had been, it was still difficult to read.

'What are we looking for anyway?' he added, gesturing to the papers before him. 'I mean, these are all receipts for liquor. Apparently Manning was quite fond of port wine. F. Potter, Wine & Brandy Merchant seems to have made quite a profitable living off the guy.' Unfortunately, Colin had got the last few sets which comprised receipts, address labels and calling cards, newspaper clippings and Manning's passports and official documents.

'Shhh!' Radha admonished him. She peered at his sets, trying to discern what else he had with him, and realised that, apart from one set comprising later correspondence, Colin didn't seem to have much of use.

'Okay,' she told him. 'Quickly go through what you have and then Vijay and I can give you some of ours.'

'We don't have to read every line of every letter,' Vijay added. 'Just scan them to see if there is anything that strikes you as important.' He grinned. 'I don't think any of us would be able to read every single word either. Colin's right, Manning's handwriting is difficult to read.'

Colin nodded, placated, and resumed his study of the documents. After about ten minutes, he held his hand out for more documents. Vijay and Radha passed him one set each from their lot.

Half an hour passed and there was silence in the room, broken only by the crackle of paper being shifted.

Finally, Colin sighed. 'I give up. I've finished going through everything I had. I couldn't find anything that could relate to …'

He broke off as he saw Radha's face.

Her phone had buzzed with an incoming message while he was speaking. She had switched it to silent mode when they entered the Reading Room. As she read the message, her face had turned white.

Vijay saw her shocked expression. 'What's the matter?' He immediately knew something was wrong.

But before he could say anything, the door to the Reading Room burst open and three men barged in, their guns drawn.

Radha knew what was happening.

The Order had found her.

And they were reeling her in now.

London Luton Airport
London, UK

Imran heaved a sigh of relief as he saw the LLA logo sparkling in white against the black facade of the airport terminal. There had been a lot of traffic on the M1, and it had taken more than an hour to reach the airport.

As the London cab slowed and came to a stop, he paid the driver and included a generous tip.

'Thanks, mate!' The cab driver grinned at him. "Ave a nice flight!'

Imran smiled back at him and alighted, oblivious to the black BMW van that had drawn up behind. He didn't have the least suspicion that Dee had tracked Radha down and that they had been under surveillance. When Imran had told Radha to disappear, she had done exactly that, leaving no trace of where she had gone to. There was no reason for him to suspect that the Order would have any idea that Radha had checked into the London Hilton.

As he pulled his strolley out of the taxi, three men dashed up to him and pinned his arms behind his back, even as one of them slipped a black hood over Imran's head.

Imran's strolley fell with a loud thud.

The cab driver jumped out of the taxi and came to the rear. "'Ere, what's 'appening?'

One of the men brandished a Glock in his free hand, pointing it at the driver, who backed off, raising his hands.

Imran struggled to free himself, but the three men were powerfully built and strong, holding him in a vice-like grip.

The few people who were around turned to look, but the guns that were being held aloft by Imran's attackers were a strong motivation to beat a hasty retreat into the terminal building or their cars.

Imran was dragged, half suffocating, as one of his captors tightened the fabric of the hood so that it clung to his face and head.

Then he was yanked into a car and flung onto the floor, face down. His arms were pinioned behind him with a zip tie.

He heard the car doors slam shut and felt feet on his back.

The car whizzed off, with Imran a prisoner.

It had all happened in a matter of seconds.

Imran was furious with himself for letting his guard down and underestimating the Order. He had thought Radha had been able to give the Order the slip. But they had both been wrong.

The Order had known.

Which meant that they knew even now where Radha was.

And they would also know about Duncan and Shukla.

The rest of the team was in danger and he had no way to warn them.

Hotan

Xinjiang Province, China

Patterson looked up in surprise as two armed guards barged into his little cell. One got busy unlocking his handcuffs and anklecuffs from the chains attached to the bed rail, while the second guard stood by, his gun at the ready.

The day had gone by quite uneventfully, leaving Patterson to his thoughts. Ever since their arrival at the secret underground facility, he had been pretty much left alone, except for a breakfast of bread and cheese, and noodle soup for lunch, both of which had been passed to him through the bean hole in the door.

Apart from that, it had been quiet.

Very quiet.

Patterson had spent the time collecting his thoughts and mentally going through the layout of the facility—whatever he had seen of it, that is. Lin's words ran through his mind again and again. There was no doubt in Patterson's mind that this place was the secret lab that Lin had referred to. But while he had, by pure accident, managed to infiltrate the place, it was not in the circumstances that he would have desired. There wasn't much he could do as a prisoner. But he still wanted more information about exactly what the CCP was doing here.

Was this a PLA operation? The presence of the Major General certainly seemed to indicate this. And despite the danger he and Iris were in and the uncertainty over what was going to happen to them, the scientist in him was curious.

What was the nature of the bug that the CCP had managed to culture? Lin had been remarkably vague about exactly what the bioweapon was. Patterson certainly had his own hunch, but it was nothing more than a guess. He needed to know more. And he would have to stay alert. The remotest possibility of being able to pass information out of this place and to his team at the GTF would have to come first irrespective of his fate and that of Iris.

Locked up in his little windowless cell, he had no idea of how much time had passed or what time of day it was.

Now he wondered where the guards were taking him.

They walked down the long corridor in silence, Patterson still in handcuffs, his hands behind his back. They were taking no chances. As they passed the door of the cell where Iris had been deposited earlier, Patterson glanced at it, wondering if she was fine. There were no guards outside her door. Then again, the cells were so secure that the PLA really didn't have any need for additional security to prevent the prisoners from escaping.

He wondered who was locked in the other cells.

They reached the lift and he felt it ascend. Then they marched down another corridor, which looked more plush than the stark, spartan surroundings he had seen so far, to a mahogany door.

One of the guards knocked on the door. A voice said something in Mandarin and the guard pushed the door open, prodding Patterson to enter.

It was some sort of a conference room, carpeted and wood panelled, with a circular table to seat five at one end, with a ceiling projector and screen and a large screen television completing the setup.

Iris was there already, teary eyed, sitting at the round table. With her were Jiang and another man who was not in the PLA uniform.

Two grim-faced PLA soldiers stood guard; their guns prepped for action.

The guards escorting Patterson hustled him towards the table.

The elderly man in civilian clothes said something to Jiang who barked an order. One of Patterson's guards quickly took off his handcuffs.

The non-uniformed man now rose and offered his hand to Patterson. 'I am Chen Gengxin,' he introduced himself. 'I am the managing director of Xia Yu Pharmaceutical Group.' He indicated a vacant chair. 'Please, sit down.'

Patterson sat down, chafing his wrists, and regarded Chen with some interest.

So this was one of the men behind the contagion.

'My apologies.' Chen noticed Patterson's action. 'But it is absolutely necessary as a precaution. I am sure you will understand.'

Patterson said nothing but glanced from Chen to Jiang. The Major General sat stiffly, his face impassive.

'So,' Chen addressed Patterson. 'I have read both your bios. You,' he looked at Iris, 'are a prodigy, as I was just saying, and we are honoured to have you here among us.' He cocked his head as if considering something, then continued.' In fact, since you are Chinese, I think it is not out of place to offer you a place on our team. Your level of expertise does not exist in Dr Barnsfield's team right now, apart from him of course. And he has told us that, with your knowledge and know-how, we could complete the final phase of our project in less than half the time we have planned.'

Patterson wondered what the final phase of the project was to which Chen was alluding.

Iris looked at Patterson, unsure of how she should respond, but the GTF director's face was inscrutable.

'I don't think I'd be able to do that,' she said stiffly, after briefly pondering how she should reply. 'I have a lab back home in the USA and responsibilities to go with it. And I'm *not* Chinese. I'm American.'

Chen's face grew dark. 'Living in America does not make you American, Dr Tsai. You were *born* in China.' He emphasised the word "born". 'And even if you had been born in America, your blood is Chinese. You owe this much to your motherland. All Chinese do, irrespective of where they are born or where they live.'

Iris said nothing but it was plain that she was uncomfortable with this line of thought.

Chen turned to Patterson. 'And you, Dr Patterson, are an enigma. A former USA Navy SEAL and a scientist. Now that is a combination that we don't see too often, do we?'

Patterson responded once again with resolute silence. Let Chen prattle on, but he was not going to give anything away. Even if they tried to force it from him. But he was more worried about what they would do with Iris. The one silver lining that he saw was that they respected Iris and wanted her expertise. And he knew exactly why, after Lin's revelations. He didn't know if and how this could be useful for the two of them, but it gave him hope. At least they wouldn't torture her for information. And this explained to some extent at least the superficially polite behaviour and good treatment they had received so far. He wondered how long it would continue once they realised they were not going to get anything from him.

A glance passed between Chen and Jiang.

Then Chen dropped the bombshell.

'So what do you want with the Owen manuscript?'

Hotan

Xinjiang Province, China

Patterson was well trained and had years of experience practising control of his emotions and expressions, but even he couldn't help but gape at Chen's words. He had been incommunicado with the rest of the GTF team, even eschewing briefings for the mission on which he had sent Vijay and Colin; the only exception being the detailed message that Imran had sent him requesting him to reconnoitre the ancient site where the Owen manuscript had been found. As a result, he had no idea of the Chinese interest in the Owen manuscript or that they had even known about its existence.

In fact, he didn't even know what the Owen manuscript was. All that he knew was that it was important for the Order.

Imran's message had been functional.

London investigation has hit a dead end. The Wilson terror threat is apparently linked to an almost 2,000-year-old text called the Owen manuscript, discovered in 1807. The text is incomplete. Suspect that the missing portion contains what the Order is after. No clues available, but Red Queen has just learnt that the Order believes the missing portion of the manuscript is in an ancient ruin near Hotan. Request you to check it out if you can. No other option I can see to close this. Confirm if possible.

Red Queen was Radha's codename in her undercover role within the Order.

The message then went on to give details of the exact location where the Owen manuscript was said to have been found, along with a description of the 'tower' within which it had been hidden.

Now Patterson was glad that he had memorised the details and immediately deleted the message.

A dark foreboding grew in his mind. Were the CCP and the Order working together?

He had by now firmly concluded that the Order was behind the ambush that had led to his and Iris's capture. There was just no other way the CCP would have connected two WHO scientists with the archaeological site where the Owen manuscript had been discovered. And since Radha was the one who had tipped off Imran about the possibility of the missing portion of the text being at the site and the fact—which he now knew to be false—that the Order believed it was there, the Order's complicity in his capture was evident.

But it still didn't explain how the CCP knew about the Owen manuscript. Chen was quite confident that Patterson and Iris had knowledge of the Owen manuscript and their surprise was evident on their faces.

Chen laughed, quite pleased at himself for having elicited a confession from them so effortlessly. 'So, it is true. Is that why you came to China, posing as members of the WHO team?'

He looked at Iris. 'Or are you not a part of this American scheme?'

Patterson thought quickly. He realised that Chen believed that the WHO infiltration was an attempt by America to search for something connected to the Owen manuscript. While the Order may have tipped off the CCP about Patterson's excursion to the archaeological site, it was evident that they had not disclosed anything else.

Nothing made much sense to Patterson at the moment. Everything was so confusing, so jumbled, that he couldn't make out what was really happening.

But he did spot an opportunity to enable Iris to dissociate herself from him. And there was no point pretending that he knew nothing about the Owen manuscript—Iris and he had already given themselves away.

Patterson decided to take the opportunity to clear Iris of any suspicion.

'She knows nothing about the manuscript.'

Chen regarded him thoughtfully for a moment. 'Is that so?' he asked finally. 'Then what was she doing there with you in the middle of the night, combing through the ancient ruins?'

Patterson stayed quiet. He was on a knife's edge here. One wrong move and Iris was doomed; he knew he was a goner anyway.

'I will ask one more time,' Chen said, the smile disappearing from his face. 'What is your interest in the Owen manuscript? What does America want with it?'

There was silence.

Chen glanced from Patterson to Iris and back again. 'I see,' he said, finally. 'You do have something to hide.'

Jiang spoke up. 'Chen *zŏng*. Leave it to the PLA. We will find out.'

Chen nodded and turned to Iris. 'And you, Dr Tsai. Whether you are complicit in this diabolical American plan or not does not matter. You *will* work with us on the final phase of our project.'

There was a mix of fear and anger on Iris' face, but she was resolute. She was not going to be steamrolled into acquiescence.

'I will not.'

Chen shrugged and looked Patterson in the eye even as he continued to address Iris. 'I don't believe you have a choice, Dr Tsai. At least, not if you have any kind of consideration for your fellow American.' He spat out the last words with a sneer. 'You see, his food today was laced with our new bioweapon. He has been infected with a heavy load of the pathogen. And it has gone straight to the gut through the food.'

Iris' eyes widened and she gasped with horror. Barnsfield had explained to her exactly how the organism worked. It operated through the gut microbiota. While it was generally spread through the air as an airborne pathogen, it eventually reached the gut where it started its malevolent work. A direct infection to the gut would be more severe and develop faster.

'Even as we speak, the organism is multiplying exponentially within him,' Chen continued. 'Within three days, the usual symptoms will start manifesting themselves. As you no doubt know by now, the incubation is seven days when it is airborne. In the gut it takes three days, maybe less.'

Patterson met his gaze and did not flinch, his expression inscrutable and unchanging.

Chen turned to her, a satisfied look on his face. 'What are you going to do, Dr Tsai? Refuse to work with us and he dies within a month. A horrible, painful death. You know what it is like. You have seen the subjects of our clinical trials here.'

He waved a hand indicating the facility they were sitting in. 'Our research shows us that fatalities happen within two months in the normal course when it is an airborne infection. Injected into the gut, it could be as little as three weeks. Or you can accept our offer, come on board and work with us to develop the antidote. Your specialised skills and expertise will be useful to create the precise molecular delivery mechanism we will need for the antidote to work effectively. And our interests will then be aligned—both of us want the antidote developed in the next couple of weeks.'

He paused.

'Don't do it, Iris,' Patterson urged her. 'It isn't worth it. You will be gifting them the means to dominate the world.'

Chen's face was grim. 'The longer you delay cooperating with us, the greater the damage inflicted on him by the pathogen,' he told Iris. He turned to Patterson,. 'I think we're done with you here, Dr. Patterson.'

Jiang barked an order and the PLA guards roughly jerked Patterson to his feet and hustled him out of the room.

As he left, he saw Iris cover her face with her hands and sob inconsolably.

Hotan
Xinjiang Province, China

Patterson's mind was full of questions, tumbling, jostling against each other, asking to be answered. But the shadow of a suspicion had begun to form in his mind. If the CCP was so interested in the Owen manuscript, whatever it was and whatever it contained, was it possible that this ancient document was in some way linked to the mystery bug that they had developed here at Hotan?

The two events—the manuscript and the contagion—didn't seem to be connected in any way at first. But the more he thought about it, the more convinced he was that there was a link.

He brushed the thoughts aside. This was not the time to be searching for answers to questions like these. From the conversation in the conference room, he had twigged that Iris had been privy to some disclosures by their captors. What they were, he didn't know, but he needed to. For her sake and his own.

Patterson believed Chen had not been bluffing when he had revealed the intentional infection of the GTF director through his food. Nor did he discount the amount of time Chen had said he had left to live. From the case histories that he had studied in the dossier about this mission, he knew that it took around seven days for the first neurological symptoms—memory loss, disorientation, confusion, incoherence—to start manifesting themselves, followed by progressive deterioration of the nervous system and other complications including organ failure and muscular dysfunction. Within two weeks of the appearance of the first symptoms, hospitalisation was required and ventilator support extended. After that it had been anybody's guess how long the patients would survive, but Chen had said two months from the date of infection.

In Patterson's case, less than a month.

He was a dead man walking.

And he had even less time as a physically fit person. Instead of the usual fourteen days before hospitalisation, he had maybe two or three days left before he would be in the ICU.

If anything had to be done, it had to be done now.

Tomorrow would be too late.

The Royal Asiatic Society
Stephenson Way
London
UK

Radha reacted in a flash, ignoring the terror-stricken faces of the other researchers in the room upon seeing the armed men.

She had anticipated this attack as soon as she saw the message and understood its import.

Even as the three other readers cowered at their tables and shrank back in fear, Radha sprang to her feet and sprinted towards the three men who rushed towards them.

Vijay and Colin watched in amazement and wonder as Radha launched herself at the man in the lead, twisting on her left foot as she leaped in the air, and lashed out with her right leg in a classic side kick, catching the man in his abdomen. Her kitten heel embedded itself in the man's solar plexus and with the momentum of her sprint and the kick, he sailed backwards and into the man right behind him.

The third man, bringing up the rear, had just enough time to skid out of the way as the two men in front of him crashed to the floor.

Before he could recover, Radha had landed on her feet like a cat and pivoted on her left foot, landing a powerful roundhouse kick to his temple. He folded like a pack of cards and crumpled to the floor.

One down.

Vijay and Colin, recovering from their bewilderment, pulled out their guns, which had been concealed beneath their jackets, and ran to where Radha stood over the three men. The first two had somewhat recovered and were scrambling around trying to regain their footing when they found they were suddenly outnumbered and outgunned.

It had all happened in seconds.

They meekly surrendered their guns, the man who had been in the lead nursing his injured abdominal muscles.

'Search them. They'll have zip ties on them for sure, meant for us,' Radha instructed.

Vijay stood guard while Colin put away his gun, patted the men down and found the zip ties, which they used to quickly truss up all three men.

As Vijay concealed his own weapon, two staff members, accompanied by Oliver Finch, came rushing into the Reading Room, having heard the commotion. They took one look at the three men, all tied up, and at the trio of Vijay, Colin and Radha, and one of the staff members scurried away to call the police.

'Did you do this?' Finch looked incredulously at them and the guns Radha was holding, which she had taken off the men when she had disarmed them.

Before any of them could answer, one of the other readers in the room, a young girl in her early twenties, came up. 'They were amazing!' she gushed. 'These men ran into the room. They had guns,' she indicated the guns that Radha held. 'It was a terror attack, wasn't it?' She looked from Vijay to Colin to Radha, searching their faces for an answer, then turned to Finch. 'If they hadn't acted quickly and bravely, I don't know what would have happened!'

Finch still looked doubtful, but he nodded. 'We'll let the police take care of them. Thank you,' he added, addressing the GTF trio.

The young girl, her hands clasped tightly with excitement, looked at the three GTF members, her eyes shining. The other two researchers had also come up and murmured their thanks.

Radha began walking away, followed by Vijay, as the girl cornered Colin.

'Are you guys from MI5?' she asked.

Colin leaned forward and whispered conspiratorially, 'I could tell you, but then I'd have to kill you.'

He walked away to join Vijay and Radha, leaving the girl staring at them. 'I always wanted to say that,' he grinned, as they shook their heads, laughing.

Radha led the way out of the room and out of the building as she dialled a number on her mobile phone. 'We're coming out,' she said cryptically.

As they reached the street, they saw two burly men walking towards them, dressed in casual clothes, their arms and shoulders knotted with muscles.

'Uh oh,' Colin said. 'I hate to break it to you guys, but our troubles ain't over yet.'

Stephenson Way
London, UK

'It's okay,' Radha told him as the two men walked up. 'They're ours.'

'They're on to us, Bruce,' Radha told one of the men who had walked up, a tall black man who towered over the others, well over six feet and five inches in height. 'Any news from your men watching over my dad?'

'Nope,' Bruce replied. 'I'll double check anyway.' He raised a questioning eyebrow. 'Trouble inside?'

Radha nodded. 'Nothing we couldn't handle. But keep your eyes peeled.'

'These guys were smart.' Bruce looked at her. 'We didn't see anyone following you. And we've been watching the entrance all this while. Sorry, Radha.'

'That's quite alright,' Radha told him. 'You're right, they were smart. They did a good job of posing as genuine researchers. Their clothes, their looks; there's no way you could have guessed who they really were.'

'I'll tell the men.' With those words, Bruce and his companion melted away.

'What was all that about?' Vijay asked. 'You got a message and then those men attacked us inside. I have a feeling you know why. Who are *these* two guys? And where did you get those close combat skills from? You took out those three men single-handedly! Colin and I were spectators; before we could react, you had them down!'

'Yeah,' Colin agreed. 'That was like out of a Bruce Lee movie or something.'

Radha let out an embarrassed laugh. 'I told you guys earlier today that the Order put me through a rigorous physical and martial arts training programme for two years during my rehabilitation. A few hours every day. I've kept it up since then and used some of it when I went on missions for the Order.'

Vijay didn't ask any questions about the missions. He knew that Radha would have had to prove her loyalty to the Order in order to fend off any suspicions they may have had about her. He was sure she didn't want to talk about that part of the four years she had been away and he wasn't very sure himself if he wanted to know.

Radha's face grew grim as she continued. 'Imran has been kidnapped. I just got a message.'

She paused, collecting her thoughts, before resuming. 'See, when I was with the Order, I never knew when an emergency could happen. I needed protection. So, I built a small personal army of my own. I helped Bruce out a couple of times, got him out of trouble and helped his brother get a job. Now, he's loyal to me. And he has a small group of men who work with him. They are my security ring when I need protection. So, when Imran told me I had to disappear, I called Bruce. They've been shadowing me ever since. And all of us after we met. The team that was following Imran sent me the message that I received inside the Reading Room. Imran was abducted just as he was about to enter the airport terminal. It happened too quickly and suddenly for them to help him and they were a couple of cars away, so they couldn't follow the kidnappers either.'

She turned to Vijay. 'Some of these men, including Bruce, were watching over you guys when you were in London two years ago. When you were with Saul Goldfeld.'

A look of comprehension swept over Vijay's face. He looked at Colin. 'So that's why our shadows suddenly disappeared the night you and Alice went to Edinburgh.'

'Ah, yes, I remember,' Colin recalled. 'We were so surprised that no one had tailed you and Harry when you acted as decoys.'

'Bruce and his men had a run-in with some men who were watching you,' Radha told them. 'After that I think your shadows just stayed away. Bruce can be very persuasive when he wants to.' She smiled.

'I wouldn't want him to try his persuasion skills on me,' Colin declared, remembering the man's thick, knotted shoulders, and arms that looked like iron bands. 'I'd be quite happy to be persuaded with a smile.'

'And then when you and Alice were at Cairnpapple,' Radha continued, addressing Colin. 'You probably didn't realise it, but it was Bruce's men who attacked the people from the Order who were already there when you reached.'

'That's why we got away so easily,' Colin realised. 'We were wondering why no one chased us.'

'The Order had Bruce's men to tangle with,' Radha explained. 'Dee was there in a helicopter, but they drove her off by shooting at the chopper.'

Vijay and Colin were silent for a moment. Even while they had considered Radha dead, she had, in her own way, been watching over them.

'Let's get my dad and Duncan,' Radha told them. 'And then figure out what we need to do next. We have to get Imran out of the clutches of the Order. They suspect the existence of the GTF. And Dee will do anything to get information out of Imran, short of killing him.'

Regent's Park
London, UK

The room was dark.

Pitch black.

Imran opened his eyes and groaned. He couldn't see a thing.

But he could feel and sense that he was bound hand and foot to a chair. He struggled against the bonds, but they held tight. Someone had done a good job of trussing him up.

He groaned again. His body ached. After being dumped on the floor of the car, he had been driven for a while until the car had stopped and he was dragged out, down a flight of stairs and into this room where he had been beaten senseless by the goons who had abducted him.

It seemed to him that they had been careful not to break any bones, but he was sure that if the lights were on he would see his body covered in bruises.

Imran realised that he had been stripped of his clothes and bound to this chair in only his underwear. He wondered what lay in store for him.

Memories flooded back. Interrogations in the dead of the night at police chowkies in Uttar Pradesh years ago, when he had been an SP. Suspected criminals beaten black and blue to extricate a confession out of them. He had had a particularly good record of getting people to confess and had cracked many cases that seemed unsolvable.

After his posting to the IB, the interrogations had continued. Only, now they were not petty criminals and murderers but suspected terrorists and their accomplices. Again, Imran had been very successful in blowing up terror plots and exposing potential terrorists, saving thousands of lives in the process. It was what had fast-tracked his growth within the IB, eventually leading to his current role at the GTF.

Now, he ruefully reflected, he knew what those people would have felt. And he knew there was more to come for him.

Would he break?

He hoped not.

As if on cue, the door to the room opened and people walked in. He heard a switch being flicked and a single, harsh, white light came on, shining directly on his face.

He flinched and shut his eyes tight, screwing up his face.

'Hurts, doesn't it?' Dee's voice came from the shadows beyond the light. 'But not as much as what I'm going to do to you.'

Imran squinted at the darkness. 'What do you want?'

'Quite a bit,' Dee chuckled. 'Well, my bosses, at least, want to know who you are working for. To whom Radha has been feeding information. What is your connection with the guy captured in Hotan?' She paused. 'Me? I only want to feel your pain.'

Through the brightness of the light, Imran saw a slim female silhouette come into his frame of view.

'Beat me as much as you want,' Imran fiercely told her, 'Waterboard me if you want. I have nothing to tell you.'

'I'm not going to beat you,' Dee said softly. 'Waterboarding is for wimps. I like the scent of blood. I like to see it flow. The rivulets coursing down, coalescing into a pool on the floor.'

She looked back at the men standing behind her. 'I should write poetry.' She laughed.

Dee's hand came into sight and Imran saw her fingers clasping a slender, wicked-looking dagger.

His blood froze as he realised that she was in this interrogation for fun. Not to extract information. The glee in her voice had been unmistakeable.

Imran took a deep breath and mentally steeled himself against what he knew was to come. This was going to be worse than he had imagined, more painful than any interrogation he himself had conducted.

'Shut the door,' Dee ordered. 'We don't want his screams to echo through the streets.'

Hotan
Xinjiang Province, China

A plan had formed in Patterson's mind as the two guards escorted him back to his cell. It was a plan strewn with hazards, but he was a desperate man running out of time. Even if it was suicidal, he would at least die knowing he had tried.

As was his habit, when he was taken out of the cell, he kept a watch on his surroundings, noting the walls, the floors, the ceilings of the corridors, the buttons pressed in the lift; whatever details he could observe and memorise. He didn't know if he'd ever be able to use the information, but experience had told him that it never hurt.

The cell bolts were shot back and Patterson was shoved inside. He glared at the soldier who had pushed him, but was ignored.

He really didn't matter to either man. He was just another prisoner and just another responsibility for them.

Good.

He automatically tensed as the handcuffs were slipped off preparatory to his being chained to the bedrail, and forced himself to relax. He didn't want the soldiers to get an inkling of what he had in mind.

The handcuffs were off and one of the soldiers moved back, out of striking distance from Patterson, and raised his gun.

The other guard worked to cuff Patterson's hands and feet to the bedrail chain, keeping the prisoner between him and the second guard to ensure that the guard with the gun was not blocked in case of an escape attempt. This was their standard drill—and it was a good one, Patterson had to admit—that ensured that a prisoner's chances of overpowering either guard were insignificant.

But was it good enough?

There was only one way to find out.

As the guard who had unlocked his handcuffs reached for one of the chains hanging from the bedrail, Patterson made his move.

The PLA soldier had the bedrail chain in his left hand, with Patterson between the two men. Patterson could only hope that his timing was right, otherwise he was a dead man.

He moved with lightning speed, kneeing the soldier holding the chain in the groin, as he grabbed his belt with one hand and one of his epaulets with the other.

The soldier standing guard over Patterson reacted with amazing swiftness and fired.

Patterson was still directly in the line of fire.

The Dorchester Hotel
London, UK

'What do you mean they got away?' There was more than just a touch of asperity in Van Klueck's voice. 'You were supposed to bring them in.'

Dee grimaced. She had been so carried away by the pain she had been inflicting on Imran that she had neglected to keep a tab on what was happening with the others. It was only when Imran was senseless with pain that she had turned her attention to the others.

And then discovered to her shock that her men had failed to bring in the others. She had been so confident, yet her men reported being driven off in one case by hired bodyguards and in the other case thwarted by the targets themselves. Three of her men were now under arrest. The police would never trace them back to her, but she had failed nevertheless.

Dee cursed at her folly in underestimating her adversaries. She remembered how, two years ago, her attempts to have them shadowed had been similarly foiled. It was that experience that had first led her to suspect that there was an organisation behind these people who professed to be only a group of friends. But she had still expected them to be soft, civilian targets, apart from Radha, whose skills she was aware of. For that reason, and in order to remain unobtrusive, she had assigned a trio of men each to the Royal Asiatic Society operation and the British Library. Now she knew she had been wrong about them. She would not make this mistake again.

She knew how close the success of this operation was to Van Klueck's heart. He had set his mind on destroying whatever organisation it was that had been such an irritant to the Order. If nothing else, he was a true, loyal servant of the Order. Even if he wasn't of the bloodline. That much she respected him for.

So she heard out his rant quietly. She knew she was at fault.

But Van Klueck hadn't finished with her yet.

He had followed up his rant with a question. 'What of your interrogation?'

Once again, Dee had to admit failure. Despite the torture, Imran had refused to divulge any more information than what she already knew: that Vijay, Radha, Colin, Shukla and Imran knew each other from a past, accidental meeting and that there was no organisation behind them.

Despite herself, Dee had found herself admiring the man's determination, as well as his threshold of pain. Lesser men had buckled under lesser pain and done her bidding. She'd known that Imran had been lying and had been holding out against the agony of the torture. She had taken it as a challenge. Her methods against Imran's endurance. And she was going to take it one step up now.

'I see,' Van Klueck said after she told him that she had no new information for him. His tone made it quite plain that he didn't see.

'We don't have time,' Van Klueck warned her. 'And we have no idea how far ahead of us the Chinese are. There is no news coming out of either Hotan or Beijing. The CCP—or at least the officials in charge of the bioweapon project—are tight-lipped about the whole operation. For all we know, they could have found the antidote by now. Where does that leave us then?'

'I'll wring it out of him if it is the last thing I do!' Dee burst out. She immediately regretted her choice of words.

'We can't wait that long,' Van Klueck countered her calmly. 'It just isn't good enough. We need results now.'

The GTF Base
Hounslow
London, UK

A grim-faced group sat around the table in the conference room located in the basement of the UK headquarters of the GTF.

At Radha's urging, Vijay and Colin had accompanied her to the British Library, where Shukla and Duncan were working on the Khandavaprastha angle, and all of them had then travelled together to Hounslow.

Bruce's men who had been shadowing Shukla and Duncan reported that they had noticed three men loitering suspiciously outside the British Library. When Bruce and his companion had joined the others, the three men from the Order had suddenly found themselves confronting six burly men, all of whom were armed and meant business.

The goons from the Order had beaten a hasty retreat, enabling the GTF team to travel to their headquarters without worrying about the Order discovering its location.

Duncan had led them to the conference room where they huddled together, trying to work out a plan of action. All agreed that the research into Manning, Humboldt and Khandavaprastha could wait. Imran came first.

'Dee will butcher him,' Radha had told the others. 'But she won't let him die. If we wait too long, we will find him in pieces, but still alive.'

Vijay had agreed wholeheartedly with this assessment, having experienced Dee's proclivity for torture and cruelty in the past.

And, apart from the humanitarian angle—and emotional case for saving Imran—there was also the need to safeguard the identity and existence of the GTF.

There was a lot at stake.

'How do we find out where Imran is being held?' Colin wanted to know.

Radha would have none of this doubtfulness. Imran had saved her life once, and was like a brother to her. 'I know the Order has a safe house in Hampstead,' Radha told them. 'We will start there. If we don't find him there, we will find someone who can tell us where else he might be held captive.'

'Okay,' Vijay agreed. He was equally keen to rescue Imran from Dee's clutches. 'When do you want to do this?'

'We have to do it tonight.' Radha was firm. 'Tomorrow will be too late.'

The discussion stretched on. Slowly, a plan began to take shape. It was risky and they didn't know if it would work. But they had to try.

Hotan

Xinjiang Province, China

Patterson cursed. He was clearly not as nimble as he had been as a younger SEAL. In those days of yore, which seemed centuries ago, he would have executed this manoeuvre with speed and accuracy and not even have broken a sweat.

Now he was older, heavier, slower and … well, rusty.

His idea had been to swing the guard around so that the soldier would be in the line of fire and take the bullet that would definitely be aimed at Patterson.

It had been a good idea. With risks, but meritorious nevertheless. In his SEAL days, it would have earned him a pat on the back from his commanding officer.

But today it had earned him a flesh wound.

He had not been fast enough in swinging the soldier around, so things hadn't gone completely according to plan, but whether on account of sheer luck or good timing, he had also moved out of the line of fire.

The bullet had nicked the overdeveloped muscle attaching his neck to his shoulders, shearing a deep furrow through it.

But he would live.

At least for another couple of weeks, until the contagion took him.

Patterson improvised as he completed the manoeuvre. He put more shoulder into his swing and brought the guard around, then let him go so that he careened backwards into the second guard who had just shot at him. He was counting on the inexperience of the two guards—it was highly unlikely that either of them had had to actually prevent an escape in this place.

Both guards crashed to the ground.

Patterson demonstrated that he had not completely lost his agility as a soldier on active duty. He swooped down and grabbed the assault rifle, wrestling it away from the guard who had shot at him. Then with the remorseless conscience of a soldier at war, he peppered both guards with bullets.

This was a do or die situation.

This was war.

It was shoot or get shot.

He sagged for a moment against the bedrail, composing himself and plotting the next steps of his plan. His neck wound was bleeding profusely, but he ignored it. There were no bones or major blood vessels where he had been shot. There was no time to staunch the flow. He would work out what to do about it once he was out of here.

Patterson had no idea what he was up against. He was going in blind. Were there cameras watching this corridor? Would they see him as he stepped out of his cell? Would an alarm go off?

He searched the men and found two more guns, both revolvers, and stuffed them into his trousers. He also found two white keycards, presumably for opening doors, though he didn't know if they would be of any use since he didn't know which doors they would open.

But he purloined them anyway.

Better to be safe than sorry.

Feeling equipped to execute the next phase of his plan, he slowly opened the cell door, looked up and down the dimly lit corridor, and slid out of the cell, cat-footing down the corridor, trying his best to keep in the shadows. Luckily the passage was not well illuminated, so he hoped that even if there were cameras, he might be able to evade detection.

He reached Iris' cell.

The bolts were shot.

It hadn't been long since he had left the conference room. Had she been brought back to her cell immediately afterward? Or had she been detained for a further round of persuasion by Chen?

Slowly, carefully, he shot back the bolts, trying to make as little noise as possible, and pushed the door open.

The room was in darkness.

He slid inside and flicked on the switch. The layout of the room and the switches was exactly the same as in his cell.

Thank heavens for standardisation.

The cell was empty.

He clenched his fist in frustration. He had intended to rescue Iris and attempt an escape with her. The thought of leaving her behind, especially if he escaped—since he was the bargaining chip—had not crossed his mind.

Patterson set his jaw and exited the cell, moving down the corridor towards the lift. He had observed the floors he had been taken to and he had originally wanted to avoid those floors.

But now things had changed. He had to check out the floor on which the conference room was located and see if Iris was still there.

Recalling the map he had stored in his mind while he had been led to the room for his meeting with Chen and Jiang, he entered the lift and jabbed the button that would take him there.

The lift doors opened and he sidled out, sticking to the walls. His shirt was now soaked in blood from his neck wound, but he kept going.

The floor seemed deserted. He poked his head around the corner of the lift landing and looked around.

No one there.

He crept towards the conference room and kicked it open, hoping to gain the advantage of surprise.

But it didn't quite work the way he had expected it to.

On the positive side, Iris was there with Chen. Jiang was missing but three PLA soldiers were in the room.

Patterson was so relieved to see Iris that he dropped his guard for just a moment.

It was enough.

Even though he recovered almost instantly and mowed down the three soldiers, diving out of their line of fire as he shot at them, they fired back at him. He had had the element of surprise in his favour but they had let loose a volley of shots. A bullet grazed his arm as he landed on the floor and rolled over to cushion his fall.

Chen sprang to his feet, but before he could do anything further, Patterson had aimed his assault rifle at the pharma CEO.

'Don't even think about it,' he warned Chen from the floor, where he lay sprawled on his back.

Iris rushed to help him stand, but he waved her away. It was a flesh wound. Nothing serious.

He got to his feet, keeping the gun trained on Chen all the time.

'We meet again, Mr Chen,' he smiled through the pain. This was something he had done before in the conflict zones he had been in, hit more than once by shrapnel or bullets, but carrying on somehow until the mission was complete. It was a soldier's job to bear pain and ignore wounds.

Chen glowered at him but said nothing. He knew when the chips were down.

'Are you okay, Iris?' Patterson addressed her without taking his eyes off Chen.

'Yes,' Iris sniffed. 'You … you're bleeding. We need to get those wounds dressed right away. You're losing a lot of blood.'

'Well, this is a medical facility,' Patterson chuckled. 'We shouldn't have a problem fixing me up.'

He looked at Chen. 'Interesting. You show no signs of fear. If I am truly infected with your bioweapon, then you should have been afraid of contagion. Were you bluffing?' He indicated the gun in his hand. 'This is not a good time to lie.'

'It is true,' Chen affirmed. 'You *were* infected through your food. But there is no asymptomatic spread of infection with this organism. It can only be transferred across hosts once the incubation period is over and the symptoms materialise. We've tested this thoroughly. Dr Tsai and I have nothing to fear from you for another day or two. After that, yes, you will be a spreader.'

'Great. That makes it easier then.'

'Where can we get Dr Patterson first aid?' Iris' voice was calm and steady now that she had got over her shock at seeing a blood-soaked Patterson burst into the room. She fixed Patterson with a steady gaze. 'You're going to get those wounds attended first.'

Her tone brooked no argument.

'There's a nursing station one floor down,' Chen replied.

'Let's go then.' Patterson's eyes bored into Chen as he spoke. 'And after that you will tell me exactly what is going on here.'

Ürümqui
Xinjiang Uyghur Autonomous Region
China

Zhu Jingting glared at Wu Xingxu, who had just burst into the room, proclaiming an emergency.

'What is it that cannot wait?' he demanded of Wu.

'The American prisoner has escaped, Zhu zǒng,' Wu bowed. 'He has taken Chen zǒng prisoner. I personally watched the feed from the CCTVs.'

'What is that miserable Jiang doing? Is the PLA going to sit around watching?'

'*Shàojiàng* Jiang is taking remedial action,' Wu informed him.

'Remedial action, my foot.' Zhu sat for a moment in contemplation. Then he rose.

'The plane,' he instructed Wu. 'It is waiting for me. Tell them the flight plan has changed. They will take me to Hotan. Do this immediately. I will have to look into this personally. I have a bunch of imbeciles in Hotan who cannot handle things the moment my back is turned.'

'But Zhu zǒng, your meeting with the general secretary? And the Politburo meeting tomorrow morning?' Wu couldn't comprehend anyone skipping a meeting with the supreme figure in the CCP or a Politburo meeting. Yet his boss seemed to intend doing just that.

'Not a problem,' Zhu waved a careless hand. 'I will reach Hotan before midnight. It will not take long to bring things under control. There is enough time for me to take care of matters there and then fly to Beijing in time for the meetings tomorrow morning.

He set his jaw. 'I will personally see that this American is dealt with appropriately.'

The GTF Base
Hounslow
London, UK

A broad smile creased Duncan's face as he read the email.

He was sitting with the others in the conference room where they were trying to while away the time until they launched their rescue plan for Imran.

Vijay, Radha and Colin were attempting to complete their study of Thomas Manning's documents, browsing the Royal Asiatic Society's Digital Library where digital copies were available. Not that they particularly felt like reading Manning's papers at a time like this, but if they found something that looked interesting or worth studying further, they could always go back tomorrow to the Reading Room at the Society and check it out.

Shukla was browsing a whole lot of resources that he had come across at the British Library. He had found links to digital editions of commentaries on different parts of the Mahabharata and was scouring the collections to see if he could dig up anything more on Khandavaprastha. So far, however, he had not found anything he had not known before.

Duncan had an operation to run and he busied himself with emails and messages, leaving the room occasionally whenever he had to make a call.

Now he had received the email he had been waiting for.

'I've got some braw news fur yer all,' he announced, breaking into his Scottish brogue in his excitement.

'I was wondering why you were grinning,' Colin remarked. 'But I thought it rude to ask.'

'Aye, this is pure barry,' Duncan agreed.

'I know that one,' Colin raised his hand. 'Pure barry. I've heard it before.'

Duncan nodded. 'So I'm sorry I didn't share this with you all before, but I wasn't sure if it would lead to anything. But it looks like my gamble paid off. Big time.' He looked around at them. Satisfied that he now had everyone's attention, he continued. 'You remember the Chinese gentleman Julie had told us about when we visited Oxford?'

Everyone nodded. Radha and Shukla had heard about the Chinese researcher who had wanted access to Humboldt's letter to Goethe when Vijay had briefed them at the hotel earlier in the day.

'Julie sent me his name the morning after our visit to Oxford,' Duncan continued. 'That was three days ago. His name is Li Ping. And he's a professor of history at Craggett University, Boston.'

'An American citizen?' Colin asked.

'Aye. He's American all right. I put my team on the job and they dug around to find out more about him. A lot of his research work is funded by China, though I couldn't find anything suspicious about his work. Everything seemed to be above board.' Duncan shrugged. 'Even the visit to Oxford and his request to examine the Humboldt letter could have been sheer coincidence.'

'So, you put him under surveillance?' Radha guessed.

'Aye, lassie. That's what I did. Initially, nothing turned up. This guy had a routine. Quite boring. Then yesterday, he flew to Poland. Krakow.'

'Krakow?' Vijay frowned. 'Why does that sound familiar? I remember coming across Krakow somewhere when I was reading about Humboldt.'

'You must have,' Duncan told him. 'The Jagiellonian Library at the Jagiellonian University in Krakow holds the second largest collection of Humboldt's papers and letters.'

Vijay clicked his fingers. 'That's right! Humboldt had bequeathed some of his papers to this library and the collection also benefited from the addition of Eduard Buschmann's Humboldt collection.'

Colin groaned. 'New guys I've never heard of keep popping up in this damn case. Who was this Edward guy now?'

'Eduard Buschmann,' Vijay explained, 'assisted both Wilhelm von Humboldt—Alexander's brother—as well as Humboldt himself, especially with Humboldt's multi-volume publication of *Cosmos*.'

'Ah, that clears up a lot. Wilhelm, *Cosmos*, I get it. Go on, Duncan.' Colin shook his head.

Duncan grinned at Colin's mock frustration. 'Anyway, the point is this. Li Ping visited the Jagiellonian Library. The moment I heard that, I knew that the first visit to Oxford was no coincidence. There *was* something happening here. Why was he checking out Humboldt's correspondence and papers in different places? Then I recalled what Radha told us—that it wasn't the Order who kidnapped Wilson. So I wrote to the librarian at the Jagiellonian Library since we don't have an operation in Poland yet.'

Vijay's eyes were shining now. His gloom at Imran's capture had temporarily dissipated. 'And the librarian told you what he had gone there for?'

'Aye, laddie. You'll never guess what he was looking at there.'

The GTF Base
Hounslow
London, UK

'This is the letter for which Li Ping had requested assistance in translation. And it is also the one for which Wilson had requested a translation.' Duncan had opened the Alexander von Humboldt Portal on the website of the Staatsbibliothek in Berlin—the Berlin State Library—which had links to the digital copies of the Humboldt collection at the Jagiellonian Library in Krakow.

He had briefed the group on what the librarian from Krakow had told him. Li Ping had used his background and connections at Craggett University to register with the Jagiellonian Library and, once there, had asked to study the extensive collection of Humboldt's papers and letters.

Apparently Li Ping had soon found what he was looking for and had then approached the library with a request to translate the letter which was in French.

Radha's face fell as she viewed the screen. 'That's practically illegible,' she complained. '*And* it is in French. Do you have someone on your team who knows French?'

'I can do better,' Duncan chuckled. 'I asked the librarian for a translation.'

'Genius!' Colin's tone was sincere, as he gave Duncan an approving look.

'What does the letter say?' Vijay asked impatiently.

'It is a letter from Alexander von Humboldt to his brother Wilhelm von Humboldt. Written in August 1818. Like Julie at Oxford, they couldn't give us a word-by-word translation, since many of the words were illegible, as Radha pointed out. But the gist is good enough for our purpose.'

Duncan pulled his laptop back towards him and opened the email he had received from Krakow.

'So,' he began, 'Alexander is telling Wilhelm about his proposed visit to London in September 1818. Apparently, Wilhelm was in London at that time.'

Vijay nodded, remembering what he had read up on Humboldt during his flight to London. 'Yes, Wilhelm had been posted to England in 1817 as the Prussian minister to Britain. When Humboldt visited London for the second time in 1817 to seek approval from the East India Company to visit India, he had stayed with Wilhelm at his house in Portland Place. I remember reading in Wilson's book about Wilhelm complaining that, even though Alexander was staying with him, he never got to meet his brother unless it was in the company of others. They were never able to spend time by themselves, just the two of them. But he was delighted to welcome him to his house and happy to see him. And then Humboldt returned in 1818 for his third attempt to persuade the East India Company to allow him to visit India. There was a fourth, final, attempt he made in 1827, but that was also futile.'

'I've never figured out how you manage to remember stuff like this,' Colin grumbled good-naturedly. He was, in fact, very proud of his friend's eidetic memory; an ability that had proven immensely useful when they had partnered in business.

'Ah, so it all makes sense now,' Duncan said. 'That puts this letter in context. I think I can now piece things together much better.' He turned back to the screen. 'So in this letter, Alexander apologises to his brother for not spending enough time with him on his last visit and promises to take out time on this trip. He also mentions that he plans to appeal a third time to the East India Company and requests Wilhelm's help, using his diplomatic status, to connect him to people.'

Duncan raised an eyebrow. 'He even asks Wilhelm to help him obtain a private audience with the Prince Regent.' He looked at Vijay. 'Did he succeed?'

'He did. Wilhelm managed to help with the private audience and the Prince Regent actually assured Alexander that he could rely on his complete support for his proposed expedition to India. I guess Wilhelm did a good job of acceding to Humboldt's request to connect him to people, since he also met George Canning, who was the president of the Board of Control and the official from the British government who supervised the activities of the East India Company. Canning also promised to help. In fact, Humboldt was so confident that any further hurdles would be removed that he sought and obtained financing from Friedrich Wilhelm III, the Prussian king, for his India expedition.'

'So Humboldt was hell bent on visiting India,' Radha remarked thoughtfully. 'There must have been something in India that he desperately wanted to study.'

'Aye,' Duncan replied, 'and that's the beauty of this letter. Alexander hints at something here. A couple of things, actually. He tells Wilhelm that he met one Thomas Manning, recently returned from India, on his trip to London in 1817. And he talks about how Manning, with the help of Frederic Fischer and one John Brereton Birch, has hidden something in Calcutta, something which is of interest to him.' He looked pointedly at Radha. 'It seems that is the something that Humboldt wanted to see.'

Duncan turned back to the screen. 'There's more. Alexander says he will tell Wilhelm all when they meet and presses him to help with his appointments.' He raised his eyebrow again.

'And here's something really interesting. He asks Wilhelm if he wouldn't be proud if his brother, Alexander, was the discoverer of a new form of life. One that could shower the world with unimaginable bounties. And he ends the letter by saying that his earlier attempts to visit India were all frustrated by Warren Hastings—the former governor general of Bengal, whom he had apparently met on his first attempt in 1814—and, if Wilhelm can help with meeting the Prince Regent and other key officials in the British government, then he is certain he will be successful this time.'

There was silence when he had finished.

'I can't believe,' Radha said finally, 'that this letter has been overlooked and ignored for so long. It is in the public domain! In a library for God's sake! Surely someone would have read the letter and wondered what it was all about? How come no one has ever tried to find out what Humboldt really wanted from India? I mean, there is clearly a connection here with the Owen manuscript!' She looked at Vijay. 'Unless I'm mistaken, wasn't Frederic Fischer the guy who translated the Owen manuscript?'

Duncan shrugged. 'Well, I guess if you read the letter by itself, it isn't really remarkable. I mean, he wanted to discover a new form of life. How extraordinary is that for a scientist who is a naturalist? He knows that something is hidden in India by Manning and Fischer. He doesn't say what, so again, why should anyone consider it exceptional? And who would take his talk of a new form of life seriously, especially in our times?'

'You're right,' Vijay agreed. '*We* can see the dots that need to be connected because we know about the Owen manuscript. We've seen the letter from Humboldt to Goethe where he talks about the Owen manuscript, so we know he was interested in that document. And *that* letter was lost for years until the Bodleian Library acquired it. And we know that Fischer translated the Owen manuscript, so we can see *that* connection as well. But someone who didn't know about or have access to any of these—never mind all of them like we have had—would never be able to see the complete picture. And even we don't really know what the complete picture is. What did Thomas Manning hide, for example? What new form of life did Humboldt want to discover? What are the "bounties" he talks about?'

'What about the Order?' Radha shot back. 'They knew about the Owen manuscript. They knew about Manning's letter to Humboldt. I'm sure they would also have known about this letter in Krakow. And what about this Chinese guy—Li Ping? How did *he* know about this letter? He seemed to know exactly what he was looking for!'

'I don't know about Li Ping,' Vijay shrugged. 'But maybe since the Order didn't know about the letter Humboldt wrote to Goethe in 1830, which is in Oxford—you mentioned that they weren't aware of this letter—they didn't connect the dots?'

'Do you think,' Colin said slowly, 'that the "unimaginable bounties" have something to do with the regeneration of the monkey's leg? Remember what Humboldt said in his letter to Goethe? He thought there was a link that existed between the Owen manuscript and the regeneration of a monkey's leg in South America. And he also said that he wanted to visit India to study this.'

'Yes, and finally his theory was validated by some Indian fakir he met, according to that letter,' Duncan completed the train of thought that Colin had embarked on.

'Logical, but fantastic,' Radha mused. 'I mean the pieces do seem to fit. But does it really make any sense? Regeneration of a monkey's limb? And, remember, the Owen manuscript is not complete. So how would Humboldt be able to see a connection between the manuscript and the monkey, even if one believes for a moment that the regeneration actually happened? From what you told me, there is nothing in the Owen manuscript about regeneration; nothing that could point to such a link.'

'Damn!' Vijay pounded on the desk with his fist. 'This is so tantalising. There's something here, we can see it. But we're just unable to connect the dots!

Hotan
Xinjiang Province, China

Patterson opened the door to the conference room and peered outside.

Strangely, it was quiet.

No PLA hordes amassing in the corridor, readying to launch an assault or even to besiege the American who had taken Chen hostage.

Surely Jiang would have learnt by now about Patterson's escape? The CCTVs in the corridor outside his cell would have captured his exit from his room without the customary escort of PLA soldiers.

So why was there no response?

Patterson held the door open and gestured to Chen to lead the way to the nursing station. Iris followed and he brought up the rear.

They made their way to the floor below without being accosted by anyone.

At every step, Patterson had expected to be waylaid by Jiang's men, but he guessed it was taking time to respond to an unanticipated situation which had no drill pre-planned. No one here would ever expect an attack from *inside* the facility. They would be geared to handle and repulse an external attack—even though that had remote chances of happening—but Patterson's internal attack would have left them nonplussed.

'It's all good', Patterson told himself. It gave him and Iris just those few minutes extra to stay ahead of the game.

The lone nurse at the nursing station was co-opted to administer first aid to Patterson once she got over her shock when Chen had been shepherded into the station by Patterson, followed by Iris.

Patterson gave Chen a grim look once his flesh wounds had been taken care of—his neck had required stitches—and the blood staunched. The GTF director had been thinking while the nurse attended to him. Even if the PLA was slow to respond to this unprecedented situation, sooner or later they would catch up with him. And while he needed to understand what was going on in this facility, the nursing station was no place to chew the fat.

No, he needed someplace more secure and they had to get there fast. Time was running out.

He eyed the CCTV in the nursing station.

Damn!

'Right,' Patterson addressed Chen. He had decided on a course of action. 'There has to be a room in this facility that does not have a CCTV. Take us there.'

Chen stared back defiantly. He knew that it was only a matter of time before the PLA rescued him. The more he delayed, the easier it would be.

Patterson sighed. 'Don't make me shoot you.'

'You wouldn't.'

'Try me.'

Chen contemplated Patterson for a few more moments, then decided that the American meant it.

'Fine,' he glared at his captor. 'But you know you are a dead man.'

Patterson shrugged. 'Either way, I am. Nothing to lose. Let's get moving.'

Chen led the way back to the lift. But to Patterson's surprise, he pressed the button to the floor above, the one with the conference room which they had just left.

'Hey, why are we going back there?' he demanded.

'I'm taking you to the room you asked for. One without cameras.' Chen compressed his lips and said nothing more.

The doors opened.

They stepped out of the lift.

And right into a group of four PLA soldiers who were standing there, waiting for the lift.

The GTF Base
Hounslow, UK

'Damn! I've been so stupid!' Vijay burst out. 'How could I have not seen it? It was right under our noses!'

After Duncan's revelations, they had all gone back to their respective reviews of material on their laptops. Silence had reigned until Vijay's sudden outburst now.

Colin frowned and looked around the room. 'Speaking in riddles again, buddy? What's right under our noses? I can't see anything.'

'Neither can I,' Radha laughed at Colin's bemused expression. 'What's bitten you now, Vijay?'

Vijay looked at them both, then at Shukla and Duncan. 'I think I know what Thomas Manning hid in Calcutta along with Fischer and the other guy mentioned in Humboldt's letter to his brother.'

Radha held his gaze, her face serious. 'Go ahead. Tell us.'

'Let's start with what we know, and follow the clues,' Vijay began. 'Humboldt wrote a letter to Goethe many years prior to his 1830 letter, telling him a story about a monkey whose leg regenerated in South America in 1800. We don't have the date of that letter, but we do know he wrote it because he refers to it in his letter of 1830.' He spread his hands and made a face indicating his disbelief. 'So the story of the monkey is unbelievable, but Humboldt told Goethe about it. Then, in 1807, the Owen manuscript is discovered. It contains mantras, medical recipes, and the incomplete copy of a text written by Susruta, who says in the portion available to us that he will reveal a secret known only to the Nagas. He talks about what he calls the Khandavaprastha Curse and mentions the Khandavaprastha *dahan*—the burning down of the forest.'

He looked around enquiringly. There were nods, indicating that the others were with him so far.

'Fine, so far,' he continued. 'But the portion of the text that actually deals with this curse is missing. According to Fischer, who translated the Owen manuscript, the missing portions were either damaged while retrieving the manuscript or left behind in the chamber where the manuscript was found. And, we know that Humboldt made four attempts to visit India—in 1814, 1817, 1818 and 1827. He was unsuccessful each time. According to Wilson, he said he wanted to visit the Himalayas. Please note clue number one.'

Vijay held up his index finger, before resuming. 'And, finally, he says in his 1830 letter to Goethe that his theory was validated by an Indian fakir who he met in Astrakan, in 1829. Clue number two.' He held up two fingers.

'So the question is, or rather the questions are, first, what was Humboldt's theory that was validated by the fakir? And second, why did he want to visit India?' He paused to collect his thoughts.

The others waited. They knew Vijay had a knack for logical and analytical thinking. This was his way of showing them how the pattern he saw emerged from the facts that they were aware of so far.

After a few moments, he continued. 'Let's look at the other facts, which have only recently come to light, at least for us. We now know that Humboldt met Manning in 1817; he tells his brother Wilhelm as much. And he also informs Wilhelm that Manning, along with Fischer and another guy, hid something in Calcutta.'

'John Brereton Birch,' Duncan offered helpfully.

'Yes, Birch,' Vijay agreed. 'That's clue number three. And Humboldt pointedly tells Wilhelm that he has an interest in what was hidden by these three men in 1817. Finally, he talks about a new life form, which is, once more, speculation, since he never did discover a new life form which had a connection with India. I'm sure I'd have remembered if it was mentioned in Wilson's book or in any of the other resources I researched.'

'Manning didn't seem to have mentioned anything about Birch or Fischer or a new life form in his papers,' Radha said. 'At least not in the papers that I was studying.'

'Me neither,' Colin agreed. 'The only interesting things that I came across in his papers were the riddles. And even those didn't have answers to them, so I couldn't even check if I had guessed correctly.'

Vijay shook his head. 'That's just the point,' he exclaimed. 'We've been looking for the wrong thing! We were searching for what Manning *said* or *wrote*. But what we need to search for is what he *didn't* say or write!'

The GTF Base
Hounslow, UK

Colin frowned. 'What do you mean? How do we search for something that isn't there?'

Vijay beamed. 'Follow the clues, buddy. Here we go. Clue number four: Thomas Manning was the first Englishman to visit Lhasa and meet the Dalai Lama. Remember what Radha told us earlier today?'

'The Himalayas!' Colin and Radha burst out together. They were both familiar with the leaps of logic that Vijay made whenever he analysed a problem or puzzle, and they immediately knew where he was going when he mentioned Lhasa.

'Exactly.' A look of satisfaction swept over Vijay's face. 'Connects with clue number one—Humboldt wanted to visit the Himalayas. Manning did. Okay, here's clue number five: Fischer translated the Owen manuscript.'

He paused.

Silence greeted him. The others were still wondering how the dots connected. They couldn't see the link that Vijay saw.

'Okay, fine, maybe I haven't explained it properly,' Vijay grumbled. 'Let me summarise what I'm thinking. Suppose there was something in the Himalayas that Humboldt knew about? And that was why he wanted to go to India? *He* couldn't, but unknown to him, Manning went to India and from there to Tibet. Remember, Manning had travelled to unexplored parts of Tibet, which upset the Chinese Emperor, and he had to leave in a hurry. Was Manning searching for something? Now, what if Manning did find something in Tibet? And he,

Fischer and Birch hid that something in Calcutta? And here's a huge leap I am making now. I know this sounds crazy, but what if Fischer *deliberately* did not publish the translation of the missing portion of the Owen manuscript? What if that was also hidden somewhere? And what if Manning told Humboldt all this when the two men met in 1817? That could have been the basis for Humboldt's theory which was verified by a fakir from India in 1829. A fakir who would have known about the Khandavaprastha dahan.'

Again, there was stunned silence.

Then Radha spoke, shaking her head. 'Too many assumptions, Vijay. How would Humboldt have known about something in the Himalayas? And how does Tibet enter the picture? Humboldt wanted to go to India, not Tibet.'

'Aye, laddie,' Duncan agreed. 'Fischer not publishing part of the manuscript is surely a leap of pure speculation. Why would he not publish it?'

'And what could Humboldt's theory have been?' Colin wondered. 'Too many gaps in your theory, Vijay. Like all good conspiracy theories, it has too many holes.'

Vijay regarded them calmly. 'I have answers to all your doubts. I've been thinking about this all morning.' He shrugged. 'Well, actually, I have answers to most of your doubts, maybe not all.'

He began ticking off the points on his fingers. 'First, how would Humboldt have known about something in the Himalayas? I have no idea. It is an assumption based on my other deductions. And I don't think Humboldt ever thought about going to Tibet. For him, it was always about going to India because he wanted to climb the Himalayas. Second, how does Tibet enter the picture? Well, I'd been doing some research of my own after I finished going through my lot of

Manning's papers.' He gave a sheepish grin. 'Actually, I should have mentioned that earlier. Clue number six. Humboldt tells Wilhelm in his letter of 1817 that Warren Hastings was responsible for the earlier rejections of Humboldt's application to visit India and that he is confident that he will be successful in 1818. Well, Warren Hastings died in August 1818—the month in which Humboldt sent Wilhelm the letter—and Humboldt visited London in September. So his confidence could have stemmed from the fact that Hastings was no longer around to frustrate his efforts to visit India. That is why he boldly went ahead and secured funding for his India expedition from the Prussian king.'

'But what does that have to do with Tibet?' Colin asked. 'I'm still not clear.'

'And despite the death of Hastings, Humboldt still wasn't able to get permission to visit India,' Radha added. 'It still doesn't add up, Vijay.'

'It does,' Vijay insisted. 'Look, even after Hastings died, if the East India Company didn't allow Humboldt to visit India, doesn't it mean they had something to hide? Something connected with the Himalayas? I first got scent of this thanks to Wilson. In his book, he explicitly states his opinion that the East India Company did not deny Humboldt the opportunity to visit India because of his anti-colonial writings. True, Humboldt had written that colonialism in South America and India was …' he screwed up his face, trying to remember, '… an unequal struggle. Yes, those were his words. And he said that the South Americans and the Hindus were subject to a civil and military despotism. But Wilson believes that the true reason Humboldt was denied entry into India was the Owen manuscript.'

'Bit of a stretch, isn't it, basing a conclusion on Wilson's opinion?' Radha sounded sceptical. 'Wouldn't other historians have come to this conclusion in the last two hundred years, if this was true?'

'Perhaps. But what if he *was* right? What if Hastings had discovered something that the Owen manuscript talked about? And the East India Company decided that they didn't want Humboldt to learn about whatever it was?'

'Wait a minute, *beta*,' Shukla interjected. 'I'm no historian, but if I remember correctly, Warren Hastings left India before the Owen manuscript was discovered in 1807. He was governor general in the eighteenth century, not the nineteenth century, as I recall.'

'Yes, uncle, that's true,' Vijay assented. 'But I'm not saying that Hastings knew about the Owen manuscript or what was in it. I think that Hastings somehow knew about something in the Himalayas—in Tibet, specifically—and that later on, when the Owen manuscript was discovered, it reinforced his discovery, so the East India Company wanted to keep it under wraps. Warren Hastings would have heard about the Owen manuscript in 1807. He would have made the connection with his own discovery. And he would have warned the East India Company against Humboldt's visit to India.'

'You know something about Warren Hastings that we don't know,' Duncan observed. 'That's why you're so confident.'

'Yes,' Vijay smiled. 'I haven't got round to that part yet. It concerns Tibet. Warren Hastings sent a mission to Tibet in 1774. It was led by George Bogle, who wasn't able to visit Lhasa, but made good friends with the Teshu Lama in Teshu Lumbo. Bogle returned to India in 1775 and Hastings actually wanted to send him back to Tibet, but got caught in a vicious power struggle with the new councillors appointed by the East India Company in 1774. In 1779, Hastings appointed

Bogle as envoy to Tibet for a second time, but the Teshu Lama died in 1780 and Bogle in 1781.'

He leaned forward. 'Here's the interesting part. Hastings never gave up. In 1783, he sent Captain Turner to Tibet—a mission that was apparently a failure. But this is where Tibet comes into the picture. Why was Hastings so keen to send people to Tibet? This is in stark comparison to his successors. None of them were interested in missions or envoys to Tibet. So why was Hastings the only one? Did he know something that, maybe, his successors didn't really believe in? Or thought it was futile searching for?'

Vijay took a deep breath. 'And finally,' he looked at Duncan, 'your point. Why would Fischer hide the missing portion of the manuscript?'

Duncan nodded. 'Aye, I don't get that part.'

'Well,' Vijay replied, 'do you remember what Humboldt said in his letter to Goethe in 1830? That he is both excited and worried for his discovery? He says that it could lead to a new and greater future for the human race but could equally become its doom.'

Duncan and Colin nodded. They remembered.

'Well, what if Fischer translated the manuscript and then decided that whatever he found there was more likely to be the doom of humanity than its salvation? What if he felt that it was something that should be hidden away? Remember, Humboldt only had a theory. He didn't actually know what was in the Owen manuscript. And he was a scientist. So he may have been excited at the prospect of investigating something new and extraordinary—a new form of life, according to him. Even today, scientists are dabbling in areas that could lead to either amazing inventions in the future or risks for humanity. Couldn't that have held true for Humboldt?'

'But what could have been so bleak in the Owen manuscript that Fischer might have decided that it needed to be hidden away?' Radha wanted to know.

Vijay's face grew dark. 'What if it had *already* been hidden away for thousands of years? What if there really was a Khandavaprastha curse?'

June 1814
London
UK

The two men sat across from each other, each taking in the other. Both were renowned in their own right.

One, a statesman, eighty-two years old, with a rollercoaster of a life which had finally given him the recognition he sought if not the title he wanted.

The other, a man almost half his age at forty-five years, acclaimed as possibly the foremost scientist of his time, with people like Simón Bolívar and Thomas Jefferson counted among his friends and admirers.

Warren Hastings.

And Alexander von Humboldt.

A liveried butler silently sidled up and served them tea in dainty china cups.

The two men had met a few days earlier during the Allied celebration of victory over Napoleon at the Battle of Leipzig in October 1813 and the fall of Paris in March of this year. As part of the celebrations, Friedrich Wilhelm III, the Prussian king, and Tsar Alexander I, the Emperor of Russia, had descended on London with their respective trains.

Hastings had been part of the train of both sovereigns, while Humboldt had accompanied Friedrich Wilhelm to London as part of his retinue, and both men had been in attendance at the Guildhall of London, the Thanksgiving at St Paul's and the Prince Regent's fête at Carlton House.

'The most deserving, and one of the worst-used men in the Empire.' The Prince Regent had, with these words, presented Warren Hastings to the Prussian and Russian sovereigns.

Hastings and Humboldt had met during the celebrations, and casual conversations had led to this private meeting.

Both men had their own agendas.

For Humboldt, it was the prospect of getting a passport to visit India—the trip he had been planning for the last eleven years, ever since his epiphany in Mexico. This was one of the reasons he had accompanied Friedrich Wilhelm to London. His plan, which was already in motion, was to meet as many politicians, British peers, scientists and influencers as possible during the two weeks he was in London, in an attempt to secure the approval of the East India Company to visit India.

He had planned it carefully. As part of the celebrations, Alexander and Friedrich Wilhelm had had academic honours bestowed upon them by the University of Oxford. Humboldt had taken advantage of this leg of the itinerary to visit the Bodleian Library and study the original copy of the Owen manuscript there, which had been purchased by Oxford in 1813 from Colonel Lawrence Owen. He had already acquired a copy of Fischer's translations of the manuscript, which the Sanskrit scholar had completed three years earlier.

While he had not expected much from his study of the original manuscript—especially since the script and the language were not one of the many languages he was fluent in—he was disappointed that he could not make headway in his attempts to connect the dots.

This was where Hastings entered the picture. Humboldt had read about the former governor general of Bengal, who had survived an impeachment motion brought against him by Edmund Burke—a nearly eight-year trial that eventually led to his acquittal—and his subsequent rehabilitation, which had been crowned in 1813 when Hastings had been summoned to London to give evidence during the debate on the renewal of the East India Company's charter. And the gist of his testimony had been to keep "interlopers" out of India and discourage missionaries amongst Indians, whom he felt were attached to their ancestral traditions. At this session in both the House of Commons and the House of Lords, he had been cheered on his appearance and, when his testimony concluded, the members of the house had stood and bared their heads as a mark of respect.

Such veneration, Humboldt had felt, was bound to add weight to his own attempts to secure his passport to India.

Hastings, on his part, had a more defensive motive for meeting Humboldt. He had tried, and failed, to unearth the secret in Tibet that George Bogle had first reported. If Hastings had one regret, it was this—that circumstances had forced him to wait four long years before he was able to appoint Bogle as an envoy to Tibet for a second time. The fierce tussle between Hastings and the trio of Francis, Clavering and Monson had resulted in this delay, since his three antagonists had stripped Bogle of every high office. That unfortunate and unavoidable deferment of his plans, and Bogle's untimely death at a young age, had robbed Hastings of the opportunity to investigate and learn more.

While leaving India, Hastings had demurred from sharing any details about the discovery with his successor. He had been expecting power and dignity on his return to England and was looking forward to a coronet, a red riband, a seat at the Council Board and an office at Whitehall. He had even harboured hopes of a peerage for his efforts in India. He did not want to ruin his chances of securing any of these by propagating a tale that, for all he knew, might turn out to be a myth with no substance or relevance.

But that did not mean that he was unafraid that someone—the Dutch or the French or even the Portuguese, all of whom harboured designs on India—might stumble upon the same secret and use it to further their ends.

And, while leading a more leisurely retired life at Daylesford, Hastings had not been oblivious to the discovery of the Owen manuscript. He had followed the news with great interest and had divined a connection between the contents of the manuscript and Bogle's discovery in Tibet.

In Oxford, Humboldt's visit to the Bodleian Library had not gone unnoticed by Hastings. A distant fear had begun to gnaw at him. Was the German scientist onto the same scent?

He had to find out.

June 1814

London

UK

'I hear that you have been meeting people and discussing plans for visiting India,' Hastings offered casually, taking a sip of his tea, after spending some time politely listening to Humboldt talk non-stop for a while about his travels in the Spanish colonies of South America.

'Indeed,' Humboldt confirmed, delighted that the very subject he wanted to broach had been brought up by his host. 'Indeed. It is my wish to visit and study the Himalayas. I told you of my interest in mountains and some part of my adventures in South America climbing the Andes, in addition to some of the volcanoes in that region.'

Hastings felt a twinge of suspicion at these words.

'The Himalayas are not the Andes, Baron von Humboldt,' he smiled. 'They will be a considerable challenge, though I see that you are extremely fit for your age. What do you hope to find there?'

Humboldt smiled back. 'I studied geology when I was in Freiberg in the last decade of the last century. Geology has always been a passion for me.' He leaned forward and placed his cup on the table between the two men, as if preparing to share a great secret with his host.

'When I climbed Chimborazo,' he continued, 'I was struck by the resemblance which we trace in climates the most distant from each other. In the Andes, for example, I found a moss growing that reminded me of a species from the forests of northern Germany, even though the two are separated by thousands of miles of land and ocean. Near Caracas, I found in the mountains, alpine trees rather like rhododendrons which reminded me of those from the Swiss Alps. In Mexico, I found pines, cypresses and oaks similar to those in Canada.' He paused for a quick breath, in his usual style of speaking fast and saying a lot at top speed, before resuming.

'Everything is connected—that is my belief. There is a web of life. Nature is a living whole. It does not recognise political or geographical boundaries. Nature is one. And I wish to extend my knowledge and research to the one range of mountains that I have never been able to study at close quarters.'

Hastings was not satisfied. While this explanation seemed to be justified, his instinct told him there was more. Humboldt's interest in the Owen manuscript, for example. Where did that fit in? Why had he made that special visit to study the manuscript? How did Humboldt even learn about it in the first place? It had nothing to do with his field of research or expertise.

Hastings decided to be direct. 'I hear that you have an interest in the Owen manuscript.'

He studied Humboldt's face, watching his expression.

To his satisfaction, Humboldt hesitated.

'Oh, yes, the Owen manuscript,' Humboldt paused for a moment, debating the best course of action. He decided to be honest without disclosing the details. After all, he only had a hunch to go on. There was no data available to support his theory, if one could call it that. And Humboldt was not accustomed to not being direct. 'It is part of the same concept of the web of life. I came across similar texts among the Incas and the Aztecs and was wondering if there was a connection, not just in nature, but also among the peoples of the world— the ancient civilisations—that we have forgotten about, or which are lost in the mists of time. And I found the Owen manuscript intriguing. Since I was at Oxford, I thought I would take the opportunity to study it first-hand.'

Hastings was not convinced. The response sounded adequate, but that moment's hesitation had raised doubts in his mind.

'And what did you find?' he enquired.

'Unfortunately, the text is not complete,' Humboldt answered honestly again. 'So it is very difficult to draw any conclusions.'

Hastings nodded. But in his mind, he had reached a conclusion of his own.

The man seated before him could reveal what Hastings had sought to keep secret. Even if the man was well intentioned, who knew what would happen if he visited Tibet and discovered what Hastings had tried and failed to unearth?

No, there was only one course of action that Hastings could see.

Humboldt must not be allowed to enter India.

PRESENT DAY

DAY SIX

October 26
The GTF Base
Hounslow
London, UK

Shukla shook his head. 'The problem is that there seems to be nothing called the Khandavaprastha curse, *beta*. I know I said earlier today that we should try and find out what the curse is as that might give us some clues, but I've gone through a whole lot of resources after that, both in the library and online, and have found no mention of such a thing.'

Vijay opened his mouth to speak, but Shukla held up his hand and Vijay closed his mouth. Clearly, Shukla had more to say; he wasn't done yet.

'Don't get completely disheartened,' Shukla continued. 'There are some interesting, shall we say, oddities, in the story, when one compares different versions and translations and commentaries, with my own translation of the shlokas.'

He adjusted his spectacles and looked at his notebook.

'So you know the story,' he peered at them over his glasses. 'I'm not going to repeat it.'

'Aye,' Duncan concurred and Colin gave a thumbs up sign. Vijay and Radha nodded their agreement.

'So let's look at these anomalies.' Shukla turned back to his notes. 'The first one is in these two shlokas:

पुरा देवनियोगेन यत् त्वया भस्मसात् कृतम् ।
आलयं देवशत्रूणां सुघोरं खाण्डवं वनम् ॥
तत्र सर्वाणि सत्त्वानि निवसन्ति विभावसो ।
तेषां त्वं मेदसा तृप्तः प्रकृतिस्थो भविष्यसि ॥

In these shlokas, Brahma is addressing Agni, the fire Deva, who has approached him with his problem of losing lustre after the twelve-year sacrifice of Shvetaki, which I told you about earlier. Brahma says to Agni: in ancient times, the scary forest of Khandavaprastha where the enemies of the Devas lived was reduced to ashes by you. There reside many living beings in that forest. Satiated by their fat, you will become normal.'

Shukla looked at the others. 'A couple of things struck me here. Mind you, when I read these shlokas earlier, they really didn't seem extraordinary. But in the context of the case we're discussing—a secret, a curse and a mystery—what I'm sharing with you really jumped out at me.'

He took off his glasses and dangled them in one hand. 'First, I never really focused on the fact that Khandavaprastha was destroyed not once, but twice, by fire. This is quite clearly stated here. The first time was sometime in antiquity. The second time was the event that is narrated in the Mahabharata. And the second thing that presented itself was this reference to the enemies of the Devas. True, in the story that unfolds in the Mahabharata, there are Danavas, Rakshasas, Nagas, Pisachas who reside in the forest, in addition to all the animals that lived there, so you could argue that these were the enemies of the Devas. But the way I read these lines, they seem to refer to enemies of the Devas living in ancient times, when the first conflagration occurred, and the forest was reduced to ashes. Because only after referring to the enemies of the Devas and the first fire does Brahma talk about the present inhabitants of the forest.'

He turned back to his notebook and slipped on his glasses. 'Then there is this very strange shloka:

अब्रवीच्च तदा ब्रह्मा यथा त्वं धक्ष्यसेऽनल।
खाण्डवं दावमद्यैवं मिषतोऽस्य शचीपते:॥

It never sounded strange to me earlier, but in our current context, it does stand out. You see, the shloka basically is about Brahma telling Agni that, while Indra—the husband of Shachi—blinks or watches, Agni can burn down Khandavaprastha, because Agni now has the means to do so. But it is not the meaning of the verse that is strange. This verse uses a peculiar grammatical rule by which it is indicated that the act of burning down the forest would dishonour Indra. Strange. Quite strange.' The last words were muttered more to himself than the others.

'Next,' Shukla continued, without looking up, 'is this very curious allusion found in this shloka:

दीप्तोर्ध्वकेश: पिङ्गाक्ष: पिबन् प्राणभृतां वसाम् ।
तां स कृष्णार्जुनकृतां सुधां प्राप्य हुताशन: ॥
बभूव मुदितस्तृप्त: परां निर्वृतिमागत:।

This shloka describes how Agni—the fire—of yellow colour, with his hair burning, drinks the fat of the living beings that are being slaughtered by Krishna and Arjuna. Now, here's an interesting thing. M.N. Dutt and K.M. Ganguli both translate part of this shloka in the same way—Agni drank the "nectar-like stream of animal fat". M.N. Dutt omits the word "animal" but, essentially, they are saying the same thing. But now that I look at this shloka closely, I feel that the word *sudham* could be translated as "to the elixir", which would mean that this verse could be translated as follows: The yellow fire, with his hair burning, drinking the marrow of the living beings killed by Krishna and Arjuna and having obtained the elixir, became very happy and greatly satisfied.'

He looked up. 'Do you see? It is all a bit puzzling, isn't it? I really don't know what to make of it.'

The GTF Base
Hounslow
London, UK

'But there's nothing about a curse,' Colin concluded.

'The fact that there are peculiarities in the shlokas only ties into my theory.' Vijay could be as stubborn as a mule when he wanted.

'So you think there was something associated with Khandavaprastha, which Susruta called the Khandavaprastha curse. And Humboldt somehow got to know about it. And this is what is hidden in Calcutta.' Radha summed up Vijay's theory.

'That's right.' When she put it this way, Vijay realised that his entire theory was based on a whole lot of suppositions and speculation. And he still had no idea how Humboldt would have known what the missing part of the Owen manuscript contained.

What if he was wrong?

But he had made up his mind. Right or wrong, he had decided on a course to pursue. Nothing was going to make him change tracks.

Vijay looked at Radha questioningly. 'Do you have Van Klueck's number?'

'No, I don't. Why?'

'I want to pass a message to him.'

'Well,' Radha considered Vijay's request. 'I guess I could pass on a message through my network in the Order. I'm sure it would reach him.'

Then the realisation of what Vijay's words meant dawned on her. 'No! You can't be serious!'

'I am.' Vijay's face was set in stone. 'This is a better option than trying to rescue Imran by storming a base belonging to the Order when we don't even know if Imran is being held there. And we don't have to wait for tonight to do this. We can do this now. Pass this message on through your network and I guarantee you, Van Klueck will call me within the hour. *He* knows my number.'

'No,' Radha's voice was firm. 'You're not doing this. You aren't sure of your theory yourself and you're going to peddle it to Van Klueck? No way!'

The others finally understood what was happening.

'What makes you think that Van Klueck will jump at your offer to help them?' Duncan was curious. 'They probably know all this already.'

Vijay shook his head. 'I don't think so. If they really had all the information we have, they would be busy looking for whatever it is that Manning and Fischer hid in Calcutta—or, at the very least, for the missing part of the Owen manuscript.' He shrugged. 'And I think we hold a card that the Order doesn't have. We know about Li Ping. The Order doesn't. But you're right. Maybe I *am* gambling that even if they do have all the information, they haven't analysed it the way we have.'

He turned to Radha. 'It is our best chance of getting Imran back unharmed,' he told her. 'Trust me.'

'He's right,' Colin chimed in. 'The odds are better than us trying to rescue Imran through force. Let's use brain not brawn.'

'And what if Van Klueck sees through your ruse?' Radha demanded.

'I'll take that chance,' Vijay replied. 'It is worth it. Imran's life is at stake here.'

Radha wasn't about to give up so easily. 'Do you remember,' she said slowly, 'what happened the last time you cooperated with him? That was only four years ago. When you offered to help him in exchange for guaranteeing my safety.'

Vijay remembered only too well. He had gambled on saving Radha by helping Van Klueck find what the Order was looking for. In the bargain, he had almost lost his own life. And Radha too.

'I remember only too well,' he replied. 'But it is a chance we have to take. You want to get Imran back safely just as much as I do. There is no other way that will guarantee that. And you know that as well as I do.'

Radha took a deep breath. She was torn between wanting to protect Vijay and getting Imran back.

Finally, she made up her mind. 'Fine, I'll do it.'

She took out her phone and tapped out a message. 'I've made it tantalising enough for Van Klueck to give this top priority.'

'Thanks.' Vijay sat back, trying to quell the storm in his head, a peculiar mixture of apprehension, fear, excitement and determination.

'Now let's wait for his call.'

The Dorchester Hotel
London, UK

Van Klueck and Vijay sat facing each other on sofas in Van Klueck's suite.

As Vijay had predicted, after Radha had sent out her message, he had received a call asking for a meeting at The Dorchester.

Vijay had duly arrived at the hotel and made his way up to the suite where he had been cordially welcomed by Van Klueck.

There was no one else in the suite, just as Vijay had requested.

If nothing else, Van Klueck was a man of his word. It remained to be seen if that extended to what Vijay had in mind.

'Well,' Van Klueck began, after both men were seated. 'Glass of wine, Vijay?'

'No, thank you,' Vijay said. 'Let's get down to business, shall we?'

'Very well. You said you could help me locate the missing portion of the Owen manuscript. And something else besides. What would that be?'

'Before I tell you anything,' Vijay replied, 'I want your word. I want Imran released and handed over to us.'

Van Klueck regarded Vijay. 'Ah, your colleague.'

'My friend.' Vijay was firm. The GTF team had anticipated that Van Klueck would try and ferret out information about the organisation. Radha had told them that, while the Order was still unaware of the GTF's existence, they suspected that there was an organisation working against them.

Van Klueck smiled. 'Still pursuing your little charade, are you? Your colleague did spill the beans about the group you work for after Dee gave him a little bit of her "treatment". I must say that you've done a great job keeping it hidden from us for so long. But no longer.'

Vijay's heart sank, but he kept a brave face. 'There's no group. We're friends, that's all.' He looked at Van Klueck. 'Okay, so if there is a group, what's it called?'

A cloud passed over the older man's face as he realised Vijay was calling his bluff.

'Never mind,' he brushed the question aside. 'That is irrelevant now. The point is that I know there is an organisation behind you. There are too many coincidences for it to be otherwise.' He ticked off the points on his fingers. 'You and the IB agent flying around in private jets. I don't think you could afford that on your own; definitely not the IB agent. Then, when we laid the trap for your group in Hotan, I thought I'd find someone flying there from India or the USA following the false lead we had passed along. I never expected to find someone already in Hotan. So who were those people in Hotan? And why did Radha pass on the lead about the Owen manuscript to them? Coincidence? I think not. But we digress. I agree to your condition. But only if I find the information you share with me worth my time.' He folded his arms and sat back, waiting.

Vijay nodded. 'I know that Thomas Manning discovered something in Tibet, which he brought back with him to Calcutta and hid there. And along with that, he hid the portion of the Owen manuscript that Fischer said was missing. And I know how to find both.'

This last bit was not pure bravado. On his way to the Dorchester, Vijay had continued to reflect and analyse all the facts and had had another epiphany. He had a strong hunch he knew how to find whatever it was that Fischer and Manning had hidden.

Van Klueck couldn't hide his elation. 'Indeed? Tell me more. I want details before I agree to carry out my part of our bargain.' He knew Vijay's gift for solving riddles, having experienced it first-hand earlier.

Vijay told him about Li Ping's visit to Oxford and Krakow, the contents of the two letters Humboldt had written to Goethe and his brother Wilhelm and about all the clues he thought fit into the right places in the puzzle. As he spoke, he hoped fervently that Van Klueck would give credence to his theory. As Radha had said, he was skating on rather thin ice.

To his great relief, Van Klueck's face grew animated, as he listened with rapt attention.

When Vijay had finished, there was silence for a moment.

Then, Van Klueck smiled. 'Quite the detective, aren't you? And what were you planning on doing after you found this little secret?'

Vijay was nonplussed. He didn't have an answer. The GTF brief had been to investigate the terror threat received by Wilson's publisher. That, in turn, had led to the link to the Owen manuscript and, eventually, to the discovery of something hidden in Calcutta. They had not anticipated any of this. And, with both Patterson and Imran missing in action, there had been no opportunity or time to debrief and decide on a course of action.

Van Klueck laughed. 'So you don't know what this is all about, do you?' He correctly interpreted Vijay's silence as ignorance. 'But tell me, how do we find this secret then?'

'I'm not going to tell you that now,' Vijay said firmly. 'Not until Imran is handed over to us, safe and sound.'

'Then how do I believe you really do know how to find it?'

'My friends and I will go in search of it.'

Van Klueck considered this. 'I don't think you are lying,' he said finally. 'I think you are quite aware of the reach of the Order and our power. None of you would last long if we really decided to come after you. Oh, I know that your little security ring has been able to repulse Dee's rather lax efforts. But then again, we really haven't tested it against the full might of the Order.' He tapped his fingers on the arm of the sofa. 'But I have a condition.'

Vijay looked at him enquiringly.

'Dee and some of our men will accompany you. Just to be sure.'

Vijay took a moment to reflect on this before answering. There didn't seem to be a way out. If he refused, Imran would still be captive. And he knew that it would be just a matter of time before the Order stumbled upon the solution to the problem. He had no illusions. The only reason Van Klueck was talking to him was because Vijay held out the prospect of achieving their goal in the shortest time possible. Not because the Order was incapable of reaching the same conclusions that he had.

'Done,' he told Van Klueck.

'Excellent.' Van Klueck picked up his phone, dialled a number, and gave instructions to release Imran.

Vijay took the details of where Imran could be picked up and messaged Radha. The other GTF team members were on standby.

'So,' Van Klueck said, when Vijay had finished. 'Do you want to know what Thomas Manning brought back from Tibet? And why we can't lose any more time in finding it?'

The Dorchester Hotel
London, UK

'You see,' Van Klueck began, 'what interests me is not the missing portion of the Owen manuscript, but what Manning discovered in Tibet, as you so astutely concluded. Because we already know what was in the original, and complete, Owen manuscript. The text that is missing is a book by Susruta, the ancient Indian surgeon, describing something amazing that happened at Khandavaprastha thousands of years ago.'

'The Khandavaprastha dahan,' Vijay murmured. 'The burning of the Khandavaprastha forest.'

'No,' Van Klueck told him. 'That's not what Susruta described in his text. It is so much more than that. According to him, the Nagas, who lived in Khandavaprastha thousands of years ago, had discovered a new form of life.'

Vijay's face brightened as he made the connection now. 'Humboldt talked about a new form of life in his letter to Wilhelm.'

'That's right,' Van Klueck agreed. 'We know that Humboldt made the connection quite early on. We have the missing portions of his journals and notebooks—the parts that he had carefully cut out and hidden away a few years before his death—in which he describes coming across ancient legends in South America and Mexico, about a pestilence that ravaged the land and how the only way to end it was to set fire to forests and, as they did in Mexico and Guatemala, even cities. Even today, archaeologists are puzzled over cities like Bahlam Jol—the Mayan name for ruins that archaeologists call Witzna—

which were burnt to ashes, and which they incorrectly ascribe to warfare. Humboldt discovered the truth and he had realised that this new form of life that was responsible for the pestilence also had some amazing benefits.'

'The regeneration of the monkey's leg.' The missing pieces of the jigsaw were beginning to fall into place for Vijay now.

'Exactly.'

'What kind of life form can induce a limb to regenerate?' Vijay shook his head in disbelief.

'I can partially answer that question.' Van Klueck rose to pour himself a glass of white wine and picked up a notebook and pen before returning to his seat and resuming his explanation. 'It started with Louis Pasteur.'

'The inventor of pasteurisation.'

'Correct. That is what he is best known for. But young Pasteur worked as a crystallographer. He discovered a property of chemicals called chirality. But first let me explain the concept of "handedness" to you. All objects can be classified as either chiral or achiral. Shoes, for example, or gloves, are chiral. They come in pairs—a left-handed glove and a right-handed one—and each is a mirror image of the other. Your left shoe is a mirror image of your right shoe. On the other hand, achiral objects do not demonstrate any kind of handedness. Take this pen, for example,' he wagged the pen at Vijay, 'this is achiral, which means that its mirror image is exactly the same as the pen itself.'

'So chirality is demonstrated when there is a pair of objects which are mirror images of each other,' Vijay summarised.

'Correct. Now let's take this down to the molecular level, which is what we are interested in, and this is what Pasteur discovered through his study of tartaric acid crystals. Chirality is also displayed at the molecular level. Here's a simple way of looking at this.'

Van Klueck set his glass on the table between them, opened the notebook and began sketching. When he finished, he twirled the notebook so it faced Vijay, who stared at the crude drawing of the molecular structure that Van Klueck had created.

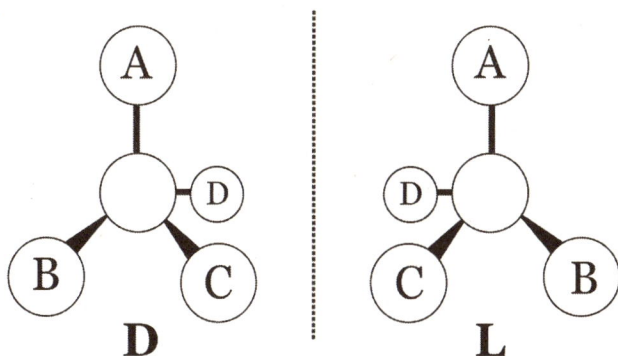

'So,' Van Klueck explained, 'this diagram illustrates chirality. Both of these show a carbon atom to which four other atoms are bonded. These two molecular configurations are mirror images of each other. Pasteur discovered that handedness basically describes how the molecule bends polarised light. If the molecule bends light to the left, it is called left-handed or L for *levo*, and if to the right, then it is right-handed or D for *dexter*.'

He leaned back and took a sip of his wine, as Vijay continued to study the diagram.

'Let's come to life as we know it,' Van Klueck continued. 'Many organic molecules are chiral which means that they can exist in mirror image forms like these which cannot be superimposed on each other. Like a left-handed glove cannot be superimposed on a right-handed one. Most of the basic molecules that are responsible for life have mirror image versions. And the two different hands can have different properties even though they are built from the same atoms. Take the drug thalidomide. It was used in the 1950s to treat morning sickness in pregnant women. But one hand cures the morning sickness, and the other hand causes severe problems in limb development in the foetus. Because thalidomide was synthesised, both hands were made and the result was a tragedy that rocked the world. You see?'

Vijay nodded his understanding. He wondered where this was leading.

'Life as we know it is single handed,' Van Klueck went on. 'In all living beings across all the kingdoms of life, amino acids are left-handed and DNA and RNA are right-handed. Glycine is the only amino acid that is its own mirror image; it is achiral. The others are all L-amino acids. And in cells, the chirality of the molecule makes a difference to how it interacts with other cell components. Think of the whole cellular system as molecular locks which can only be opened using a key that has the correct handedness. That is the basis of life as we know it. So, for example, proteins which bind to D sugars will fail to recognise the L versions because of the difference in the chirality.'

A shiver ran down Vijay's spine as a cold realisation dawned on him. He had begun to connect the dots. He remembered the briefing that Patterson had given them about the assignment from the White House, the China Telegrams, and the mysterious contagion that had originated in China.

'The new form of life that Humboldt talked about,' Vijay ventured. 'That was described in the Owen manuscript as being discovered in Khandavaprastha—it was not life as we know it.'

'I've learnt not to underestimate you, Vijay Singh. You are right. The organism that was discovered by the Nagas was a form of what is today called "weird life" by scientists—an alternative form of life on earth, specifically in this case, mirror life.'

'With its amino acids right-handed and DNA or RNA left-handed,' Vijay breathed.

'Exactly.'

Vijay hesitated. He had to ask but was afraid of the answer.

'Is this the organism that is causing the pandemic that originated in Hotan?'

'I'm afraid so,' Van Klueck replied. 'Because the organism is a mirror image of normal life, it enters the body without rousing the immune system since its biochemistry is completely different. The antigens it carries cannot be recognised by our immune system. And no vaccine or drug that has been developed can kill it because they are all designed for the molecular interactions that are based on the chirality of life as we know it. For our bodies and our immune systems in particular, it is not a genuine life form that they can recognise as one that can invade and infect us.'

Vijay frowned. There was one problem with this explanation. 'But if it is a chiral twin—if I can put it that way—it would also be incompatible with life as we know it. If it can evade our immune systems, then it cannot chemically affect our bodies. Why are people falling ill then? This doesn't add up. And this still doesn't explain how this mirror life microbe has the ability to make limbs regenerate.'

The Dorchester Hotel
London, UK

Van Klueck shrugged and sipped his wine. 'I told you I could only partially explain. We don't have the answers to your questions, because we never had the organism with us. The Susruta text describes it quite clearly as a mirror organism or a mirror microbe, if you will. There's no doubt about that. And we never thought that it still existed after thousands of years. That is why we never bothered to study Humboldt's papers or journals to figure out what was happening. But then we learnt a few years ago, through our sources in China, that the CCP had found samples from an ancient archaeological site and that they had cultured the microbe. Two years ago, we even offered to collaborate with them. But they turned us down. So, we decided to try and obtain a sample for ourselves to study it and get to know more about it. Unfortunately, the PLA somehow got to know and there was a shoot-out in Hotan when our source in the Hotan lab was supposed to deliver the samples to us. We got our samples, but there was a leak in the container as a result.'

Vijay was horrified. 'So *you* were responsible for the start of this pandemic!'

'China was responsible!' Van Klueck snapped. 'We stayed quiet for centuries. *We* didn't go looking for this organism. *They* are the ones who developed it as a bioweapon. Would you rather that we had done nothing and allowed them to gain full control over this organism?'

Vijay was silent. There was truth in Van Klueck's words. But he still couldn't help feeling angry that the Order had allowed the microbe to escape from the laboratory in Hotan.

He decided to change the subject. There was no point in arguing any further. Water under the bridge.

'So this is the true story of Khandavaprastha,' he mused. 'A mirror organism somehow ravaging life in the forest. Presumably it affects all life forms, since it is a mirror image of all life as we know it.'

'Apparently not. Like I said, I can only partially explain. So I don't know why it doesn't affect all life forms. So far, we only have the case of the monkeys that Humboldt found and now humans being infected. If it could infect all life forms, we'd have known by now. But you are wrong about Khandavaprastha,' Van Klueck said, draining his glass of wine. He dangled his empty glass at Vijay. 'Are you sure you won't have some wine? This is really good South African stuff.'

Vijay shook his head. He was more interested in the truth about Khandavaprastha.

Van Klueck poured himself another glass of wine and settled down on the sofa again. 'Khandavaprastha is not just another story about a pestilence. Think about it. It wasn't just the contagion.'

'Then why did Krishna and Arjun kill every living being in Khandavaprastha, except for the seven who survived?' Vijay wondered. 'I thought it was because this organism infected every single one of them, including the trees, which is why the forest had to be burnt down. Just like the forests and cities that you said Humboldt came across, which were burnt down to end this pestilence.'

Van Klueck shook his head. 'That's only part of the story,' he told Vijay. 'There's more to it. Haven't you read the story of Khandavaprastha dahan?'

He rose and walked to the bookshelf which had, among other books, the complete Mahabharata. He picked out the first volume and returned to the sofa.

'Here,' Van Klueck told Vijay, after flipping through the pages. 'Let me explain. Indra protected Khandavaprastha. That much is clear. And once the forest begins to burn, and the slaughter begins, there is a fierce battle between Krishna and Arjun on one hand and all the Devas on the other. All, that is, except two of the most important Devas—Varuna and Agni. Agni is the one who burns down the forest. And Varuna is the one who provides the weapons for the slaughter and the battle against the Devas—Gandiva and the Sudarshan Chakra.'

He leaned forward and looked Vijay in the eye.

'Haven't you ever wondered why the two most important Devas after Indra were in the camp that fought *against* the Devas?'

November 1, 1817
London, UK

Alexander von Humboldt put the tips of his fingers together and regarded the man sitting opposite him with interest. Both men were around the same age; Manning was just three years younger than Humboldt and, with his flowing beard, made quite an impression on everyone he met, including Lord Amherst, who had led the failed embassy to Peking earlier that year. Amherst had objected to Manning's beard and had wanted to exclude him from the team, but the intercession of George Staunton had secured Manning his membership among the company that comprised the embassy.

Humboldt, on his part, was eager to meet Manning after reading the contents of the cryptic letter he had received mentioning the Owen manuscript. The Prussian scientist had arrived in London to venture a second attempt at petitioning the East India Company to allow him to travel to India. He had a packed schedule in London, with plans to visit the Royal Observatory in Greenwich, drop in at Joseph Banks' house in Soho Square and visit the celebrated German-born astronomer William Herschel, who had discovered Uranus in 1781 and was a legend even now at the age of eighty. Humboldt was particularly interested in seeing the enormous forty-foot telescope Herschel had built. And, of course, Humboldt was keen to discuss Herschel's idea of an evolving universe, which resonated strongly with him and which he would write about years later.

It was an exacting schedule—not that Humboldt did not enjoy it. He was happiest when going from one engagement to another even late at night, revelling in the warmth, respect, adoration and interest that he received from his admirers.

Yet, he had found time to meet Manning who had come in to London from his little cottage near Dartford especially for this meeting. The missive indicated that Manning knew more about the manuscript than was available in the public domain. Humboldt didn't know how that was possible, but it was worth meeting the man to find out.

'So,' Humboldt decided to get to the point; he had another meeting to go to shortly—Joseph Banks had invited him to the exclusive Royal Society Dining Club, and Humboldt was keen on reconnecting with the chemist Humphry Davy, who had visited him in Paris three years earlier.

But Humboldt also wanted to find out exactly what Manning had had in mind when he had written that letter. 'What manner of advice do you seek from me?'

Manning hesitated. He had sworn secrecy to Fischer and Birch when he had agreed to undertake the mission they had entrusted to him. He did not wish to violate that oath. Yet, he was torn. The reality of what he had discovered in Tibet, if what the Owen manuscript said was true, was just too unnerving to let it be. He wanted—rather, needed—validation that what he had done and agreed to had been the right thing to do.

Who better to give that validation than someone like Humboldt? Someone who was an expert. Who knew, even if he didn't understand, what they were dealing with.

'Go ahead. You can trust me.' Humboldt noticed Manning's hesitation and sought to reassure him.

Manning nodded. 'I know I can. It is why I reached out to you. But I cannot disclose everything I know. You have to understand. I am sworn to secrecy.'

Humboldt considered this. It was not good news for him. It meant that he would not get all the details he had expected from this meeting. But he was curious to know what Manning did have to say. The admission of an oath of secrecy meant that Humboldt had been correct in his guess that there was more to the Owen manuscript than was available at the Bodleian Library. What really mattered was what was in the portion of the manuscript that he now was sure had been deliberately hidden by someone. Clearly Manning had been privy to the concealment.

'I understand,' Humboldt's voice was gentle. 'I will help in any way I can.'

Manning took a deep breath as if steeling himself. 'If the Owen manuscript were a true account of what happened in the past.' He looked at Humboldt. 'I'm not saying it is, but suppose it is.'

Humboldt nodded.

'Well, then,' Manning continued, 'what would you do if you knew that, thousands of years ago, someone had discovered a new form of life? One that could annihilate the human race?'

PRESENT DAY

DAY SIX

October 26
Hotan
Xinjiang Province, China

The four soldiers immediately raised their guns and aimed them at the trio.

Patterson leaned closer to Chen and whispered in his ear. 'If they start shooting at us, remember, you will be our shield. I'll make sure they riddle you with bullets before anything happens to either of us.' His voice was as hard as steel.

Chen said nothing, but nodded, his face grim. He had no doubt that Patterson would do exactly what he had threatened. Then he barked out something in Mandarin to the soldiers.

Patterson didn't know what Chen had said, but the four soldiers looked at each other, clearly confused. From their expressions, it seemed that they couldn't reconcile Patterson's blood-soaked shirt with whatever Chen had told them. Slowly, they lowered their assault rifles.

Chen slowly led the way past the soldiers, nodding to them as he passed.

The soldiers seemed to relax, until one of them spotted Patterson's assault rifle. He immediately yelled something to the others and their rifles were up again.

Patterson whirled around, holding Chen in front of him and pulling Iris behind him, covering her. He realised that Chen had said something disarming earlier to the soldiers, not wanting to appear a hostage.

But now the situation had changed.

Chen barked out something again. This time, the soldiers did not budge. The guns remained levelled at them.

'Tell them,' Patterson breathed, 'to put their guns on the floor, and get into the lift. Now.'

Chen said something to the soldiers, his voice hard. Patterson was sure he had threatened them with action by the CCP.

Whatever it was that he said, the soldiers seemed to understand that they would have to shoot Chen to get to the Americans. Slowly, they placed their rifles on the ground and backed off, their hands raised.

Chen spat out angry words again.

One of the soldiers jabbed at the lift call button and the lift doors opened.

The four soldiers disappeared inside and the lift doors closed.

'Iris, get a couple of those assault rifles,' Patterson instructed, and Iris dashed forward, grabbed two of the guns that the soldiers had left behind and sprinted back, while Patterson covered her in case the soldiers reappeared.

But the threat had passed, at least for the time being.

Patterson discarded the rifle he was carrying. It was running low on ammunition and he was grateful for the new guns. He slung one on his back and held the other one pointed at Chen.

'Now,' he told Chen, 'take us to the room you told us about.'

Chen nodded wordlessly and led the way back into the conference room. He walked to the conference table and pressed a button. One section of the wood panelling on the walls slid aside, revealing a hidden lift.

Patterson raised an eyebrow, but said nothing as Chen jabbed the call button and the lift doors slid open soundlessly.

Inside the lift, Chen pressed the single button on the panel and the lift descended before it came to a halt and the doors opened again.

They walked out into another wood-panelled office, much more luxurious than Jiang's modest office had been. There was a large mahogany desk in one corner of the room, which had plush carpeting and a couple of leather sofas in the opposite corner from the desk. Banks of monitors covered the walls, showing feeds from CCTVs across the facility. Some of the monitors—which displayed scenes from some offices and workstations—had keypads attached to them, probably to facilitate communications with those workstations and offices.

As Iris walked in, she saw Barnsfield on one of the monitors with a keypad attached, sitting in his office and studying something on his laptop screen.

'Wow!' Patterson exclaimed, as he took in the room and its opulence, noting that there were no cameras installed here. Clearly, this was some sort of a VIP room where secret meetings were held. 'Whose office is this?'

Chen frowned but replied, 'Zhu Jingting. The CCP Committee Secretary, Xinjiang Uyghur Autonomous Region.'

'Well, I guess we can sit and talk here for a while without anyone disturbing us then,' Patterson observed. He knew they didn't have much time before the PLA swung into action. Yet, without information, his escape would be worth nothing. And when they had a senior functionary like Chen in their grasp, it would be throwing away a golden opportunity to understand what was happening here if Patterson did not interrogate him.

Escape could wait. It would be no easier to try and escape now than it would be half an hour later. The place was crawling with PLA soldiers anyway. Either way, he would have to think of a plan.

Patterson dismissed the thoughts on his mind and focused on what he needed to do now.

He looked at Iris. 'Do you know how to handle a gun?'

Irish shook her head. 'I hate guns.'

'You can skip the assault rifle,' Patterson told her. 'Here, take this handgun.' He showed her how to use it. 'Just remember, shoot before anyone else shoots at you. If you hesitate, you're dead.' He fixed her with a steely gaze. 'You may need this if we are to get out of here alive.'

Iris nodded, but her face showed her uncertainty about being able to comply with his instructions.

Patterson gestured to Chen to sit on one of the sofas. Chen sat down with a resigned air. But inwardly, he was exulting. While this was not what he had planned, he had succeeded in leading the American to the most secure room in the complex; the one room which was impossible to enter without authorised access. But it was also the most difficult to get out of without the appropriate level of security access.

Chen had led Patterson into a trap.

Hotan
Xinjiang Province, China

'When we realised that Wilson was privy to information about Humboldt and the Owen manuscript, we decided to kidnap him and get the information from him,' Chen told Patterson and Iris.

He had explained the technical nature of the labs in this facility as well as the details of the experiments conducted here, taking Patterson on a tour of the facility without stepping out of the room.

Iris had assisted him with the specialised scientific explanations based on her understanding of what Barnsfield had told her, since this was her field of specialisation.

Patterson had listened, horrified at what the CCP, with the help of Howard Barnsfield, had accomplished.

He also realised that there was a flaw in the plan he had come up with. When he had decided to make a break for it, Lin's words in Beijing had echoed in his mind.

The lab had to be destroyed.

So he had run over different options in his mind to ensure that the facility was destroyed even if it meant he went down with it.

But after listening to Chen, things had changed.

There were thousands of people housed here; subjects of all the experiments and clinical trials being conducted as part of the bioweapons programme. If the lab was destroyed, they would die with it.

That was not part of the bargain. He was a soldier, accustomed to killing, but that was on the battlefield. There were rules of engagement. He could not—would not—kill innocent people. Every one of the subjects incarcerated here was an innocent victim.

No, Patterson had concluded during Chen's explanation, he could not destroy the lab. Instead, he now had to find a way for Iris and him to escape with the information that they had collected.

The world must know.

But there was still one missing link that he did not understand.

'Where does the Owen manuscript come in?' he had demanded, finally. 'Where does a two-thousand-year-old text from India fit into all of this?'

Chen had explained and was just concluding his account of how they had discovered the means to achieve their ends.

'Wilson told us about Humboldt's letter which was in the Bodleian Library at Oxford and we got one of our sleepers at Craggett University—the one who recruited Barnsfield for us—to check out the letter.'

Chen told Iris and Patterson about the contents of Humboldt's letter to Goethe. 'Then,' he continued, 'we realised that we needed more information. Wilson was of little help. We also realised that someone else was interested in Wilson's research and perhaps the Owen manuscript. We had to be careful. We went a bit slow after that and tried to find out who we were up against. But we failed to come up with any information on our unknown rival. So we decided to retrieve Wilson's notes from his house and managed to acquire them before his house was burnt down, probably by the ones who had issued the terrorist threat to Wilson's publisher.' He grimaced. 'We lost a week in the process. A week we couldn't afford to lose. In another week or so, the first patients in the USA and elsewhere will begin dying in the most horrible manner. Two months are almost up since the Hotan accident. We have to find the antidote before that.'

Patterson recalled what Lin had told him about the manner in which the Chinese archaeologists had met their end, and shuddered. It wasn't just he who was running out of time. The countdown had started for the biggest extinction the planet had ever seen.

Chen looked at Iris. 'That is why we need you on our team.' He spread his hands. 'If you won't do it for China, do it for the world.' He pointed at Patterson. 'And for your friend here.'

'Like you care about the world!' Patterson spat. 'Once you have the antidote, you will use it as leverage. I think the world has wised up to the CCP. You aren't the demure, flexible, welcoming entity, open to change, that we thought you were. When China was admitted to the WTO, we thought that the CCP would change. That democracy had a chance in China.' He scowled. 'We were wrong. You used the WTO to strengthen your position in the world economy, grow rapidly, all the while appropriating—while pretending to welcome— Western investment and technology, and simultaneously consolidating the CCP's position within China. The world has yet to realise how dependent on China it has become, but you will not hesitate to use your dominant position to force your own agenda through. And democracy, freedom of speech and human rights don't fit in that agenda.'

'Even if I do help you,' Iris added, 'you still don't have the recipe to create the antidote.'

Chen held up a finger. 'Ah, but that's where you are wrong.' A beatific smile crossed his face, a smile of triumph. For a moment he forgot that an assault rifle was pointed at his chest.

'You see,' he told them, 'we have made a breakthrough. Among Wilson's papers, we found a reference he had made to another letter that Humboldt had written, this time to his brother Wilhelm. Our man at Craggett University has checked out the letter for himself. It was in a library in Krakow. His report has come in. This letter is the missing link we were seeking. It will lead us to the antidote.'

Hampstead
London, UK

Dee listened bitterly as Van Klueck outlined his plan to her. He had called her to update her on his decision to release Imran, and his discussion with Vijay in which they had agreed that Dee and a few of her men would accompany Vijay and his friends to Calcutta.

The plan wasn't one that she liked, or even agreed with, but she didn't have a choice.

The only thing that was of some comfort to her was that even with this new plan, one thing would not change.

Her intention to kill Radha in the most painful, horrible way possible.

Nothing would give her more pleasure.

London
UK

Vijay stood at the foot of Imran's bed in the hospital suite as engineers scurried in and out, installing cables, equipment and monitors where Imran could easily view them.

'I'm glad you are in one piece,' Vijay grinned.

'Oh, that I am. I'm just a little cut up with Dee,' Imran joked, wincing with pain as he laughed at his own pun. He had greeted Vijay by berating him for the deal he had made with Van Klueck.

'You will hand over what Van Klueck wants on a platter,' he had upbraided Vijay. 'The exchange was just not worth it! You should have let me stay in their custody and conducted the search yourself!'

Vijay had allowed himself to be hauled over the coals with no remonstrance. He had expected nothing less from Imran, having known the IB officer for so long. In fact, it was just the thing that he had expected Imran to do—put the safety and well-being of others over his own.

Imran had eventually subsided, having got his feelings off his chest. He had also realised that there was no going back now.

And, truth be told, both men were relieved that Imran was out of the clutches of the Order. Or, rather, of Dee.

While Vijay and Van Klueck had been closeted at The Dorchester , Radha and Duncan had gone to the rendezvous that Van Klueck had mentioned. They were horrified to see Imran's condition and had rushed him to the hospital, Duncan making frantic calls along the way to ensure that emergency attention and blood supplies were available the moment they reached.

After Imran had been attended and his wounds taken care of, he had been wheeled to this suite, where his immediate request was to set up a command and control centre so he could monitor the operations of the GTF from his hospital bed.

Duncan had tried to argue, but Radha knew the futility of any discussion with Imran on matters like this and had advised him to acquiesce.

Duncan had then dropped Radha and Colin at the airport, while Vijay dropped in to see Imran after his meeting with Van Klueck. The plan was for them to fly direct to Kolkata along with Dee and her men, while Vijay would accompany Shukla to Delhi. Vijay also wanted to drop by Jaungarh Fort for something, but had been tight-lipped about what he wanted to do there. He would join the rest of the group in Kolkata. Van Klueck had consented to this plan, knowing that Vijay would not risk the safety of his friends while Dee was with them.

Radha had initially been flabbergasted when she heard that Vijay had told Van Klueck he knew how to find the location of the missing portion of the Owen manuscript. All their discussions had centred on the theory that something had been hidden. There had been absolutely no speculation about how to find it. But she knew Vijay well and, after getting over the initial shock, realised that he had a hunch.

'So what is it?' she had demanded. 'What's your hunch? I know you have something up your sleeve.'

'I'll tell you once I'm absolutely sure. I'm reasonably sure right now, but I want to research a bit more.' Vijay grinned at her. 'But I'll give you a hint. Something Colin said earlier today set off the lightbulb.'

'Me? What did I say?' It was Colin's turn to be bewildered. He couldn't think of anything he had said that was connected with a means to find the location of the secret.

Radha shook her head. 'You won't get it out of him until he's good and ready to tell you.'

Hotan
Xinjiang Province, China

Zhu Jingting glared at Jiang Zitao. '*Shàojiàng* Jiang, you have disgraced your position!'

The CCP committee secretary had arrived in Hotan a short while ago and was immediately ushered into Jiang's office. When he had expressed surprise at not being taken immediately to his own office, he had been informed that the American prisoner, who had escaped and taken Chen captive, had occupied the office along with Chen and the Chinese American scientist.

Zhu had been furious. 'You allowed them to commandeer my office? Were you sleeping when all of this happened?' he had thundered.

Jiang had initially tried to explain. 'Zhu *zŏng*, we are fully equipped to repulse any attack on the facility from the outside. But we do not have a standard drill for an internal assault. No one had ever anticipated a military grade attack from someone inside the complex.'

'Yet it has happened! Were safeguards not in place?'

'Our cells are secure. We have never had this problem before. The American was handcuffed when taken out of the cell and his hands and legs secured when he was inside. All standard precautions were taken.'

'And still the American escaped!'

After that, Jiang had given up and he now stood quietly, shamefaced, listening to Zhu rant. The Major General knew where the centres of power lay—they were always with the party; here, in Xinjiang, it was with the CCP committee secretary. Crossing him would mean a fate worse than death.

Finally, after fulminating for a while, Zhu calmed down somewhat.

'What is your command, Zhu *zŏng*?' Jiang asked obsequiously.

'Let me think.' Zhu sat with his fingertips together and reflected. If the American was with Chen, then he would have extracted information from the Xia Yu executive. Zhu had little faith in Chen's ability to withstand any form of interrogation, even a mild one. With a gun to his head, he would have spilled the beans. Zhu had no doubt about that.

Under the circumstances, the only thing that mattered now was that the American soldier should not be allowed to escape. He should either be captured or killed.

There was only one problem. Whether by design or accident, the American was holed up in the most secure room in this complex. It had been intentionally built that way for Zhu's own security. Like most ambitious men in China, he trusted no one. So when the factory and the lab beneath it were being built, he had ensured that he had a sanctuary within that was impregnable. There was no way to reach the American as long as he remained in the room.

And like it or not, there was truth in Jiang's words. No one had ever contemplated an attack from within the lab. The only people who ever came here were the Chinese staff who worked here and had been thoroughly vetted, or the subjects for the experiments, who had no choice in the matter.

Even he, Zhu, had never dreamed that, one day, a foreign armed soldier opposed to the CCP would occupy the safe house he had built for himself within the lab.

Zhu rose. He had made a decision.

He gave Jiang a hard look. 'Evacuate the complex. All staff. I want it done in the next ten minutes. Then we activate the safeguard.' He swung away and strode towards the door.

Jiang stared at Zhu's retreating back, uncomprehending. 'But ... Zhu *zǒng* ...'

Zhu swung back. 'Yes, *Shàojiàng?* Do you have a problem with my order?'

Jiang swallowed. 'No Zhu *zǒng.*' He finally summoned up the courage to speak his mind. 'But to destroy everything that we've built ... all the work of decades ...' his voice trailed off. He was unnerved by the implications of Zhu's command.

Zhu nodded. 'Yes. It is a waste. But we have a full back-up of all our experiments, records, results. Our staff will continue their work at another facility. We will find new subjects—those are not hard to come by. The ones here ... well, they're going to die anyway, so they won't be missed. I had the safeguard built precisely for a situation like this. Though I never dreamed it would actually happen, I foresaw a possibility that a Western power might infiltrate this complex and try and thwart our plans. Who knows what Chen has told the American? And there is a fully equipped communications centre in that room. If Chen has told the American about it, the world will know about this facility.'

He shook his head. 'No. There is only one way to save the CCP from embarrassment. We can never let the world know what we've been doing here. Everything China has done over the last fifty years would go down the drain. *That* would be a tragedy ... to destroy everything we have built over the decades—our power, our strength, our position in the world, stronger even than the Soviet Union ever was.'

'And what about Chen *zŏng*?' Jiang realised what Zhu intended to do.

'He is dispensable,' Zhu told him. 'He is no lynchpin for our plans. We will find another to take his place.' He pointed a finger at Jiang. 'Do it. Now.'

Hotan

Xinjiang Province, China

Suddenly, a klaxon went off in the room, startling Patterson and Iris. Chen, too, looked surprised.

The sound of the klaxon was accompanied by an announcement that emanated from concealed speakers in the ceiling of the room. It was in Mandarin.

Patterson looked enquiringly at Iris, who translated for him. 'It's an alert for evacuation. It says that all staff are to evacuate within ten minutes. And that this is not a drill; the countdown has begun.'

'What countdown?' Patterson's gaze bored into Chen.

The Chinese man had looked surprised at the announcement, but was now chuckling with obvious glee. 'Zhu *zǒng* has arrived, I see.' He laughed. 'So this is the end of the road for you, American. You will die here. Zhu *zǒng* has activated the safeguard procedure. In ten minutes, this facility will be reduced to a pile of rubble. No one will ever know that it existed. And you will die with it.'

Iris paled as she heard Chen's words.

'Get us out of here,' Patterson commanded Chen.

The Xia Yu managing director just laughed in response. 'I'm not going anywhere,' he told Patterson. 'Kill me if you will. I am prepared to die for my country, protecting its secrets. Are you?'

'Then we'll just leave without you,' Patterson muttered, his head awhirl with thoughts of how to extricate himself and Iris from this predicament.

'You'll never find your way out,' Chen chuckled, clearly pleased with himself. 'You are at the lowest level of the complex. Even if you do find your way to the exit, you will never reach it in ten minutes!'

Patterson's forehead creased with worry as he realised that Chen was right. This place was a maze of corridors. Without a map or a guide, there was no way to make a swift exit from the building.

They would never make it.

To his surprise, Iris suddenly placed her gun on a table next to her and bounded across to the monitor where Barnsfield could be seen bundling some papers into a briefcase and preparing to leave like the rest of the staff.

Iris looked at the keypad. It had notations in Chinese, but she could read them. She jabbed at the call button. Barnsfield heard the ring and looked at the screen in his room, astonishment clouding his face as he saw Iris's face there.

He pressed the button to talk on his monitor. 'Iris! Where are you? This place is going to blow up in less than ten minutes!' He knew that if she had accessed the facility's communication system, she couldn't be in her cell. And he could see the wood panelling behind her. 'Wherever you are, get out of there now!'

'I don't know the way out.' Iris was surprised to find her voice calm and steady despite the circumstances. 'Can you please help, Howard?' She thought fast. 'I know my way to the conference room.'

Barnsfield hesitated, then nodded. 'That's not far from where I am. We can make it. I'll meet you in the conference room in two minutes. Don't dawdle. The countdown has started.'

He disconnected and left his office, clearly on his way to meet Iris.

Patterson was watching, relieved. Now that they had a guide out of here, things were looking up.

But he had let his guard down. He had taken his eye off Chen.

He turned around to see Chen lunging for the gun Iris had left on the table.

'You're not going anywhere!' the Chinese man shouted as he grabbed the gun.

Patterson brought up his rifle and pumped a volley of bullets into Chen, but he was too late.

The Xia Yu managing director, clearly incensed by the prospect of Iris escaping and betraying her people, had fired two shots at Iris before slumping to the floor in a pool of blood.

One had found its mark.

Patterson watched, horrified, as Iris toppled backwards with the impact of the bullet, going limp and collapsing, her arms flailing as she fell.

Hotan

Xinjiang Province, China

Patterson rushed to Iris and was relieved to see her breathing. Blood seeped through her trousers. She had been hit in the leg. He hoped it was not a major wound. If the bullet had hit any of the major blood vessels in the leg, she would bleed to death before he could get her to safety.

But his first priority was to get Iris to the conference room. Otherwise both of them were dead anyway.

He put one arm around the back of her neck, intending to pick her up and carry her, when her eyes fluttered open, her face screwing up with pain.

Iris saw Patterson's face looking down at her and felt his arm supporting her.

'I ... I think I can walk,' she said weakly. She felt her trousers and her hand came away covered in blood. 'Just grazed my leg,' she told Patterson. 'I should be fine.'

'You were lucky.' Patterson helped Iris to her feet and supported her as she limped to the lift. 'Chen was diving for the gun and was off balance when he fired at you. And perhaps he was not a very good shot either. But you did well to talk to Barnsfield.'

'Thank you.' Iris gave him a wan smile as they stepped into the lift and Patterson jabbed the button to go up.

Barnsfield was waiting for them in the conference room, pacing up and down.

He rushed to meet them when he saw them exit the lift and enter the room. 'We have to be quick. There's just five minutes left!' he began, then stopped short as he saw Iris' leg drenched in blood. 'Oh my God! You've been shot!'

'Let's go,' Patterson instructed Barnsfield. 'We need to get her to a hospital as soon as possible.' He set the countdown timer on his watch.

'This way,' Barnsfield led the way out of the conference room and down the corridor, in the opposite direction from the lift that served the floor.

'Hey, the lift is this way!' Patterson thought that the scientist was going the wrong way.

'There's a VIP exit from here,' Barnsfield called over his shoulder, without breaking stride. 'Only a few of us have the keycards to access it. It's the fastest way to get out of here. We will never make it in time to the main exit.'

There was a steel door at the end of the corridor. Barnsfield swiped at the electronic lock on the door and pushed it open.

Patterson and Iris followed him into another lift. Another swipe of the keycard and Barnsfield pressed the sole button on the panel of the lift and it rose to stop one floor above.

The lift doors opened into a spacious garage in which there were four SUVs—a couple of BJ2022s, a BJ2020 and one BJ80.

'The key will be in the ignition for all of them,' Barnsfield informed them helpfully.

Patterson nodded and headed for one of the BJ2022s. He helped Iris into the passenger seat in the front, fastened her seatbelt, then clambered in behind the wheel.

Barnsfield hopped into the passenger cabin, as Patterson started the SUV and pressed the accelerator to the floor. The SUV lurched forward and fishtailed with a screech of tyres, then steadied and raced down the garage towards the exit.

'It's shut!' Patterson shouted, looking at his watch.

Less than a minute to go.

'Don't worry!' Barnsfield called back, looking around nervously. 'There's a sensor!'

To Patterson's relief, Barnsfield was right and the doors began opening as the SUV approached the exit.

Thirty seconds to go.

Patterson changed gears and accelerated, willing the SUV to go faster.

Twenty seconds.

The door was just metres away.

Ten seconds.

Almost there.

There was a series of loud explosions.

The floor beneath the SUV shuddered, then began to give way as the vehicle hurtled towards the exit.

The charges to blow up the complex had been built into the foundation of the structure. The entire building had been designed to implode when the safeguard was triggered.

Then the floor behind the SUV disappeared just as the SUV flew over the threshold and into the darkness of the night outside and the entire garage came crashing down behind the vehicle.

Above them, the sound of a helicopter came to their ears, its rotors slicing the night sky as it headed away from the complex.

Patterson raced the SUV away, relieved.

Next to him, Iris had a stricken look on her face that gradually gave way to relief.

They had made it.

Just about.

In the air over Europe

'I've got it!' Colin yelped.

Radha and Dee looked at him curiously.

Dee and five of her men were the other passengers in the jet provided by the Order to ferry them to Kolkata. While Radha and Colin had sat together, Dee sat with her team at the rear of the aircraft, half resting, half watching over the other two. Without saying a word, she had made it very clear that she was not interested in the hunt for the Owen manuscript. She was going along only to ensure that the interests of the Order were protected.

Which was fine with Radha. She could sense the resentment that Dee bore towards her, even though she never quite understood why. Not that she liked Dee, but considering that they hadn't met more than a couple of times while Radha had been with the Order, and had never worked together, there really didn't seem to be any logical reason for Dee's hostility. Still, there it was, and Radha was quite happy that Dee had stayed away from her and Colin.

'Vijay thinks he's really smart, eh?' Colin pouted. 'Well, I'm going to show him this time.'

Radha laughed. 'It's really been gnawing at you, hasn't it? I could see that you've been thinking hard all this while.'

Colin had not been his usual garrulous self ever since they had parted with Vijay. He had been lost in thought, his forehead furrowed for most of the trip to the airport and on the flight, until now.

Radha had known why. He had been busy trying to work out what it was he had said that had given Vijay a clue to finding the location of the secret.

'Riddles,' Colin told her now.

'Riddles?' Radha looked flummoxed. 'What do you mean?'

'Do you remember when we were talking about Manning's papers? When Vijay was telling us his theory?'

Radha nodded. She recalled the conversation. Vijay had been talking about Manning hiding something in Kolkata.

'Well,' Colin continued, 'I had mentioned riddles. In the bunch of Manning's papers that I had been studying at the Royal Asiatic Society and later online, I had come across a whole lot of riddles he had written. I have no idea whether he had created them or only noted them down, but there were some interesting ones. I tried to guess the answers to some of them but, infuriatingly, Manning only provided the riddles and not the answers. And some of them were really tough ones.'

Radha sat up, interested now. This was a constructive line of thought. 'Go on.'

'So what if Manning cannily sneaked a riddle in that lot that can lead us to where the Owen manuscript is hidden? It would be the best place to hide something. No one would ever guess. I mean, there's a whole bunch of riddles which are pretty pointless unless you want to pass your time by racking your brain.'

'You do have something there,' Radha agreed. 'And it sounds like just the kind of thing to get Vijay all worked up. He loves puzzles.'

'Yup. That's why he was being so cagey and mysterious. I know Vijay. He wants to solve the riddle himself.' Colin grinned. 'Let's show him, shall we?'

He pulled out his laptop and booted it, then connected to the jet's Wi-Fi and began browsing through the Royal Asiatic Society's Digital Library, angling the laptop screen towards Radha so she could see it. He found the Thomas Manning collection and clicked on the link *Notebooks and Notes*.

'There's a bunch of them,' he told her as he opened the first lot of riddles.

Thomas Manning's right-slanted, fine handwriting filled up the screen and they began scanning the riddles to see if any of them fit the bill.

Each riddle was preceded by a number, but there was no order to the numbers. The riddles seemed to be randomly numbered. Some of them were simple one-line questions like: *Where was the first nail struck?* Most, however, were three- or four-line riddles, with a handful exceeding five lines, asking the reader to guess the identity of someone or something.

Manning's handwriting was difficult to read, and they pored over the riddles, trying to figure out the words in each line.

They finished one set of riddles, not having come across anything that looked even remotely relevant. The set ended with a list of anagrams, which were interesting, but useless for their purpose. They looked at each other.

Had Vijay been wrong about this?

'There are a couple more sets of riddles,' Colin pointed out. 'We've only gone through TM/9/8/01—the exercise book containing riddles.' He was referring to the catalogue number of the scanned text they had been reading. 'Let's look at this set of ten riddles on slips of paper.'

'The handwriting seems different,' Radha murmured.

Colin agreed with her. It still slanted to the right, but was less angular, not as fine, and easier to read.

These riddles were longer than the last lot; most of them had four lines, and one had as many as eight.

> 'My first is his—Whose? Mine?—No, His
> My 2nd is a Tory
> Who writes my whole, writes sometimes lies
> And calls it all his story.'

Radha read out the second of two riddles on the second slip of paper. 'It would be nice to try and figure out some of these if we had the time,' she muttered. 'You were right, Colin. Nice stuff to aimlessly while the hours away.'

'He was quite creative,' Colin remarked. 'Some of those anagrams were pretty good. And these riddles are tough brainteasers.'

He sighed as they finished the second lot of riddles and opened the third set. Their hopes were dwindling now; after this lot, there was only one more set of riddles in the collection.

'They're getting longer now,' Colin commented after a while. They were halfway through the collection of riddles. 'These are all five lines or more unlike the earlier ones and some of them are almost like poems. Look at this one:

> 'My first is a sign of eight that kindled an empire
> My second, where lightning struck a holy spire
> My third is the key where the ruler fought a duel
> My fourth where the first rests among equals
> My fifth is the outpost that lay between two faiths
> My whole is the weapon used to vanquish the wraiths …'

He broke off as Radha gave a cry. 'What?' He looked at her, startled.

'Sorry,' Radha apologised. 'Didn't mean to interrupt you. But look … look at this next line!'

'I was going to read it,' Colin frowned at her in mock irritation, 'if you'd only let me.'

He turned back to the screen and continued reading.

'In the forest where the two fought the gods and the beasts.'

He broke off again and looked at Radha. 'Well, what about this line? I don't see anything extraordinary …'

'But don't you see?' Radha interrupted him, her eyes shining with excitement. 'The forest. The two who fought the gods and the beasts.'

'Now you're making leaps of logic like Vijay does,' Colin observed. 'Just because a forest is mentioned? Who are the two? And where do the gods and beasts come in?'

Radha realised that Colin probably didn't know the entire story of Khandavaprastha from the Mahabharata. She remembered that her father had talked more about the burning of the forest than the battle that had followed the conflagration.

'Didn't Papa tell you about the battle between Krishna and Arjuna on one hand and the Devas and all the inhabitants of the forest on the other?'

Colin thought hard, then shook his head. 'Nope. He told us about how the forest burnt, and the slaughter of every living being in the forest. But that was all.'

'Okay, so there's more to that story. I'll give you a synopsis. Indra, the king of the Devas, was protecting the forest because his friend Takshaka, the king of the Nagas, lived there. And among the inhabitants of the forest were not only animals and Nagas, but also Danavas, Rakshasas and Pisachas, loosely called demons and ghosts by Western scholars. Now, when the conflagration began and Krishna and Arjuna began rounding up the inhabitants and killing them, they were attacked not only by the residents of the forest but also by a contingent of Devas or the celestials, the gods.'

'Ah!' Colin understood. 'So you're thinking the reference to the wraiths is the ghosts and the demons that lived in the forest and the gods and the beasts also joined in the battle.'

He studied the verse on the screen. 'You could be right,' he said, finally. 'Look at the last few lines:

From my second to my fifth is my shaft facing east
Be true to your faith and you will without doubt
Find the secret I hide by unearthing the key
If you see my whole, if my whole you find out
If not you're the same as you plainly will see.'

They exchanged looks. It didn't make much sense, but then again, it was a riddle.

Had they found it?

Was this the key to finding the secret of Khandavaprastha?

DAY SEVEN

October 27
Kolkata
India

'What took you so long? Whatever were you doing?' Colin voiced what everyone else was thinking.

On their arrival in Kolkata earlier in the day, Radha and Colin, along with Dee and her goons, had been whisked off to a bungalow in Alipore that the Order had leased. Van Klueck was not taking any chances. He had insisted that they use the Order's jet, and use this house as their base in Kolkata. Vijay had agreed. He had seen no harm in acquiescing, since he had agreed to Dee tagging along anyway.

The original plan had been for Vijay's flight to take off not long after the others had left, giving him some time to catch up with Imran. And then there was the layover in Delhi, which would take a few hours, given the travel time from Delhi to Jaungarh and back. In any case, the original scheduled time of arrival for Vijay at Kolkata airport had been around 2.30 p.m.

But the deadline had passed and Dee had been begun to get agitated over Vijay's nonappearance. Her innately suspicious nature had been kindled by 3 p.m., and with every minute that passed, it grew more intense. And the constant stream of reports she kept getting from the two men posted at the airport to pick up Vijay and bring him here hadn't helped. Knowing her nature, they were bordering on panic, not wanting to be held responsible for somehow missing Vijay when he arrived. All her men knew what Dee was like when she was furious and none of them had any desire to cross swords with her.

Then, suddenly, she got a call to inform her that Vijay had arrived with another person in tow.

Dee had announced to Radha and Colin that Dr Shukla had accompanied Vijay to Kolkata, even though that had not been the original plan. Shukla was to disembark in Delhi.

To everyone's surprise, however, Vijay turned up on their doorstep accompanied not by Shukla, but by none other than a cheery Scotsman.

'What the devil are you doing here?' Colin hadn't been able to help himself.

'Aye, couldn't miss a treasure hunt,' was all that Duncan would say.

Vijay was equally tight-lipped about the change in plans. 'We can do with another hand on this search' was the only thing he said to Dee by way of explanation.

After arriving at the safe house, he had locked himself in the room allotted to him and refused to come out. He hadn't even exchanged words with Radha or Colin.

But both of them knew Vijay well. It was clear to them at least, if not to Dee, that Vijay was on to something. He was working out something in his mind. At times like these, he would ignore everyone else and focus only on what he needed to resolve. Love, friendship—even sustenance, since there were times when he had spurned food and drink as well—were irrelevant when he was working on a problem. Both Radha and Colin had experienced this before.

For them, it was good news.

It meant Vijay was making progress on delivering on his promise to Van Klueck.

They had racked their brains on the flight after they had discovered the riddle, but had been unsuccessful in deciphering it. Both of them had some ideas about what it could mean—clearly it had some references to locations in Kolkata—but they still couldn't figure out how the pieces fit together.

If anyone could solve this riddle, it was Vijay.

When Vijay had finally emerged from his room, the first thing he had done was give Radha a warm hug and a long, passionate kiss. Then he had turned to Colin and given him a high five.

It was then that Colin had burst out, frustrated.

The plan—and the commitment to Van Klueck—had been to locate the secret before the day was over and return to London where he awaited them.

Vijay's tardiness had put this at risk. There were less than twelve hours to go before midnight, UK time. How were they going to complete their mission by then?

But Vijay only grinned back at Colin. 'Okay, buddy,' he said. 'Tell me what you thought of the riddle.'

After discovering the riddle, Radha and Colin had immediately sent off an email to Vijay, informing him of their deductions. He had promptly responded with a congratulatory message, thanking them for validating his own thoughts.

If the three of us think the same thing, there must be some substance to it. Ergo, this has to be the riddle that Manning created, that can lead us to the location we seek.

Both Radha and Colin had been thrilled to hear that Vijay too had arrived at the same conclusion. They had spent the next few hours before landing discussing what it possibly meant.

'Well,' Colin said, hesitantly, 'we figured that the riddle refers to locations in the Kolkata of Manning's time.' He looked at Radha for support with the explanation.

'That's right,' Radha joined in. 'Manning had many riddles like this one in his notebooks. And we thought, since we believed that the riddle was a clue to a location where something was hidden, that we should also look for five locations, each of which is described cryptically in each of the first five lines of the riddle. The second line of the riddle also uses the word "where", which strengthened our conviction that each line refers to a different location.'

'Very good.' Vijay was genuinely impressed. 'This is great stuff. So did you manage to work out what each line means?'

'We'll tell you what we worked out,' Colin said. 'Then you can tell us what you think.'

Kolkata

India

'Well,' Colin began, 'we already told you how we figured out that this was the riddle we were looking for. The two lines about the wraiths and the forests and the gods and the beasts. So that meaning is clear—the reference to the forest is obvious. And the weapon, well ...' He looked at Radha and said, 'You'd better explain. I can't pronounce all those names.'

Radha smiled. 'Sure. So if we find all five locations, then we should get either the Gandiva—Arjuna's bow that was given to him by Varuna—or the Sudarshan Chakra—which was given to Krishna by Varuna. And based on the reference to a shaft—we understood that to mean an arrow—it is probably Gandiva. But what that means, we really couldn't work out. I mean, are we looking for the Gandiva? An ancient bow from the Mahabharata? And how will that lead us to the secret that Van Klueck told you about?'

'We took a leaf out of your book and spent the remaining hours of the flight surfing the internet and trying to find historical locations in Kolkata that match the descriptions in the riddle,' Colin took up the explanation again. 'So we decided to start with the second line, assuming that the holy spire being referred to is the steeple of a church. Since Manning was a Christian, it was more likely that he was talking about a church than a temple. We discovered that St Anne's church stood next to the Old Fort William, and its steeple was struck by lightning in 1724.'

'Apparently the church was badly damaged during the fighting in 1756, when Siraj ud-Daula and his forces attacked the fort,' Radha added. 'Today the Writers' Building stands where the church once stood. That's the second location in the riddle.'

'Brilliant,' Vijay enthused. 'What else?'

'Uh, that's it,' Colin confessed. 'Oh, there's one more thing we figured, but it's probably stating the obvious. The second location—St Anne's church, or rather Writers' Building as it is today—should be located to the west of the fifth location—the outpost between two faiths, whatever that means. Because the shaft—or arrow— is facing east, from the second to the fifth.'

Radha and Colin looked at Vijay expectantly. They had been quite ecstatic that in the seven hours it had taken them to reach Kolkata after they had discovered the riddle, they had actually managed to find one location and decipher a few lines.

'We have no idea what the last four lines mean,' Radha added, glancing at Dee, who had walked up and been listening to them. 'What did you find?'

Vijay watched Dee turn away disdainfully, her disinterest in their conversation apparent. 'Well, you guys did a pretty good job. My guesses were the same as yours so I think we're on the right track. I did manage to work out a couple of more things, but there's still a lot of work to do. And I did have a bit of an advantage over you guys. I had some more time than you to meditate on the riddle with the flight to Delhi, the trip to Jaungarh and back, and then the flight here. I didn't sleep during either flight, but spent my time researching. And I spent a couple of hours at the Reading Room of the British Museum, where Duncan helped me get immediate access to some research material and old books, which I photocopied to read while travelling.' He nodded to Duncan, who had been listening intently to the discussion, and Duncan nodded back.

'You look like you haven't slept for a week,' Colin commented gratuitously. 'Look at the bags under your eyes.'

'So I agree that we are looking for Gandiva,' Vijay continued, ignoring Colin's wisecrack. 'Even I can't imagine what that really means, but it is hard to believe that it is the actual bow that Arjuna used. More likely it is a symbol or representation of some sort; I really don't know. I guess we'll only know when we solve the entire riddle. But I *did* work out a couple of things. First, if you remember the general pattern of Manning's riddles, there were some riddles that had eight lines, and were divided into two verses of four each. Like this one.'

He referred to his notes and read aloud from them.

> *'My 1ˢᵗ is found in midst of froth*
> *Like to Venus, sea-born Queen*
> *In Venus self, excepting us*
> *By all mankind my second's seen.'*

That is verse one. Verse two is:

> *'Venus each day, when warm'd with play*
> *Is drawn by doves, for that's her rule;*
> *So is my whole drawn every day,*
> *But not till it begins to cool.'*

He looked up at them from his notes. 'This is just one example. There are more like this. So if we apply a similar rule of logic to the riddle we are trying to decipher, we can break it up into two verses based on the rhyming scheme, like in the riddle I just read out. So, the first verse, comprising the first eight lines, would read:

> *'My first is a sign of eight that kindled an empire*
> *My second where lightning struck a holy spire*
> *My third is the key where the ruler fought a duel*

My fourth where the first rests among equals
My fifth is the outpost that lay between two faiths
My whole is the weapon used to vanquish the wraiths
In the forest where the two fought the gods and the beasts
From my second to my fifth is my shaft facing east.'

Vijay shrugged. 'I could be wrong, but this is my best guess. The last line in this verse is also related to the first seven, all of which describe the weapon, which we have all guessed as Gandiva, Arjuna's bow. And it rhymes with the seventh line. That leaves the remaining four lines in the second verse:

'Be true to your faith and you will without doubt
Find the secret I hide by unearthing the key
If you see my whole, if my whole you find out
If not you're the same as you plainly will see.'

He paused, studying their faces to see their reaction.

'That is interesting,' Radha said slowly. 'Quite a bit of lateral thinking. It never occurred to us. But now that you have divided the riddle into two parts, it does seem obvious. The first verse talks about the weapon—Gandiva and its arrow. The second verse is completely unrelated. But what does it mean?'

'I have no idea,' Vijay shrugged. 'But I also managed to guess the meaning of two other lines in the first verse.'

Kolkata

India

'The reason I went to Jaungarh,' Vijay told them, 'was because I remembered that my dad had created a file where he had compiled newspaper cuttings from archaeological excavations all over India.' He looked at Radha. 'You saw the file, remember?'

'I do.' Radha recalled sitting with Vijay among the cartons and packages containing the possessions of Vijay's parents that were carefully stored in one of the upper rooms of the fort. 'So that's why you had a bee in your bonnet about going to Jaungarh. To find a clipping on Kolkata in that file.'

'I wasn't sure about it,' Vijay admitted, 'but I thought I'd take a chance. After what Van Klueck told me, I thought we'd need all the help we could get.'

'And you found something,' Radha smiled.

'Yes. I found a clipping that described the demolition of an outpost of Raja Man Singh, who was the governor of Bengal and Bihar during the rule of Akbar. Apparently, Man Singh had an outpost which stood at the location where Sealdah railway station stands today. The British called it "Man Singh's chowkey" and demolished its ruins. Apparently there wasn't much left of it anyway, and the station had to expand after its first track was laid in 1862. The article also referred to something called the Consultation of 15 November 1749, which describes Man Singh's chowkey as the outpost of the Raja.'

'The outpost that lay between two faiths!' Radha exulted, connecting the dots. 'Vijay, that's amazing. No one would ever make the connection unless they had all the clues. Which I guess is what Manning intended. But it adds up.' She was looking at the map of Kolkata on the table. 'See here. Writers' Building—the second location—to Sealdah—the fifth—is west to east.'

'I would never have guessed if it hadn't been for Dad's file,' Vijay admitted.

'Wait a minute,' Colin held out his hand. 'You're going too fast for me.'

'Aye, for me, too,' Duncan chimed in. 'I dinnae ken how you reached that conclusion.'

'Oops, sorry,' Radha smiled sheepishly. 'Let me explain. Akbar was one of the Mughal emperors who ruled India. I think this should help you connect better—he was the grandfather of Shah Jahan, who built the Taj Mahal.'

'Ah,' Colin nodded his understanding and was joined by Duncan.

'So,' Radha continued her explanation, 'Akbar was a Muslim. And Raja Man Singh was a Rajput king, the ruler of Amber—today known as Jaipur—who served under Akbar. He was a Hindu.'

'The two faiths—two religions.' Duncan understood.

'And Man Singh's chowkey was the outpost,' Colin added. 'Manning must have been the one who invented cryptic crosswords. You really have to think deeply to understand his riddles.'

'You said you'd worked out the meaning of two lines,' Radha observed.

Vijay understood the question implicit in her remark. 'Yes. I also worked out the first line. One of the books that had been referred to me at the British Museum was *Echoes from Old Calcutta*, by H.E. Busteed. By a stroke of luck, it was the first book I looked at. It had a map of Calcutta as it was in

1756-1757. When I first looked at the map, it seemed pretty useless for our purpose since it shows a large area with little detail—I guess there probably wasn't much to show at that time anyway. Luckily, I didn't discard it right away, but had it photocopied along with some of the other books that I wanted to study during the flight. Then, when I was going through the books I had photocopied and musing over the riddle, it struck me that the "empire" Manning was referring to *must* be the British Empire. Which other empire would he know of? The Mughal Empire, which was gradually disintegrating by that time? I didn't think so. As an Englishman, he would be talking about the British Empire. And we all learnt in school—or at least Radha and I did,' he looked apologetically at Colin and Duncan, 'that the foundation of what would eventually be the British Empire in India was laid in 1757, with the Battle of Plassey, in which Robert Clive defeated Siraj ud-Daula.'

'Oh, yeah, I recall *that* Indian name,' Colin said promptly. 'Radha and I came across it when we were checking out St Anne's church. He was the Nawab of Bengal.'

'That's right,' Vijay assented. 'So I first started thinking that I had to find something associated with the Battle of Plassey that fitted the description of a "sign of eight". I spent quite a while thinking about it and searching for clues, but I drew a blank.'

Radha understood where Vijay was going with this explanation. 'The riddle talks of kindling the empire. You kindle a fire using a spark. The Battle of Plassey was the first flame, if we use that metaphor. It wasn't the spark. It was decisive. The actual spark came in 1756, when Siraj ud-Daula attacked Calcutta and destroyed the church and the fort and much else. We read about it when we were researching St Anne's church.'

'Exactly.' There was now a twinkle in Vijay's eyes. 'That's what I thought. I recalled reading about it when I was reading about Warren Hastings; he was one of the Englishmen who had been taken prisoner during the assault on the East India Company's factory at Kasimbazar in 1756—just twenty-four years old at that time. And *that* was when I remembered Busteed's map of 1756-1757. I wondered if I could find any clues in it. Hang on.'

He disappeared into his room and emerged with a photocopy of a map.

'Here,' he laid it on a table so they could all see it clearly. 'What do you see?'

It was a sparse map of Kolkata, depicting the area north of the old Fort William, showing the bend in the Hooghly river—spelt Hugli—and with large open spaces marked out, with labels for locations.

There was silence as they all pored over the map.

'Can you see anything that relates to the number eight?' Vijay asked, when no one ventured any suggestions.

'Only this thing here,' Duncan peered at the map. 'Kelsall's Octagon. An octagon has eight sides.' He looked doubtful. 'But is that a sign of eight? And how does an octagon kindle anything, least of all an empire?'

Vijay grinned. 'Let me now give you some context. Another set of books that I photocopied at the British Museum was three volumes of *Bengal in 1756-1757*. And in all three volumes, guess what is repeatedly referred to as one of the reasons—or excuses, as it is presented in these books—that Siraj ud-Daula gave for his attack on Calcutta?'

'Kelsall's Octagon?' Radha guessed. 'But what was the Octagon?'

Vijay shrugged. 'A summer house built, or rather repaired or rebuilt, by a merchant called Henry Kelsall, according

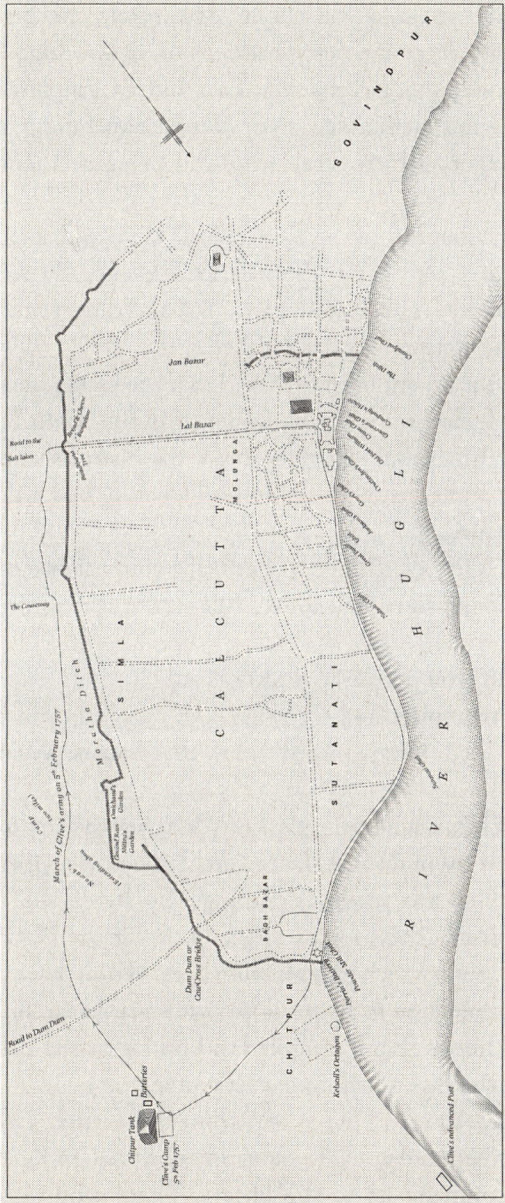

Map of Calcutta 1756–57

to the books I just told you about. Apparently, the Nawab took umbrage at some fortifications—a drawbridge and other construction works that the East India Company had undertaken—and demanded their demolition, along with Kelsall's Octagon, which Siraj ud-Daula presumed to be a fortification.'

'The spark that led to the Kasimbazar siege and then the devastation of Calcutta in 1756, leading eventually to the defeat of Siraj ud-Daula by Clive in 1757, and the start of the creation of the Empire,' Radha finished.

'Yes. There is no doubt in my mind that the Octagon is the sign of eight. It featured quite prominently in the books I read as one of the things that really got under the Nawab's skin.'

'Manning really made it hard to find what he had hidden,' Colin complained.

'That's it,' Vijay concluded. 'That's all I could figure out. I couldn't crack the third and fourth lines and the meaning of the second verse.'

'So what do you propose?' Radha asked.

'Well, I have a plan.'

Colin groaned. 'Okay. I know what that means. Work or trouble.'

Vijay shot him a withering glance. 'We have work to do.' He gestured to his room door. 'I wasn't catching up on my beauty sleep in there. I was organising things. So here's the deal. Imran's organised access for us to the books in the National Library in Alipore, which isn't far from here. We go there now, there will be someone to help us, and we start researching. I have a list of books that I compiled in London at the British Museum, on the flight, and even after coming here.'

He nodded towards the group from the Order. 'I don't think any of them are going to be of any use, though I'm sure they will accompany us to the library. That's why I asked

Duncan to join us. Between the four of us, I think we should be able to go through the books on my list and crack the riddle tonight. And then all we have to do is follow the clues.'

'You make it sound so simple,' Colin grumbled.

Duncan didn't understand. 'But it is logical.'

'You don't know him,' Colin shot back. 'Nothing he does is ever simple. I can already see us tying ourselves up in knots and getting into trouble.' He fixed Vijay with a questioning look. 'How can you be sure that we'll find our answers to the riddle in the books you've listed?'

'Because I did my research in London before catching my flight and on the way here, dumbo,' Vijay retorted. 'Trust me.'

'That's just the problem,' Colin muttered.

'What are we waiting for then?' Radha asked. 'Shouldn't we be on our way?'

Bhasha Bhawan
Belvedere Estate
Alipore, Kolkata
India

The lights blazed in the section of the library that Vijay, Radha, Colin and Duncan occupied as they browsed through the books that Sushanta Dasgupta, the friendly library staff member who had been assigned to assist them, had helped them locate and carry back to the table which they now occupied.

The rest of Bhasha Bhawan was shrouded in darkness since it was well past the library's closing time. It was here that all the books from the National Library, which had been previously housed in Belvedere House, the former residence of the governor generals of India, had been shifted in 2005.

There was complete silence in the library, even more than usual. The only sound that could be heard was the occasional rustle of paper as a page was turned.

The four of them had been at it for almost two hours. Stacks of books were piled up beside each one of them.

Vijay stared at the map in front of him, his frustration gnawing at him. He had been so confident that they would find what they were looking for.

But so far, none of them had made a breakthrough.

Dee and her men were around and about. Vijay had explained to Dasgupta that they were part of their security detail. Since the library was closed and they had been conferred VIP status, there had been no metal detector checks, so Dee's men had been able to carry their guns in with them.

Vijay shuddered to think of the consequences if they—no, he—failed to deliver on his commitment to Van Klueck. The man would not hesitate to let Dee loose on them. It was a grim prospect and not one that he wanted to dwell upon.

He turned his attention back to the book he was perusing, willing something to happen.

But another half an hour was to pass before Colin whispered his discovery.

'I found something!'

The other three looked up from their books, immediately hopeful.

'According to this book, *Rulers of India* by Captain L.J. Trotter, Philip Francis, a councillor appointed by the East India Company in 1774, challenged Warren Hastings to a duel in 1780 because Hastings had said something about Francis's behaviour being "void of truth and honour". I'm guessing that Hastings is the ruler mentioned in the third line of the riddle. And the place where the duel was fought,' his voice betrayed his excitement, 'is this very place where we are sitting! Belvedere Estate! This place is the third location!'

Vijay frowned. 'Sound logical all right,' he agreed. 'But what about the key mentioned in the line?'

Colin shrugged. 'I don't know. Could it be something Manning put in to throw people off the trail?'

Vijay looked uncertain. 'Let's keep it as a potential candidate for now,' he suggested. 'We'll revisit all our options later and see if they make sense.'

Duncan spoke up. 'You know, I've been thinking about the fourth line. It is very ambiguous. But I did have an idea which might help us narrow it down a bit. Of course, I'm not sure if I'm right or not, but you can tell me what you think.'

'Go ahead, shoot,' Vijay replied. 'We're all in the same boat. We're all guessing.'

'Well, call me morbid,' Duncan mused. 'But I can't get it out of my head that the fourth line refers to a graveyard.'

'A graveyard?' Colin gaped. 'What makes you think that?'

'Well,' Duncan hesitated, then decided to go ahead with his explanation. 'Everyone in a cemetery is equal, right? They're all dead; rich or poor, commoner or king; death is a leveller. And the word "rests", I thought, is what indicates a graveyard as well. That's the one place where we all eventually rest, don't we?'

'Not if you're Hindu,' Vijay told him. 'We cremate our dead. And there's no rest for us—the soul undergoes a cycle of rebirths based on our deeds in the last birth. The phrase "rest in peace" is Christian.'

'Aye, that may be right,' Duncan agreed, 'but Manning was a Christian and he would have been thinking like one. I'm also inclined to think that there is a hint about this in the first line of the second verse. "Be true to your faith", he says. What's *his* faith? And what if he assumed this riddle would be read by Englishmen and no one else? We've seen before that he's used the word "faith" to indicate religion, when he talked about the Hindu king and the Muslim emperor. So, it wasn't used just to rhyme with "wraiths". This guy is canny. He hasn't used random words even to complete a rhyme. There is a meaning in each word of the riddle. I think we will find our fourth clue in a graveyard in this city.'

Radha regarded him with a new respect. She hadn't seen this side of Duncan until now. Clearly, the operative was as brainy as the other members of GTF. 'Let's look for a graveyard then.' She was convinced. 'Kolkata must have quite a few Christian graveyards, but there can't be many that are two hundred years old.'

A new rush of exhilaration seemed to sweep through the room as they turned back to their books to find what was, hopefully, the last clue that would point them in the direction of Manning's secret.

Bhasha Bhawan

Belvedere Estate

Alipore, Kolkata, India

'I think I've got it!' Radha cried.

More than an hour had passed since they had decided to find a graveyard in Kolkata that fit the riddle. They had focused on looking for mentions of old Kolkata's cemeteries in the books they were now reading.

No words had been exchanged ever since.

Dasgupta had come around and placed bottles of packaged drinking water for them, which they accepted gratefully.

Apart from that, there had been silence. And more reading. Until now.

'Spill it,' Colin told her jovially.

'I think it is the South Park Street Cemetery,' Radha told them. 'It was referred to as the Great Burial Ground. It was opened in 1767 and was active at the time Manning was in Kolkata and met Fischer. According to this book, there are burials there going all the way up to 1837.' She looked at Duncan. 'I think you were spot on with this.'

'Why the South Park Street Cemetery?' Vijay asked. 'According to the book that I'm reading, which lists inscriptions on tombstones and monuments in Bengal, there were quite a few Christian cemeteries operational at that time. The North Park Street Cemetery, for one. Then there was the Tiretta Cemetery. Okay, no, that was a French cemetery, so he couldn't have been referring to that. There's Mission Cemetery; the graveyard at St John's Church—the old cathedral; St John's churchyard—funny, I can't seem to make out the difference between the two, but they've been separately listed—which were also functional during Manning's time in Kolkata after Tibet. There are probably more; I'd need to go through this list to be sure which ones were operational in 1811, when Manning returned to Kolkata from Tibet.'

'I'll tell you why.' There was a gleam in Radha's eyes as she spoke. 'As Duncan said, "rests among equals" signifies a graveyard. I think we all agree on that. That leaves us with the "first" who rests there. Someone buried in that graveyard. But why use the word "first"? What does it signify?'

She looked around, but found only blank faces.

'Okay, so here's how I figure it,' she continued. 'It struck me that Manning himself was a "first"—the first Englishman to visit Lhasa and meet the Dalai Lama. Could that have been at the back of his mind while he was composing his riddle? I mean, wouldn't that naturally have occurred to him and set the context for this line? So if you take that reasoning to its logical conclusion, who else could be a first in that context?'

Vijay had been glancing at his book and flipping through the pages while Radha spoke. Now, he looked up, his face bright, and jabbed a finger at the page before him. 'George Bogle!' he exulted. 'He was the first Englishman to visit Tibet. And he is buried in the South Park Street Cemetery!'

Dee, who had been aimlessly loitering around the rows of bookshelves, heard his raised voice and came over to investigate.

'Exactly. I had come across a reference to Bogle's tomb in another book I read earlier, which spoke of his death, possibly due to cholera, and his burial there. The facts fit, don't they?' Radha glanced at Colin and Duncan to gauge their reactions.

'Sounds plausible,' Colin agreed and Duncan concurred as well.

'Well, then,' Duncan said, 'we've got all five lines then; all five locations, if our initial assumption was correct. Now what? Where's the bow?'

'You've found it?' Dee enquired, a trifle impatiently. She was getting tired of hanging around doing nothing. It was not in her nature to chaperone people. She was an expert operative of the Order and a skilled assassin, and preferred to carry out covert operations, direct missions for the Order, and kill anyone who got in the way. She was getting restless now. Nothing seemed to be moving. All that seemed to be happening were endless discussions.

'I think so,' Vijay's voice rose slightly in pitch with his excitement. 'I think I know where the secret is buried.'

'Buried?' Radha frowned. 'What do you mean?'

'Look at the second line of the second verse,' Vijay told her. 'It's the tenth line of the entire riddle. It says you can find the secret by unearthing the key. What does "unearthing" mean?'

'Ah,' Colin saw the point Vijay was making. 'You mean dig up the earth, right? To get at something that is buried underground.'

'Correct.' Vijay wagged a finger at him. 'What this could mean is that the secret is buried in the South Park Street Cemetery!'

Dee's face brightened. Finally it looked as though there was something to do other than skulk around while these four discussed and debated the riddle.

'Where in the cemetery?' she wanted to know.

'I don't know about this,' Radha said doubtfully. 'What about the last two lines then? Where do they come in? And what about the Gandiva? I thought we had all agreed that the "whole" that Manning refers to is Arjuna's bow? Shouldn't we be looking for that?'

'I don't know about the last two lines,' Vijay admitted, 'and it could be that the bow itself is hidden in the cemetery and will yield another clue when we find it.' He shrugged. 'But look at this. Manning buried another clue in this line, which makes it obvious now that we've identified the graveyard. He says: "find the secret I hide". He looked around the group. 'Would you believe that there is a John Hyde buried in the South Park Street Cemetery? Could Manning and Fischer have hidden it in John Hyde's grave, which dates to 1796?'

DAY EIGHT

October 28
South Park Street Cemetery
Park Street, Kolkata, India

Vijay and Dee watched as Dee's men worked by torchlight on digging a channel without destabilising the massive monument that towered above them.

The tomb was imposing. It was built on a raised, cube-shaped plinth, with four principal faces topped by pediments and four thin, rectangular, two-faced pillars set between the principal faces, giving the edifice multiple corners and edges and the appearance of steps between one face and the next. Above the pediments, a narrow pyramid soared into a tree whose branches had grown around it like protective hands around a child.

Its black tombstone was split in half, dividing the long inscription on it into two unequal parts.

'You had better be right about this,' Dee warned Vijay. 'I'm not going back empty-handed.'

'Don't worry,' Vijay reassured her. 'I am confident that this is it.'

It had been a couple of hours since they had arrived at the cemetery. The first thing that Dee's goons had done on breaking into the cemetery was to swiftly despatch the gardeners who tended to the upkeep of the cemetery and its flora, and their families, who lived within the walls of the graveyard.

John Hyde's Tomb

No survivors. No witnesses. That was the motto of the Order.

That problem having been taken care of, they turned their attention to finding space around the monument, which had tombs on three sides, just a few feet away. The idea was to avoid weakening the foundations of the monument by digging some distance away rather than directly under the monument.

They had eventually settled on using the open space behind the tomb, which would provide enough room for both the furrow as well as the effort of digging it. They would need to skirt a few trees that stood there, and a large pile of freshly cut wood that lay in the clearing, but this was a minor inconvenience.

In the time since their arrival, they had excavated a deep furrow that led under the monument, minimising the surface area of the monument that would lose support in case there was no vault beneath it, but just an open grave. But given the shape and size of the edifice, it was reasonable to expect that there would be a solid foundation in the form of an underground vault in which John Hyde would have been laid to rest. This assumption also fit with the expectation that something had been hidden there; it would have been far easier to hide something in a vault than in a small grave.

The men were at the monument now, digging slowly and carefully at the earth packed around it.

There was a clunk as one of the shovels hit something solid.

Dee and Vijay approached the men, treading carefully, and shone their torches into the narrow furrow.

Ancient bricks were revealed in the light, exposed where the men had dug the earth away from them.

'It's a vault,' Vijay's voice was triumphant. He had been correct.

The men got to work, carefully dismantling the wall of the vault, putting solid timbers in place to ensure that the support provided by the wall to the monument above remained intact.

Slowly, painstakingly, they created a hole in the wall.

Finally the hole was big enough for a person to squeeze through.

Dee indicated the entrance to the vault that had been created. 'In there,' she commanded Vijay. 'Tell us what you find.'

Alipore, Kolkata
India

Radha had an uncomfortable feeling. Despite Vijay's confidence in his conclusions and the forcefulness of his arguments, she had deep misgivings.

'We're on the wrong trail,' she had argued at Bhasha Bhawan. 'I cannot believe that Manning and Fischer did something as egregious as breaking into a tomb to conceal something from the world. It is impossible.'

'Why is it impossible?' Vijay had demanded. 'The value of what they were seeking to hide was so great, even if they had no clue about its true nature, that they would have gone to any lengths to conceal it.'

'What about the Gandiva?' Radha had countered, unconvinced. 'Shouldn't we have found some trace of it, if not a reference, after deciphering all five clues hidden in the first verse? Since we haven't, either we have goofed up while solving the riddle, or if we have, indeed, solved it correctly, we're missing something.' Her voice was firm. 'And what about the last two lines of the riddle? Surely they must mean something? I refuse to believe they are there "just because".'

'I am confident my reasoning is correct.' Vijay had stood his ground. 'We'll probably find the weapon buried under John Hyde's tombstone.'

'What do you guys think?' Radha had turned to Colin and Duncan.

But the two non-Indians saw merit in both arguments and, being unfamiliar with the country and the history, they felt that Vijay and Radha were better placed to figure things out.

After much discussion, Dee had intervened, irritated by the arguing, and decided that Vijay would accompany her and some of her men to the cemetery where they would dig up John Hyde's grave.

Accordingly, Dee and her men, with Vijay, headed off to the cemetery, after picking up shovels and timber to support the digging, the Order having made arrangements using their connections in the city. Dee could have recruited more men for the operation, but Van Klueck had been very clear that none of the Order's associates should get even a whiff of what was being planned. Given the historical and mythological context of what they were seeking, this would have been akin to the Holy Grail for the local associates of the Order, and Van Klueck didn't want to take any risks. Dee, on her part, didn't think that she required additional muscle either; with the guns and brawn she had at her disposal—not to mention her own skills in a skirmish—she feared nothing.

Now, as Radha sat in the safe house of the Order, her head swam with all kinds of possibilities that might ensue if Vijay was wrong.

Dee was feared within the Order for her temper. She knew she was privileged by virtue of her bloodline, and that made her arrogant and supercilious. And when she was angry, she lost all capacity for reasoning. Her logical faculties were hijacked by a deep-rooted desire to lash out at people around her.

Vijay was a soft target.

Without thinking, Radha picked up Vijay's iPad, which was lying on the table. He had loaned it to her, since she didn't have a device of her own, having left everything behind at the Order when she fled.

With nothing to do but wait, Radha started mapping the five locations they had discovered in the riddle.

Kelsall's Octagon in Chitpur. Writers' Building. Sealdah railway station. Belvedere House. South Park Street Cemetery.

Why hadn't they found the bow?

She looked at the pins that marked the five locations on the map. There was nothing extraordinary about them. The only thing she could see was that the locations spanned all four directions of the city.

She opened up the photograph of John Hyde's tomb, which they had earlier downloaded from the internet, and gazed at it. While it was architecturally elaborate, there was nothing remarkable about it; a grey monument from a time long past, strangely unaffected by the ubiquitous green moss that grew on almost all the other monuments they had seen in photographs while searching for Hyde's tomb.

Radha inclined her head to one side as she studied the photograph, which had been taken from an angle. Behind the tomb, and off to its right as she viewed it, rose two more large pyramids, one almost black with age, and the other pristine white. The white pyramid was the tomb of William Jones, the founder of the Asiatic Society. According to the sites they had browsed, it had been restored by the Asiatic Society. There were two smaller pyramid-capped tombs, between Hyde's tomb and the two large pyramids, and a tomb with a moss-

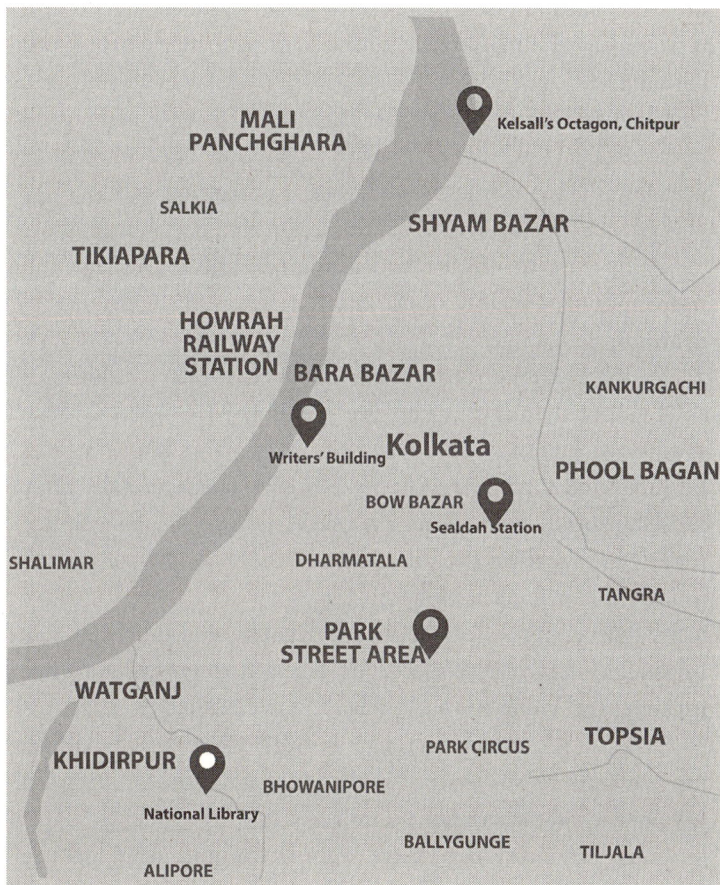

MALI PANCHGHARA

Kelsall's Octagon, Chitpur

SALKIA

SHYAM BAZAR

TIKIAPARA

HOWRAH RAILWAY STATION

BARA BAZAR

KANKURGACHI

Writers' Building

Kolkata

PHOOL BAGAN

BOW BAZAR

Sealdah Station

SHALIMAR

DHARMATALA

TANGRA

PARK STREET AREA

WATGANJ

PARK CIRCUS

TOPSIA

KHIDIRPUR

BHOWANIPORE

National Library

BALLYGUNGE

TILJALA

ALIPORE

infested dome that appeared in the photograph, just in front of the inscription-bearing face of Hyde's tomb.

For the life of her, she couldn't figure out why John Hyde's tomb would have been chosen to hide the secret. It still didn't make sense to her. Something had been nagging away at her, but she couldn't put a finger on what it was. She sighed and returned to the map with the five locations marked out and stared at it.

Maybe Vijay was right after all. He usually was. His logical mind and analytical skills made him good at working out puzzles, like the riddle they had been confronted with.

'Would you believe it?' Colin interrupted her thoughts.

With time to kill, he had immersed himself in learning more about the history of the city that featured so remarkably in Manning's riddle.

Radha looked up from the iPad. 'What?'

'I've been reading up on the history of Belvedere House ever since I read about it in the library. You know, an old building and stuff like that. I was interested, especially after learning about the duel. So I've been checking on the internet for any information about Belvedere House. And guess what I found? It is really amazing.'

'What did you find, Colin?' Radha couldn't keep the impatience out of her voice. She wanted to get back to her musings and work out exactly what was troubling her.

Colin realised that she was worried about Vijay. All the more reason to share what he had found with her. It would take her mind off worrying about Vijay.

'You remember that there were three guys who hid the secret, according to Humboldt's letter to his brother in 1818. We've been talking only about Fischer and Manning, but there was also this guy,' he looked at his laptop screen, 'John Brereton Birch.'

Radha nodded, remembering Duncan's exposition of the letter. What Colin said was true. All this while, they had talked about two men hiding the secret, when in reality, there had been three.

'Well, this is what blew my mind,' Colin told her. 'Believe it or not, John Brereton Birch also lived in Belvedere House! He bought it in 1810 and lived there until 1824, when he sold it to ... to ... an Indian guy whose name I can't pronounce. Here.' He showed the laptop screen to Radha.

'Shambhu Chander Mukherjee,' Radha read the name aloud.

'Yup. That's the guy.' Colin took the laptop back and shook his head. 'Can you believe it?'

But Radha had frozen like she had been struck by lightning. She was staring at the iPad screen like it was something she had never seen before.

'Hey, you okay?' Colin asked, concerned.

Radha unfroze. 'Yes ... yes, I'm fine,' she muttered. 'Give me a minute please.'

Colin sat back and looked at her, his forehead creased with worry. Had her stress affected her somehow?

Then she smiled, and he heaved a sigh of relief.

'Oh wow,' he said. 'Never thought I'd be so happy to see you smile.'

But her smile disappeared as quickly as it had appeared.

'We have no time to lose,' Radha said. 'Vijay is in danger.'

'With Dee around, we're all in danger,' Colin tried to comfort her. 'Not just Vijay.'

'You don't understand,' Radha said. 'He's wrong about John Hyde and the tomb. There's nothing buried there.'

South Park Street Cemetery
Park Street, Kolkata, India

Vijay fashioned his handkerchief into a mask and knotted it behind his head. He was about to step into a small room that had been sealed for more than two hundred years with a corpse inside it. The air would not be breathable, even if nothing remained of John Hyde's body after the passage of the centuries.

He jumped into the furrow as Dee's men clambered out to give him space. There was room for only one person to stand in it.

'I'm waiting for a couple of minutes for the air to circulate inside.' His voice was muffled by the handkerchief as he spoke to Dee.

Dee repressed her urge to get on with it, recognising the danger inside the vault, and nodded her assent. She needed Vijay alive.

For now.

After waiting for a few minutes, Vijay took a deep breath—he had no idea why, but it felt like he was about to dive into something that would not allow him to breathe—and entered the vault.

He shone his torch. It was a small room, smaller than he had imagined, with Hyde's rotting and almost disintegrated coffin placed in the centre on a raised platform of bricks. There was barely any place to move around the sides of the casket.

But what really took the wind out of his sails was the obvious fact that, apart from the coffin, there was nothing else inside the vault.

Vijay shone the torch around on the walls, the floor and the casket, desperately hoping to find some sign of the bow, or anything that could point to the fact that he had found what he had come here for.

But there was nothing.

He could not believe for a minute that Manning and Fischer would have desecrated the coffin by placing something inside it. He had been prepared to buy the argument that they had broken in to hide the secret in the vault where it would be safe. But no more than that.

Despite his misgivings, he flashed the torch onto the crumbling coffin. It was virtually empty. Most of John Hyde's body had long turned to dust, leaving only a few bones and what looked like teeth scattered on the floor of the coffin.

Now as he looked around, he had to admit it.

He had been wrong.

There was nothing hidden here.

And he knew how Dee would feel about that.

Alipore, Kolkata
India

Duncan sat bolt upright. He had been lounging in a chair, half asleep, when he heard Radha's words.

He was instantly awake. 'Are you sure, lassie?'

Radha nodded. 'Hey!' She called to the lone guard who stood in one corner, a bored expression on his face. He was upset about being given the job of babysitting these three. Dee had left one single guard to keep an eye on them, confident that the three of them would not attempt anything foolish as long as she held Vijay hostage. She knew that Radha would not do anything to risk Vijay's safety.

'What?' the guard demanded. 'If you want anything, wait till Dee comes. I ain't doing nothing till then.'

Radha sighed. 'I just got a message from Dee. Fine, if you don't want to see it, we'll just wait for Dee to return. You can be the one to tell her that you refused to read her message.'

The guard's expression changed from indifference to fear. 'What does she say?'

Radha got up and walked over to him with her phone, fiddling with it. 'Take a look for yourself.'

She handed her phone to the guard.

'Hey, there's nothing ...' the man began after taking the phone from her and looking at the screen, but he was unable to complete his sentence.

Catching him off guard, Radha punched him twice in the face, breaking his nose, then whirled around and delivered a roundhouse kick to his temple, knocking him out instantly.

The man slumped to the floor, blood flowing from his broken nose.

Radha picked up his assault rifle and threw it to Duncan. 'All yours. Let's go before it is too late.'

She knew only too well what Dee would do when she learnt there was nothing hidden in the cemetery.

South Park Street Cemetery
Park Street, Kolkata, India

'Well?' Dee called to Vijay. 'What did you find?'

Vijay poked his head out of the vault. He didn't know how to break it to Dee. 'I ... I don't know ...' he stumbled over his words.

'Don't tell me there's nothing in there.' Dee's voice could have sliced through steel.

A numb feeling took hold of Vijay. He shook his head.

Dee sighed. 'Come on out, then.'

Vijay couldn't believe his ears. He hadn't expected her to be so understanding. He had expected all hell to break loose.

'Get him out of there,' Dee commanded her men, who helped Vijay out of the furrow they had created.

It was only when they did not let go of him but walked him to Dee, his arms pinned behind his back, that he realised her cool demeanour was just a facade. Beneath it, she was a seething cauldron of hate and fury.

Her next words confirmed this. 'Of what use are you if you cannot deliver on your commitment?' Her voice was low, but her rage was palpable. 'You made a promise to Christian. And you have failed. If I have to go back empty-handed to face Christian and the Order, then so be it. But you're not getting off so easy.'

Dee's eyes bore into him. 'The last time we met, you tried to kill me. And the mistake I made was leaving before I was sure you were dead. I don't know how you managed to escape and survive, but I'm not going to repeat that blunder this time.'

Vijay's heart sank, but he inwardly steeled himself for the bullets that he was sure had been reserved for him. His only regret was that he had not had time to spend with Radha after getting her back.

To his surprise however, at a gesture from Dee, the men holding him wrestled him to the ground, face down.

Two of them began tying his feet together and the other two bound his wrists behind his back.

Vijay struggled to break free of their grasp, but the men were big and strong and with grips like iron bands.

Once they were done, Dee knelt as he lay prone, trussed up and unable to move a muscle.

'Goodbye, Vijay.' There was a note of grim amusement in her voice. 'Let's see you get out of this one, Houdini.'

Dee gestured to her men and they picked Vijay up and began dragging him back to the furrow. Towards the vault.

Vijay realised what they were going to do. Dee was going to finish what she had left incomplete the last time. She had probably planned this earlier and had intended to go ahead with it even if they had found something in the tomb.

They half dragged, half carried Vijay into the furrow and heaved him through the hole in the tomb wall into the vault. One of his shoulders hit one edge of the brick platform on which John Hyde's coffin rested, sending a bolt of pain shooting through his neck and back, and he landed heavily on the floor.

Without the torch, it was dark inside. Just a glimmer of light seeped in from the torches held by the men who stood outside.

Slowly, even that dim glow faded as the men bricked up the tomb again.

Darkness fell inside the vault.

Vijay struggled against his bonds, but the men had done a good job. The cords cut into his wrists and ankles but remained as fast as ever.

There was absolutely nothing he could do, immobilised as he was.

And even if he wasn't, how on earth could he get out of a place as secure as this? He was certain the men would replace the earth they had excavated, covering the furrow and the portion of the vault that they had exposed and burying the vault once more.

He fought the despair and panic that hovered at the fringes of his mind. But no matter what he did, the certainty of one thing was clear.

There was no way to get out of this vault.

John Hyde's tomb would now also be Vijay's tomb.

Kolkata
India

Radha drove like a maniac through the deserted streets, grim determination on her face. Colin and Duncan were stony-faced as well.

After knocking out the guard, they had searched him for the keys to the second SUV that the Order had used to transport the team around Kolkata. Radha had grabbed his torch as well since they would need something to light their way in the cemetery.

They had then commandeered the vehicle which Radha had insisted on driving. She could only hope that they were not too late. She was sure that Dee would kill Vijay in her anger and frustration at not finding what they were looking for.

The car screeched to a halt at the gates of the cemetery.

It was dark and silent.

Dee's men had picked the locks on the two sets of gates and they were still open. But there was no sign of the SUV that had taken Vijay and Dee to the cemetery. It was unlikely that the SUV would have been driven into the colonnaded portico through which the cemetery was accessed.

Radha's heart sank.

She raced through the gates, Colin and Duncan close on her heels, and into the dark cemetery which was clearly deserted. They stopped at the portico and looked around.

Three paths diverged from there and into the cemetery. One led straight ahead and the other two were at right angles to this path, leading off to the left and the right.

Radha glanced at her companions, her face betraying her despair. Two glum faces stared back at her. They were thinking the same thing.

This was a large cemetery, with more than one thousand five hundred tombs. It would be easier for them if they could split up. But they had only one torch between them, and a pall of darkness hung over the tombs.

Radha sprinted down the path to their right, which had been cemented at one time, but was worn out with the passage of time and feet. The two men followed close on her heels.

Suddenly, she stopped short, numb at the sight that greeted her eyes.

Bodies lay across the path, their arms outstretched, contorted, blood pooling in the crevices of the track where the cement had worn away. Men, women and children; no one had been spared.

Colin gave voice to their shock. 'They've been shot. Looks like a couple of families.' He couldn't keep the horror out of his voice.

Radha grimly pursed her lips. This had to be Dee's doing.

She thought for a moment. These people had been killed to eliminate all witnesses and to prevent anyone from raising an alarm. But, while Dee would have ordered their executions, she would have considered the dead to be too insignificant to have spent any time here.

No, these people would have been killed by Dee's men.

Which meant that Dee would have been occupied elsewhere.

Radha flashed her torch around, illuminating the tombs on their left and the boundary wall on her right.

She immediately turned back towards the portico and raced back to the entrance. Colin and Duncan followed her without hesitation.

This was not the time to ask questions.

Radha knew where she wanted to go. Without missing a step, she dashed through the portico and sped down the path that led straight ahead from the entrance gate.

And stopped. She had reached a crossroads.

Radha swung her torch helplessly, trying to illuminate the three paths that branched off before her, at right angles to each other, from the path where she stood.

Which one should she take?

Alipore
Kolkata, India

Dee stood and listened, her frustration mounting, as Van Klueck responded to the report she had just given him.

After leaving the cemetery, she had rushed back to the safe house with her men. Even if the Order's mission had not succeeded, she was determined to fulfil her mission to kill Radha.

But Radha and her two companions were missing from the safe house when she arrived to find the guard lying unconscious and bleeding from his broken nose.

Dee had smirked. Though she had no way of knowing that Radha had realised that Hyde's tomb hid no secret, Dee had guessed that Radha had gone to the cemetery. She put it down to a misguided attempt by Radha to turn the tables on the Order.

No matter.

She would return to the cemetery and ensure that Radha died in the same place as Vijay. How appropriate, Dee chuckled to herself, that it would be in a cemetery that both met their end.

Just as she was about to leave the safe house, however, Van Klueck, impatient for an update, had called.

And Dee had had to bring him up to speed on what had happened.

To her great surprise, Van Klueck had not sounded angry, or even upset. He seemed to have taken the bad news with composure.

'It doesn't matter,' he had told her. 'Vijay was not our only hope to find the secret. He was our best hope to get there earlier than we had expected. There was anyway no guarantee that he would succeed. It was a chance we took. A worthwhile chance, but a chance nevertheless. But we have other irons in the fire. It is just a matter of time now.'

But it was what he was now saying in response that was a blow to her plans to terminate Radha.

'You must return to London immediately.' Van Klueck's tone made it clear that he would brook no argument. 'If there is an organisation backing them, as we suspect, they will come after you. And they know the location of the safe house. Get out of there right now. Cover your tracks. No one should know what happened at the cemetery. And I don't want you going after Radha.' Van Klueck knew Dee only too well.

'Christian,' Dee couldn't help herself. 'No. You promised me.'

'We are racing against time on this project and there's work to do. This isn't the time to be running around carrying out petty personal vendettas,' came the brusque response. 'The purpose of the Order is more important.' Van Klueck paused. 'Unless you believe otherwise, of course.'

Dee bit back a sharp retort. She would not rise to the bait. 'Of course not, Christian. You are right. The Order is more important. I'll see you in London.'

Radha may have escaped her fate today.

But for how long would she be able to elude it?

South Park Street Cemetery
Park Street, Kolkata, India

Radha forced herself to calm down, to suppress the waves of panic that crashed against each other in her mind, amplifying her anxiety. She closed her eyes and took a deep breath, slowing her breathing, stilling her thoughts. She had to think straight, think clearly.

Even as Radha struggled with her decision of which road to take, Colin and Duncan strained to pick up the sound of digging or breaking, which would tell them where Dee and her men were.

If they were still here.

But the silence that enveloped the cemetery was deeper and darker than the night.

Had Dee left this place? Had she achieved what she had set out to do? Had she found what they were searching for?

But neither Colin nor Duncan, like Radha, could contemplate calling off the search for John Hyde's tomb.

If Radha was correct, then Dee would have found nothing. She would have vented her frustration and rage on Vijay.

Their biggest fear was that Dee had indulged in her favourite pastime of bloodletting before killing Vijay.

Radha had told them what Dee was capable of. And she was certain in her mind that Dee would not have left the cemetery with Vijay alive. The fact that she and her men were missing meant that they had dug into Hyde's tomb and discovered Vijay's error, and were now gone.

Vijay had to be here. In the cemetery.

They could only hope that they would find him alive and in time to save his life.

They were walking a razor's edge and running out of time.

'This way,' Radha said, her voice interrupting the thoughts of the two men. She had reached a conclusion. And lost precious seconds in the process.

'Why are you shining your torch on the treetops?' Colin wanted to know.

All this time, Radha had been focusing the light of the torch on the ground or on the tombstones around them.

Now, as they ran down the path that led straight ahead, she was directing the light above their heads, illuminating the upper branches of the trees around them.

'The reason I decided to abandon the first path we took, where we found the bodies,' she explained, 'was because it ran along the wall that adjoins Park Street. I recalled what I had seen in the photograph of Hyde's tomb and there was no wall in sight. Which is also why I didn't choose the other path that also runs along the wall. This is the only path that doesn't run along a wall. And when we reached the crossroads, I realised that we are never going to find a pyramid by shining the torch downwards. Hyde's pyramid is on top of a plinth that looked pretty high in the photograph—probably seven feet or so above the ground.'

'Aye, lassie,' Duncan agreed. 'Better to shine the light where we can see the pyramid then.'

'Not that it helps,' Colin complained. 'There are so many tombs here that are topped by pyramids. It's like looking for a needle in a haystack.'

'That's the other reason,' Radha continued. 'In the photograph, I remembered seeing two large pyramids behind and off to the side of John Hyde's tomb. One was white, probably the tomb of William Jones. The other was dark grey, almost black. I'm betting that there's only one pure white pyramid in this entire cemetery, because none of the other tombs look, in the least, like they have been restored.'

'If we find that white pyramid, we find John Hyde's tomb!' Colin finished her train of thought.

'Exactly.' Radha quickened her pace, then stopped again. They had reached another path, this one perpendicular to the track they had followed until now. Beyond the perpendicular path was another row of tombs, with an open space that stretched into the darkness.

But there was no white pyramid in sight.

Time was running out.

Radha turned and sprinted back in the direction of the gates. 'Doesn't seem right,' she muttered, but she knew that she was only acting on instinct.

They reached the crossroads again, and this time Radha turned left, the light from the torch piercing the darkness, lighting up the green-topped slabs, domes and pyramids around them.

They were all hoping that a white pyramid would suddenly appear.

It was Duncan who spotted it.

'There!'

Off to their left, an enormous pyramid soared towards the sky, glittering white in the light of the torch.

Radha sucked in her breath. A second almost equally large pyramid stood next to it, blackened with age.

She swung the light of the torch onto the path.

A track leading off the path they were on came into view, paved with red tiles.

Without breaking stride, the three of them raced onto the tiled path and past the white pyramid. There was no time to stop and gape in awe at this marvellous monument.

They passed the black pyramid, then another tomb capped by a dome on their right and a large decorated plinth on their left and came upon a clearing that was overgrown with weeds, grass and shrubs and a scattering of trees. To one side of the clearing was a half-ruined tomb, and a circular domed tomb with rectangular arches.

A large pile of wood lay almost in the centre of the clearing.

Radha swung her torch to the left of the clearing and her heart skipped a beat.

Standing next to two small tombs with mini-pyramid caps, black with age and green with moss, was a solemn grey structure, with pediments topping the faces at the foot of a narrow pyramid that rose into the branches of the trees around it.

The tomb of John Hyde.

With a cry, she rushed towards the tomb, flashing her torch on the ground.

If she knew Dee, Vijay would have been left to bleed to death on the ground.

They scoured the clearing and the ground around the tomb, Radha's heart quickening at the thought of finding Vijay.

But there was nothing there. No Vijay. No blood either.

The ground around one corner of the tomb looked like it had been recently cleared, dug and refilled, and four shovels were still lying there, left by the labourers who had done the digging—perhaps a fresh grave that had yet to get a slab put over it to mark the burial. But apart from that, nothing seemed to have disturbed the peace and tranquillity of this cemetery.

'Where is Vijay?' Colin's voice was despondent. 'There's no one here.'

Radha desperately shone her torch around the monument, scouring the ground, hoping to find some trace of Vijay, some clue to where he could be.

Had Dee killed Vijay and taken his body with her?

Radha pushed the horrid thought away and tried to think positively.

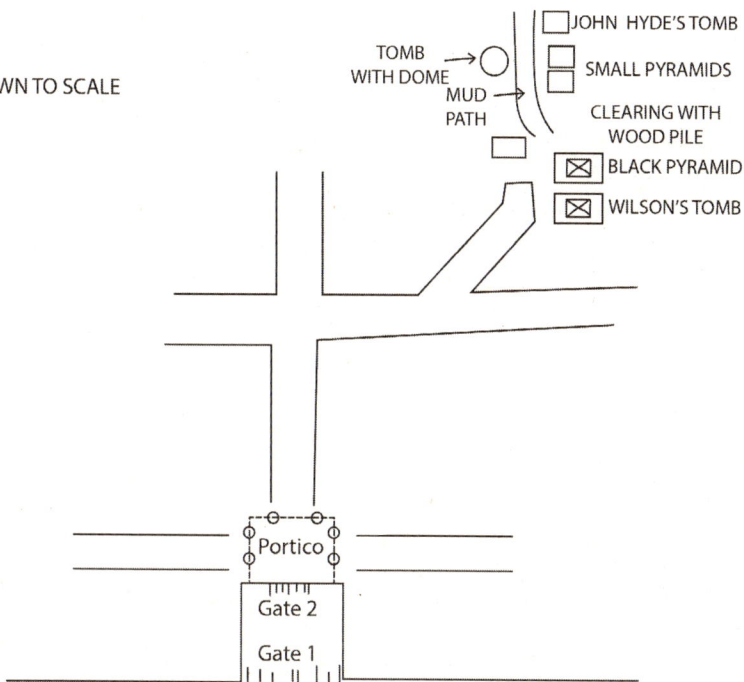

*NOT DRAWN TO SCALE

JOHN HYDE'S TOMB

TOMB WITH DOME

SMALL PYRAMIDS

MUD PATH

CLEARING WITH WOOD PILE

BLACK PYRAMID

WILSON'S TOMB

Portico

Gate 2

Gate 1

Rough map/layout of South Park Street Cemetery showing areas covered by Radha, Colin and Duncan

Then it struck her.

No one had been buried in this cemetery for close to a hundred years.

So why was the ground dug up?

And why had a trail been cleared in the open space behind the tomb, snaking back almost to the half-ruined tomb they had passed on the way?

She suddenly realised that the rest of the cemetery, indeed, the rest of this very clearing, was overgrown with weeds and shrubs and had dead branches and twigs in a thick carpet on the ground.

Unlike the trail behind the tomb.

Her voice caught in her throat as realisation dawned on her.

No!

It couldn't be.

London

UK

Imran listened with horror as Radha described how Colin, Duncan and she had exerted themselves to excavate the underground vault in which John Hyde was buried, and extricated Vijay from there.

Fortunately for Vijay, he hadn't been buried alive for too long. Even then, confined in the small space of the tomb, he had lost consciousness and had required hospitalisation.

'But he'll be okay,' Radha told Imran happily. 'The doctors say he'll need a few days in hospital to recover. But otherwise, he's fine.'

'Thank God for that!' Imran was truly grateful for Vijay's narrow shave. His voice had taken on a gloomier tone. 'I sent a team to the address you messaged me, but there was no one there. I suspect Dee and her team flew the coop once they reached the safe house and discovered that you had escaped.'

At the cemetery, Radha's first priority had been to dig Vijay out once she realised what Dee had done. But she had also wanted to apprehend Dee before she vanished into thin air. While Colin and Duncan had busied themselves with excavating the vault, she had messaged Imran the location of the house where they had been held, before joining them in digging Vijay out.

But she knew they would never find Dee now. The Order would have spirited her away.

Radha sighed. But there was one silver lining. She knew where the secret was hidden.

London
UK

'Are you sure about this?' Imran asked.

'Yes.' Radha's face on the monitor radiated confidence. 'See this.'

Her face disappeared and a map of Kolkata filled the screen. On the map were five location pins marking the places that had been concealed in the riddle.

'We know,' Radha explained, 'that we have to find a weapon—a bow—and since Manning also talks about a shaft facing east—an arrow. Why haven't we found it yet? Because we were looking in the wrong place. We missed the meaning of Manning's line: "my whole is the weapon". What is the "whole"? We thought the whole weapon would be found in John Hyde's tomb. But what if the "whole" refers to the five locations we have identified? When I was looking at the map on the iPad, I suddenly saw it. And here it is. The bow of Arjuna. The weapon used to vanquish the wraiths.'

Lines appeared on the map connecting the five locations.

'And this could also explain the last two lines of the riddle,' Radha finished. 'We thought they were redundant, but this assumption contradicted the kind of riddles in Manning's notes. What if the final two lines were Manning's way of giving us a means to validate that we had correctly deciphered the first five lines of the riddle and identified the locations he was alluding to? If you "see the whole" and find out the whole, you unearth the secret. If not, you're the same as you were before you tried to crack the riddle—clueless, "as you plainly will see".'

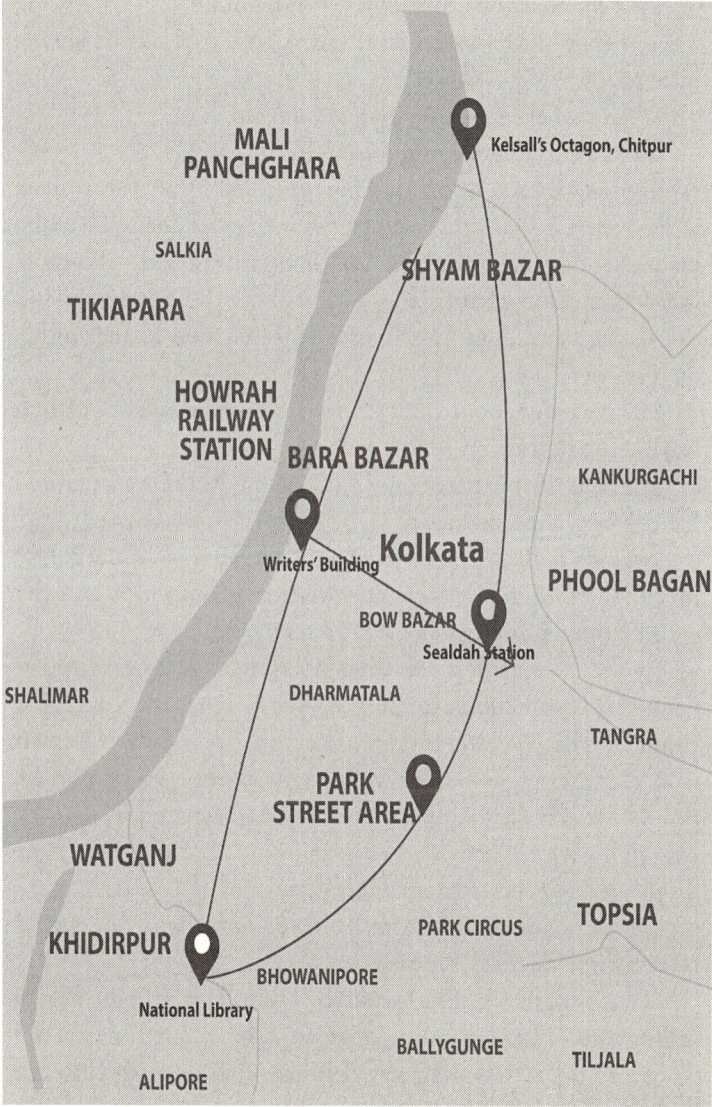

MALI
PANCHGHARA

Kelsall's Octagon, Chitpur

SALKIA

SHYAM BAZAR

TIKIAPARA

HOWRAH
RAILWAY
STATION

BARA BAZAR

KANKURGACHI

Writers' Building

Kolkata

PHOOL BAGAN

BOW BAZAR

Sealdah Station

SHALIMAR

DHARMATALA

TANGRA

PARK
STREET AREA

WATGANJ

KHIDIRPUR

PARK CIRCUS

TOPSIA

BHOWANIPORE

National Library

BALLYGUNGE

TILJALA

ALIPORE

'Amazing,' Imran agreed. 'But this only means that you've guessed the locations correctly. Nothing more.'

The map disappeared and Radha appeared on the screen once more.

'That's where Colin helped,' she smiled.

From behind her, Imran heard Colin say, 'Me?'

'It was when Colin said that John Brereton Birch lived at Belvedere House that things fell into place for me,' Radha resumed her explanation. 'We had all missed the most important clue—that Birch was one of the three men who hid the secret away. And what better place to hide it than in his own house?'

She told him about what Colin had discovered about Birch buying the house and selling it in 1824.

'He was living there in 1811, when Manning returned from Tibet,' she concluded.

'Sounds logical,' Imran frowned, 'but Birch sold the house in 1824. Wouldn't he have removed the manuscript and the secret from its hiding place before selling it?'

Radha shrugged. 'I can only guess. Maybe it would have been too conspicuous for him to break open the concealed room in which it was hidden. Everyone would have known that something had been hidden in there. Or maybe he thought it was secure and no one would ever find it. And he was right, wasn't he? No one ever found it, even when they discovered the secret room a few years ago.'

Imran raised an eyebrow. 'A secret room was discovered recently in Belvedere House?'

'That's right,' Radha replied. 'I checked it out before calling you. There are tons of newspaper reports about the discovery. In 2010, archaeologists working on restoring the building discovered a mysterious underground room. Because the building is a heritage monument, they could not break in—and the room had no entrance. They were certain that the room housed some secret—and the media took up the story—but when they did manage to peer inside, they found it filled with mud. They assumed it was built to strengthen the foundations of the building.'

'Still.' Imran was not entirely convinced. 'There are five locations in the riddle. Why should Belvedere House be the one where the secret is hidden? It could have been part of the riddle only because of the connection with Birch. There's nothing to say that this is the one—it could be any of the others as well.'

'But there *is* a clue!' Radha exclaimed, a trifle impatiently. 'See the third line of the riddle: Belvedere House is where the "ruler"—Hastings—fought a duel, right?'

'Okay.'

'And the same line says it is the "key". Now, look at the tenth line: "find the secret I hide by unearthing the key". The "hide" did not refer to John Hyde's tomb. But what if the "key" in the tenth line is also the "key" in the third line? And "unearthing" means exactly what Vijay thought it was—digging up a buried secret. So the secret is interred underneath Belvedere House. Is the discovery of the secret room under the building a coincidence? I don't think so. I believe this is what Manning was pointing at in his riddle.'

Imran was excited now. 'This does sound promising,' he told Radha. 'Okay, I'm going out on a limb here, but I think you're right about this. I'm going to call the PMO and ask for two things. One, permission to break into that underground room. I think the urgency of the situation demands it. Two, I'm going to ask for a team to help us retrieve the contents of that room. Since we are dealing with a protected building, I think it's best to go through the proper channels rather than break in on our own.'

Belvedere House
Kolkata, India

Radha, Shukla, Colin and Duncan stood with the archaeologists, as the last of the mud was shovelled into a container and carried out of the room.

Imran had been as good as his word. And he had also demonstrated his connections in the government as a highly regarded member of the Indian Intelligence Bureau. People had snapped into action with one phone call, and the prime minister was roused. The result was a directive from the very top of the government, and the entire state machinery had swiftly swung into action.

Two archaeologists were assigned to the classified operation, along with a crew to do the heavy lifting. The prime minister himself had given written authorisation to the Ministry of Culture who, in turn, approved the partial demolition of the wall of the hidden room in Belvedere House.

Now, the stage was set for entering the room.

Radha felt a tingle run down her spine as she led the way inside. She wished Vijay could have been here to witness this momentous unveiling of the secret they had worked so hard to find.

But Vijay, with his customary bull-headedness, had not only got himself into trouble this time, but also missed being present for this discovery. Not that Radha wanted to change him. Not only did she love him the way he was, warts and all, but his innate stubbornness had led to multiple breakthroughs in the past. So what if he had failed on one occasion? He was human after all. Like her and the rest of them.

The room itself was bare.

'There.' Duncan pointed to a small archway set in one wall of the room. 'Through there, I think.'

Radha, followed by the others, headed towards the archway, which led to a short, narrow tunnel which, she reckoned, lay beneath the lawns of the Belvedere Estate. The tunnel, in turn, opened into another chamber, smaller than the first one.

There was a stone pedestal in the centre of the chamber, on which rested a lead casket.

With trembling hands, Radha unfastened the clasp on the casket and opened it.

Nestled within were three things.

A bunch of ancient birch bark strips, on which were inscriptions in the Brahmi script. A sealed vessel made of a strange black metal. And a sheaf of loose papers, roughly stacked, with fading handwriting in English.

'The missing part of the Owen manuscript.' Shukla's voice was tremulous with emotion. 'And Fischer's translation.'

Radha was more pragmatic. 'And the antidote.'

Gurgaon, Haryana
India

'Imran has made all the arrangements,' Radha told Iris as they sat in the conference room of Titan Pharmaceuticals' medical research facility. 'Your team and the additional equipment you requested are already on a plane on its way here.'

The GTF team had had a quick discussion after the antidote was retrieved from its hiding place in Belvedere House.

There weren't many options. The world was running out of time.

While Fischer had translated the recipe for the antidote from the Owen manuscript and Shukla had corroborated the translation, it was too difficult to understand, with its archaic and esoteric references to different ingredients. Even Shukla had struggled to identify the modern names for some of the constituents.

There was only one way to develop the antidote. The sealed black metal vessel had to be opened and whatever was in it had to be analysed.

The decision had been quick, though difficult to make. Iris and Patterson had also been involved and Iris listed the equipment she needed for developing the antidote. She had also insisted that she needed her team to be able to deliver results swiftly.

The harder decision had been to use Titan Pharmaceuticals' facilities to analyse the antidote. But the pharmaceutical company had the best research and laboratory facilities in

India. It meant giving the Order what they had always sought, but as Imran put it, the GTF could gain solace from the fact that the antidote was now in the public domain.

'If they had found it and spirited it away, they would have monopolised it and that would have given them leverage over the world,' Imran had argued. 'We have denied them that opportunity. Even if they do get the formula now, it doesn't matter. Once Iris develops the antidote using modern ingredients, we can make it freely accessible to all nations in the world. The Order will have no leverage at all. It will be useless to them.'

The plan had made sense and that was why Iris had flown from China to India and was now in Titan Pharmaceuticals' research facility.

Patterson, on the other hand, had flown back to Washington, DC, quarantined in a private jet, to ensure that he was isolated before his symptoms began materialising.

The good news was that the contents of the black metal vessel were still intact after thousands of years. Whether it was because of the freezing conditions in the Himalayas or just the nature of the contents, no one knew, but it didn't matter. And if it was good enough for reverse engineering, it was good enough for use as a cure. There was a lot of it since the container was quite large and the dosage required minuscule in comparison. Enough for the treatment of all the patients who were the earliest affected by the events in Hotan.

Including Patterson.

November 5
Intelligence Bureau Headquarters
New Delhi, India

Vijay looked around with satisfaction at the GTF team assembled in the conference room. Imran was there after having spent the last week recuperating from his injuries at the hands of Dee. Finally mobile, he had returned to India and insisted on attending this debriefing in person rather than by video conference. Radha, Shukla, and Colin were also present. Vijay himself had spent time in the hospital recovering from his ordeal in the tomb.

From other screens on the walls of the conference room, Patterson, Duncan and Iris stared out at them, along with Percy Galipos, the genetics expert at the GTF. Duncan was back in London and Iris had returned to her lab at Craggett University. She and her team had worked round the clock and developed the antidote in less than thirty-six hours, after which doses were airlifted to be administered to patients in hospitals all over the world.

Patterson was admitted in a hospital in Washington, DC, still in quarantine. The antidote from Khandavaprastha had worked its magic and, since it had been administered before his symptoms began showing up, he had been spared the ravages of the disease.

'You must all have seen the news.' Patterson brought the meeting to order after initial pleasantries had been exchanged, with everyone expressing their happiness at seeing each other safe and well, following which he had given a quick debrief on how he and Iris had escaped from the secret lab in Hotan and rushed to the nearest hospital, where Iris had been treated for her gunshot wound. It had been—as she had insisted it was—a flesh wound, Chen's bullet having only grazed her leg, missing the major blood vessels. She had been very lucky, as Patterson had told her.

Imran had already heard the story, when Patterson had called him a week ago, immediately after their escape.

'An Islamic terrorist attack on a factory in Hotan,' Vijay scoffed. 'Do they seriously expect the world to believe that?'

Patterson shrugged. 'It is plausible. Face saving. It also gives China the justification to tighten the screws on Xinjiang. And it was the only reason they were prepared to share all their research on the mirror organism they cultured and call off their search for the antidote. That is also why you didn't encounter any Chinese agents in Kolkata. Otherwise, you would have had them hot on your heels or, worse still, they might have got to the prize even before you.'

'How would they have deciphered the clues in the riddle?' Colin wondered. 'It was difficult enough for us.'

'Don't underestimate the CCP,' Patterson warned. 'Especially when a prize as big as this is at stake. Anyway, I think all is well that ends well. At least we managed to get them off your backs in exchange for allowing them to save face.'

'What about Zhu?' Imran wanted to know.

'He probably wishes he went out like Chen did.' Patterson's face was grim. 'It would have been faster and less painful. Merciful, in fact. I think he overstepped in his zeal to show his dedication to the Party, and also because of his own ambitions to rule China someday. But quite apart from the ethical and moral considerations of what he did, he is also an embarrassment to the CCP now that the cat's out of the bag. The general secretary was very vocal in his disappointment at Zhu's behaviour and actions. Zhu has been arrested and stripped of his powers and rank. He's lost everything. For a man like Zhu, that's probably a fate worse than death; especially since he will spend the rest of his life in prison in China. Not a pretty place, from what Lin told me.'

'And Barnsfield?' Duncan asked. Patterson had only mentioned the American scientist's role in helping him and Iris escape and the fact that he accompanied them in the SUV out of the facility. He hadn't mentioned the scientist after that.

Patterson shook his head. 'I don't know. He accompanied us to the hospital since he knew the senior medical staff there, helped Iris get immediate medical attention and then, when we were busy getting Iris attended to, he disappeared. I know why he would not have wanted to return to the USA, but I wonder what his fate will be in China.'

He turned his gaze to Imran. 'There are still a lot of blanks that need to be filled in for me. I know bits and pieces but I don't know the whole story yet.'

Imran nodded. 'And we need you and Iris to fill us in on what you discovered in the lab. Right now, all we know is that the organism that the lab in Hotan cultured, and which Humboldt was interested in, is a mirror organism. Van Klueck explained that much to Vijay. But we still don't understand how it works, since a mirror organism should be completely harmless and no threat to life as we know it. So why the contagion? Why the neurological disorders? That is truly mystifying.'

'Yes, please do explain, Director Patterson,' Colin chimed in. 'I took a look at the paper in the dossier explaining exactly how this organism works and what it does, and I got lost in a maze of words like quorum-sensing systems, epinephrine-signalling pathways, and ...' he referred to the papers before him, 'dysregulated microglia activity.' He shook his head. 'It will be nice to get an explanation in English.'

'Iris?' Patterson shifted his gaze to her face on his screen. 'Would you like to take the lead on this?'

Intelligence Bureau Headquarters
New Delhi, India

'Sure,' Iris smiled. 'I'll try not to make it too technical, but you must understand that some terms we use have a completely different meaning from the way those words are used in common parlance. For example, in everyday usage, people use the words "toxins" and "poisons" interchangeably. But in technical usage, there is a difference, even though both can harm living beings.'

'Go ahead,' Colin grinned. 'I'll be sure to stop you if it goes over my head.'

'Okay, so let's start with the gut microbiota—all the bacteria, archaea, fungi, protists that live in our digestive tracts. We are only now slowly beginning to comprehend the immense importance of the incredibly biodiverse environment in our guts. Simply put, a delicate balance exists in our stomachs and intestines between the microbiota and our physiological system. Any disruption to this system can produce all kinds of medical conditions, as explained in the dossier.'

Colin put up his hand. 'Sorry, I was kidding earlier, but now I really do have a question. What are protists?'

Iris thought for a moment before answering, trying to find the right words to simplify the answer. 'Okay. Every living organism is either a prokaryote or a eukaryote. Prokaryotes are unicellular—they are single-celled organisms—and do not have a nucleus or other membrane-bound structures. Bacteria, for example. Eukaryotes have a nucleus and other cell structures enclosed by a plasma membrane. They can be unicellular or multicellular. A protist is a eukaryotic organism that is not an animal, plant or fungus. Protozoans, like amoeba, are protists, amongst others.'

'Thanks.' Colin subsided, satisfied.

'We know,' Iris resumed, 'that the symptoms begin with neurological disorders, cognitive loss, behavioural changes and develop further into a range of symptoms that manifest in different individuals according to their individual physiology and genetic make-up—psychiatric disorders, muscle atrophy and even organ failure. Before I explain exactly what the mirror organism does once it reaches the gut—which is really its theatre of activity—let me quickly describe how these symptoms are generated.'

She paused to see if everyone was following her. Not receiving any questions, she continued.

'I'm not getting into the details of the mechanics—that's in the dossier. I'll keep it simple. Let's start with the commensal microbes in the gut microbiota—the ones that do not harm us—which produce neurotransmitters like dopamine, norepinephrine, serotonin, GABA and others. When there is an excessive presence of these neurotransmitters the health and fitness, and maybe even behaviour, of the host can be altered. Second, virulence genes, which are normally shut off in the gut bacteria, are activated. Okay, so what are virulence genes, you may be asking.'

Colin grinned and nodded.

Iris smiled and nodded back. 'Virulence genes, simply put, are genes in bacteria, in our case in the gut bacteria, that can cause damage to the host when active. Mind you, this is a very simplistic definition, but the technical stuff is in the dossier. Normally, these genes are switched off, but in this case, they get activated upon infection.

'Third, some commensal gut microbes start secreting chemicals that either block our natural neurotransmitters or mimic their function, which leads to either paralysis or spasms. Fourth, all commensal gut microbes produce metabolites as end products of their metabolism. These can be amino acids, fatty acids, lipids and other products. As a result of the infection, these microbes begin to alter the metabolites they produce, in some cases even producing metabolites that are toxic for the host. Fifth, life as we know it is unable to digest mirror microbes. As the mirror organisms excrete waste, there is a build-up of toxins. Also, as they die naturally, the accumulated material cannot be cleaned up by our bodies. That also leads to high levels of toxicity, which can lead to organ failure and death. Essentially, what happens is that the delicate balance in our guts is disrupted. Now, the gut microbiota interacts with the enteric and central nervous system, and this imbalance leads to the neurological disorders we see. This is why the first symptoms are neurological. The nervous system is where the initial and maximum impact of the infection is.'

'So that is why Zhu and company were interested in culturing this organism,' Radha murmured.

'Yes,' Patterson affirmed. 'Lin confirmed this to me. If they could find a way to control the impact of the organism and its neurological effects, they would have a means to control restive populations and ensure that people were docile. Even a mild impact would be sufficient to ensure this, especially with cognitive loss. The antidote would have helped them control the impact exactly the way they wanted since they could have timed the administration of the antidote to suit their purpose.'

'And there's the commercial jackpot as well,' Iris added. 'Some of the most valuable drugs are proteins, which include wrong-handed amino acids, like the immunosuppressant cyclosporine. With a readymade organism that is immune to infection by regular viruses, drugs, biofuel, and all kinds of products can be manufactured without the biological issues that have to be managed today.' She told them about all the benefits that Barnsfield had listed while justifying his work with the lab in Hotan.

'That's one thing I never understood,' Vijay said on hearing about the possibility of limb and organ regeneration that Barnsfield had extolled. 'Limb regeneration. How on earth does that happen? How is it even possible? I read the dossier, but it was too technical for me.'

'I'll take this one,' Patterson told Iris and Galipos. 'One of the main reasons why higher eukaryotes like mammals cannot regenerate limbs and organs is because scar tissue forms at the site of an amputation. The moment that happens, regeneration is not possible. In lower animals like the axolotl or amphibians like the salamander, limbs and even entire organs like the heart can be regenerated because scar tissue doesn't form. And in even simpler animals like the hydra or the planarian worm, the *entire organism* can be regenerated. One of the effects of the mirror organism is the regulation of scar tissue and the inflammatory response at the site of the amputation or limb loss, which prevents a build-up of scar tissue. And that enables regeneration. You see, our bodies already have the means to regenerate. The effect of the organism is to trigger the changes that allow the regeneration to take place. And the beauty of it all is that the regeneration happens with all the controls in place to stop the cell proliferation from developing into cancer, just the way it happens in the lower animals.'

'Wow,' Colin was amazed.

'Percy, do you want to take over now?' Patterson asked.

'Sure.' Galipos cleared his throat and began. 'Another interesting implication of infection by this organism is the effect on Long Non Coding RNAs or lncRNAs. I'll start by explaining what they are. Ninety-eight per cent of the DNA in a human cell doesn't code for proteins—what was earlier called "junk

DNA". But now we know that the major role of so-called junk DNA is to regulate gene expression. In fact, more than eighty per cent of the genome is transcribed. Which means that while only two or three per cent of the genome is transcribed into protein-coding mRNAs—messenger RNAs—the majority is transcribed into what we call lncRNAs.' He waved a hand. 'The technical details are in the dossier, so I won't elaborate on that now. But what is important is that this mirror organism alters the expression of lncRNAs, which leads to cognitive loss and/or psychiatric disorders. The regulation of lncRNA expression by the organism also leads to a cytokine storm, which disrupts the blood brain barrier, allowing neurotropic chemicals and toxins to access the central nervous system, which causes neurogeneration and physical disability. This clears up a mystery that had baffled experts when the first patients started coming in—the fact that even though the mirror organism is not detected by the immune system, we still witness cytokine storms, which are basically an inflammatory response triggered by the immune system in response to normal pathogens.'

'And the mirror organism's regulation of lncRNAs can also affect gene expression,' Patterson added, 'which will facilitate limb regeneration.'

Vijay frowned. 'But if my understanding is correct, a mirror organism is completely different from normal life—that is why it cannot be detected by any tests that are designed to identify normal pathogens. So how does it cause all this havoc? Shouldn't our bodies be unaffected by it for exactly this reason? And how does it feed? Where does it obtain its nutrients from? I understand that the bacteria and other organisms in the gut microbiota get their nutrients from the host or from each other. And the viruses are phages which live off the bacteria. But how does a mirror organism live when it cannot metabolise anything produced by normal life?'

Intelligence Bureau Headquarters
New Delhi, India

'Good questions,' Patterson answered. 'Let me address the question of nutrients first. We still have a long way to go—the CCP may have cultured it, but a lot of research lies ahead of us before we understand much about the mirror organism. But there are signs that this is a canny, adaptable little organism, which is probably why it has survived for so long alongside normal life. We believe, based on the research in China, that there are two nutrient sources. All cells have enzymes called isomerases which can transform specific molecules into their mirror image versions. Our mirror organism, either through evolution, or by virtue of developing parallel to life as we know it, has the right set of isomerases to break down normal nutrients—fats, sugars, proteins—and convert edible matter in the gut into the appropriate mirror forms that supply it with nutrients. The second nutrient source is rather breathtaking. It appears that the mirror microbe can eat and breathe electrons when normal nutrients are not available. This is quite common even among bacteria with normal chirality. *Halomonas, Idiomarina, Marinobacter, Thalassospira* and *Thioclava* are examples of electron-eating bacteria. *Geobacter* and *Shewanella* breathe electrons. And we're just scratching the tip of the iceberg—it is just a matter of time before we find bacteria that do both. That the mirror organism seems to have perfected this back-up source of energy is no surprise. And this was one of the commercial applications that excited the CCP—the most effective "green" energy source!'

Vijay knew a thing or two about electrons from his engineering days. 'That's fascinating,' he mused, 'but there's no source of electrons in the human gut.'

'Yes, there is,' Patterson disagreed with him. 'Many bacteria in the gut microbiota generate electricity. You have to understand that life is essentially a flow of electrons. The food we eat provides us with electrons that are used to generate energy. The mirror organism can accept electrons from gut bacteria that generate them and need to find another electron acceptor. And it then uses these electrons to generate energy in the absence of nutrients that can provide electrons. Again, this is nothing new. Such symbiotic relationships have been found between microorganisms with normal chirality.' He paused. 'Iris, maybe you should explain the real secret here.'

'Um ... okay.' Iris took a few moments to collect her thoughts so that she could give an explanation that was simple and clear. 'Dr Barnsfield was instrumental in making this discovery. It revolves around the concept of symbiogenesis, which I can best explain using an example—*Mixotricha paradoxa*—a protist that lives only inside a termite species called *Mastotermes darwiniensis* or the Darwin termite. Now, termites can eat wood, but *they cannot digest it*. It is the bacteria and protists that live inside its gut that help the termite to digest wood. Without them, the insect dies from starvation. Coming back to the protist, one *Mixotricha* cell is made up of half a million individuals—nine different types of prokaryotic microbes that make up a single protist. Similarly, within our gut microbiota, Dr Barnsfield discovered a protist that is a mirror organism, which is actually a compound of multiple organisms, and is harmless to life as we know it. It is a great example of symbiogenesis. We never knew of its existence before because we didn't know where to look or how to look or even that we had to look for something like this in the first place. A lot of work needs to be done in order to learn exactly what role this protist plays within our gut, but it does have a role to play—that much is certain because it is *this mirror protist* that gets infected by the mirror pathogen that was accidentally discovered in China and cultured in Hotan. While the pathogen is harmless to normal life, it is deadly for the mirror protist. And once it gets infected, there is a severe imbalance in the delicate ecosystem of the gut microbiota, which leads to a devastating cascading effect of all the symptoms that we see in patients.'

There was a hushed silence as everyone in the room mulled over this revelation. The fact that we still don't know so much about our own bodies and the trillions of microorganisms that live within us—most of which are still unidentified—was a sobering thought. And the fact that these microscopic creatures could actually control life and death was an epiphany for a species that has considered itself to be a dominant species on this planet.

'What I still don't get,' Imran mused, 'is where the mirror pathogen came from. I mean, we now know that the CCP accidentally stumbled upon it, but how did it come to be in Miaozigou in the first place?'

'Dr Barnsfield said that the CCP had given him the samples in the pieces of a meteor,' Iris responded.

Patterson nodded. 'Chen corroborated that. It was a carbonaceous chondrite that landed in Miaozigou, God knows how many thousands of years ago. Apparently these meteor fragments often contain organic molecules like amino acids. Chen told us that, even today, there are ancient legends about a conflagration in antiquity that destroyed a forest in Miaozigou.'

'And its presence in Khandavaprastha—is that a coincidence? How did the Nagas discover the mirror organism there?'

'I think I can guess,' Shukla spoke up. 'The answer may lie in the Mahabharata. In the story of the burning of the Khandavaprastha forest.'

Intelligence Bureau Headquarters
New Delhi, India

All eyes turned towards Shukla.

'Well,' he began, 'I'm connecting some dots here, but I think it is a fair guess on my part. We know that there was an ancient inferno in Miaozigou. Van Klueck also told Vijay that Humboldt, in the missing pages of his travel journals which the Order possesses, had mentioned finding ancient pre-Incan texts in Bogota, which mentioned the burning of an ancient rainforest, and a connection with the Himalayas. Humboldt was deeply convinced that it was not a myth, but a true story from deep in the past. He also came across a similar story among some indigenous tribes south of Chimborazo. And then, if we look at the Mahabharata,' he opened a thick tome on the table before him, which he had carried with him for this meeting, 'we find this shloka, barely noticeable, which almost everyone has disregarded as abstruse, unimportant or irrelevant. I must admit that I too ignored it. Here it is:

पुरा देवनियोगेन यत् त्वया भस्मसात् कृतम् ।
आलयं देवशत्रूणां सुघोरं खाण्डवं वनम् ॥

This is Brahma speaking to Agni, after the sacrifice of King Shvetaki, when Agni approaches the Creator for advice upon losing his lustre. In this shloka, Brahma tells Agni: 'In ancient times, in accordance with the plan of the Deva— *devniyogain*—the very fearful Khandava forest, the abode of the enemies of the Gods, was reduced to ashes by you.'

He peered over his spectacles at Vijay, Colin and Radha, and then at the screen showing Duncan. 'You will remember my telling you about this shloka in London. I had registered this as an anomaly, but even then I didn't realise the significance of this verse.

Radha connected the dots. 'So there was a series of ancient conflagrations—Miaozigou, South America, Mexico and India. You're thinking it is possible that the same meteor carrying the spores of the mirror organism broke up into fragments and struck the planet in these spots, causing the infernos and delivering the organism to Earth?'

'Indeed. It is a possibility,' Shukla answered.

Colin frowned. 'But that seems implausible. Why would a meteor target only forests?'

'Maybe not only forests,' Radha turned over the idea in her mind, thinking aloud. 'Maybe other places as well. But the forest fires stuck in humanity's memory and were perpetuated as legends. In other places—deserts and mountains, for instance—there may have been no conflagration or no populations to witness any devastation, so there are no stories about them.'

'It could have been a series of meteors,' Vijay agreed. 'Who knows? The fact is that the mirror organism landed on earth in a meteor. We know that from Miaozigou. And if it was present in other places, this seems to be the only explanation.'

'There is something that puzzles me,' Radha spoke up. 'If this mirror organism is so deadly to life as we know it because of the mirror protist which it infects, then how come it never spread across the world earlier? Why is it only happening now? I mean, we know that the monkey Humboldt rescued in the Amazon forest was infected. But life as we know it in the Amazon forest was unaffected. And why didn't Humboldt and his companions get infected by the monkey?'

'I think I can answer that,' Iris offered. 'The original mirror pathogen that was delivered in the meterorites was buried for thousands of years, until it was dug up, probably accidentally, in Miaozigou, five thousand years ago. I guess the same thing happened in the Khandavaprastha forest, where it was accidentally discovered. Again, in the Amazon forest, it is possible that a troop of monkeys somehow dug up the mirror organism, which had lain undisturbed for thousands of years. And it seems that this mirror pathogen either has a proclivity for the mirror protist present in the guts of primates like the titi monkeys and humans, or there isn't an equivalent mirror protist which it can infect in the guts of other species or life forms. Another possibility is that, even if other life forms do contain a similar mirror protist, the pathogen in the meteorites cannot infect them. We don't know. We don't even know if all primate species have this commensal mirror protist in their gut microbiota. We'll need to undertake studies to find out and that will take time. But this is probably why it did not spread to other animals in the Amazon forest. Coming to the question of why it is spreading so fast now, in our modern world, it is very easy for any pathogen to spread fast to all corners of the world, with the world being connected so well, by air travel and other means of transport. Finally, I'm guessing here, but I think the reason Humboldt and his companions were not affected by the pathogen was because they were probably not exposed too much to the monkey once it became a spreader. And, even if they were exposed, the pathogenic load was probably insufficient to cause a serious infection. I mean, there would be no response from the human immune system to any amount of pathogenic load, but a load threshold would be required to be crossed in order to breach the defences of our commensal mirror protist, which is the real target of the mirror pathogen.'

'I think you're right about this, Iris,' Vijay cried. 'I remember reading about how they had travelled by boat for seventy-five days through the Amazon forest, without falling ill, but when they reached Angostura, all three were taken by a strange fever and spent two weeks recovering from it. Do you think that they did get exposed but, as you put it, the load was not sufficient for a serious illness and they got away with just a fever?'

'I'd be speculating,' Iris said with a smile, 'but, yes, this could be possible. If it was a fever for which no cause or infection was detected, it could have been our mirror pathogen at work. In which case, they were really lucky.'

Vijay turned to Shukla. 'Dr. Shukla, I think you should explain your report in the dossier regarding the Owen manuscript and the Khandavaprastha curse.'

'Oh yes.' Shukla smiled at Vijay. 'I think we have Van Klueck to thank for some of the details, which helped me piece together the other parts of the puzzle. Again, let me be clear about this: there is some amount of speculation on my part to explain what happened and I guess we will never know, but I think this is the best guess about the truth of the Khandavaprastha curse.'

He adjusted his glasses and continued. 'The big mystery in the entire Khandavaprastha story has always been the fact that even with Lord Krishna being part of the story, every single living being—with the exception of seven inhabitants of the forest—was killed mercilessly. Of the seven that either survived, or were allowed to live, five—the four Sharangaka birds and their mother, Jarita—were from one family. One—Ashvasena, Takshaka's son—escaped with the help of Indra. One—Maya, the Asura—was given protection by Arjuna, and even Krishna did not seem to want to kill him. Mysterious indeed. And then there is the fact that Van Klueck had pointed out. Very relevant, but mostly ignored: while most of the Devas were amassed on Indra's side and against Krishna and Arjuna, why were Agni and Varuna helping them and not aligning with the other Devas? Agni consumed the forest and Varuna provided the weapons to kill all the living beings. You must remember that Agni and Varuna were the most important Devas after Indra. So why were they aligned against Indra and the other Devas?'

He paused before resuming. 'This is where Van Klueck's explanation helps. It seems the Order knows much more than we thought they did. We always knew they are ancient, but I think we underestimate their reserves of knowledge. So, according to Van Klueck, the Nagas discovered the mirror organism and were conducting experiments or trials—he was a bit vague about this point—in the Khandavaprastha forest. And they also developed the antidote. According to Van Klueck, while the mirror pathogen does not infect all life forms, as Iris has just explained, something sudden had happened which exposed every living being in Khandavaprastha, except for the seven survivors of the fire, to the mirror pathogen. While it did not harm them, it could have spread beyond the forest, to the world outside, where it would have been devastating. According to the Order, this is why all the inhabitants of the forest had to be killed—so that they did not carry the pathogen to the world outside.'

'That makes sense,' Iris nodded, 'even if it is speculative, as you have clarified. While the disease spreads only through symptomatic transmission, the mirror pathogen could have jumped from animals to humans even if any human living outside the forest hunted and butchered an animal from the forest which was a carrier.'

'So the massacre at Khandavaprastha was essentially for containment,' Radha mused, pondering the answer to one of the biggest mysteries of the Mahabharata. 'Similar to the culling that we do nowadays for things like bird flu and swine flu; except, in Khandavaprastha, it was the carriers and not the infected who were culled.'

'Dr Shukla,' Patterson said, looking thoughtful, 'why *was* there a division in the ranks of the Devas? You haven't really delved into that part in your report.'

Shukla shrugged. 'Because it is speculation on our part, based on what Van Klueck told Vijay. We have no way of validating this, unlike your scientific report which can be easily corroborated. But I will explain. Indra, the king of the Devas, was a friend of Takshaka. But I refuse to believe that he was guided by friendship in protecting the forest from Agni's attempts to burn it down. I think there was more happening there, on which Van Klueck did not shed light. For some reason, Indra wanted the Nagas to continue their experiments. But Agni and Varuna were against it. Remember Agni's ailment that affected his lustre? Some translators like K.M. Ganguli and M.N. Dutt have interpreted this as a stomach problem. Was that an infection with the mirror organism? Remember that Agni lost his lustre because he consumed too much ghee during Shvetaki's sacrifice and was ill. It is strange that the antidote to that malady is consuming more fat! Shouldn't that have made him even more ill? But there is one shloka,' he flipped the pages, 'here it is:

दीप्तोर्ध्वकेशः पिङ्गाक्षः पिबन् प्राणभृतां वसाम् ।
तां स कृष्णार्जुनकृतां सुधां प्राप्य हुताशनः ॥
बभूव मुदितस्तृप्तः परां निर्वृतिमागतः।

'And, here's the translation: The yellow fire, with his hair burning, drinking the marrow of the living beings killed by

Krishna and Arjuna and having obtained the elixir, became very happy and greatly satisfied.'

He looked at Vijay, Radha, Colin and Duncan in turn. 'You will recall my confession that I was baffled by this shloka. But if we translate this shloka the way I just did, we could say that there was an elixir that cured whatever ailment Agni was suffering from.'

He looked around the room and at the screens before continuing.

'So, Agni and Varuna probably decided to take matters into their hands and destroy the forest, its inhabitants and everything the Nagas were doing there. The only problem was that Ashvasena escaped thanks to his mother, who sacrificed her life to save him, and he was the one who carried the antidote to Tibet, where he hid it. That is the true story of Khandavaprastha. And this story was captured in Susruta's text that was part of the missing pages of the Owen manuscript. Susruta had explained this entire story in detail—the mirror organism, the antidote and the location of its hiding place in Tibet. He even included the formulation of the antidote in his text. I think he was foresighted. He probably knew that at some time in the future, this contagion would rear its head again.'

'So that is how Manning was able to find the antidote in Tibet and bring it back to Calcutta.' Patterson finally understood.

'Yes,' Vijay affirmed. 'The Order knew about the antidote, but never tried to search for it because it was of no use to them. The original mirror organism had been destroyed in the fire. Why would they waste resources on a key to a lock that did not exist? Until they heard that the CCP had cultured this mirror organism. Then they swung into action and tried to co-opt it at first. When that didn't work, they decided to steal it, which led to the Hotan incident. And when they read about Wilson's revelation, they knew they had to act. They burned down Wilson's house as well to try and ensure that the CCP didn't get hold of his papers. But they were too late.'

'I have a question,' Imran spoke up. 'Why did the CCP have Wilson kidnapped? How did they know that the Owen manuscript had what they were looking for, when they didn't have access to the portions that were hidden away?'

Intelligence Bureau Headquarters
New Delhi, India

Patterson had the answer. 'Chen told us. In 2003, Wu Haoling, a Chinese Sanskrit scholar from Beijing University, came across a text consisting of fourteen yellowed palm leaves at Drepung monastery in Tibet. It spoke of an ancient book written in antiquity by an Indian surgeon called Susruta. But being a philosophical text, it didn't reveal anything more that was of much use. Woven into the philosophy however, the CCP saw glimpses of the mirror organism that they had by this time identified. So they scoured all sources possible, trying to find this ancient text by Susruta. That was when they came across the story of the Owen manuscript. And then they heard about Wilson and his book. So, they kidnapped him. They sent Li Ping to check out the Owen manuscript, and he did. But the key portion of the manuscript was missing. They searched Wilson's house for clues to finding the text they needed. You know the rest of the story from there.'

'I guess that connects all the dots,' Imran said.

Colin raised his hand. 'I'm sorry, but I do have one last question.' He looked at the monitor showing Iris' face. 'I read your report on the antidote, and I have to confess that it blew my mind, even though I didn't quite understand how the antidote really works to kill the mirror organism. Molecules derived from snake venom as a key ingredient of the antidote? Seriously? I thought snake venom killed people!'

Iris laughed. 'I was wondering if that was going to come up. Venom-based cures have been around for centuries. Cobra venom has been used for centuries in traditional Chinese medicines. The toxicologist on our team tells me that ancient Indian texts mention them as well. Dr Shukla, would you know something about them?'

Shukla nodded. 'I've read some of the ancient medical treatises, and after seeing your report on the antidote, I went back and looked at them again. They are mentioned by Charaka and Vagbhata. Susruta has also discussed the uses of snake venom, apart from the formula for the antidote that he provided in the text that was part of the Owen manuscript. Snake venom is harmless if it is swallowed. This is well known in Ayurveda, which prescribes snake venom for therapeutic purposes. The venom needs to be injected into the tissues or into the bloodstream in order to produce toxicity. Snake venom was usually prescribed along with other Ayurvedic drugs.'

He looked around at the group. 'And quite apart from the fact that snake venom as an ingredient for an antidote is unexpected, we really should not be taken aback by this discovery. After all, who better to know about snake venom and its application than the Nagas? There are plenty of stories in the Mahabharata about the venom of the Nagas themselves.'

'Even in modern medicine,' Iris took up the explanation again, 'venom-based cures came into prominence in the 1960s with Arvin, a drug that destroys blood clots, derived from the venom of the Malayan pit viper. In the 1970s ACE inhibitors, which are used today to treat hypertension, were developed from the venom of the Brazilian pit viper. Advances in molecular biology have enabled scientists to work on researching the application of toxins in snake venom to treat cancer and many other diseases. Other examples are Enalapril, Eptifibatide and Tirofiban—all molecules derived from snake venom—which are approved by the FDA in the USA.'

She paused before adding, 'Bill, I think you're the best person to describe exactly how the snake venom derivative works as an ingredient at the molecular level.'

Patterson nodded, the molecular biologist in him coming to the fore. 'To understand how the antidote works, you first need to know about ion channels, through which ions pass into and out of a cell, through the cell membrane. Let me try and simplify it for you. Think of an ion channel as a protein with a hole in it, which functions as a gate or a valve, to allow or stop ions from either entering a cell through the cell membrane or leaving it. Our cells have a high concentration of potassium ions, but they are low in sodium ions. Outside our cells, there is a high concentration of sodium ions, but not of potassium ions. I'm sure you are familiar with the fact that ions move from areas of high concentration to areas of low concentration in order to equalise the concentration and remove the concentration difference. Ion channels regulate the movement of these potassium and sodium ions into and out of the cells. Ion channels are found in every organism on Earth— including the mirror organism from Khandavaprastha—and they are responsible for maintaining the relative concentration of ions inside our cells as well as in the extracellular fluids.'

He looked around to see if there were any questions. But everyone seemed to have followed his explanation. 'Why are ion channels important for life?' he resumed. 'Because it is important to maintain this ion concentration gradient—to maintain the difference in ion concentration levels. Remember, I had said earlier, that life is a flow of electrons. Without this flow, we die. Think of it this way. In a hydroelectric dam, as long as water is trapped behind the dam, potential energy is stored. It is when the water is released from the dam that the energy is also released, which is used to generate electricity. Something similar happens inside our bodies at the cellular level. The differences in concentration of ions within our cells and outside them is used to generate electrical impulses, which are transmitted along our nerves and to our muscles, which are then used to control every biological process needed to sustain life, including the development and regeneration of cells. And ion channels are the gates or valves of the cells, through which this bioelectric current is generated. Consider this: around one-third of the oxygen that we breathe and half of the food that we ingest is used to maintain the ion concentration gradient across our cell membranes. If the ion concentration gradients collapse completely, and the difference in ion concentration levels inside and outside the cells disappears, no electrical impulses can be generated. And we die.'

Patterson paused to allow this to sink in, before resuming. 'The antidote doesn't contain snake venom per se, but—as Colin rightly said—molecules derived from it; peptides to be specific. A peptide is, putting it simplistically, like a mini protein. It is made up of amino acids, like a protein, but a smaller chain of amino acids than a protein. Our antidote contains what we call a chimeric hybrid peptide—essentially a combination of two peptides—which form ion channels or pores in lipid membranes. I won't get into the technical details of how this peptide works—the technical details are in the dossier. The snake venom peptides essentially work as molecular hole punchers, inserting themselves into the membrane of the mirror organism, and forming a huge hole through which the ion gradients are disrupted, essential nutrients leak out of the cell, and the organism dies. And this is the best part. The structure of the peptides ensures that they are not harmful to any other cells—they target only the mirror cells. We've seen similar cases in antibacterial research: chimeric cecropin A-melittin hybrids do the same thing with gram positive and gram negative bacteria without harming other cells. Again, all the technical details are in the dossier, and they are a bit difficult to explain, so I'll stop here.'

There was silence as everyone mulled over the breathtaking mechanics of nature, which enabled a natural cure for an unnatural disease.

Then Patterson spoke again. 'I think we have filled in the blanks. But I still have one last question. Vijay?'

Vijay looked at the camera, wondering what Patterson wanted to ask him.

'Why did you do the deal with Van Klueck? You could have easily found the antidote yourself. You had no need of the resources of the Order. Why did you not just go ahead and finish the search by yourself with the help of your colleagues?'

Vijay took a deep breath.

Am I in trouble again?

He decided to be honest. 'I knew that even if the Order did get the antidote, it would find its way to Titan Pharmaceuticals thanks to Varun Saxena, who is part of the Order.' He held up his hands. 'I know you and I disagree on this, but this was my opinion. And Van Klueck was very clear about this. The Order wanted to save the world as much as we did. Eventually, the infection would wipe out the Order as well—nothing would stand in the way of this contagion. It was a matter of survival as much as having a world to dominate.'

He paused, thinking, then continued. 'Director Patterson, for me the deal was never about finding the antidote or trying to understand what the mystery was about. It was about Imran. I hope this will resonate with you. When you, as a soldier, are on the battlefield, and one of your comrades falls to a bullet or shrapnel, would you leave him there? I don't think so. You would risk your own life to get him to safety so he has a chance to live. That's what I did. I couldn't let my comrade fall by the wayside and leave him at the mercy of the Order.'

Patterson stared him from the screen as silence descended once more upon the room.

Then the GTF director spoke up. 'Well done, Vijay.' There was a measure of respect in his voice. 'You are right. I would never leave a comrade to die. I never did.' There was a strange inflection to his voice, almost as if he was recalling something. 'So I understand what you did.'

He looked around. 'Well, if there are no more questions or comments then this debrief is at its end. Let's all take a well-deserved break, shall we?'

Everyone agreed wholeheartedly, even though something about the mystery still felt incomplete.

There were still so many questions that would never be answered.

But the important thing was that the world was safe. And it would never know how close it had come to ending.

EPILOGUE

November 5
Intelligence Bureau Headquarters
New Delhi, India

Patterson stared grimly out of the monitor at Imran. All the other members of the GTF had left and Imran was alone in the room. The Director of the GTF had asked him to stay back after the debrief.

'So, they know.'

Imran nodded. 'That much is clear from what Van Klueck told Vijay. And Radha had also told us earlier that the Order suspects the existence of an organisation like the GTF.'

'Then it is only a matter of time,' Patterson grunted. 'It's great that we managed to stay under their radar for as long as we did. With the kind of resources the Order has at its disposal, and with their tentacles spread wide, it is just a matter of time before they know all about the GTF.' He shrugged. 'We need to put our contingency plans in place before they do.'

'You are right, Director. I'll get on it right away,' Imran said with a brief nod.

Jaungarh Fort

'Well,' Colin sighed. 'That's that. What a beautiful night.'

He and Vijay were sitting on a balcony of Vijay's ancestral fort. The weather was pleasant and there was a slight nip in

the air, a harbinger of winter. The lights of the village at the
foot of the hill upon which the fort was built, were like little
stars scattered on the ground.

Vijay looked at the dark expanse of sky above them, the
stars like pinholes in a dark canvas through which light was
shining, almost like a reflection of the little village below them.

His expression was morose.

Colin had a fair idea of what was eating Vijay up. He decided
to tackle it head on. 'What's going on between you and Radha?'

Vijay gave a start. 'What do you mean?'

Colin sighed. 'Come on, pal. You think it isn't obvious? All
these years you believed that she was dead, while hoping for
a miracle. And now, the miracle has come to pass. I mean you
two should be walking hand in hand, with flowers showering
from heaven and music playing in the background. What's
with the cold vibes between the two of you then?'

It was Vijay's turn to sigh. 'I don't know, buddy. It's
complicated.' He paused to reflect, before resuming. 'Radha's
changed. I don't know how, but she has. Haven't you noticed?'

'Yeah, you're right about that.'

'So, first I was upset that she called Imran and not me,
to tell him she was alive. But then, I reasoned with myself.
I understood that they have a very special relationship and
maybe she didn't want me charging headlong into danger to
find her and help her.'

'That's true,' Colin agreed. 'You'd have gone and got yourself
killed for sure. I know you, pal.'

Vijay shrugged. 'So, I got over her not telling me she was alive
and calling Imran instead. But I can't seem to be able to get close
to her again. Not like it was, you know? There's this gap between
us; and it isn't the gap of four years. It's the change in her.'

Colin pondered this. 'It will take time,' he said finally. 'Time
and work.'

He looked at Vijay. 'For both of you. I've noticed that she, too, is hesitant. Both of you need to work on it.'

'Why is she hesitant?' Vijay wondered.

'Who knows? We have no idea what she's gone through in the last four years. She may have done stuff for the Order that she hated doing. I don't even want to think about it.'

'Neither do I,' Vijay concurred.

'Just give it time.' Colin stared at Vijay, trying to assess his reaction.

Vijay held Colin's gaze, but said nothing.

'So,' Colin decided to change the topic. 'D'you really think that China is going to turn over a new leaf?'

'Director Patterson doesn't seem to think so.' Vijay shrugged. 'Personally, I have my doubts too. The CCP is too strongly entrenched. And judging by what Lin told Director Patterson in Beijing, they've got a good reason not to change tack now.'

'All I can say is that,' Colin began, sounding thoughtful, 'if the CCP continues to exert the kind of iron grip they have over the country and suppress everything the way they are doing now, not only will they reverse all the gains they have made over the last few decades, but they will trip up sometime. Democracy is not perfect. But, neither is an autocracy. The freedom to disagree is priceless. And it is something that humans long for. It is probably what makes us human as well.'

Vijay grinned at him. 'Quite the philosopher today, aren't you?'

Colin grinned back. Then a thought struck him. 'By the way, there's one question that still hasn't been answered, at least for me.'

'What question?'

'What exactly is, or was, the Khandavaprastha curse?'

Vijay looked at Colin in surprise. 'You didn't stumble over the name this time! How come?'

'Been practising.' Colin grinned. 'Can't have you gloating about that. But answer me, what do you think was the curse?'

'I don't really know.' Vijay looked at the stars as he composed his thoughts to answer Colin. 'And I guess we'll never really know. Susruta was quite enigmatic about it, according to Dr Shukla. He just mentions it a few times and then talks about the antidote and its ingredients.'

'And the surgeon dude, in turn, got it from some ancient texts that were passed down,' Colin added. 'I'm sure those texts wouldn't have survived, like the texts about the Druids from ancient Greece and Rome.'

Vijay nodded. 'True.'

'But I want to know your guess,' Colin pressed. 'I think it is the mirror organism. The one that arrived on earth in the meteorite.'

'Possible,' Vijay mused. 'Or it could be the mirror protist that is within all of us. A curse and a boon at the same time.'

'Or even the infection of the mirror protist by the mirror microbe.' Colin warmed up to the speculation that they were indulging in. 'Or the experiments by the Nagas.' He paused for thought. 'Actually, it could be any of these. You're right. We'll never know.'

Vijay was silent. He had a nasty suspicion that Van Klueck hadn't told him everything. That he had cannily concealed information about Khandavaprastha that was not really required for finding the antidote.

He didn't know why, but Vijay had a feeling that, whatever it was the Nagas were doing in Khandavaprastha, it was not limited to the weird life organism that had now been rediscovered.

And whatever it was, he had a hunch they would get to know.

Sooner or later.

Extract from the GTF Dossier reporting on the China mission (prepared by Bill Patterson, Iris Tsai and Percy Galipos)

Simply put, the mystery superbug, which was released at Hotan is a form of weird life, specifically mirror life, with its chirality opposite to life as we know it.

That is the reason why it causes a mystery infection with symptoms but no immune response (the cytokine storms are due to other possible reasons as explained below), since the immune system does not detect it. That is also the reason why we have been unable to detect antigens or antibodies post infection. And it is impossible to detect by pure observation since we never knew what we were looking for. Especially in this particular case, where convergent evolution would naturally disguise the pathogen.

The mirror microbe can have two effects: direct and indirect.

It may be noted here that we are positing the effects of the superbug based on contemporary research into pathogens which are life as we know it. Further research is required in order to validate our theories.

The direct effect comes from the fact that it cannot be digested and, as the mirror microbes excrete waste, there is likely to be a build-up of toxins. Moreover, as they die naturally, the accumulated material cannot be cleaned up by our body.

It also appears that the mirror microbe has a set of isomerases that break down normal nutrients—fats, sugars, proteins—to convert edible matter available in the gut into itself. It also seems to have the ability to eat and breathe electrons, giving it a back-up supply of energy from bacteria in the gut that generate electricity.

Therefore, the mirror microbe seems to be able to use normal gut microbes as food sources and vice versa, enabling it to survive in a eukaryotic system.

To explain the indirect effect, we will need to resort to symbiogenesis. It is now evident, based on Dr. Barnsfield's research, that there is, within all of us a holobiont which has, at its centre, a mirror organism that is benign. This mirror protist has probably been a key part of our physiology for thousands, if not millions, of years. And, just as our physiology has adapted and evolved to depend on our symbiotic gut microbes, it appears to have also evolved to depend on the fine balance with the mirror protist that resides in our gut (but which has never been identified because, firstly we would not be able to distinguish it from regular life and secondly because we still don't have a comprehensive database of all the bacteria, viruses, protozoans that are critical components of the gut microbiota). Moreover, just as the balance of our gut microbiota can influence normal brain function, the balance with this mirror protist would also influence normal brain function.

The mirror microbe (cultured by China at Hotan) infects the mirror protist when it enters the gut. Both have the same biochemistry and this infection disrupts the fine balance in the gut microbiota. This leads to a devastating cascading effect, described below, eventually leading to the death of the host.

The symptoms that are manifested can differ among individuals, based on their individual physiology and genetic make-up. These are some of the symptoms that have been commonly observed:

a) Neurological disorders like schizophrenia, depression, anxiety, multiple sclerosis, amyotrophic lateral sclerosis

b) Behavioural changes like aggression

c) Cognitive loss

d) Psychiatric disorders with symptoms including psychosis, delusions, motivation loss, repetitive behaviours, uncontrolled anxiety, cognitive issues, dissociation

e) Inflammatory response (cytokine storms) leading to damage of nerve cells (also through excess production of glutamate)

f) Regeneration, including the reparative regeneration of limbs and organs as observed in the experiments conducted by the secret laboratory in Hotan.

The broad mechanisms which can lead to the expression of these symptoms upon infection are described below.

1. Impact on the gut-brain axis:

The mechanisms for gut bacteria to influence the nervous system are:

i)   alteration of the activity of the stress associated HPA axis
ii)   vagal nerve stimulation
iii)   secretion of short chain fatty acids (impacting microglial cells)
iv)   affecting permeability of the blood-brain barrier
v)   modulating neurotransmitters directly or through biosynthesis pathways

These mechanisms may be exploited by the mirror pathogen in the following ways:

1.1 The infection of the benign mirror protist may alter the behaviour of commensal microbes in the gut microbiota, which can have the following (multiple and simultaneous) effects:

a)   some commensal microbes produce neurotransmitters which can lead to excessive presence of these neurotransmitters, thereby impacting the health/fitness of the host as well as possibly altering behaviour

b)   activating virulence genes in gut bacteria by disrupting the bacterial quorum-sensing system and/or the epinephrine host signalling system

c)   causing some commensal gut microbes to secrete chemicals that bind to the same sites as native neurotransmitters—either blocking or mimicking their function and blocking or opening ion channels leading to paralysis or spasms (as explained earlier, the mirror organism itself may possibly be responsible for toxins detected, either through waste material excreted or by accumulation of dead cells that cannot be cleaned up by natural processes)

d)   causing commensal gut microbes to alter metabolites they produce, leading to neurological disorders and even possible modification of behaviour

1.2 The infection of the benign mirror protist disrupts the delicate balance of the gut microbiota, possibly leading to the following effects:

a)   the imbalance in the gut microbiota, which interacts with the enteric and central nervous system, and leads to neurological disorders listed earlier. These disorders are associated with both dysregulated microglia activity and dysbiosis of the gut microbiota. The gut microbiota also modulates astrocyte activity which, if impacted, can lead to loss of blood-brain barrier integrity, ion gradient balance and glycogen storage in the brain

2. The mirror organism may be able to travel to the muscles and brain

It may be transported through the bloodstream—entering RBCs and WBCs—thus carrying them to neurons, or by entering peripheral nerves. Through mitochondrial dysfunction—triggering an inflammatory response in the cell, it can lead to nerve cell damage, neural dysfunction or even death.

3. Regeneration (specifically epimorphosis as distinct from compensatory hyperplasia):

3.1 The infection by the mirror pathogen evidently switches on a molecular pump that transports protons across cell membranes (perhaps the mirror organism can use some of the current produced by the proton flow, for its own energy, since it does eat and breathe electrons). This proton pump produces a long-range electric field that helps to direct what happens to nerve cells that pour into the site of the regeneration.

3.2 The infection by the mirror pathogen also appears to lead to a regulation of scar tissue formation and the inflammatory response (at the site of an amputation/limb loss). This conclusion is based on the connection between macrophages and scar tissues (macrophages appear to prevent a build-up of scar tissue based on contemporary research). So, if the infection by the mirror pathogen can influence a response (to amputation/limb loss) where macrophages as well as pro- and anti-inflammatory cytokines invade the site at the same time (M1 and M2 macrophages peaking at the same time), regeneration may be possible. This is what we believe the Chinese experiments on regeneration of limbs revealed at Hotan.

3.3 The infection by the mirror pathogen seems to turn on genetic switches which activate the complex networks needed to construct an appendage or complicated organ (e.g., Lin28a, EGR and other genes). For example, during regeneration the compacted portions of the genome physically become more open to allow regulatory switches to turn genes on and off—LINEs (for example) may act to decompact chromatin. This point is linked to point 4.2 below. Another possibility is the activation of genes associated with Extra Cellular Matrix remodelling.

4. Mirror pathogen induced regulation of lncRNAs

4.1 The infection by the mirror pathogen appears to alter the expression of lncRNAs, which disrupts fine synaptic tuning, leading to cognitive loss and/or psychiatric disorders (point d of the symptoms, above).

4.2 Mirror pathogen induced regulation of lncRNAs possibly also affects gene expression leading to limb regeneration (e.g., lncRNA controlling EGR).

4.3 Mirror pathogen induced regulation of lncRNAs can also lead to a cytokine storm which disrupts the blood-brain barrier allowing neurotropic chemicals/toxins to access the CNS (we know this is possible with viruses like H5N1 and H1N1 using infected leucocytes in a Trojan horse mechanism, but it looks like chemicals or toxins can also have the same effect, in the case of the mirror organism). This can lead to neurodegeneration and physical disability.

The Antidote

To begin with, snake venom, like all animal venoms, is a cocktail of pharmacologically active components, which include proteins, enzymes, peptides, lipids, carbohydrates, metal ions and some other non-protein compounds which have not yet been identified.

The principal mechanism through which the antidote works is based on the way in which naturally occurring ion channels in the body function to maintain ion concentration gradients across cell membranes, which is responsible for generating electrical impulses.

Our antidote contains a chimeric hybrid peptide—essentially a combination of two peptides—which forms ion channels or pores in lipid membranes.

The mirror organism has a lipid bilayer membrane. Normally, the bilayer lipids and the membranes are chiral, so a specific chirality of a peptide would be required for it to be active for a membrane of a specific chirality. For example, the right-handed lipids in the mirror organism would require the peptides to also be right-handed if they are to work. But the chimeric hybrid peptides derived from snake venom are based on L amino acids, since all normal life works with L amino acids. And, in this case, it seems that the peptides associate with the membrane by electrostatic forces and then form the channels that kill the organism. There is no specific interaction required with chiral receptors or enzymes.

The snake venom peptides essentially work as molecular hole punchers, inserting themselves into the membrane of the mirror organism and forming a huge hole through which the ion gradients are disrupted, essential nutrients leak out of the cell, and the organism dies. The pores are composed of aggregates of seven peptide chains which are present individually in the venom and co-assemble to form the pore that punches a hole in the mirror organism. This ensures that the chimeric hybrid peptides are not harmful to any other cells—they target only the mirror cells. We've seen similar cases in antibacterial research: chimeric cecropin A—melittin hybrids do the same thing with gram positive and gram negative bacteria without harming other cells.

AUTHOR'S NOTE: I prepared this extract specifically for the scientifically inclined, so that the general reader does not get bored by or lost in the scientific terms that underpin the very real science that lies at the heart of this book. The bibliography available at The Quest Club provides more resources that substantiate the scientific explanation provided above.

Last Notes

There are a lot of facts—scientific, historic and others—that I have used to craft this story. However unbelievable some facts may be, they are true. Here's where I help you to distinguish fact from fiction, and also provide more details on the science that has been used in this book for the sceptical or scientifically inclined reader. If you want to know more, there's tons of information at The Quest Club, which is free to join, if you are not already a member. And, of course, do check out the readings in the detailed bibliography available at The Quest Club.

And, before I forget, there are free bonus chapters available at The Quest Club as well!

The Science

Synthetic organisms (including microbes): There is fascinating research happening in this field and the possibility of a completely synthetic organism—even a synthetic microbe—i.e., one designed and assembled by humans is not far-fetched. More on this and the details behind Barnsfield's experiments and research on The Quest Club website.

Radha's treatment after being shot: The described treatment is based on a real treatment that was given to at least one patient that I came across in my research. Believe it or not, the entire procedure is scientifically accurate. If Radha survived, it was because of science, not because I wanted her to live. More details are available on The Quest Club.

Weird Life: This is a fascinating subject which serious scientists have researched and written about. No weird life has yet been found, but that doesn't mean it does not exist. See The Quest Club for a bibliography which lists books and papers to learn more.

Bacterial Spores: This is real science. If bacteria can survive through spores, there is no reason a mirror organism cannot do so as well. More on this at The Quest Club.

Carbonaceous Chondrites: The Earth is littered with pieces of these kinds of meteorites, many of which carry amino acids of all types. For more details, check out The Quest Club.

The Gut Microbiota: Everything mentioned about the gut microbiota in this book is real science. We are only just scratching the surface of the subject here. More at The Quest Club.

Limb Regeneration: Patterson's explanation, especially about scar tissue and axolotls and salamanders during the debrief (and in the dossier), is based on real science. More on this at The Quest Club.

Long Non-coding RNAs: Galipos describes real science in his explanation (and in the dossier). This is still a very nascent field and research will uncover more about how lncRNAs work. More at The Quest Club.

Electric Bacteria: Believe it or not, they are real. Yes, including the bacteria in our gut. More at The Quest Club on these fascinating creatures.

Life is a flow of electrons: This is true—real science at work. I have provided a detailed explanation at The Quest Club (including some fascinating information on quantum biological effects in our bodies!)

Symbiogenesis: This is a fascinating subject. *Mixotricha Paradoxa* is a real protist in the Darwin termite. And, yes, termites eat wood but cannot digest wood. They need their own gut microbiota to help them digest the wood they eat. See The Quest Club for more fascinating examples of symbiogenesis.

Chirality: It is true that Louis Pasteur discovered chirality. I have attempted to simplify the explanation of chirality, especially in biology, to make it less technical and to ensure that the flow of the story is not interrupted. If you would like to understand the concept better, there is more information at The Quest Club. And the example of thalidomide given by Van Klueck is real, and very tragic.

Mirror organisms: The benefits outlined by Barnsfield to Iris are very, very real, if a truly mirror organism is ever created. Van Klueck's explanation is real science. It is true that the immune system cannot detect a mirror organism. Does mirror life exist? Who knows? It is extremely difficult to detect with the current equipment that is geared towards detecting normal life. For more information on detection of mirror organisms, please see The Quest Club. And regarding the mirror organism within our bodies (see 'Dossier' for details), while researching this subject, I observed that everyone was looking for weird life on our planet, on other planets, and the thought occurred to me: what if our scientists are looking in the wrong place? Instead of weird life existing externally, what if there was a mirror organism *within* us? What if weird life had developed together with life as we know it, but inside our bodies? That radical thought led to the hypothesis that is at the heart of this book. Today, we haven't even been able to identify most of the normal life forms that live in our guts. And it is difficult, if not impossible, to identify a mirror organism within our guts, if there is one, for the reasons mentioned in this book. So while the mirror protist within us is a product of my imagination, there is no scientific research or test available today that can rule out this possibility.

Decay and Degeneration: In case you are wondering why John Hyde's body and coffin decayed, while the birch bark strips of the Owen manuscript and the papers in the secret room at Belvedere House did not, there is an explanation. Simply put, even in the same humid climate, the secret room was at a much lower level than John Hyde's coffin. And the manuscript was in a lead casket, for added protection. That is what helped preserve its contents better than the tomb.

Snake venom: All the examples quoted from ancient texts as well as modern medicine are factual. Snake venom has been used in Ayurveda and Chinese traditional medicine and it is true that it's harmless if swallowed. Though I wouldn't recommend that you try it!

The Antidote: While the antidote itself is fictional, the manner in which it works is not. So, if you felt that a molecular hole puncher composed of seven parts, which then assembles to form the pore, as described in the dossier, is far-fetched, then think again. I was inspired by defensins (found in our skin) and alpha toxin (produced by *Staphylococcus aureus*) that work in this manner. For details and diagrams, check out The Quest Club.

The History

Miaozigou: There was an excavation between 1985 and 1987 (see Bibliography) at this site. More than seventy skeletons were discovered, most of them hastily buried in pits around the remains of the dwellings. Archaeologists concluded that a pestilence had struck the village and it was hastily abandoned in the manner described in the Prologue. However, the incidents described in the Prologue are fictional. More on this excavation at The Quest Club.

Alexander von Humboldt: Humboldt did find a monkey as he journeyed along the Rio Apure and the Orinoco. But the regeneration of the monkey's leg is fictional, as is the incident in Angostura, though Humboldt, José and Bonpland really did develop a mysterious fever when they reached Angostura. Humboldt also did make four attempts to visit India and was denied each time by the East India Company. He did meet a fakir in Astrakan in 1829. He was a close friend of Goethe and wrote several letters to him. All the facts about Humboldt's discoveries and things named after him, that are listed in this book, are true. Darwin, Simón Bolívar and Thomas Jefferson were admirers of Humboldt, and Wordsworth and Coleridge drew inspiration from him. It is also true that, a few years before his death, Humboldt had reorganised his journals and notebooks, cutting out a lot of parts, which have never been found. Whether they contained anything about a new form of life, we'll never know, but I had fun imagining that they did. He was an interesting person and you can discover more about him at The Quest Club.

The letter from Alexander Humboldt to his brother Wilhelm in August 1818: The letter is fictional, as are its contents about the secret in Calcutta, though the two brothers did correspond and Humboldt had disclosed to his brother his desire to visit India. It is true that Wilhelm had also told his wife, Caroline, in a letter, that Humboldt and he were never alone together during Alexander's visit to London in 1817. The meeting between Humboldt and Hastings in 1814 is a product of my imagination, though there really was a celebration of the Allied victory over Napoleon just as I have described.

Goethe: He and Humboldt were close friends. And Goethe was a passionate botanist. More on this aspect of Goethe at The Quest Club.

The Owen manuscript/Fischer: The Owen manuscript and its discovery is inspired by the discovery of the Bower manuscript in 1890. The account of the discovery in the Prologue is fictional. The Bower manuscript was undecipherable by several Indian Sanskrit scholars. It was finally translated by A.F. Rudolf Hoernle. Read all about it at The Quest Club. Oh, and Friedrich Fischer, like the Owen manuscript, is fictional, though Henry Thomas Colebrooke really was the President of the Royal Asiatic Society in 1807. And the *British Medical Journal*, in 1895, actually did describe the Bower manuscript as a collection of complex farragos, which I adapted for use with the Owen manuscript, though at an earlier date. For the actual article in the journal, please see The Quest Club.

Susruta: I've mentioned Susruta in my TEDx talks, including a section about a technique of plastic surgery used by him which is still in use in the twenty-first century. The *Susruta Samhita* is an amazing, if slightly tedious, read. The text by Susrata that is part of the Owen manuscript is, of course, fictional.

Thomas Manning: A fascinating person, though little known or remembered. Everything mentioned about him in this book is true—he was the first Englishman to visit Lhasa and meet the Dalai Lama, he didn't publish his travel journals, he didn't report to the East India Company when he returned to Kolkata from Tibet, he did meet Napoleon, he really did write those riddles(!) and he lived the life of an eccentric recluse after returning to England. But he didn't meet Humboldt in 1817 (at least there is no record of it) and the letter to Humboldt is fictional; and he didn't get back a secret from Tibet or hide anything in Kolkata. A trove of his letters was discovered in 2014 and acquired by the Royal Asiatic Society. For more on Thomas Manning, check out The Quest Club, including scanned copies of his riddles and notebooks and, yes, the receipts from F. Potter, Wine & Brandy Merchant (Just for kicks!).

John Brereton Birch: He was a Magistrate of Calcutta (now Kolkata). He died in 1829 and is buried in the Old Cemetery at Barrackpore. Everything else about him in this book is fictional.

Warren Hastings: Everything about Warren Hastings in this book (including the two missions to Tibet) is true except for his opposition to Humboldt and his getting to know about a secret in Tibet. That is a product of my imagination. And, yes, Warren Hastings did die in August 1818.

George Bogle: Everything about George Bogle in this book is factual, including his burial in the South Park Street Cemetery. The Quest Club has photographs and a video of his tomb.

Bahlam Jol: Apparently the city of Bahlam Jol really was burned down. Archaeologists ascribe this to warfare. Read more about it at The Quest Club.

St Anne's Church: The church did get struck by lightning in 1724. It was almost destroyed in 1756 during the battle between Siraj ud-Daula's forces and the East India Company. Writers' Building stands on the foundations of the church today.

Man Singh's Chowkey: The outpost did exist in Sealdah according to the Consultation of 15 November 1749.

Belvedere House: All details mentioned in this book, including the duel with Philip Francis and the secret room that was discovered in 2010, are factual. Unfortunately, that room was never excavated because it was filled with mud. And John Brereton Birch did live in Belvedere House and he did sell it to Shambhu Chander Mukherjee in 1824.

Cemeteries in Kolkata: The details of the cemeteries, including John Hyde's tomb, are real. North Park Street Cemetery and Mission Cemetery don't exist anymore—they have been built over. However, the details of the underground vault in John Hyde's tomb are fictional. For photographs of South Park Street Cemetery, check out The Quest Club.

The Bodleian Library: The original Bower manuscript is in the Bodleian Library at Oxford. Humboldt's visit to the library is fictional. Learn more about the Bodleian Library, with photographs, at The Quest Club.

The Mahabharata

Indraprastha and Khandavaprastha: The Sanskrit shlokas quoted by Dr Shukla throughout the book are real and taken from the Chitrashala Press, Pune, edition of the Mahabharata, though I also consulted the M.N. Dutt, K.M. Ganguli and Bibek Debroy (Critical Edition) translations, along with a Sanskrit scholar, who is my advisor. There is no fictional element to the translations. The story of Khandavaprastha, the anomalies mentioned by Dr Shukla and the perspective provided by Van Klueck are all present in the Mahabharata and are not fictional. However, the shlokas that tell the story of King Shvetaki and of Brahma advising Agni to consume Khandavaprastha are missing from the BORI Critical Edition of the Mahabharata. Indraprastha was, indeed, built before the Khandavaprastha forest was burned down, just as Dr Shukla explains. For more details about these shlokas, check out my non-fiction web series called *Revealed: Mysteries of the Mahabharata*, available exclusively at The Quest Club Gold.

The Khandavaprastha fire: There were seven survivors according to the Mahabharata, not six as many people think: Ashvasena (Takshaka's son), Maya the Asura, the four Sharangaka birds and Jarita (the mother of the birds).

Nara and Narayana: According to the Mahabharata, Arjuna and Krishna were incarnations of Nara and Narayana. For more information on Nara-Narayana, including stories about them, you can check out my non-fiction web series called *Revealed: Mysteries of the Mahabharata* available exclusively at The Quest Club Gold.

Other Notes

Radha's call to Imran two years earlier: For those of you who missed it, at the very end of Chapter 1 of *The Secret of the Druids*, Imran receives a call from a private number. That is the call that Imran refers to in this book, when he tells Vijay about Radha. All the clues are there—you may want to go back and look up *The Secret of the Druids* to see if you missed this the first time you read the book.

Hotan: The description of the market is authentic. Fact, not fiction. What Beth witnessed (she's also fictional, by the way) is fiction, of course. Nothing like this ever happened in Hotan.

China: It is politics that has led to the 'China vs the world' situation that we find ourselves in today. We must not confuse the CCP with the Chinese people, who have traded their freedom for political stability. And there are very real issues with the CCP and the Chinese government, especially related to secrecy, espionage, and the repression of minorities. But the China Telegrams are fictional as is the bioweapon and the laboratory in Hotan. Nothing of the sort has ever been found. Put it down to my imagination running riot. However, in 2019 the International Consortium of Investigative Journalists, which is a real organisation, revealed the China Cables, which documented the very real atrocities being inflicted on the Uyghurs. Fortunately, it does not extend to the extremes described in this book, but the repression of the Uyghurs is a real, saddening fact. And, there is such a thing as the Autonomous Region State Organ Telegram. There's a write up at The Quest Club, if this interests you. It is true that the Chinese have never had global colonial ambitions (though they have conquered and occupied various parts of South East Asia over the centuries). It is also true that the Chinese government has, over the decades, embarked on global domination through economic means, while building a military to rival that of the USA. China's Thousand Talents Plan is a well known initiative to recruit foreign intellectuals and their intellectual property, while it is also well known that the Chinese government has placed people in USA colleges and institutions, over the years, whose loyalties may lie with the CCP. It is also true that there are many Chinese Americans, like Iris, who are fiercely loyal to their adopted country. All nationalities have their share of good people and bad people and the Chinese are no different. I have tried to present a balanced view in this book to represent this fact.

Radcliffe Camera/Bodleian Library, Oxford: The Bodleian Library is where the Bower manuscript can be found, so I used it for the Owen manuscript as well. The storage of the Humboldt letters in the Radcliffe Camera is fictional. Old manuscripts are never kept there, it only serves as a reading room. For more information and photographs, including layouts of the Bodleian complex and locations of the various buildings, please see The Quest Club.

Duncan's English (or, rather, Scottish!): If you go to Scotland, say Edinburgh, you'll hear the brogue that Duncan breaks into, on occasion, in this book. Many Scotsmen (think of Sean Connery or David Tennant) can speak with a perfectly good English accent. But their normal speech resembles what Duncan uses at times in this book.

The CCP and PLA: It is true that the PLA is not an army of the Chinese government. It is the army of the Chinese Communist Party (CCP).

The Jagiellonian Library: It is a real place and does hold the second largest collection of Humboldt's papers, including the Eduard Buschmann-Humboldt collection. Scanned copies of some of Humboldt's documents are at The Quest Club.

Drepung Monastery: This is a real monastery and a trove of ancient manuscripts was, indeed, discovered there in 2003. More on this at The Quest Club.

To My Reader

In 2015, when I first thought of the idea that led to this book, it seemed utterly fantastic and highly improbable. The science—the biology—that underpins the story was nascent, though real, and inspired by the books and work of George Church, Paul Davies and David Toomey (see the Bibliography for details). However, after my initial excitement at what seemed to be a great idea wore off, the biology was just too incredible. I wasn't sure if readers would believe that the science was real.

So, I decided to shelve the idea.

In hindsight, though, I am glad I waited all these years to write this book. Not only has COVID-19 demonstrated that a lot of the epidemiological facts that I had thought of at the time (which may have been ridiculed had I written about them, back then) could actually transpire in the real world, but these years have also seen a lot of cutting-edge research that has shed light on how the biology of disease and contagion works, thus providing a solid scientific basis for my initial hypothesis/book idea (see Last Notes and bibliography at The Quest Club for details). The passage of time has also demonstrated how little we know about the human body and our microbiome. We have a long way to go.

There is also the fact that, owing to COVID-19, most readers will now be more familiar with some of the scientific terms used in this book than they may have been in 2015. So while there is still a chance that some readers will find the book a bit scientific (it is, after all, based on real science), I think that probability has significantly diminished now. I'm keeping my fingers crossed.

In 2020, when my international research trip (for another line of research I had intended to use for this book) was cancelled at the last minute due to the pandemic, it didn't take much for me to dust off my notes, dive deeper into research and pull the science together, to develop the original idea into this book.

Now, you hold the book in your hands. A book that describes a chilling possibility that is all too real. A story that cannot be easily dismissed as fiction (though it is) because the science is very, very real …

Our world, our future, is fragile. This book shows you why.

On the Bibliography

A book like this is not lightly written. Given the various subjects it covers, a lot of research is required in order to be historically and scientifically accurate.

After the first two books in this series, I received a deluge of emails from readers wanting to know more about my research. I got requests to publish a bibliography.

So, for this book, I thought I'd share a detailed bibliography, for those of you who want to go deeper.

Unfortunately, there is not enough space in this book to publish the bibliography, since there are about 300 readings that I have listed. But the complete bibliography is available at The Quest Club. So, if you are interested, please log into your Quest Club account or join The Quest Club for free to access it.

I have organised the bibliography by subject, so you can easily find the books and papers on the topic of your interest there.

Acknowledgements

This book has been, in a way, six years in the making (as I mentioned in the Author's Note at the beginning). And I acknowledge the solitary toil that has gone into the writing of this book. However, as always, once the toil is done with, it is all about teamwork and there are people without whom this book would never have seen the light of day.

As always, I begin with my wife, Sharmila, and my daughter, Shaynaya. The last few years have been extremely demanding, in many ways, and their support has been rock-solid, while I went through the vicissitudes of a cancelled research trip due to the pandemic and losing all the money that I had spent on that trip; and then spending most of my time away from them, researching hard and writing to make up for lost time.

Artika Bakshi, as always, read the first draft and gave me her frank feedback and suggestions, cross checking spellings, grammar, omissions, facts, locations and historical references, which has always helped me stay accurate and true to facts. Thank you, Artika.

Anand Prakash, my friend and genius designer, who has designed the cover of every one of my books, and who has, once again, come up with a brilliant cover.

My thanks also go out to Dr Nivedita Awasthi Mishra, who took out the time to review and challenge my scientific hypothesis. Her expertise was valuable in ensuring that I did not propound a theory that was scientifically inaccurate, even though it is fictional. It is always a great experience to explain to a scientist what my assumptions and interpretations are. And, while explaining my theory to her, my own clarity on the science increased manifold. Her endorsement of the plausibility and of the scientific hypothesis presented in this book in no way implies that she necessarily agrees with any of my theories, application or interpretation of scientific facts and their correlation with the Mahabharata.

My thanks go out to Patricia MacEwen, Brenda Clough, E.M. Prazeman and Patricia Burroughs—fellow scribes in my writers' research group, who answered difficult questions regarding topics that were hard to research.

Mrs Dhanashree Shejwalkar, my Sanskrit advisor and translator, who painstakingly provided me with detailed translations of many more shlokas than have been shared with you in this book.

Dr Ambarish Khare, who translated verses from the Rigveda which puzzled me, even though I have not directly included any of those verses in this book.

Debalina Das, whose inputs helped me with my research.

A big thanks to Saurabh Garge from Westland, for his inputs on the cover design and also for creating the illustrations which have brought critical parts of the book to life and made it easier for the reader to visualise some of the happenings in the book.

A big thank you to all the people at Westland, especially Gautam Padmanabhan, for their unstinted support. I appreciate the support of the sales team, the marketing team and everyone else at Westland who was involved in bringing this book to you.

As usual, my editor, Sanghamitra Biswas, did a wonderful job of polishing my writing and challenging me where required. We had some interesting discussions during the edit process and I felt reassured that she was editing the book. I thank Karthika V.K. for her valuable inputs while finalising the manuscript.

My acknowledgements cannot be complete without expressing my deep gratitude to my parents, who inculcated the joy of reading in me and ensured that I always had a ready supply of new books to read. Without that foundation, I would never have been able to dream, as a child, of one day being an author.

Finally, I cannot express enough gratitude to my readers. It has been a long time since the publication of the previous book in this series. You have waited, patiently, and supported me through everything in the intervening years. I feel blessed. Thank you.

And, as always, all errors and omissions rest squarely on my shoulders.

Don't miss your FREE bonus chapters at The Quest Club (membership is FREE)!

That's right! Due to limitations of space and in order to keep the story fast-paced, we decided not to include a few chapters that I had written for this book. And I have decided to make those chapters available for FREE to all members of The Quest Club, along with all my research and additional information about the history, science and information about the Mahabharata that I have used for this book.

So, if you are a member of The Quest Club, log in today to read the FREE chapters and get access to all the other fascinating information that I have posted there for you.

If you are not yet a member, then you can become a member for FREE today by registering, using this link: www.authorchristophercdoyle.com/the-quest-club.

What do you get as a member of The Quest Club?

1. Free bonus chapters — like the ones for this book — for all my future books!

2. The opportunity to interact with me face to face at Quest Club meetings in different cities in India, and online during virtual Quest Club meetings (recordings of the online meetings are available at The Quest Club for free viewing). At these meetings, we discuss my books, the Mahabharata, science, ancient legends, history—oh, and this is a great place to get your copies of my books signed by me!

3. Access to my research and site visits (photo-tours, videos of my onsite research in India and overseas) and also my research notes. Learn more about characters, events and locations which I feature in my books!

4. The opportunity to post comments and ask me questions online — and I answer every one of them!

5. Exclusive previews of my future books, puzzles, contests and quizzes and advance information and updates of my new books, cover reveals and more!
6. There will also be free eBooks over the coming years which I will release exclusively at The Quest Club (the first one was A Secret Revealed, which is still available to read for free at The Quest Club).

So, what are you waiting for? Log into your Quest Club account today to read the free bonus chapters or join The Quest Club to get all these benefits completely FREE with your Bronze membership!

The Quest Club Gold

While everything listed above is free, in January 2022, I launched a paid channel at The Quest Club called The Quest Club Gold. For a nominal subscription (the price of a book or the cost of a couple of Starbucks coffees!) you can gain access to exclusive online content, starting with my non-fiction web-series called Revealed: Mysteries of the Mahabharata, which is an exploration of the original text of the Mahabharata with stories from the Puranas and the Vedas. If you ever wanted to read the original Mahabharata, and didn't know where to start, this web-series is for you. This series answers all your questions about the Mahabharata and gives you insights which are not available elsewhere. Simply join The Quest Club (for free) and then upgrade yourself to Gold to enjoy this web-series and more in the years to come!